PRECIPICE
OF DOUBT

By the Authors

Mardi Alexander & Laurie Eichler:

To Be Determined

Precipice of Doubt

Mardi Alexander:

Twice Lucky

Spirit of the Dance

Laurie Eichler:
Written as Laurie Salzler:

A Kiss Before Dawn

Right Out of Nowhere

Positive Lightning

In the Stillness of Dawn

After a Time (YA)

The Day Cagney Lost Her Wag (Children's)

Visit us at www.boldstrokesbooks.com

PRECIPICE OF DOUBT

by

Mardi Alexander
and Laurie Eichler

2018

Credits
Editor: Ruth Sternglantz
Production Design: Stacia Seaman
Cover Design by Sheri (hindsightgraphics@gmail.com)

Acknowledgments

Mardi Alexander:
Writing with Laurie is never work, although there have been times we have certainly labored. Our collaboration continues to be fun, exciting, and paved with discoveries, heaps of laughs, and midnight conversations built in and around joey feeding times. Laurie, your friendship and generosity in sharing this writing adventure is a gift I regard as most precious. From the bottom of my heart, thank you. xx

Every animal and person is unique and comes into your life at just the right time, for just the right reason. There have been few more special than Bonnie, who was my inspiration for Lucille. A more gentle, loving soul, with a magical heart and disposition I have yet to meet. To have known you, and have loved you, for ever so brief a time, has been one of the greatest gifts that I have ever received.

To all the crew at BSB, and for Sandy and Ruth who both pushed to make us, and the story, better—thank you.

To Michelle, who continues to share my crazy life, the long hours, rescue callouts, and helps me appreciate all that we have. Thank you, babe. xxx

Laurie Eichler:
Mardi, it's all your fault, you know. You planted that seed to make me fall helplessly in love with those joeys, and you're doing it again with koalas. *smile* And then we started writing together and what a journey we've begun. "Get out of my head" is synonymous with "we've got a good thing going, let's write another." And so we shall. Your friendship, camaraderie, and guidance in all things we manage to get ourselves into is something I will forever treasure and could never thank you enough. xx

Thank you to Ruth and Sandy for getting this book exactly how we wanted it.

To those of you who follow me as Laurie Salzler as well as Laurie Eichler, thank you for your support and desire for more. And there will be more.

I'd be remiss if I didn't mention my wonderful cohorts from WIRES (Wildlife Information, Rescue and Education Service, Inc.) You guys are a wealth of knowledge and experience that I so appreciate. I don't know what I'd do without you, Viv, Tony, Teresa, Robyn, Sandra, Vickii, Chris, Pam, and you too, Mardi (to name a few). A simple thank you is not enough, but it'll have to do for now.

Dedication

MA: Bonnie—The cuddliest koala, ever. (17.09.2007–01.03.2018)

LE: As wildlife carers, we're forced to make sometimes difficult life and death decisions on behalf of some of the most unique and beautiful creatures on this planet. I have been extremely lucky to partake in the lives of ten orphaned kangaroo joeys (thus far). Every single one of them was a teacher…in life, love, and letting go. This book is for you, Willow, Ash, Rizzo, Zelda, Rizzi, Sampson, Martin, Dorothy, Jamie, and Annie.

PROLOGUE

L oud pounding on the front door of the veterinary clinic surgery shocked Jodi Bowman into wakefulness. She blinked a few times in the muted light radiating from her computer screen. She had fallen asleep at her desk. Again. The second time this week. She yawned and wiped drool from the corner of her mouth. *Blurgh. Very classy, Bowman.* The pounding continued. She stretched in an attempt to wake her body up as she made her way to the clinic's front door, rubbing tired eyes with one hand, while she disconnected the security alarm and opened the door with her other. A frantic husband and wife team, shadowed by two children aged somewhere between eight and ten, met her at the door. The husband's arms were full of a small tan and white body wrapped in a bloodstained white towel.

"Please, Jodi. Our Penny needs your help."

Jodi opened the door up wide. She loved her job, but some days it smacked of never ending. She smiled wearily. "You'd best all come on through then."

CHAPTER ONE

Ninety-eight, ninety-nine…One hundred laps of the seawater baths were part of Jodi's morning routine, rain, hail, or shine. It was a peaceful start to the day. No thinking, no planning, just stroke, kick, and breathe. No one to talk to, no questions to ask or answer, no phones ringing. Tap the wall, tumble, push off the wall, and feel the rush of watery fingers drag along her limbs. The tickle of bubbles ran along the underside of her body before her head broke the surface and the physical mantra started again. Stroke, kick, and breathe. Touch the wall. One hundred. She gripped the stainless steel handles alongside the diving block. She emerged halfway out of the water, closed her eyes, and willed her breathing to slow. The early morning sun warmed her shoulders and back as water sheeted off.

She hefted herself the rest of the way out of the pool, grabbed her towel, and walked around the edge of the pool's perimeter. There was no dallying this morning. She briefly stood under the freshwater outdoor shower and rinsed off the salt. Her swim was slightly later than usual. She needed to get home, change, and grab some breakfast before she started work at her veterinary hospital clinic in the seaside town of Yamba.

Turning off the water, she towelled her hair briskly and wrapped it around her waist. When she turned towards the car park she spied a familiar face. Cole Jameson, her veterinary nurse, held two takeaway cups of coffee while sitting on the park bench overlooking the baths.

Jodi walked quickly to erase the distance between them and laid a hand on her heart.

Cole wore a mock-exasperated look, although it was slightly unconvincing given she also appeared to be nervous. Wordlessly, Cole held aloft a coffee cup as Jodi approached.

Jodi sat down heavily, accepting the offered steaming cup. "You're a lifesaver. What would I do without you?" She took an appreciative sip and luxuriated in the warmth travelling down to her toes. She hummed in delight and closed her eyes to savour the flavour...and Cole's presence. Although Cole had worked in her practice for going on five years now, she had to admit that being with Cole outside of the clinic environment was somewhat intimate, for lack of a better word. Which felt strange. Cole was straight.

Rarely did they see each other outside of work. Which was probably why she had really never noticed how attractive Cole looked out of her baggy scrubs. And that surprised her. She mentally shook her head and wondered when the last time was she'd noticed *any* woman for that matter. She reckoned it was probably back in her first year at university, maybe. But Cole...

Cole held up a paper bag, interrupting Jodi's thoughts. "You'd starve to death and the clinic would be a mess."

Jodi looked inside and spied a toasted ham sandwich and proceeded to stuff one half of it into her mouth. "Mm. You're most likely right."

"I know."

They sat in companionable silence as Jodi finished her surprise breakfast. "Why are you up so early?"

"I figured you'd need some refreshment after your early start—or, should I say, late night."

"How did—?"

"And I need to apologize. I picked up the practice mobile by mistake and took it home. So I know you got a call from the Petersens a bit before two a.m. I take it the puppies arrived then?"

"Mm. Six. By caesarean." Jodi drained the last of the coffee and put the scrunched up paper bag into the cup.

"You should have called me."

"No point both of us losing sleep."

Cole sighed. "Perhaps not, but if you'd have called me you might have gotten home earlier."

"Next time."

Cole snorted. Jodi acknowledged calling Cole in the middle of the night to meet her at work was most unlikely to happen. Jodi looked after her staff.

They stood and headed towards the car park. Jodi scrunched up her nose. "Don't feel bad. You can still be a part of it. I'm pretty sure I left an awful mess behind." Jodi laughed as Cole rolled her big brown eyes. "Thanks for brekkie. I owe you."

"Yeah, yeah. Go home, get changed, and get your butt back to work so you can help me clean up *your* mess before we open the clinic." Jodi waved. "See you directly."

Cole secretly enjoyed surprising her boss after her early morning swim. She'd long known Jodi was a fitness freak but found it funny how she'd never really taken much notice of Jodi's *body* before. But watching her glide up and down in the water and stepping out to stand under the shower to clean off after her swim, there was no denying Jodi's muscle tone and fitness. Perving on her boss in her swimmers was an unexpected bonus to the day.

The morning had gone better than Cole had a right to expect. In truth, she had expected Jodi to take her to task for taking the practice phone home. Although she'd had a slight ulterior motive, she wasn't about to voice that to her boss and risk losing her job over it. She and Jodi got on well, working comfortably together in the small but demanding practice. Cole had learned the hard way to tread lightly when it came to employer and employee relations—her last position had cost her everything, engagement, job, and home. Never again would she take things for granted. Work was work. Love was love. Oil and water didn't mix. Simple.

Cole entered the vet clinic via the back door and turned on lights as she went. She rounded the corner into the surgical room and came to a halt. She put her hands on her hips and shook her head. Jodi hadn't lied. It looked like a bomb had gone off in the room. Bloodied gauze, towels, and discarded tubing were scattered on the table and on one side of the floor. She couldn't stay mad at her boss for long though, as she knew Jodi had stayed back until late to make sure another of their patients, a Doberman puppy, had stabilized after surgery when it had been brought in by its owners right on closing time. The puppy had been accidently run over with the family car and had sustained internal injuries. It had been a long and tricky surgery and she knew Jodi had stayed on long after she had been sent home.

Cole decided to leave the mess until last, after she had everything else cleaned and sorted. She checked on the animals who had spent the night. Several had near fresh IV bags, meaning Jodi had overseen their care in addition to the puppies' the previous night.

One of the kennel doors rattled loudly as Popcorn impatiently pawed to be let out. A client, Mrs. Rosa, had asked Jodi if she'd give her beloved dog a home if she became too infirm to care for the little Pomeranian herself. Jodi agreed, never thinking that in a few short years, the elderly woman would succumb to a series of strokes.

Cole lifted Popcorn down from her cage and let her have the run of the office while she refreshed water bowls and bedding, booted up several computers, and gave the floor a quick mop. With Popcorn at her heels, she set the coffee machine up, knowing it would be in much needed service throughout the day.

She was midway through putting a load of soiled bedding into the washing machine when she heard the turning of a key in the back door lock, announcing Jodi's arrival. Popcorn ran in anticipation to the door, her nails clicking on the tiles.

Jodi's hair was still damp from her swim and neatly tied up into a loose bun. Her outfit was rounded off with fresh surgical scrubs. Despite the dark circles under her eyes, Jodi had her business face on and strode straight over to the nearest cage. She scanned the patient's sheet and talked to the matching hospitalized animal. Only when she was satisfied did she look up and smile a greeting to Cole. "Good morning."

Cole grinned back at her. "Again."

Jodi smirked. "Yes, again. Thank you, again, for my breakfast." She picked Popcorn up and gave the dog the attention she craved.

Cole winked at her. "You're welcome."

"On the proviso I shout lunch, and you hand my phone back."

Cole held up her left hand, her little finger pointing to the sky, which Jodi interlocked with her own. They pinkie-shook. "It's a deal."

Cole held nothing but respect and admiration for Jodi, knowing how she took each and every patient to heart and gave them the very best care. Long days and nights never seemed to diminish her abilities or her dedication to the job. Silently she retrieved the mobile from her bag and handed it over, albeit sheepishly.

With a last look around, bar the surgical room, it was time to open the front doors to the public. She looked to Jodi for confirmation. "It's time. You ready?"

Jodi straightened her shoulders and rolled her neck. "Too right. Open sesame." She disappeared briefly to take Popcorn back to her kennel.

Cole grinned at their long-standing joke that they were a cave that people came to visit, expecting relief, confidence, help, or, sometimes, even miracles. She turned the sign to *Open* and unlocked the wooden door as well as the screen door. By chance, she looked down and spied an old shoebox on the doorstep with holes punched in its sides. She grimaced briefly, nervous at what the box might contain. No box left on a doorstop ever boded good tidings and good fortune. She retrieved the box and carefully carried it out the back.

Jodi walked around the corner with two fresh mugs of coffee in her hand. "Whatchya got there?"

"A delivery. On the doorstep."

"Oh." Jodi stepped closer and Cole cut away the tape holding the box lid down. She opened it up and was greeted instantly by two black and white magpie chicks, necks extended, mouths open wide, screeching and demanding food.

Cole sighed. "Oh, dear. I better dig out some insectivore mix."

The mooing door chime announced a customer. Jodi set the mugs down and patted her on the shoulder. "I'll get that. I'll leave you to see what we've got in stock to feed these two."

Cole mixed up a powdered portion with pre-boiled warm water just as Jodi came through the door with another box.

"Hope you made plenty."

Cole looked up. "Huh?"

"We got another one." Jodi lifted the lid to reveal a grey fluffy magpie chick wobbling about and demanding food.

"Oh, for heaven's sake."

"I know." The door chime sounded again. Jodi waved. "Got it."

Cole took the box from Jodi and set it next to the first one.

"You are not going to believe this." Jodi put another towel-covered box on the bench.

"Don't tell me…"

"Uh-huh."

"Oh, for Pete's sake! What? Is it raining magpies?"

Jodi shrugged and grinned. "Looks like it's gonna be one of those days."

The door chime mooed again and Cole rolled her eyes. "You better bring me in a cute puppy or kitten next or you'll owe me dinner as well as lunch."

A few minutes later Jodi returned, laughing. "Hope you're hungry!"

"You can't be serious." Cole looked up from feeding the four already in the box.

"Serious as a heart attack. Here's two more for your collection." Jodi carefully added the newcomers to the box.

Cole snagged a piece of food with the tweezers and held it over the birds. "Damn! I can't keep track of which of you buggers I've fed and who to feed next." Cole stared into the box where six magpies screamed with gaping beaks, pushing against each other for the mouthful.

Jodi joined her at the counter and peered in, catching a whiff of Cole's scent and feeling the warmth of her shoulder against her own. She smelled like sunshine and rose geranium. She surprised herself by thinking she actually liked it. "You've already fed that one and that one. I'd feed those two next as they're hungrier."

Cole looked at her incredulously. "You're not kidding, are you?"

"Nope."

"Can I ask how in the hell you can tell?" She offered nuggets of insectivore to the birds that Jodi had indicated. The birds grabbed at the morsels in the tweezers and eagerly gulped them down.

"Have a look at them. See any differences?" Jodi leaned her hip against the counter to put some space between her and Cole.

"Aside from the fact that one has poop on its wings and another on its feet, they all look black and white to me."

"Look at their gapes."

Cole squinted and studied the fledglings. "Mm. Most are pinkish, but two have beet red mouths."

"Uh-huh. Those are the two you need to feed next."

"Ah, the proverbial light bulb just went off. The hungrier they are, the brighter red the gape."

Jodi pursed her lips and nodded. "That's how the parents figure out which of their brood needs to be fed."

"Interesting."

"Interesting enough to venture into the bush for a hike one day?" The words were out of Jodi's mouth before she could stop them, knowing full well what the answer would be.

Cole huffed. "Not *that* interesting."

Her brief musing about not minding Cole's company ended quickly. "While you're feeding the hordes, I'll have a quick look at the schedule and ring Pip and Charlie." Jodi quickly turned and walked towards the front of the clinic, puzzled at the unexpected new interest in wanting to spend time with Cole outside of work, and the flash of disappointment at her offer being shut down.

❖

Jodi put the phone on speaker to free up her hands while she flipped through the patient files.

"Hello. Pip speaking."

"Hey, Pipsqueak. Whatchya doing?" Jodi put a file down and leaned back into the chair.

"Hey, Jodes. Charlie and I are heading out to pick up a possie."

"Good, you're on the road then. Will you be anywhere near Yamba?"

"We could be. Why? What do you have?"

"What makes you think I have anything?" Jodi bit her lip in amusement.

"Could be that I heard the mischief in your voice because you're more than likely biting your lip."

"Okay. Busted. I have a box of magpies for you."

"A box. Of magpies." Pip paused. "And how many maggies constitutes a box?"

"Six." Jodi worked hard not to giggle.

"*Six?*" Charlie and Pip said at the same time.

"It was like an assembly line today. There were two left in a box by the front door when Cole got here this morning. Four different people came in nearly right behind one another."

"Christ," Charlie grumbled.

"I know," Jodi said. "I commend people for wanting to do what's best for wildlife, but this year they seem to be all too keen, picking creatures up too soon."

"All right. We'll be there after we finish the possie rescue."

"Plan on a cuppa when you get here."

"Will do."

Jodi heard Charlie say something. "Hey, Charlie. What did you say? I couldn't hear you."

"Hi, Jodi. Yeah, sorry. I asked Pip what you meant by too soon."

"Pip, do you want to explain?"

"No, no. You go ahead. I want to see if you've been listening to me at all."

"Right. I'll give it a go. So, it's normal for magpies to leave the nest without knowing how to fly yet. They spend a while on the ground, and that's where the parents feed them. People don't realize the parents are still caring for them during this time. The fledglings hop onto low branches and begin experimenting with their wings. They ultimately grow tail feathers and start following one of the parents around, begging for food. People see the babies on the ground, assume they've fallen out of the nest, and become intent on rescuing them. What they actually achieve, in most cases, is taking away the babies from their best caregivers, their parents. How'd I do, Pip-smartarse-squeak?"

"Not bad, Stretch. We'll see you in a while."

CHAPTER TWO

I'm stuck." Charlie Dickerson's muffled voice echoed from the darkened recess beneath the weatherboard house.

Pip Atkins bent over and squinted in an attempt to see what was wrong with her partner. "What do you mean, you're stuck?"

"Oh, you know, as in can't go forward and can't go back kind of *stuck*."

"Oh. Well, why didn't you say so?" Pip grinned when she heard Charlie's groan.

Native wildlife rescuers, Pip and Charlie had received a call for help just after breakfast from the elderly lady who owned the house, who had called them about a possum her terrier had chased under the house. "Mrs. Billings, would you mind holding this towel for me please? As soon as you see the cage come out from under the house, if you could drape the towel over the top to block out the light and stop the possum from getting any more frightened, I would be most grateful."

"Of course, my dear." Mrs. Billings accepted the towel from Pip with her gnarled, lived-in hands. "Only too happy to help."

Pip touched Mrs. Billings lightly on the shoulder. "Thank you so much."

"A pleasure, my dear."

Pip lowered herself flat onto the ground. She commando crawled behind Charlie. "Hey, Yank, any chance you can move to the left just a smidge?"

"Well, I would if it wasn't for that *stuck* thing we were talking about a minute ago."

Pip half smirked. If Charlie's humour got any drier she'd light a fire. "Not to worry. Just get ready to get a bit squeezy in a minute." With a few grunts and twists, Pip pulled herself along the ground until she was wedged in right up against Charlie and one of the house supports. With a slight incline of her chin, Pip leaned forward and kissed Charlie.

She smiled as a small sigh escaped Charlie's lips. Sliding half a foot past Charlie, Pip looked back and saw that Charlie's belt was caught on a metal hook supporting some electrical wires. "Ah, I see the problem." She moved enough ahead to turn around until she faced Charlie and could reach the snag. With a twist and pull she managed to free her and steal another kiss. "Better now?"

"Much. That'll teach me to be so gallant and come under the house first instead of you. Stuff the possibility of meeting up with a snake. Next time it's all yours, short stuff."

"Well, if there were any snakes in here, I reckon you've probably scared them off by now. What say you head on out and help Mrs. Billings and I'll pick up possie."

"I'm happy with that. I've got more than enough dust up my nose for one day."

As Pip surged forward, Charlie dragged herself back out.

Ten seconds later, Charlie's brief gasp stopped Pip still. "Thank you, Mrs. Billings," Charlie said, "but we might save the towel for throwing over the *crate* when it comes out."

Pip stifled a giggle as she pictured Charlie's head covered in the bath towel.

Pip surveyed the ground ahead. The possum's eyes reflected off her headlamp. She retrieved Charlie's catch pole, and after several missed attempts, managed to loop the noose around the possum's head and shoulders. She pulled the growling and hissing creature towards her while dragging herself backward towards the more spacious area under the house where the possum cage waited. She sat up and swung her knees underneath her. With a firm grip and a deft swing and stuff motion, she manhandled the cranky struggling beast into the cage and snapped the lid shut.

Pushing the pole and cage ahead of her, Pip crawled out from under the house, squinting at the harsh onslaught of bright sunlight. She was pleased when Mrs. Billings successfully covered the cage, as opposed to capturing another rescuer.

Pip stood and slapped her pants legs. She coughed as plumes of dust wafted in the air and tickled her nose and throat.

Charlie patted her on the back. "Man. You really did get down and dirty, didn't you?"

Pip grinned. "I have a magnetic ability when it comes to dirt."

Charlie dusted her down some more. "So it would seem, sweet."

"Would you two like a cup of tea?"

Charlie shook her head. "Thank you all the same, but we might take this little one back and get started on his assessment. If it all goes well, when he's recovered, maybe we could take you up on your offer of tea when we bring him back for release."

"Oh, that would be most suitable. Thank you again, girls. You have both been quite marvellous."

"You're very welcome." Charlie picked up the cage and Pip the pole, and together they packed the gear into Pip's white Toyota Hilux dual cab ute. Pip threw Charlie the keys.

They drove in companionable silence for a bit, appreciating the spectacular view of the mighty Clarence River that ran parallel to the road. Charlie pulled the truck onto the river ferry and turned off the engine. When the other waiting vehicles joined them, the ferry pulled out onto the water.

"Thanks for unhooking me."

"No probs. Did you like the rescue technique, by the way?" Pip got them each a fresh bottle of water.

"What do you mean?"

"It's a little used practice."

Charlie looked puzzled as she took a sip of water.

Pip bit the inside of her lip trying to keep a straight face. "Mm. It's called the Billings Method."

Charlie sprayed water all over the inside of the window. After she left the ferry, Charlie turned left onto a drive that spread out into a staging area for cane trucks. She scowled at Pip.

"Would you please hand me a towel? I need to wipe the window down so I can see."

Pip reached behind her seat and pulled one from a rescue bag. "Here you go, my darling." She batted her eyes innocently, grinning inwardly because Charlie now got her Aussie jokes at least half the time.

"You need to eat something." Charlie handed Pip the muesli bar she retrieved from the centre console.

Pip's Labrador nosed her shoulder and whined softly. "You're getting nearly as good as Chilli."

"Your face tells all when your sugar is getting low."

Pip held the vet surgery door open as Charlie carried the possum cage inside.

Jodi and Cole looked up from the service counter. "Ah. If it isn't the dynamic duo." Jodi winked at them.

Pip scrunched her nose up. "I'll swap you—a possum for some magpies."

Charlie lifted the cage to show Jodi. "Possible dog bite."

"Why don't you take it on through, Charlie? You know the way. Cole'll give you a hand getting things set up. I'll be there in a minute."

Charlie nodded just before she headed down the corridor. The hissing, wriggling cargo let everyone know that it was not happy. Cole followed right behind them.

Jodi rounded the counter and gave Pip a hug. "We've both been so busy since the flood that we haven't had much of a chance to catch up. You doing okay, my friend?"

"Yeah. I'm good. We're both good. Thanks to you. That beer I owe you? I reckon I might need to make it a case. Thanks for, well, setting us straight."

"As long as you're happy."

Pip kissed Jodi on the cheek. "I am. How about I go and freshen up the jug while you and Charlie see to our none-too-happy guest?"

With an affectionate squeeze of her hand, Jodi headed out the back, leaving Pip to make the familiar way to the surgery's kitchen. So much had happened in the space of a few short months, changes she had never envisaged, let alone believed were possible. She, an intensely private and confessed loner, had been paired up with an exchange work program person from the States for a whole year by the head of the Wildlife Rescue and Education Network. She had gone from objecting to Charlie, to enjoying her company, to finally—after months of working together, the drama of an ex-girlfriend, and a major flood event—admitting she was falling in love.

She stirred a spoonful of sugar into Jodi's coffee. Thanks to Jodi's intervention, well… Pip tapped the spoon on the edge of the sink and carried the steaming mugs over to the table. Theirs could so nearly have been a very different story altogether. Yep. Jodi easily deserved that case of beer.

Pip sipped her tea and waited for the rest of the team to join her. Easy laughter preceded their entry into the room. She pulled a chair out for Charlie and received a touch on the shoulder in response. "How'd your assessment go?"

"He has a couple of small, not very deep puncture marks between his shoulders and a bit of bruising. Jodi's given us some antibiotics, just in case, but thinks they should heal well in the next few days."

"Uh-huh. And your box of maggies?"

"One still has a touch of down on it, but the others have feathered up. A variety of ages, but all close enough."

Pip rubbed her eyes. "Well, I suppose it'll make release a bit easier as they'll have already formed a group." Pip couldn't help but notice that Charlie was a tad quiet. She took a guess that it might have something to do with the upcoming release of her eagle, Big Bird.

Charlie sipped her coffee quietly, smiling and nodding at the appropriate times while the others conversed. Big Bird's release weighed heavily on her mind. Yes, she'd been attached to other raptors in her care at the Wildlife Rehabilitation Service in Cody, Wyoming. She'd never before stopped to think about why she favoured the bald and golden eagles, but it was more than likely due to the intensity of their personalities as well as their power. However Big Bird topped them all in those qualities, and in size as well. His wingspan was wider than she was tall, and he was simply magnificent. To bond with such a majestic creature and have him show affection was a high compliment and a gift from the gods. And now she had to make plans to release him back into the wild.

"...party, Charlie."

Charlie looked up from her empty mug. "I'm sorry. I was kind of lost in my thoughts."

Pip nudged her with her shoulder and laid a hand on her thigh. "I think we should have a Big Bird release party. What do you think?"

"Oh." Charlie lifted one shoulder non-committally. "Sure."

"I know you're going to miss him. It was clear right from the beginning that you two shared a special connection." Jodi smiled with empathy.

Charlie nodded. "He's a very special bird. Pip knows I've been struggling with having to release him."

"All the more reason to have a party when we get back. Hopefully it'll help take your mind off it." Pip patted Charlie's forearm. "What do you say, sweet?"

Charlie sighed. "Okay. I knew I'd have to do it eventually. Maybe a few drinks afterwards will help."

Jodi giggled. "If you put all the maggies together, they're sure to make a big bird."

"Funny, Jodes." Pip chortled. "Hey, do you want to come along? You have some investment in him as well."

"I'd love to. I've never seen you release anything, and it'd be an honour to have it be Big Bird. This'll all have to be on a Sunday, though, if that's okay."

"Perfect. Cole, you're invited as well," Pip added. "After all, you're the one who rescued him in the first place. Want to go for a hike?"

Cole threw her head back and laughed. "I think I'll pass. The wilderness and I do not at all see eye to eye."

"That's for sure," Jodi said. "She called me one night after work because a green frog was sitting in front of her door and supposedly wouldn't let her in."

"He wouldn't," Cole squeaked. "Every time I'd take a step forward, the monster would jump at me. Stop your laughing. He had mean eyes. It was quite scary at the time. Besides, all that exercise thing, traipsing around in the bush, running into spiderwebs and stepping on sticks that all look like snakes. Until they're not sticks. No, thanks. Just let me know what Sunday you pick. And now I've got to go get the surgery room prepped. The boss gets kind of cranky if it's not set up beforehand."

Jodi swatted her leg. "You love your job and you know it."

Charlie saw the affectionate softening of Cole's face when she smiled at Jodi.

Cole cheerfully replied, "I do, and there are several reasons why, but mainly the fact you don't make me clean the toilets here." She cringed and shuddered.

"Ah, but that could change."

Pip and Charlie left the clinic with the possum and box of magpies while Jodi and Cole playfully bickered with one another.

Charlie tossed the truck keys to Pip. "Your turn to drive."

"You okay?" Pip got in and slid the key into the ignition. She reached over her shoulder and ruffled Chilli behind the ears.

"Yeah, I'm fine. I have a load of work to do on my immigration application when we get home. Think later on we can look at the map and decide on a release location?"

"You bet, lovely."

When they got home, Charlie went directly to the massive aviary that housed Big Bird. Pip had had it built for her as a present last year. He greeted her with excited chirps and feather fluffing. "Hey, beautiful boy. Let's have a look at you." She slid a heavy leather glove onto her left hand and entered the cage. "Come on. You can fly to me."

Big Bird continued chirping as he crouched, spread his wings, and glided over to Charlie's outstretched arm. After he had folded his wings close to his body, she rubbed the feathers behind his head. The eagle bowed his head lower to give her better access to where he liked to be scratched best.

Charlie carried Big Bird to the training perch in the middle of the aviary, the open roof of which they'd erected under the tight but high canopy of gum trees. Not only was the location shaded from the intense sun, but also Big Bird couldn't see any other birds of prey flying overhead, which could cause him unneeded stress. Once she'd looped the tether around the perch, she removed her glove and watched him settle.

"I'll be back with some mice in a few minutes."

She walked back to where Pip had just finished rearranging branches inside a second, smaller aviary to accommodate the new residents. Charlie placed a shallow pan of fresh water inside on the floor and waited while Pip brought the box of magpies in. She opened the lid and together they removed each bird individually, assessed it, and set it on the ground.

A few of the fledglings hopped onto branches and chose a spot to perch. The others squabbled and pecked at each other before finally settling.

"They all look healthy. I'm going to give them a good feed."

"I'll walk with you. I want to feed Big Bird some mice."

"Righto. I'll meet you back at the house afterwards."

Charlie grabbed Pip's shirt and stopped her. "Thanks for understanding. I know I'm being a bit of a baby about letting him go."

Pip took Charlie's face in both her hands and kissed her. "There's nothing wrong with being sooky. You have an amazingly huge heart, my love. Some animals tend to occupy a bigger part of it than others. As you well know, I'm a sucker for the joeys. You'll always remember your first. I think it's because they're the first to put a big hole in your heart when you let them go. But fortunately, the memory stays even though that hole eventually heals."

"Good grief! Could immigration make these forms any more complicated?" Charlie tossed the twenty-five page bundle onto the table. "I have to remember every job I had since birth? Seriously?" She pursed her lips.

Pip rubbed Charlie's back as she set a mug of coffee next to her. "Since birth?"

"Yes." Charlie picked the forms up and flipped through the pages until she found what she was looking for. "See? Right here—since birth." She rubbed the back of her neck.

Pip pulled a chair closer to Charlie. "Australia is very picky about who we let in."

Charlie stared at her in disbelief. "Didn't England send all their convicts out here in the way back? That doesn't seem very selective to me."

Pip chuckled softly. "They didn't send them all. Even back then there was a pick and choose process as to who came over. So, see? Nothing much has changed."

"Okay, look at this." Charlie rustled through the papers again. "I not only have to list those jobs, I have to describe them in detail." She ran her hands through her hair.

"Charlie," Pip said in a soothing voice, "you can do this. Just focus on one form at a time. I'll help as best I can, and together we'll work through it until it's done."

Charlie rested her head on Pip's shoulder. "You're already helping by being here. This is so overwhelming."

"Is it what you want?"

"Yes."

"Then it'll be worth the effort, won't it?"

Charlie sat up and kissed Pip's cheek. "Every single gut-wrenching, teeth clenching, headachy moment."

Charlie suddenly felt too hot. Her stomach churned and her breathing increased. The telltale signs of an anxiety attack. She closed her eyes and willed calmness. Heart palpitations thundered in her ears. She got up and paced the kitchen floor.

Under the visa extension Teresa, the WREN coordinator, had obtained for her, she had to leave Australia every three months. Where would she go? Back to the United States each time? That would cost a lot of money she didn't have. And what was the guarantee customs would let her back in each time? She and Pip had watched hours of a TV show about border patrol over the course of her time here. They would laugh at the poor sods that got turned away. What if that happened to her?

"Charlie?" Pip sleepily padded to her side. "What's the matter? You look like you've seen a ghost."

"What if I'm not allowed back in after I visit the States? What if—"

"Sweet, it's late. You shouldn't be worrying about this right now. Let's go to bed, baby."

"Pip, my original visa is up in *seven* weeks. I have to leave then, or I'll be deported."

"And you'll come right back on the new visa. It will all work out. I promise." Pip stood and took Charlie's hand. "Come on. I'll hold you while you go to sleep."

Charlie took a deep breath. "Okay."

She let Pip lead her to bed. Although she heard the steady beat of Pip's heart beneath her cheek, it still took her a long time to relax and nod off.

Chapter Three

Jodi couldn't remember the last time she'd foregone the endorphin rush of swimming for three cups of coffee before she went to work. But she just couldn't get her head into it. It was easier to keep the kettle hot. She poured a cup as soon as she rolled out of bed, and another while she still had a towel wrapped around her after a shower. Dressed in scrubs, she carried the third out to the car. When she realized she'd forgotten her keys, she went back in, refilled the half empty mug, grabbed her keys, and continued on her way to the clinic.

She hadn't been able to find the clinic's mobile the previous evening when getting ready to head home. It had annoyed the crap out of her that Cole had taken the mobile home again last night, although probably an honest mistake. Cole was meticulous, and for her to have taken the wrong phone home, twice, seemed out of character. There'd been few nights since she'd opened her practice that she hadn't gotten emergency calls. She'd actually woken up twice convinced she'd heard the phone ringing. But it'd only been the jingle of the chimes outside as wind preceded the summer storm that blew in in the early hours of the morning. She chewed her lip in thoughtful suspicion. She was sure Cole would've called her if there'd been anything she couldn't handle on her own. In a way Jodi hoped Cole had been woken several times by concerned owners, then reneged on that thought. No use having both of them sleep-deprived and exhausted.

Jodi yawned and swallowed the remaining coffee while waiting for traffic to move past the roundabout. It seemed Yamba had one at each intersection, and while efficient most days, there were times it took several minutes to get through one. Not everyone drove straight through and often there were traffic jams within the circle. The car behind her honked its horn, rousing her out of her thoughts. She waved an apology over her shoulder and moved into the circle and continued on her way.

Jodi's personal mobile rang through the Bluetooth connection in her car. She pressed the button on the steering wheel to connect. "Good morning, my thieving assistant." Jodi smiled to herself.

"Where are you?"

Jodi tightened her grip on the wheel. "I'm about three minutes out, if the traffic cooperates."

"Mr. Hanson was waiting at the door when I got here. Rocky had a paralysis tick on him. It was fairly engorged and came off easily."

Jodi didn't miss the concern in Cole's voice. "I'll be right there. Get a weight and then put an oxygen mask on him."

"Already done. Seven point nine kilos and he's on O2 now."

"Good woman." Jodi disconnected the call. She knew Cole would have already given Rocky a sedative so he didn't become anxious as a result of the paralysis. "Damned paralysis ticks. Why couldn't you have evolved somewhere other than Australia?"

Jodi was out of her car before the engine finished its shutdown. She strode into the surgery and took the stethoscope Cole handed her. Rocky's heart rate was steady. She was pleased to see his leg had already been shaved and a catheter inserted into the vein, which was connected to an intravenous drip to keep him hydrated.

"I looked him over with a fine-tooth comb. There was only the one. Good thing he has such a short coat." Cole prepared a syringe with the antiserum and handed it to Jodi, who removed the protective cap from the needle and pushed the yellow medication into the injection port.

"Okay, little man, Cole is going to put you in a nice quiet cage so you can work on getting better." She nodded at Cole. "I'll go talk to Roger."

Jodi walked out into the waiting room and found an obviously distraught Roger Hanson. He pushed himself up on arthritic legs that had steadied him on a prawn trawler for fifty years. "Hi, Roger."

"Oh, Doc, how is my little Rocky?" His voice was low and gravelly.

Jodi took him by the elbow. "Come on into my office. I'll get us some coffee and we can talk."

Roger's watery eyes were bright against his salt-weathered face. White stubble peppered his cheeks and jaws and complemented his bushy grey eyebrows. He'd been one of the first clients to step through her doors when she'd first opened the surgery. Back then Roger had held a tiny brown and white Jack Russell puppy, barely seven weeks old. He'd found the pup abandoned near his boat, clinging for his life on rocks exposed by a very low tide. Rocky was aptly named and developed his sea legs to accompany Roger on his boat for the past twelve years. The two had never been separated. Until now.

Roger sat rubbing his gnarled hands against one another. Jodi set a mug of coffee on her desk in front of him, which he lifted with crooked fingers, bent and misshapen from arthritis.

Jodi pulled a chair up next to him. Roger was a favourite client. He'd regaled her with story after story of his and Rocky's adventures on the sea. Over time, they'd become quite close.

"We're getting him stabilized now."

"What's wrong with him? He wouldn't eat this morning and when I put him outside he got to gagging. Then he had problems standing. I got in the truck and brought him right over. Sorry I didn't call ahead, but he started panting real hard."

Jodi patted Roger's leg. "You did the right thing. Cole found a paralysis tick on him."

"A tick? I haven't seen one of those bloodsuckers in years."

"We've been having lots of storms lately which probably instigated a hatching. Unfortunately, even if you'd found it and pulled it off, Rocky would've still needed treatment. As the female tick feeds, it injects a neurotoxin that binds to where nerves meet muscles. That's why he was having coordination problems."

"He'll be okay now though, won't he—since you got it off?"

Jodi offered him a deep sigh and what she hoped would be a comforting expression. "It's good you got him in here early. But unfortunately, even though we removed the tick, the toxins will continue to affect him. He has the antiserum on board and what he needs is quiet and rest. So I'm going to keep him here for a couple days and monitor him. He's not a young dog, and Cole tells me the tick was quite engorged, so in all likelihood he'll need a couple more injections of antiserum before it's all said and done."

"Well, you know best. Bloody hell. It'll be a right bugger not having him with me." Roger wiped his lips with the back of his hand. "But it'd be worse if he never came home. You just do whatever you need to do for him, Doc." He nodded as if in agreement with himself. He finished his coffee, set it on Jodi's desk, and pushed himself out of the chair.

"I promise, he'll be back with you as soon as we get him over this hump. Rocky is a special little guy. Nothing but the best treatment for him." Jodi rubbed his arm and smiled.

Roger nodded. "You've always been so good to me and ol' Rocky, Doc. I thank you kindly for that."

"It's no drama at all. You two are a couple of my most favourite clients. I'm not about to let anything happen to the seafaring dynamic duo."

Jodi accompanied Roger to the door and patted his back reassuringly before he walked out. "I'll call you later."

Roger waved over his shoulder as he made his way to his truck.

Jodi was fairly certain he was working hard to hold back tears. In all the years she'd known him, she'd never seen the old man cry, even when he'd brought Rocky in with a bloody big shark hook that had pierced clear through his flank, barely missing his intestine. There'd been blood everywhere, yet Roger hadn't blinked an eye. But even then, she'd been able to send Rocky home that same day with antibiotics and some anti-inflammatory medication. He'd never had to leave his faithful dog behind.

A woman appeared at the door with a young boy who held a small kitten in his arms.

"Good morning." Jodi forced a smile to her face.

"Hello. I have an appointment for our kitten to be vaccinated." The boy possessively held the kitten closer.

"Of course. Please have a seat and I'll have my vet nurse check you in."

Cole anticipated that Jodi would spend the night at the surgery to keep close tabs on Rocky. Mentally she shook her head, knowing the previous night's reprieve, in the guise of secretly kidnapping the phone, would hold little benefit with another potential sleep-deprived night for Jodi.

After making up a new client card and patient file, Cole showed the mother and son into one of the clinic rooms. Jodi met them and proceeded to undertake the tiny feline's first physical exam in preparation for the vaccination. Cole loved the way Jodi included the small boy in the conversation and the way he responded to whatever question Jodi asked him.

Cole scrubbed her knuckles over her tired eyes. She loved her life. A happy life. A busy life made all the busier by a boss who burned the candle at both ends. Jodi had been the best thing that had happened to her. When she and her fiancé had split and he'd fired her, she had no choice but to leave town and start again. She had moved from New Zealand to Australia and the seaside town of Yamba in New South Wales. Upon arrival, she'd read a help wanted ad for a new vet clinic in the local paper. Within hours of meeting Jodi, she had a contract drawn up and they had set to building up the practice. Jodi helped her study to turn her human nursing skills into qualified veterinary nursing skills, and together, they had never looked back. What with Jodi's skill and customer service reputation, the practice had grown quickly. It was now busy enough, in Cole's opinion, that a second vet could be accommodated comfortably.

But Jodi was both proud and particular in the care she offered her patients and their families. Cole had watched her work her fingers to the bone to set the clinic up. She'd been younger then. They both were. But here they were now, a few years down the track, and Cole's concern was that Jodi's current pace couldn't be continued in a healthy long-term way. The greatest challenge now was how was she going to sow the seed and convince Jodi to ease up on the reins and hand over a portion of control to someone else. Cole sighed. An emergency caesarean at three o'clock in the morning was so much easier by comparison.

The phone rang, interrupting her inner musings. She recognized the number. "Hi, Charlie." She smiled upon hearing her American friend's accent. She'd been lucky enough to get to know Charlie when she'd spent several weeks working at the clinic and living in the flat above. "I know. I miss seeing your ugly face every day too." Charlie laughed in response, and Cole smiled. "What can I do for you, my friend?" She listened on and glanced at the closed door. "Jodi's still with a client, but I don't imagine she'll be much longer. I don't know about her, but I for one definitely want to come over for a sticky beak and to see what you've done with the big cage. Will you be home this arvo?" Cole scribbled some notes down. "Uh-huh. As soon as she's free, I'll get her to call you. Okay. Bye."

Jodi swerved the Land Rover right and then quickly left to avoid another pothole carved out of the dirt road by the recent rains. She tried to avoid another immediately after, but the tyres lost their grip on the washboard surface. The hole was too big for the shock absorbers to do their job and the truck bounced and nearly went off the road.

"Far out, Jodes. Why'd you come down this road? It's horrible." Cole had a death grip on the door handle and another on the bag of fish and chips.

On a whim, Jodi had stopped at the fish co-op in Maclean to grab tea for Pip, Charlie, and the two of them.

Jodi grinned. "It's a shortcut." She stole a quick glance over at Cole. Truth told, she loved to put the truck through its paces. And to have someone with her made it doubly fun. Although it didn't look like Cole would agree. Jodi had a sudden impulse to slow down and take Cole's hand in reassurance. She blinked hard, not exactly knowing where the desire to make such intimate contact came from.

"By what? A minute?" Cole grunted when they hit another pothole.

Jodi refocused on the task. "When it comes to fish and chips, every minute counts. You can't eat them when they're cold. Yuck."

"I'm pretty sure Pip and Charlie have a microwave."

Jodi shook her head vehemently. "Oh no. It's not the same." She hit the brakes. The truck slid to a sudden stop. "Shit. Big one." She let off the brakes and let the Rover roll down the six inches of hole and crawl back up again after crossing the five-foot washed-out expanse. "Ah. There we go. See? We'll be there in no time."

"I won't have any teeth in my head by the time we get there."

Jodi signalled for a left turn. "Dentures aren't bad. Dad's had them for a long while. Once Mum got him the right glue to keep them from flying out every time he sneezed, everybody was happy. Sure was funny though."

"Mm."

Jodi had been torn about leaving Rocky alone to make the trip to Ashby to see Pip and Charlie's new eagle aviary. But he'd been resting comfortably and was stable. And Cole had grabbed her arm and refused to let go until she got in the truck.

"It'll be good to see those two. It's been a while since I've been over." Jodi tried to recall exactly when her last visit had been and couldn't.

"This is my first time, actually."

Jodi looked over incredulously. "Serious?"

"Yeah. There's just never been an occasion to."

"Mm. I suppose you're right. Before Charlie hit the scene, Pip pretty much kept to herself. For a long time, I only saw her when she brought something into the clinic."

"I don't remember you ever saying you'd been to Pip's."

Jodi swallowed as a rush of sadness wormed through her chest. Before Charlie, when she and Pip were both solo, there'd been a few Sundays when she'd felt pent up with the need to get out. So she'd showed up unannounced at Pip's and they'd tossed back a few beers after hiking Pip's property.

"Only a handful of times, really. The first time I went over was to drop off a whiptail wallaby joey. Poor Pip was so busy with the ten joeys she already had in care that she couldn't get away for five minutes to pick it up."

"But heaven forbid she'd ever say no to another orphan. Sounds just like her." Cole shook her head. "But now she has Charlie."

Jodi smiled. "Yeah. She does." A wash of envy brushed over her when she thought of Pip and Charlie. She gripped the steering wheel in resolution. No point thinking like that—she barely had enough time to do her own laundry most weeks. She certainly didn't have time to go looking for, or entertaining, a date. "I'm so glad they sorted out their differences. They deserve each other. And I mean that in the best way possible. And here we are." Jodi slowed and turned right onto the barely perceptible path that was Pip's driveway. Shrubs and leafy vegetation scraped and squeaked against the Rover's side as Jodi navigated through.

"I would never have found this place if I was on my own," Cole said.

"Trust me, the first time I came out here, I drove past it about a zillion times before I finally saw the barest hint of a tyre tread in the dried mud. Sure keeps the place private though."

"Just like Pip likes it."

After a few minutes of carefully avoiding low hanging branches, Jodi finally drove out of the thick bush into a small clearing, and the house came into view. The roof peaked sharply over weatherboard walls. A huge veranda wrapped around three of its sides. The windows were all rectangular six-sectioned library glass. Adjoining the house and looking over the enclosures in the backyard was the prep room that Pip had designed wholly for the animals. Jodi knew it was Pip's pride and joy.

"Wow. It's gorgeous. What a cute place. I love the old schoolhouse look."

"That's because it *is* an old schoolhouse, ya duffer. The building was for sale in Chatsworth. She fell in love with it, bought it, and had it moved here." Jodi parked in front of the house.

The prep room door opened up and Chilli bounded out in front of Pip.

"Hey, Pipsqueak." Jodi wrapped her arms around Pip and squeezed her tightly.

"Cole! Welcome," Pip said looking around Jodi's shoulder.

"Hi, Pip. Good to see you."

"Charlie is feeding the magpies, Jodes, if you want to head down there. I know she's been busting for you see this eagle aviary."

"Yeah, sure."

"Cole and I will meet you down there with drinks." Pip sniffed the air. "And I'll put the delectables you have in a warmer. We can eat down there."

"Perfect." Jodi walked around the prep room towards the shed in back. The outline of the eagle aviary stood out in the distance. "Far out."

"Is that you, Jodi?" Charlie called from a large cage attached to the shed.

"The one and only." Jodi didn't know how Charlie could've heard her amongst the hungry pleading from the magpies. She stopped beside the cage and peeked in. "How many do you have in there?"

"Eight. The six you gave us, and then two others we got calls about." Charlie plucked a piece of meat from the Tupperware container with tweezers and offered it to one of the birds. It gaped widely and flapped its wings against its sides.

"They're all doing good then?"

"Oh, yeah. They're mostly a healthy bunch. One has a small healed ulcer on its eye. I'll have to wait and see if it impacts his coordination and ability to fly or not."

Jodi nodded.

Charlie quickly fed two other magpies before coming out of the cage. She spread her arms wide and hugged Jodi. "Hi."

"Pip tells me you want to show me something?"

Charlie's smile broadened and her eyes twinkled with excitement. She grabbed Jodi's arm. "Oh my gosh! Wait until you see it. Big Bird loves it." She bounced from foot to foot. "Let me run this food back up to the prep room and I'll be back."

Jodi laughed as Charlie took off like a shot. Her exuberance was infectious and some of the stress and fatigue slid from her shoulders. The clinic and its patients were a constant presence in her mind, especially lately, no matter how hard she tried to push them aside. Even now, while waiting for Charlie's return, she hastily calculated when Rocky would need his next injection of antiserum.

"Ready?" Charlie suddenly appeared in front of her.

"Absolutely."

As they passed the other cages and pens that sheltered koalas, out-of-pouch kangaroo joeys, and an assortment of birds, a round building made a sudden appearance. It was so well structured that it seemed more part of the natural surroundings than something man-made.

"It's beautiful, Charlie." Jodi marvelled at the sheer height of the cage.

"Come on inside. I want you to really look at it and see if you have any feedback or suggestions from a vet's point of view."

Charlie opened a sliding door and they went in.

Jodi spun around in awe. "All I can say is wow. This is magnificent. And it'll be perfect for all raptors, not just your eagles."

"I know, right?"

"I only have one suggestion. You may want to mount some perches at different heights on a couple of the poles so the birds get used to landing in various situations."

Charlie tapped Jodi's arm. "You're starting to sound like a regular WREN person. Sure you don't want to change your career path?"

"No, thanks. I'll let you and Pip wrestle the wild things."

"Speaking of wild things," Pip said from behind them, "Charlie, do you want to show them how much your giant budgie likes it in here?"

"Yes. You all can watch Big Bird fly as a healed bird. In fact, it's fitting you're all here. Big Bird is here because of you, Cole, for finding him, Jodi, for putting him back together, and he's got the ability to do this"—Charlie spun around in a circle with her arms outstretched—"thanks to my darling Pip." Charlie kissed Pip on the cheek.

"And you, love. He's at this point largely because of all the work you put in to him."

Charlie smiled and nodded in proud acceptance of the recognition her efforts had contributed to the bird's recovery. "Be right back. He's in the adjoining outside pen so you could see it without him raising a fuss."

Jodi accepted the bottle of beer Cole handed her. "Impressive, hey?"

Cole shook her head. "This whole place is incredible."

Pip cleared her throat. "Um, we may want to watch from over by the bird care shed and the safety of the double-glazed window. You know how Big Bird gets around anybody that's not Charlie."

Jodi laughed as Cole sprinted over to the small building. The long side of the shed had been accommodated into the structure of the cage. Two sliding doors opened up into a light filled room.

Charlie arrived with Big Bird perched on her arm. He sat quietly and unmoving with his long wedge shaped tail draped over the back of her arm. He wore a hood and couldn't see anything. She closed the doors behind her and walked to the centre of the cage. She glanced over at them and said, "Here goes."

After removing the tether from the eagle's feathered leg, she carefully slid his hood off. The eagle blinked, looked around, but showed no signs of wanting to take flight. His cream coloured bill showed brightly against his reddish-brown head and wings.

Charlie raised and lowered her arm. Big Bird spread his wings and chirped. Jodi caught a glimpse of the one white primary feather that had grown back over the incision site. It was a stark contrast to the rest of his very dark ones. Suddenly, he crouched and pushed himself up, and with several powerful wing flaps, he lifted off and into the air. He flew the length of the cage, spread his tail feathers to slow, and banked right. After a few minutes, he flew to the top of the cage and circled overhead.

Jodi tore her gaze from the eagle and looked at Charlie who glowed like a proud parent. She knew Charlie was absorbing every detail of Big Bird's flight and committing it to memory. It wouldn't be long before the eagle was freely soaring the skies.

CHAPTER FOUR

With Cole's help, Pip collected the empty plates and stacked the dishwasher. "Thanks for dinner. That was really sweet of you guys, to bring out the fish and chips."

"Living out here, I don't suppose you eat too many takeaway meals."

"Not really. Tyranny of distance and all that. Which made dinner such a treat. And I got a night off cooking, so I feel like a right winner."

"I can appreciate that."

Pip poured them each a wine and leaned against the counter. "I owe you an apology."

Cole choked slightly on a mouthful of wine. "Sorry? Come again?"

"It occurred to me when we were walking around earlier, that I've never invited you out here before. And for that I apologize."

"Oh no. You don't have to—"

"Yes. I do. I'm afraid I have been a bit of a crap friend these past few years, what with one thing and another. And I'm sorry. I should have had you both out here a long time ago for lunch, or dinner, or something social. So"—Pip raised her glass in Cole's direction—"I hereby rescind my troglodyte ways and would love it if you both would come out here one night for wining and dining. And now that we've repaired the cabin, you're both welcome to camp overnight so you won't have to worry about being tired or drinking and driving."

Cole grimaced. "Jodi told me the cabin got hammered pretty badly from the flood."

"Mm." Pip looked off into the distance to where she knew Charlie would be settling Big Bird in. "When I organized help for building Charlie's big budgie cage, I had some engineers and builders come in and sort out the foundations to the cabin and set it back on stronger, stabilized supports. Easier to have all the workmen come out at the same time and choof off when they're done. Fingers crossed, it should be right from here on out."

"I'd love that. Charlie used to rave about the cabin with the tree and everything growing in the middle of the house."

"Well, any time you come over, or need a place to hide out, the place is yours."

"I might just take you up on that."

They both took a seat at the breakfast bar. "Charlie tells me you built the cabin yourself."

"Largely, although I cheated with the house. I bought it and had it moved out here. It was in a pretty sore and sorry state, so I managed to pick it up for a song. It's been a labour of love."

"I can see that. It really is quite amazing."

"Thanks. I like it."

"And the prep room is choice."

"You like it?" Pip grinned with pride. "I knew what I wanted and had it all planned out. Jodi was gold, helping me with suppliers or showing me some neat tips and tricks that would be cost effective."

"You two must go back a ways then."

Pip thought about Cole's remark. It felt like she'd known Jodi forever. "Thirteen or fourteen years." She shrugged. "Something like that. I met her when she first came to town. I'd only been here a few years myself when I ran into her. She was trying to feel her way into the town, and I was in need of a good vet. We're a similar age and it was nice to connect with someone. We've been mates ever since."

"You seem pretty tight."

"We are."

"You've never been more than just friends?"

Pip chortled softly into her wine. "No. There was no time for relationships. Friendship was more important for both of us. We were both married to our dreams. Still are."

"But you have Charlie now."

Pip sat back in her chair and reflected to the recent past. So much had changed since Charlie had come to Australia on a work exchange visa. Her entire life had changed. "Yeah. I do."

"And has your dream changed?"

"Yes. And no. Now I have someone to share it with. I never thought that would happen."

"That must feel pretty nice. To have someone to share with, I mean."

"It is. It truly is. It's not been easy, but then, somehow I think that makes it all the better. Life is still busy, yet it's less hectic, if that makes sense."

Cole furrowed her brows as she glanced at the doorway. "Has Jodi ever talked to you about getting a business partner?"

The conversation was interrupted by the sound of footsteps at the doorway, as they were joined by Charlie and Jodi.

"Ooh, wine. Yes, please. Did we miss anything?" Charlie kissed Pip as she handed over a glass.

Pip held up the bottle to Jodi in question, but Jodi shook her head. "Can I nab a coffee instead?" Jodi looked at her watch.

"Sure. I'll put the jug on." Pip looked up at the wall clock. It was late afternoon, and Jodi wanted coffee. It didn't take much to put two and two together. "You expecting a late night?"

Jodi frowned. "I'll need to head back to the clinic soon. I want to check on Rocky. Roger Hanson's little dog. Paralysis tick."

Pip winced. "Nasty bastards." She handed over a mug of coffee. "Will he be okay?"

Jodi scrunched up her nose, her back straight and tense. "He's not a young dog. Hopefully we got it in time."

"Fingers crossed then, hey?"

"Hm." Jodi sipped her coffee.

"Big Bird looked really strong today, yeah?" Pip rubbed Charlie's back.

"I know, right? I think the direct flights I had him taking from the perch to me have made all the difference."

"When will you release him?" Jodi leaned against the counter. She didn't bother sitting at the table knowing they'd have to get going shortly.

"Well..." Charlie bit her lip. "Relatively soon. I need to find a release site for him first though."

"We need to do it before Charlie has to leave the country." Pip linked her fingers through Charlie's.

"You're leaving? I thought you were guaranteed another year." Cole moved next to Jodi.

Charlie sighed. "That's the sticky part, I'm afraid. I have to leave every three months. Returning effectively renews my temporary visa for another three months."

"Wow. That's a pain. Does it matter where you go?" Jodi saw a flash of sadness in Pip's eyes.

"No. I can go anywhere, actually. This time I'm going back to the States to visit my dogs. I miss them terribly."

Jodi smiled. "Do you think you'll bring them here?"

"Absolutely. That's one of the things I want to accomplish while I'm there. I've looked into what importing them entails." Charlie blew out a big breath. "It's a lot. But the first thing that's required is to have a rabies titre drawn. Then a hundred eighty days after that, they can get on a plane."

"Ah, that's right. I knew they'd changed the rules and put the burden of work on the owner instead of Australia being responsible for it. That also shortens the amount of time they have to stay in quarantine, from six months to ten days."

"How do you know all this?" Cole nudged Jodi.

"I'm a vet. I have to." Jodi set her empty mug next to the sink.

Cole huffed. "Or it's something you read, and having a photographic memory helps."

Jodi screwed her nose up. "Or something." She pushed away from the counter. "I have a few ideas of where you could release your eagle. I'll email some maps to you tonight, if you'd like."

"That'd be champion, Jodes," Pip said. "Thanks. I'd forgotten about your avid knowledge of the area and your obsessive hobby of bushwalking. I told Charlie I could think of maybe one area that doesn't have a dominant wedgie pair, but I haven't been there recently to really check it out."

"No worries." Jodi checked her watch again and frowned. "Hey, I have to get going. Rocky will need another injection as soon as I get back to the clinic."

"I can't imagine having to leave every three months," Cole said after they'd turned out of Pip's driveway and onto the main road headed back to Yamba.

"I guess it's the price Charlie has to pay until she's granted permanent residency. I know Pip will be more than supportive through it all. But I also know she's going to really feel Charlie's absence, even if Charlie is only gone for a few days."

"Did she say something?"

"No." Pip used to talk to her a lot, but since Charlie, well, Jodi had to admit she missed her friend. "I saw it on her face." She shrugged half-heartedly. She couldn't deny feeling a bit envious of what Pip and Charlie had, despite the immigration issues. She was more than happy for Pip. At the same time Jodi wondered if she'd made a mistake somewhere along the line by focusing exclusively on her career, disallowing herself a chance to meet someone and fall in love. Oh, well. It seemed like a moot point. It was what it was.

It was past dark when they arrived at the clinic. Jodi parked the Rover next to Cole's car. "See you in the morning." Jodi turned the truck off and released her seat belt.

"Promise me you'll go home at a decent hour and get some sleep." Cole opened the door and slid out.

"You know it'll depend on how Rocky is doing. I'm going to monitor him for a while after I give him this next antiserum. If I think he can be left for a few hours again, I promise I will go home." Jodi met Cole's eyes and smiled tiredly.

Cole shook her head. "I have no doubt that you'll fall asleep in your office chair for an hour, if not all night. But, okay. You're the boss. Call me if you need me to come back in."

Jodi grinned. They both knew Cole's words were wasted. There'd only been a handful of times that she'd requested Cole's nonsurgical help in the middle of the night. But she'd also lost count of the times when she'd worked as both surgeon and anaesthetist. Jodi justified her decision because time was of the essence and she couldn't wait for Cole to make the hour drive into Yamba.

Jodi had already unlocked the door to the clinic before Cole drove out. Rocky was first and foremost on her mind, so she headed straight towards where the Jack Russell was housed.

When the practice began treating more cases of paralysis tick a few years ago, she and Cole had devised a special oxygen crate. They'd covered a cage in clear plastic, so the animal could see out. Oxygen was pumped in via a tube attached to the side, the flow calculated based on the size of the crate and the dog.

Rocky seemed to be resting comfortably. He lay on his side, and at first glance the rise and fall of his rib cage seemed normal. Jodi pressed the stethoscope to Rocky's side.

"Looks can be deceiving, hey, little man?"

Rocky lethargically thumped his tail once.

Jodi closed his cage and increased the oxygen flow. She double-checked Rocky's IV site before drawing antiserum into a syringe and administering it through the port. "We'll see how you go with this next one." She traded the near empty bag of lactated Ringer's with a fresh one and adjusted the flow.

She was unwilling to leave him, and pinched the skin at her throat. She'd promised Roger an update. Before she went to the office to make the call, she made a cup of coffee. Although the heartburn was starting to make itself known, she couldn't do without the boost of caffeine. She had a feeling it was going to be a long night.

As Cole drove away from the surgery, she automatically glanced in the rear-view mirror. As she'd expected, Jodi had gone inside the moment she had dropped her off. She sighed. Her heart felt heavy with increasing concern for Jodi and the continuous long hours she was putting in with little respite. Cole squinted at the sudden harsh assault of car headlights as she passed a knot of oncoming traffic.

Cole slowed the car at an intersection. Her mind balked at her heavy introspection. Why was she taking such a personal interest in Jodi's life? After all, Jodi was simply her boss. But that was too flippant. Too easy. Jodi was more than that. She was also her friend who'd helped her get back on her feet again.

She shook her head. Too involved. They spent more time together than an average married couple, simply because of the nature of their work. She needed to take a step back. Jodi was, after all, a big girl who could take care of herself. She needed to draw a line and not get so involved. That had been her undoing in her last relationship, and look where that had gotten her—nowhere, unless you counted engaged, dumped, penniless, unemployed, and with nowhere to live as progress in life. She drew in a big breath and pulled her shoulders back in an attempt to relax. It worked for all of about ten seconds. Cole frowned. Dammit if she didn't want what was best for Jodi. It wasn't a crime, was it?

She drummed her fingers on the steering wheel. The practice currently had two vet nurses on the books working a variety of hours. If Jodi took on another vet, there would be more work available. They were a tight-knit group, a happy, well-balanced team. Whoever came in would need to fit in to that. Cole nervously bit a fingernail. If she was going to present some options for Jodi to consider, then she needed to make them good ones. She racked her brain about the last few vets that had blessed their doorstep with their presence. They'd had a few locums in for brief stints, but none that shone from memory.

Cole looked up in time to see a shooting star flash across the horizon. *Reminds me of the flaming arrow they used one time at the Olympics to light the cauldron.* Arrow. Of course—Fletcher! Cole laughed and slapped the wheel at the pleasure her own cunning gave her. Catherine Fletcher. Cate had been a mature student in her final year of veterinary science who'd served her last six months in the surgery, gaining valuable hands-on time with clients and animals under Jodi's guidance. She still had Cate's number somewhere. Cole decided to call her when she got home, to catch up, to see how she was going, and to maybe get a feel for where she was and what she was doing.

A small nagging feeling chewed away at the back of her mind. She felt slightly guilty and devious for plotting behind Jodi's back. But something strange, alien almost, was hinting to her subconscious that this was an important thing for her to pursue. And if there was one thing her grandmother always taught her, it was to listen to her inner feelings—she might not understand what they were saying at the time, but she knew they were there for a reason.

"Hey, babe. Look what Jodi sent over." Charlie clicked on each of the three maps and enlarged them.

Pip set a cup of tea on the table next to Charlie's computer and peered over her shoulder. "Jackadgery, Dorrigo, and Nymboida. Those are rough and remote places, just where the wedgies like it best."

"Now we need to find out if there are any breeding pairs in those areas." Charlie shook her head. "I don't know if we'll have time enough before I leave." She put her head in her hands. "Damn immigration. I hate this." She drained her cup. "Tell me again why we can't release Big Bird near where Cole found him."

"Because there's going to be some fairly wide scale clearing happening there to make way for hobby farms later in the year. He'll only have five minutes to settle in before everything gets torn to pieces. We need to find him someplace not only where he'll be safe, but also that you'll be happy with long term." Pip rubbed Charlie's back and sat down next to her. "Leave it with me. I'll make a few calls to Parks and Wildlife, and to Raptor Care and Conservation. They'd know better than anyone what's out there."

Charlie leaned her head against Pip's. "See? In one swift move, you've managed to make things better. What would I do without you?"

"Probably get deported because you'd be hiking all over looking for the perfect place to release your budgie, and then be late leaving Australia."

"Please, don't even go there. I'm nervous enough as it is."

"You'll be right, sweet. Things will work out. You'll see."

Charlie nodded and sighed. "Deep down, I know that. But my pessimistic side, which also runs the anxiety department, is sitting in the driver's seat."

"Well, knock the chair out from under her then." Pip wrapped an arm around Charlie's shoulders and squeezed her close. "Come on, lovely. Let's go to bed and work on those chair tipping techniques."

CHAPTER FIVE

Jodi woke up still sitting at her desk in front of the computer. She looked at the screen, which of course was black because it had gone into sleep mode. She drew a big breath, pressed a hand to her back, and tried to stretch some of the stiffness out. She checked the time. "Oh, shit. Cole'll be here in fifteen minutes."

Jodi grabbed a fresh pair of scrubs and changed quickly. She rolled her dirty clothes up, sprinted out to the truck, and tossed them onto the floor in the back where they'd be out of sight.

After a quick freshen up in the bathroom, Jodi filled the coffee maker with water and switched it on. While the coffee brewed, she pulled Rocky's chart from the active file and went to the kennelling area. Her heart sank when she found him on his side breathing heavily. Jodi increased the oxygen flow, injected another dose of antiserum, and noted the time on his chart. "Damn ticks. Mongrel things, aren't they, Rocky?"

"Talking to yourself again, I see," Cole said from the doorway. "How's the little man doing?"

Jodi scowled. "Not as well as I'd hoped. I just turned the O2 up. We'll need to watch him very closely from here on out."

Cole cocked her head and Jodi was sure she was being scrutinized. "You spent the night here, didn't you?"

Jodi widened her eyes innocently. "Why would you say that? I'm not wearing the clothes I had on last night. Doesn't that say something?"

"Oh yes. But contrary to what you're *trying* to make me believe, it's easy to throw on fresh scrubs and hide your old clothes in your truck. Which, by the way, hasn't been driven since yesterday when we got back."

"And you would know this, how?"

Cole crossed her arms over her chest. "The hood of the truck is cold and there aren't any tyre tracks in the dew."

"You should've gone to detective school instead of vet nursing," Jodi groused and handed Cole Rocky's chart.

"I hardly see any need for that. I've already got you figured out, Doc."

Jodi laughed. "It seems you do. Come on, let's have a cuppa and you can tell me what's on today's agenda." She walked past Cole and gave her a playful little shove. "Smart-arse."

While Cole logged on to the computer to bring up the day's schedule, Jodi poured two mugs of coffee. The headache between her eyes spoke loudly of lack of sleep and needing a caffeine fix. She put Cole's mug on the desk and sat down on one of the lounges in the waiting room.

"Speak to me, Detective Impresario." Jodi made herself comfortable and sipped her coffee.

Cole rolled her eyes but stayed focused on the screen. "Okay. Appointments this morning, and then this arvo you're going to Hodder Stables to vaccinate, check teeth, and lastly check on my favourite horse."

"*Your* favourite? When have you ever stepped foot on that horse stud?"

"Never. But if they have a horse named Coal, then it would have to be my favourite."

"Okay. I'll give you that. Anything fancy this morning?"

"Same old, same old—stitches out, needles in, surgical and annual health rechecks."

The majority of the morning passed uneventfully. The appointments were fairly straightforward, other than the big old tomcat admitted into surgery. He was sporting a painful abscess on his cheek, no doubt from fighting with another cat. She would lance and drain it before she left for the horse stud later in the afternoon.

"Ah, there you are. I thought you'd already fed the girls earlier this morning." Charlie unlatched the gate to the koala pen and affectionately ran the back of her fingers over the coat of Alinta, a female koala wedged into a Y section of housing who was watching her with sleepy eyes. She squatted next to Pip on an upturned milk crate, where Pip cradled another of the long-term residents, Lucille, in her arms.

"I did. I just came back to check on them."

"Something wrong?"

A frown marred Pip's normally relaxed face.

"Not sure. Lucille wasn't really interested in the fresh red gum this morning, and that's always been her favourite. And she seems super cuddly."

Charlie knew Pip had a big soft spot for Lucille, who had come into her care after being hit by a car and sustaining significant head injuries. No one had expected the koala to live, but with a joey in her pouch, Pip gave her and the joey every chance to pull through she could afford. Lucille rallied and Pip nursed her back into health. Months later, the joey grew into a fine young koala who was released back into the wild to carry on Lucille's genetic legacy.

Left with some residual brain damage, and mildly uncoordinated, Lucille was unable to be returned to her natural habitat, and she now lived her days out in comfort with abundant fresh food, milk treats, and regular cuddles whenever she requested them. And since being taken into care and returned to health, Lucille had proven to be a wonderful surrogate mother to orphaned joeys.

Charlie scratched the back of Lucille's neck. The koala raised her head from Pip's shoulder and stretched her arms out for a cuddle, crossing bodies to snuggle into Charlie's embrace. She inhaled Lucille's sweet, clean eucalyptus odour and smiled. Koalas were truly magical, wondrous creatures, unlike anything else she had ever encountered, and Lucille was one in a million. She was going to miss cuddle time from Lucille when she headed back Stateside.

Pip walked over to a fresh bucket of leaves, plucked a stem, and brought it back. Lucille reached out and munched on the offered leaves happily.

"Well, if you're worried, why don't you ask Jodi to come over and take a look at her?" Charlie hefted Lucille back into the fork of the tree stand in the enclosure. "She seems to be eating okay now."

"Hm. Might be nothing."

Charlie took Pip's hand and gave it a light squeeze as they walked back. "Have you heard anything yet from your friends in Parks and Wildlife, or Raptor Care?"

Pip chuckled. "Not yet, love. But then, it's only been a little while since I sent off the emails. I've seen you studying the files Jodi sent over. Do you have a spot in mind?"

"I rather like the look and sound of Jackadgery. And it has the added bonus of being the closest."

"Is that why you picked it? Because it's closest?"

"Oh no. It has some marvellous escarpments and a variety of forestation, from dense to light sclerophyll with the odd pocket of clearing. It's sparsely populated, with only a handful of roads in the area. And the climate is pretty much the same as where he originally came from. But"—Charlie couldn't help but smirk guiltily—"it just happens to be the closest, which is a bonus, I'll admit."

Pip laughed. "I'm just pulling your chain a little, but as your mentor, I had to ask and make sure you had thought it out with more than just your heart, even though I knew you would."

"Heh. Sucks to be boss, huh?" Charlie felt a slight twinge of discomfort that Pip felt the need to revert back to a supervisor's role instead of trusting her.

"Oh, I don't know, it has its perks."

Charlie stopped walking. Pip's flippant attitude puzzled her.

Pip stroked Charlie's jawline tenderly. "I wouldn't be doing either of us any favours if I went all soft on you just because you're my bed buddy. Besides, I need to make sure you're up to speed if ever I should decide to retire and put my feet up."

Charlie playfully coughed. "You could never retire."

Pip kissed her lightly before resuming their walk back to the house. "You're probably right. But I needed to ask, just as I think you needed to say those reasons out loud to yourself."

Charlie pondered Pip's words. She was right. She hadn't stopped thinking about all the options since Jodi's email first came through, compiling lists and poring over maps to justify her choice. She wrapped her arm around Pip's shoulders. "Dammit. I hate it when you're right."

Pip winked at her. "I know."

Jodi left Cole to keep an eye on the cat while he woke up from the sedation. She'd considered putting a drain in to facilitate the healing, but given he lived in a cowshed, she gave him a sufficient injection of antibiotics.

She donned overalls over her scrubs and settled a baseball cap onto her head. Cole had already supplied the tackle box with everything she needed for the horse stud visit. Although her clinic was primarily a small animal surgery, there were a few clients whose livestock she tended to as well. She didn't mind tending to horses or the odd sheep or cow as it sharpened her familiarity with large animal husbandry.

"Rocky will need another injection before you leave, Cole. Can you just text me the time you give it and how he's doing?"

"No dramas. I just checked him and he's stable."

"Good. Okay, then I'll see you tomorrow. You know how Mr. Hodder likes to ramble on about his Percherons."

"About as much as he does when he brings his kelpies in, I reckon." Jodi grimaced. "Yep."

"How many times have you heard the same stories now?"

"I've lost count. But every once in a while he does add a new titbit in." Jodi juggled the truck keys and walked out the door.

The drive to Casino was one she enjoyed. The widespread sugar cane fields gave way to national forest on both sides, eventually spilling out onto rolling paddocks, where hundreds of cattle grazed, an assembly of different breeds, from Simmental, Charolais, and Hereford to Angus, Brangus, and Brahmas.

Jodi passed a McDonald's in town and considered getting a coffee. She decided against it, figuring it was only another ten minutes, and Lord help her if she had to interrupt Frank Hodder to ask if she could use his toilet.

The driveway to the Hodder Stud was framed by three huge poles. Metal silhouettes of a Percheron horse on one side and a kelpie on the other faced the Hodder Stud sign, which hung proudly in the middle.

The road was lined the entire length with purple flowering jacaranda trees. Despite the winter rains, Frank Hodder kept his five kilometre dirt drive impeccably smooth.

The house came into view first, dazzlingly white where the afternoon sun touched it. The solar panelled roof peaked sharply, giving the structure some adornment to make up for the lack of windows on this western facing side.

Jodi followed the circular drive around to where the main entrance had been built to take full advantage of the morning light as well as the 1,800 stunning acres, which fanned out in front of it. A huge, marble floored veranda, lined with potted plants of all shapes and sizes, gave host to a number of Adirondack chairs. Frank Hodder stood up from one of them and approached Jodi's truck.

"G'day, Doc. Room in there for me to catch a ride down?"

"Indeed there is." Jodi waited while Frank got into the truck. "Where to first?"

"I reckon we'll head over to the yearling barn, then to the training barn, then the foaling barn. I made sure Bob brought everybody in that needed tending to. He'll be happy you're on time because he's going to have to clean every one of them stalls again." Frank rubbed the stubble on his chin. "We'll get the yearlings done quick to be nice on him. Them young horses don't know how to keep a clean stall yet."

Jodi drove down the westward sloping lane to the barns. White vinyl fencing surrounded huge, empty paddocks that had been cropped close and trampled hard and bare in spots where the Percherons congregated in the shade or at water troughs.

"After you're done, we'll be running the yearlings up into the green paddocks near the river. They'll stay up there until they graze them out or the rains start again, whichever comes first, I reckon. I bought a solar powered irrigator from a bloke in Western Australia. Decided to try it out in the brood mare pasture. It's damn near the greenest part on the farm."

Jodi smiled and nodded. Frank was always looking for ways to maintain a green lifestyle, for his horses and dogs as well. Every time she visited his farm, there was always some new contraption he was trying out.

"You'll want to turn left for the yearling barn here, Doc."

Jodi pressed her tongue into her cheek. She'd been here enough times to know her way around, but Frank always thoughtfully reminded her.

She parked the Rover close to the open entrance of the Zincalume cladded barn. Everything about Frank's barns spoke of keeping his horses cool in the summer heat, and out of the cold rain and wind in the winter. The ceiling was high, and each of the ten stalls was occupied by a grey or black muscled individual looking out over the stall door.

Bob walked out of the feed room and engulfed Jodi's hand in his. "Always an extreme pleasure to see you, Jodi." He was a small lively man with dark leathery skin like an old well-polished boot. His sparkling brown eyes were full of naughtiness and his grin was too innocent to be true.

Jodi rolled her eyes at Bob's politeness. "Good to see you as well."

"Come on, come on, Doc has work to do, so quit your flirting. Let's start with Ringo."

"Yes, sir." Bob winked at Jodi. He slid the ever-present lead rope off his shoulder and opened the door to the first stall. "Do you want me to bring them into the aisle?"

"That won't be necessary. I just need to give them a quick once-over before I vaccinate them."

Ringo was a big strapping yearling. He sported a straight profile, broad head, large eyes, and small ears. His dappled grey hide shone even in the low light of the barn, speaking loudly of the intense grooming and excellent diet Frank made sure he and all the other horses received.

While Jodi listened to Ringo's heart and lungs, checked his teeth, and gave him his needle, Frank rambled on how the breed originated in France, in the Perche province. Although this was the umpteenth time she'd heard it, she continued on with the rest of the yearlings, nodding and exclaiming at the appropriate times. She'd learned early on she wouldn't get a word in edgewise anyway. Even Bob remained politely quiet, responding with little grunts whenever something was required of him.

Not much changed in the training barn, except the horses were much bigger and more mature. Frank explained his training techniques and even bragged a little about his success at the Casino agricultural show.

The brood mare barn was their final stop. A few of the mares had already foaled earlier in the week. With Frank holding the seemingly unconcerned mares and Bob attempting to hold the already strapping foals, Jodi gave them their first real health exam.

Frank pointed towards the back part of the barn. "These last four mares are due to foal within the month. Bob brings them in at night to get them used to their stalls. We like them to foal in the stalls so we can keep an eye on them. I sure don't need them disappearing into the scrub and then having a problem."

"No, you sure don't." Jodi quickly peeked into each stall as she followed Frank down the cement aisle. The mares' bellies were enormous from the growing foals within.

"Coal here is a week late, Doc," Frank said as they stood in front of her stall.

The mare was jet black with just a hint of white hair on her upper lip. Long hair grew down from her fetlocks and covered her enormous pancake shaped hooves. To Jodi, she looked miserable with her head hanging low. The mare shifted her hind feet every few seconds to seemingly give them a break from the extra weight she carried.

"Frank, I'll do Coal last. I want to look at her closer."

"Righto."

The other three mares were alert and eager to go back outside. The fact that Coal wasn't as anxious to join her herd mates bothered Jodi.

As with the other horses, Jodi waited until Bob put a halter on Coal before she entered the stall. But the mare didn't seem to even notice their presence.

Jodi rested her hand on Coal's neck when she placed the stethoscope against the horse's chest. Her heart rate was elevated and she was sweating lightly beneath Jodi's hand.

"Frank, I'm pretty sure this mare is in labour."

"Nah. Can't be. Every foal she's ever dropped here has been in the wee hours of the morning." Frank swiped a hand down Coal's neck. "She *is* sweating more than usual."

Jodi bent over and checked the mare's udder. "She's waxed."

"Bob, we better wrap her tail." Frank took the lead rope from him.

Jodi lifted Coal's upper lip and pressed a finger against Coal's gum, then released it. The tissue was slow to return to a healthy pink. "This mare's in trouble. She needs fluids. I'll be right back." Jodi jogged out to the truck and opened the back. She grabbed two bags of Lactated Ringer's and an IV set, then hurried back to the stall.

She quickly plunged the end of the IV set into the fluids bag and handed it to Bob who stood ready to give a hand. Jodi inserted the needle into the mare's jugular and adjusted the flow to wide open.

Suddenly the mare's legs gave out and she dropped to the ground. She rolled onto her side with a groan and pushed as a contraction took hold of her.

"Bob, make sure that line doesn't kink." Jodi pulled on a long plastic glove. She squirted a generous amount of lubricating gel onto it and knelt behind the mare's hindquarters. She was just about to insert her hand when the mare pushed. "Oh, crap." Jodi stared in disbelief as two noses appeared at the vulva opening.

"What's going on, Doc?" Frank squatted down next to her. "Bloody hell. She has two in there?"

Jodi nodded wordlessly and waited until the contraction ended. She eased her hand inside, closed her eyes, and pictured what she was feeling. One of the foals reacted with its tongue when she touched its nose. The other seemed sluggish. She reached in further and pushed against the lively one's chest to try to give the other more room to come out. Her arm and hand were suddenly crushed with the onset of another contraction. Jodi gritted her teeth and waited it out.

The mare hoisted herself onto her belly and threw her front legs forward.

"Bob, keep her down!" Frank rose quickly and went to the mare's head. Within moments they were able to push Coal back down onto her side.

The mare groaned loudly. Her huge belly rose and fell heavily as she worked to breathe.

Jodi offered up a silent prayer that her arm wouldn't be broken while she tried to deliver these foals. She pushed again, to no avail. The foals weren't going anywhere. She followed one of the foals' neck until she located a tiny hoof, which she slowly drew forward. After waiting out another bone crushing contraction, she found the second front leg. Once she had them together in her hand, she pulled. But when two tiny right shoulders emerged, she quickly realized she was pulling on both foals. "Dammit." Jodi glanced up and saw Frank lowering his mobile from his ear. She let go of the legs, re-lubricated her arm, and pushed against the foals and the strength of the mare, who was intent on working against her. Sweat ran down her face into her eyes and dripped off the edge of her nose. Somehow she had to find a way to untangle them. She closed her eyes and, by touch, tried to map out which body part belonged to which foal. Just when she thought she had them figured out, she'd realize she was wrong. Again. And again. Jodi lost track of time. Her entire focus was on what was happening inside Frank's prize mare. Her fingers tingled and went numb. Despite resting and flexing, all she felt was the pressure of the powerful contractions as they constricted the blood in her arm. But after a few minutes, it was apparent the mare was tiring and the birth canal was dangerously drying out. She had to get these foals out before they suffocated.

"Jodi." A voice sounded far off.

"Jodi." She felt a strong tap on her shoulder. "Come on. Let me have a go."

Jodi opened her eyes and focused on the figure squatting next to her. Jeff Callahan, the area's horse specialist, squeezed lubricant onto his already gloved arm.

"There isn't much time. You need to move out of the way so I can save this mare and her foals."

Jodi silently nodded, withdrew her arm, and scuttled back on her haunches. Her arm ached and needles of blood rushed back into her fingers.

Within moments, Jeff had the first foal delivered. "Bob, give the fluids to Frank and come back here." Bob was instantly at Jeff's side. "Give this foal mouth-to-mouth and try to get it breathing." He dragged the lifeless body away from the mare to give them both some room to work.

Jeff reached back inside for the second foal.

Coal gave one final push and deposited the remaining foal at Jeff's knees. Although the mare was covered in sweat and breathing hard, she rolled up and managed a nicker to her babies.

Jodi stood up, feeling completely useless. Bob had gotten the first foal breathing on his own and was rubbing him dry with handfuls of straw. Its nostrils flared and its tiny tongue slipped out and disappeared again. A wave of relief washed over her when she saw the regular rise and fall of its chest.

Jeff stripped his glove off and quickly wiped the second foal's mouth and nose clear and compressed its chest. But after several moments, it was clear to everyone that the filly would never take a breath. "Too bloody late," Jeff muttered as he closed the foal's sightless eyes with a gentle swipe of his hand.

Frank couldn't spare a glance her way. She knew he blamed her for the loss of the second foal. Hell, she knew it was her fault. In a daze and completely deflated, she quietly slipped out of the barn while Jeff spoke with Frank. Bob was still focused on his foal. A heaviness settled over her as she drove back to Yamba.

CHAPTER SIX

In the car. That was where Cole found her. Staring straight ahead, sitting behind the wheel, the Land Rover's windows beginning to fog up. Cole had spied the lights turning into the surgery's driveway just on dark, twenty minutes before, and had come out to investigate when Jodi hadn't come inside.

Jodi sat in the driver's seat with her hands sitting limply in her lap, her face pale in the glow of the torchlight from Cole's mobile phone. Cole tapped on the window. Jodi didn't blink, let alone respond to the noise. She tapped again. Nothing. Cole slowly opened the door and gasped. Jodi's overalls were stained and wet. The cloying smells of urine, manure, and sweat engulfed her briefly as she pulled the door open.

Cole squared her shoulders. She needed to get Jodi out of the car. She squatted, cupped Jodi's jaw, and slowly turned her head until their eyes met. "Looks like you had a big afternoon."

Moisture welled and glistened in Jodi's eyes. "Yeah." Her voice was raspy. Her words almost choked out.

Cole's chest cramped "C'mon, love. Come with me. We need to get you out of these clothes and into something clean and warm."

Jodi nodded mutely.

Jodi's consent and her return to awareness pleased Cole, who was shocked to see her strong, resilient, calm-under-pressure boss so flat and beaten by the day's events. Her curiosity burned with the need to know what had happened, but she swallowed it down. Right now, Jodi needed her help, not an inquisition—question time would come later. She helped Jodi from the car and together they went straight upstairs to the one bedroom flat above the surgery. Cole guided Jodi into the bathroom and turned the shower on. Jodi stood motionless as the steam gathered and built in the tiny room. Cole smiled tentatively. "Let's get these overalls off and get you in the shower."

Cole peeled the heavy cotton garment off, followed by Jodi's scrubs, and Cole winced when she saw the mass of blotched bruises from mid-upper arm down to her wrist. She turned Jodi's arm to get a good look and sighed. "Looks like a tough day at the office, huh?" Cole undid the tie on Jodi's scrub pants and let them fall to the floor, before gently turning her to remove her bra and underpants. Cole cupped her hands underneath Jodi's elbows, mindful of the bruised right arm. "Into the shower, love. The warmth will do you a power of good. Did you need a hand, or are you right?"

"I'm okay." Jodi's voice was flat and lifeless.

"That's good then. You just soak awhile and I'll be back in a few minutes."

Jodi turned around and faced her through the clear glass shower screen. "Thank you."

Cole dipped her head in acknowledgement. "You're welcome." She scooped up the dirty clothes and closed the door behind her. Jogging down the stairs, she tried to bleed off some of the nervous anxiety that had built in her body after finding Jodi in such a state. She threw the clothes into the washing machine and set it to soak. Quickly assessing all the animals in care, she locked the doors and set the surgery's alarm for the night. As she ran back up the stairs, she could still hear the shower going. There was food in the kitchen—she could whip something up if Jodi wanted it. Cole set the jug to boil and went in search of the fresh clean clothes she knew Jodi kept for the odd occasion when she stayed in the flat. Pulling out some soft flannel pyjama pants and a cotton long-sleeved top, she snagged an old soft brushed-cotton dressing gown from the cupboard and a hot water bottle. Cole's choices were all about warmth and comfort.

Once Jodi was dressed, Cole settled her on the couch, hot water bottle snugged in tight and a blanket over her lap. She handed Jodi a steaming mug.

Jodi took a sip and her eyebrows shot up at the first taste.

Cole sipped her own mug and winked at her. "I figured some hot chocolate might be better than a coffee."

"There's more than just chocolate in that mix."

Cole batted her eyes innocently. "And I might have added a slurp of brandy for good luck."

Jodi huffed as she took another sip.

"Do you want to talk about this afternoon?" Cole took a mouthful and held the liquid warmth in her mouth for just a moment before swallowing.

"I screwed up."

"What do you mean?"

"I killed one of your favourite horse's babies." Jodi's flat hard tone sent shivers up her spine.

"I'm going to need more information before I can believe that." Cole carried the bottle of brandy over to the coffee table and sat down on the couch next to Jodi.

Jodi stared off into space. The silence stretched out uncomfortably.

"I got to Hodder's, checked over all the young stock, and finally the brood mares. The mare worried me from the outset. I left her till last. I should have looked at her first. She was in labour. She didn't look good."

"Did Frank know she was in labour?"

Jodi shook her head. Even though she was obviously reliving the afternoon, her body was definite in its response. "No. But I *knew* something wasn't right. I took too long. I should have gotten to her sooner."

Cole needed Jodi to focus on facts, not what-ifs. "What happened?"

"She had twins. I no sooner set up an IV than she went down. The foals were stuck and trying to come out at the same time. I tried to push the big one back in and give the smaller one a chance to get out. Their legs were everywhere, all caught up in each other. I took too long."

"Did you do your best?"

Jodi nodded.

"And?"

"And I should have seen the signs sooner. Reacted faster. Done something more to save her. But I didn't. I was too slow. Too arrogant. I knew how much those foals were worth. Frank called Callahan. He didn't screw it up. Both foals were on the ground in minutes."

Cole knew Jeff Callahan was the Northern River's go-to equine specialist. With his many years of experience, she didn't think there was much he hadn't seen or treated. "Were you responsible for the ultrasound and pregnancy confirmation?"

"It doesn't matter."

"Were you?"

"No."

"Did you ever palpate that mare?"

"It doesn't—"

"Did you?"

Jodi closed her eyes briefly, her right hand opening and closing. Cole knew Jodi was recalling the mare's contractions against her arms, as evidenced by her bruises. If Jodi was to stop blaming herself, Cole needed her to go over the facts. "Did you?"

"No." Jodi's voice was barely audible.

"But there were twins?"

"Yes."

"How many have you delivered?"

"Only a handful of twin foals. But I have a lot more experience in cattle."

"Horses with their long legs are just that little bit more difficult. And that second embryo should have been pinched to protect the mare and increase the viability of a single healthy foal."

"I should've been able to deliver them."

"Frank did what he had to by calling Callahan."

Jodi shook her head. "*I* should have called Callahan."

Cole put a hand on Jodi's arm. "Jodi, you can't blame yourself for the death of that foal. You know as well as I do that one foal will always be weaker and smaller. Was the second one smaller?"

Jodi shivered under her touch and nodded slightly. Cole poured straight brandy into the now empty mug and gave Jodi a nudge to take a sip of the liquor panacea. "If you *hadn't* been there, Frank might have lost them all. You said it yourself, that no one had picked up she was already in labour."

"Frank couldn't even look at me."

Jodi finished the brandy. Cole poured her a last nip and placed the bottle onto the coffee table. "I think what you both had was a bloody awful day. A sad, horrible day. But one that was already playing out before you even got there. Your job today was to stabilize the mare long enough for Callahan to save the one strong, healthy foal. You gave Frank something to hang on to, rather than losing them all, which is what might've happened if you weren't there."

Jodi sculled the final measure. Cole took Jodi's empty mug, set it next to the bottle, and wrapped her arm around Jodi's shoulders, drawing her in against the side of her body. She didn't need to wait long for the day's events and the brandy to help Jodi relax against her. "You had a bad day, my friend. But because of what you did, you stopped it from being the worst possible outcome for Frank. And as that foal grows, he will look at it and know that it is here only because of all you did today."

Jodi's body let go of the day. Her breathing became slow and deep. Cole knew she should probably encourage her to get up and go to bed rather than fall asleep on the tiny couch. But for some reason she wanted to hold Jodi for just a little bit longer. Looking down at their entwined fingers, Cole thought she really should get ready to go home but found herself not wanting to break the contact or lose the warmth between them just yet. Cole kissed Jodi on the top of the head before relaxing against her and allowed the day to close as it might, wrapped in warmth and compassion.

"Oh! You little shit, you." Charlie set the milk bottle on the table and grabbed the tea towel she always kept at her side when feeding.

"Kick the teat out of her mouth again, did she?" Pip shot a wry grin over her shoulder as she pulled clean pouches from the washing machine.

Charlie exhaled loudly. "Yes. Damned milk is everywhere now." She mopped a pool of milk from the wallaby joey's belly and then her hand.

"How much did she drink?"

"Who the fuck knows? It's like she knows I'm in a hurry to get her fed." She dipped a cotton ball in the mug of warm water and gently cleaned the sticky milk off the joey's fur.

Pip touched her lightly on the shoulder. "Take your time, lovely. We're not in any rush." Pip picked up the full wash basket and opened the door. "I still have to hang these and then make sure the koalas have enough fresh leaves to last the day."

Charlie sighed. "I know. It's just that I want to make sure we pick the perfect place."

"You know, of course, that all we can do is give him an ideal place with which to start. In all likelihood he'll end up flying hundreds of kilometres from his release site."

"You're right. And I suppose I'm just being silly."

"Not silly, love. Just a typical concerned parent." Pip winked. "I'll be back by the time you've finished cleaning everything up. The joey, you, and the bottles."

Charlie laughed and waved her out. She made sure the joey was completely wiped of congealed milk dots and then toileted her. After twisting the pouch closed she slid the wallaby back into the canvas bag to sleep until the next feed.

She ran hot water into the sink and added a sizeable squirt of dishwashing detergent. There were some days when she felt that all she predominantly did was clean out the bottles and teats. She took her time, knowing she was essentially putting off the inevitable.

Her emotions fluctuated. Of course she would miss the eagle that had bonded with her so strongly. But the goal had always been to rehabilitate and then release. The same as it was with all the animals they had in care. Charlie would openly admit to anyone that she was happy for the bird. But his release also meant something that she absolutely was not looking forward to. The first in a series of goodbyes. In the span of three days, she would be saying goodbye to Big Bird, Pip, and Australia, boarding a plane, and returning to the States for two weeks.

It would be the first time she and Pip would be separated since the flood. And that had been months ago. When she'd come to Australia, she never thought she'd love it so much, let alone *fall* in love and want to stay permanently. Now, she couldn't imagine being away from Pip and the animals even for five minutes. Living here was as natural as breathing. The days they'd be apart already felt nearly unbearable. Charlie took a shuddering breath and slumped against the counter, an increasing burn behind her eyes.

Pip snaked her arms around Charlie's waist and pulled her close. "It'll be all right, love. Big Bird will be just fine."

Charlie hadn't even heard her come back into the room. Somehow it was like Pip always knew when she was upset. Charlie turned around and Pip held her, her embrace reassuring. She nodded against Pip's shoulder and cried. She sniffed and tried to laugh. "Oh, it's not just him."

"I know. But we're not going anywhere. All you gotta do is make sure you get that cute arse back here quick smart, so we can keep working on getting you permanency."

Charlie wiped her eyes. "I wish I didn't have to go."

"Me too. But if this is what you have to do until you finish your application and immigration evaluates it, then I reckon we just need to suck it up and get on with it. It'll be over in the blink of an eye."

"Ha. I wish it were only that short."

"Me too, love. Me too." Pip rubbed her back. "Hey, Jodi'll be here any second. So we should probably get ready."

"I didn't think Jodi was coming. I'm surprised she's taking some time off. She seemed pretty busy the last time she was here." Charlie turned the cold water on, splashed some on her face, and wiped it dry.

"She *was* going to bail out but Cole managed to convince her to come along for the ride by offering to hold the fort at the clinic. Cole called me while I was outside to give us the heads-up. Seems Jodi had a bugger of a week. She lost a horse and Rocky's still crook."

"Poor Jodi. Sounds like she needs a break. Good thing it's Sunday," Charlie said, thankful that she could focus on something other than her own challenges.

"That's exactly what Cole figured. But you know Jodi. It doesn't matter what day of the week it is. Her patients are always foremost in her mind."

"I do. I've seen it first-hand. Well, good. Between the bushland, some hiking, and Big Bird's release, let's see if we can't get her mind off things for a while."

When Pip winked at her, Charlie knew Jodi wasn't the only one who needed some deflection and distraction.

Charlie slid the empty raptor cage into the back of the truck. She secured it by clipping the floor-mounted straps onto each side. They'd made this cage especially for Big Bird, although it would prove useful for any large birds they cared for in future. The exterior was lined with dark shade cloth to decrease the amount of light entering, to keep the bird quiet. A second layer of cloth on the inside also protected flight feathers in the event the bird panicked and tried to fly around inside.

The crunching of gravel pulled her attention to the driveway. Jodi's Land Rover slowly crept down the drive. Charlie waved and smiled when Jodi flashed the lights in acknowledgement. When the vehicle came to a stop, Charlie walked over and opened the driver's door.

"Hi, stranger."

Jodi offered her a tired smile. Dark circles hung below her eyes and her face was pale and drawn. Her shirt hung from her fit body.

"Pip's in the house making us a lunch to eat on the way. Why don't you go on in and see if you can mooch a cuppa and a biccy off her."

"Thanks. I'll take you up on the coffee."

"Good. I'll be right in."

Jodi nodded and slid out of the truck. Her shoulders seemed to curl over her chest as she rubbed at her arms.

Charlie pulled Jodi into a side hug. "Hey, sorry about the past few days. I heard it's been rough."

"Mm. Ta." Jodi gently brushed Charlie away and walked to the house.

Charlie frowned. This was certainly not the vibrant Jodi she knew. Her eyes had lost the mischievous sparkle continually born of a bright smile. Jodi looked emotionally drained and Charlie could only hope Pip could bring some light back into their friend.

While Pip and Jodi were in the house, Charlie walked down to the aviary. Big Bird chirped a greeting when he saw her coming. His high perch gave him ample view of the house. His new gold leg band from National Parks and Wildlife winked in the sun.

She made a slight detour and brought out his hood and some mice for him to eat. He'd have a lot to take in once he was on his own. A full crop would give him one less concern. The eagle flew down to his eating perch and started gobbling down the mice. While he fed, she sat with her back against the wall and watched him.

He hadn't really grown any since he'd been in her care. When Cole had rescued him from the side of the road, he'd been nearly full-grown. But his plumage had gone from mid-brown in colour with a reddish brown head and wings, to a richer, darker chocolate. He would become progressively blacker for at least the next ten years until he was mostly a dark blackish-brown.

Charlie got to her feet when he swallowed the last one. He spread his two-metre long wings and flapped them gently.

"Okay, big boy. This is the last time you'll ever have to wear this thing." She put the leather hood over his head. He ruffled his feathers into place and settled. She slid her hand into a thick leather glove, pulled the tether between her fingers, and pushed gently against his belly until he stepped up onto her arm.

Pip, Jodi, and Chilli were already waiting in the ute. She walked to the back, set him on the perch, then quietly closed the door and the back of the ute.

"Doing okay, love?" Pip handed her a sandwich when she slid into the passenger seat.

"Yep. Let's get this over with before I change my mind and keep him."

"Oh no, you don't!" Pip clutched her heart. "That would mean *I* would have to take care of him when you fly off someplace."

Charlie grinned. "It wouldn't be that hard. You'd just have to put up with him dive-bombing you when you brought him his mice."

"Uh-huh. Not exactly my idea of fun."

Charlie laughed. "Sook. Where's your sense of adventure?" She turned around in her seat. "Jodi, why don't you ride up here? You know the route better than either of us."

"Nah. I'm okay back here. I'll tell you where to turn or whatever." Jodi's voice was flat and quiet.

"I think she thinks Chilli is better company than we are, babe." Pip reached back and ruffled Chilli's neck.

From Ashby, they followed the Pacific Highway through Maclean and south to Grafton, where they turned onto the Gwydir Highway. The road wound through mostly thick bush and some forested paddocks.

"You'll want to hang a left, just up here on Purgatory Trail," Jodi said.

Charlie grimaced a little. "That's kind of an ominous name."

Fittingly the asphalt road ended as Pip turned left onto the oddly named dirt road. Several eastern grey kangaroos watched them go by from the shade of some very large gum trees.

The rough road narrowed the further they went. From time to time branches scraped the truck's sides making screeching sounds of various pitches as they swept past. The ground fell away to the right and rose sharply to the left, giving it a no-turning-back feel. Pip's knuckles blanched to white as she clung to the steering wheel.

Charlie thought the road was more of a path, dubious and uncertain, winding back and forth on itself. It led them along a ridge of high bluffs. Through the trees, far below, the sun reflected brightly off the surface of nameless meandering streams.

Finally they came down off the mountain ridgeline and heavily forested escarpments. The trees thinned before opening up to a flat grassy plain.

Pip let the truck drift to a stop. "Wow. This is remote."

Charlie realized that none of them had spoken a word the entire drive in. "I'll say."

"It's ideal for your budgie." Jodi opened her door and got out. She raised her face to the sun and took a deep breath.

Charlie caught Pip's eye and smiled. It was perfect for Big Bird, and if Jodi's reaction was anything to go by, it was exactly what Jodi needed too.

Chilli whined to be allowed out.

"Go ahead, bub." Pip took an apple from the console and bit into it.

Chilli bounded out and raced around to the driver's side. She sat down quickly, wagged her tail, and smiled in the classic Labrador style.

Charlie opened up the back of the ute. Big Bird appeared to have made the trip fine. To her relief, he sat secure on his perch with not one ruffled feather.

"Okay, my dear boy, it's showtime for you." She slid the protective glove on and opened the cage. When she held her hand against his lower breast, he calmly stepped onto her forearm.

Charlie came around the side of the truck. Pip gave her a reassuring smile. Jodi shaded her eyes against the sun and leaned against the front of the truck.

Taking a deep breath, Charlie walked a fair distance into what she figured was the middle of the field. Her chest tightened and heaviness settled in her stomach. She loved this bird. If only she could think of a better way. No. Big Bird deserved to be released back into his wild world. This is what they had all worked so hard to achieve—his release. It wouldn't be fair to keep him in captivity. Nor would it be fair to Pip, who would be tasked with caring for him while she left the country on these stupid immigration related trips. This was the next big step. For both of them.

Charlie removed the tether from his leg before loosening the ties of the hood and sliding it off his head.

Big Bird looked around, clearly assessing his surroundings. He cocked his head and peered into the sky.

"This is it, big guy. It's time." Charlie felt the familiar burn behind her eyes and blinked. She wanted to see him fly away with clear sight, not blurred by tears.

The eagle crouched as if to take off. He spread his wings slightly and seemed to reconsider. He ruffled his feathers and tail and settled, apparently content to sit on Charlie's arm.

She waited several minutes, the muscles in her arm burning from holding his weight. Suddenly, in a burst of power, Big Bird pushed off. His flight feathers stretched like fingers reaching for the sky. In ten heavy flaps, he rose. Each metre he gained in altitude made it easier for him to get his heavy body higher and higher on slow, powerful wing beats. He rose until he was soaring with ease, circling on an afternoon thermal. In a few minutes, the wedge-tailed eagle became but a speck in the sky before finally disappearing amongst the clouds.

Charlie turned around and there was Pip right behind her. "I feel like a part of me is gone."

"It is, sweet. It's on the wing in that wide-open sky. Exactly where he was born to be, thanks to you."

"You look like you caught some sun on your face today. It suits you." Cole crossed her arms and leaned against one of the surgery's side countertops, as she supervised Popcorn consuming her dinner meal.

Jodi put her hands to her face and felt the still warm flush on her cheeks from an afternoon spent in the sun. As much as she hated to admit it, Cole had been right sending her away for the day. Although still physically tired from too many nights of poor sleep, her mind and body felt a lot more relaxed and peaceful.

After Charlie's eagle had been released, the trio spent a couple of hours hiking along one of the short pathways near a picnic spot that Jodi had trekked before. An avid bushwalking enthusiast, Jodi knew the area reasonably well and enjoyed not only the physical outlet of the hike but also sharing it with friends. They spotted who they thought was Big Bird a couple of times. But who knew? It could've been another eagle. Nevertheless, it had been a most enjoyable and successful day. And she felt much better for it.

"I had a lovely day. Thank you for bullying me into it."

"I wouldn't have had to resort to such tactics if you'd given in earlier. As my karani Heke would say, *You are too stubborn for your own good.*"

"Who?"

"My granny, Heke. She helped raise me. She was a good judge of character."

"I take it *karani* is Maori for grandmother?"

"Where I come from, it is. As with a lot of cultures, including the aboriginals here in Australia, words differ across the tribes and where you come from."

Jodi pondered Cole's statement. Language was such a diverse and complex thing the world over. She had never really given it much thought. "Do you miss it?"

Cole picked up Popcorn's empty dinner bowl and rinsed it in the sink. "What? My grandmother, or New Zealand?"

"Both."

"Yes and no. I love Australia. I can't imagine going back to New

Zealand to live. There are too many shadows there for me. I might go back one day, to visit, but this is my home now."

Jodi nodded. She knew of Cole's largely absentee parents, and that she had been raised by her elderly grandparents who had since passed on.

"And of course I miss my grandparents. But I carry a piece of them with me, always." A soft, sweet smile stole across Cole's face at the mention of her grandparents. A twinge of envy pinged briefly in Jodi's chest as she found herself captured by the serenity and beauty of Cole as she spoke so lovingly.

Cole picked up Popcorn and returned her to her cage next to Rocky. "You do know you're staring, don't you?"

"Huh? What?" Jodi checked herself. "Sorry. Been a long day."

"Uh-huh."

Jodi didn't quite know what to make of Cole's remark. The phone rang and saved her from any further mildly uncomfortable analysis. "I'll get that." She answered the phone. "Hello, Jodi Bowman." Jodi ran a hand through her hair. "Hi, Roger. I was just going to give you a call. I figured you'd want an update on Rocky." Jodi strolled over to Rocky's chart and read through it while she made small talk with Roger. Scanning over the results, Jodi steeled herself for what she needed to say next. "Are you doing anything tonight? Would you like to come in and see him? I know he'd love to see you...All right. I'll see you then." Jodi disengaged the call. Her heart felt heavy for Roger's sake.

"When will he be here?"

"In an hour."

"Then come on upstairs with me and I'll whip us up some dinner."

Jodi opened her mouth to protest.

"I'm not taking no for an answer." Cole's voice was gentle but firm. "You go on up and shower, and by the time you're out, I'll have something on the table."

Jodi stopped and squinted at her. "Are you bullying me again?"

Cole crossed the room and chuckled softly in her ear, placing a warm hand in the small of her back. "If that's what it takes to get you upstairs, then whatever blows your hair back, my friend. Now go."

As Jodi climbed the stairs up to the apartment above the clinic, she marvelled at how easily Cole had taken the burden of control off her shoulders, albeit temporarily. She had not only done it all day, but here she was doing it again, so that she could be rested, fed, and ready to be with Roger and Rocky. She had jokingly told Cole she felt bullied, but that was far from the truth. She stopped halfway up the stairs when she realized what she felt. Cared for. Huh. Jodi smiled tentatively, and that smile built as surprise sank in and she continued upstairs.

Roger nodded when Jodi opened the clinic door a short time later. He clasped the brim of his old sweat-stained Akubra with both hands. His gaze was pained and watery and it seemed his smile was strained.

"I'm sorry, Roger. I hope you weren't waiting long." Jodi swung the door wide.

"No, no. Just a minute or so, I reckon." Roger walked past her, his posture more stooped than usual.

"Would you like a cuppa? I was just about to make one." Jodi gently patted his shoulder.

"Yeah, that'd be great, mate. I haven't been sleeping too well."

"I understand perfectly. Worry keeps me up at night too." Jodi added fresh coffee to the machine.

Roger nodded. "Not only that, but I miss the little bastard's snoring. He sleeps next to my head on the pillow, and I've kind of gotten used to it. I'm missing him something fierce."

"Just like a dripping tap you can't do anything about and so you get used to it." Jodi added the water and flipped the *on* switch. "How about I take you back to see your little man. I'll bring the coffee in when it's done brewing."

"Righto. He's doing good, ain't he?"

Jodi's heart fell. She had no real good news to give him. "I had hoped he would be showing some signs of improvement by now, but all things considered, like his age, he seems to be holding his own. I'm hoping a visit from you might perk him up a bit. He still has to stay in the oxygen tent though." She bit her lip knowing she hadn't really answered his question.

When they entered the kennel room, Jodi retrieved a chair for Roger to sit on. "He's just over there."

"Behind all that plastic?" Roger walked over and peered in. "Hey, Rocky," he said in a gravelly voice. "How're you doin', bud?"

"I'll be right back. Have a seat. And you can stay as long as you like." Jodi stuck her fingers in Popcorn's cage as she walked by and received a quick flick of her tongue.

The smell of freshly brewed coffee was immediately enticing

when she entered the waiting room. She poured two mugs, both black, as she remembered Roger's preference. She yawned and blinked. The combination of lack of sleep and the fresh air from her time in the mountains was beginning to take its toll. But having been through it before, she knew coffee or no coffee, she probably wouldn't sleep well anyway. So she might as well enjoy a cuppa with Roger.

When Jodi entered the kennel room, she gasped in horror. Roger had Rocky's door open wide enough to slip his arm in, and the gap was letting out the precious oxygen Rocky needed. She put the mugs on the washing machine and rushed over. "Roger, we need to keep the door closed."

"But look, he's smiling. He must be feeling better."

"He might be, but we still have to keep him in there so the antiserum works its magic." Jodi didn't have the heart to tell Roger that what he had mistaken for a smile was actually the poor dog trying to breathe.

"Aw, bugger. I should've asked first." Roger rubbed his hands on his pants legs.

Jodi closed the cage door and readjusted the plastic cover. "No worries. It wasn't that long, so there shouldn't be any harm done." She hoped. She studied the dog for a few minutes and was relieved to see him lick his lips and stop panting.

"Who's this furball?"

Jodi drew her gaze from Rocky to find Roger standing in front of Popcorn's cage. "That's Mrs. Rosa's dog. You knew her, right?"

Roger smacked his lips. "I know she made a right nice chocolate and coconut slice."

"That she did, my friend." Jodi opened Popcorn's door and lifted her out. "This little girl belonged to her. When she passed, her daughter asked if I would take her."

"Hm. I'd heard something about her being crook. But I didn't realize she was gone until I overheard the ladies talking about it in the checkout line at the grocery." He stroked the Pom's soft coat.

"Would you like to hold her for a bit? It'll do her good to be out of that cage. We get so busy here during office hours that she doesn't always get the attention she deserves."

Roger smiled affectionately and reached to take her. "Hello, little one. Do you want some company?"

Jodi couldn't help but smile at the change in Roger. The furrow between his eyes relaxed and his worried frown transitioned into a small smile.

"She's a real sweetie, isn't she?"

Roger hugged Popcorn close and nuzzled her head with his stubbly chin. "I hope my Rocky gets better soon."

So do I, so do I, Jodi thought.

CHAPTER SEVEN

The rhythmic chopping of the fruit helped calm her somewhat. It was late. Or rather, it was early. Two a.m. early. Pip's mind tumbled over and over. Unable to sleep, she'd carefully untangled herself from Charlie's arms and crawled out of bed. Tomorrow—no, she checked herself, *today*—was going to be a big enough day for Charlie without her being disturbed or woken up from Pip's tossing and turning.

She grabbed a fresh banana, peeled it, and rapidly sliced it from end to end, robotically reaching for an apple when she was done, and proceeding to slice and dice it to fine cubes and slivers. Unshed tears blurred her vision. She slowed her frantic movements to avoid slicing the ends of her fingers off. Charlie had already taken her to hospital once to have stiches for that. Neither of them needed a repeat performance. Not now. And certainly not today. She sniffled. Charlie would fly out of the country in a few hours. She sniffed again and cleared her throat, which was rapidly tightening with the growing emotions. It wasn't that she was worried about being alone or lonely. She would miss Charlie. Of that she had no doubt. They had barely been apart for the best part of the year. But that wasn't what troubled her and kept her awake at night.

Ever since Terese raised the idea of Charlie applying for a permanent visa, a small knot of dread had sat low and heavy in her gut. What if they refused Charlie's application and she had to go back to the States permanently? Or worse, what if, when Charlie went home, she realized how much she missed America and her hometown and stayed, never to return to Australia? Or her.

Pip stopped chopping. She raised the back of her hand to her mouth to stifle a sob, trying desperately to contain the fears that threatened to spill over and undo her. She had schooled herself to be calm and supportive, all the way through the months of Charlie's form filling, the late night telephone calls, and the meetings with immigration lawyers, gathering testimonies of her character, all the while keeping Charlie positive and reassured. But here she was, on the eve of Charlie going, and all her nerves were unravelling. Just a couple more hours was all she needed. Long enough to get Charlie on the plane. She could fall apart later. Just not now.

She scooped the fruit salad mix into containers and was in the process of putting the lids on when she heard the toilet flush, followed moments later by the sound of bare feet padding down the hallway. She hastily swiped at her damp face and drew her shoulders back in a vain attempt to keep it all together.

A yawn preceded Charlie's entrance. "What time is it? And why are you cutting up fruit in the middle of the night?"

Charlie wrapped her arms around her waist from behind. The heat of Charlie's body pressed up along the length of her back. Pip closed her eyes briefly, her chin quivering with the still raw emotions floating precariously at the surface. *Just a few more hours.* Space. She needed some space. She eased away from Charlie's embrace, stacked the filled containers, and carried them to the freezer. "Don't mind me. Go back to bed, love."

"I woke up. You weren't there." Charlie yawned again. "You know I can't sleep when you're not there."

They'd both have to get used to sleeping alone over the next little while. "I'll be there in a minute. I won't be long." Pip kept her back to Charlie as she moved to the sink to rinse the chopping board and knives. She couldn't look at her. *Just concentrate on washing the dishes.*

"You've been up nearly every night this past week."

"Just trying to stay ahead." Wash. Rinse. Stack.

"Sweetheart. We have enough food in the freezer to feed everybody for a month."

"You can never have enough." Pip's breath caught in her throat as Charlie's arms once again reached around her. Charlie slid her hands down Pip's forearms and coaxed her to release her death grip on the washing-up brush.

"What's the matter, Pip?"

Pip's throat threatened to close over. "Nothing," she said in a strangled whisper. "Go back to bed."

Charlie's breath was hot on the back of her ear. "Not without you." She curled one of her arms around Pip's middle and held her tight against her body. "Talk to me, babe. Why aren't you sleeping?"

Pip shook her head. She had no voice. Charlie's body was threatening to effectively melt what little resolve she had left with which to remain stoic.

"Are you worried about tomorrow?"

Pip squeezed her eyes tight. "No." That much was true. Tomorrow, although hard, would be the easy bit. It was what came after that made her heart cramp with fear and uncertainty. She'd been abandoned before by someone she had loved. Echoes of past fears rang mockingly in her brain.

"I am." Charlie's quiet confession caught her off guard.

A sob escaped her lips before she could stifle it. Charlie held her tighter in her embrace. Pip felt her lover's cheek against the back of her head.

"I know you've lived on your own perfectly fine for years. But when I close my eyes, all I see is you, lying on the kitchen floor unconscious, that time when your insulin pump failed. Something so simple, and yet, something so frail and tenuous. I'm scared that something will happen to you while I'm away and there'll be no one here to help you."

Pip heard the tremble in Charlie's voice. She shook her head. She realized then that they both held fears of the what-ifs. The maybes.

Charlie nuzzled her ear. "What's worrying you, love? Please. Talk to me."

Pip crumpled in Charlie's arms, her defences spent. Charlie held her up and turned her around to engulf her in her arms and rock her gently in comfort.

"I'm...I'm scared."

"Of what, sweetheart?"

"That you won't come back. That you'll realize how much you've missed America. Your home. That you'll stay." Pip burrowed into Charlie's chest. She fisted her hands tightly in Charlie's sleep shirt. She wept freely, staining the soft cotton. Pip hated herself. She had worked so hard to stay brave and supportive for Charlie and she was failing miserably at the last hurdle. "I'm sorry," she mumbled. "I'm sorry."

Charlie brushed her thumbs softly against Pip's cheeks and paused to kiss the damp pathways. "Every day I'm away from you, from here, will feel longer than the one before. But I have to do this. For me. For us." Charlie peppered her face with kisses. "I don't want to go. But I have to."

Pip's heart ached. "I know."

"I'm in this for the long run. This is where I want to be. Here.

With you. But I'll do it with a happier heart if I know you'll look after yourself."

Pip nodded again. "I will." Her heart still cramped, but looking into Charlie's eyes, she saw the truth she needed. They had both voiced their long held fears and found the answers they needed in each other.

Charlie must have sensed it too. She sealed their affirmations with a crushing kiss. It was desperate, raw, and primal and Pip answered in kind. With that came a sense of urgency. Pip needed to feel Charlie's skin, to crawl inside her. She couldn't get close enough. Charlie whipped Pip's shirt off over her head, pausing briefly at Pip's sleep shorts where her insulin pump was attached. Pip took matters into her own hands and unplugged herself from the device. She didn't want there to be any distractions or anything to separate her from Charlie. Not tonight.

Charlie's mouth feverishly moved over every surface before it. She wrapped her hands under Pip's butt cheeks and lifted her up onto the kitchen bench before resuming hot trails up her ribs and across her hips.

Pip thought her heart would burst clean out of her chest it pounded so hard as Charlie's lips latched on to an exposed nipple. Pip wrapped her legs around Charlie's waist, rocking her hips against Charlie's lean body. When her walls of defence gave way, a part of her had been torn open and she was powerless to stop the flood of emotion. She threw her head back and a cry wrenched itself free as Charlie entered her. Never before had she experienced anything as overwhelming. She clutched tightly to Charlie, her fingernails scoring Charlie's back as their movements and breaths increased, raced each other, and strove higher and higher. Pip was lost. Her mind emptied as animalistic need drove her, and she rode Charlie's body, wave after wave until she stopped breathing, stopped thinking, and felt a blinding wash of light, emotion, and energy crash over her, ripping a cry from her throat, leaving her so spent she dissolved into sobs, her body shuddering in the aftermath.

Charlie cradled her and kissed her face, rocking her gently. Pip felt Charlie's heart pounding beneath her, its heightened pace matching her own as did the moisture glistening on her face. "I love you." Charlie's voice buzzed in her ears. And with every beat of their hearts, Pip knew it to be true.

With shaky legs, Pip slid from the bench top, took Charlie's hand, and led her back to the bedroom. Standing at the side of the bed, Pip wrapped her arms around Charlie's neck and drew her down for a languid kiss. "I love you too." As she disrobed Charlie, she was determined to use the remainder of the early morning hours to show her just how much.

Charlie stood in the bedroom with her hands on her hips and looked around. Her duffel bag gaped open on the bed. She was nearly done packing the clothes she'd need in the States. She'd purposely left a few shirts hanging in the closet, hoping to give Pip some comfort and the security that she would indeed be coming home to her.

She closed her eyes and took a calming breath, trying to slow her anxious heart. She zipped the duffel closed and set it on the floor. She slid her laptop into the computer bag, along with the charging cords, passport, plane tickets, and a copy of the visa she'd come over on originally. According to immigration she had to return to Australia before midnight the day it expired. The entire process made her nervous as hell.

The time on her mobile phone read six a.m. Her flight out of Coolangatta was scheduled to leave at ten. It would take her to Sydney where she'd board the plane bound for Los Angeles. It was time to go. She took a long look at the bed she shared with Pip, recalling the intense love they'd shown each other until dawn when red and yellow streaks coloured the sky.

Charlie loaded her bags into the truck, making sure to leave one side clear for Chilli who would be good company for Pip on the ride home.

"Pip?" She scanned the area around the house and took a quick look inside the prep room. She memorized the sweet scent of kangaroo milk and freshly washed linen, hoping it would hold her over until she returned.

The room was empty, so she closed the door and walked out back to where the wildlife enclosures were. The huge aviary sat empty and quiet but for a few brown honeyeaters that were busy picking spiders and other bugs off the netting.

Charlie caught a flash of white to her right and found Pip staring into the koala pens.

"Hey," Charlie said, wrapping an arm around Pip's waist and kissing the side of her head. "You about ready?"

"It's time, is it?" Pip's focus stayed on the koalas.

"Mm. Are you still worried about Lucille?" Charlie let go of Pip to get a closer look at the koala. "She looks normal."

"Yeah." Pip shook her head. "I know. But. There's just something... but I can't quite put my finger on it."

"Babe, when you get home, why don't you see if Jodi'll come have a look. You've been worrying about Lucille for a while now. If you think there's something wrong, then trust your instincts. Talk to Jodi."

Pip smirked at Charlie. Dark circles under her eyes bore witness to her sleepless nights. "You're right. I'll call Jodi on my way home and set something up."

"Good girl." Charlie checked her phone. "I'm sorry, sweetheart, but we really need to get going."

Pip sighed. "Okay."

"You're worse than a teenager. You've been looking at your phone on and off all afternoon." Cole tried to keep her voice light. Jodi had been quiet and reserved most of the day, which was most out of character for her usual bubbly self. Dark shadows sat heavily under Jodi's eyes earmarking yet another sleep-deprived evening. "Must be something good. Anything you want to share?"

"Actually, yes. Come into my office and I'll put it on the big screen and you can have a look."

Cole blinked in surprise. That wasn't quite the response she was expecting. But given the seriousness on Jodi's face, she swallowed any remark she might have had. She quietly let Mandy, the other vet nurse working today, know where they were in case someone came in.

"Pull up a chair while I load this file." Jodi's hands shook as she attempted to connect her mobile phone to the computer, which wasn't surprising given how much caffeine Cole had seen her consume during the day.

"I've got a better angle to work with," Cole said after a few aborted attempts. She relieved Jodi of the cord and plugged it in.

"Thanks." Jodi's reply was short and slightly gruff. She uploaded the file and opened it on her large computer screen.

"Oh, hey, it's Pip." Cole smiled. Pip was the last person she was expecting to see in the video. Lucille, one of Pip's koalas, was in the background.

"Watch this." Jodi fast-forwarded the video where Pip swung the camera around, focusing on Lucille eating and crawling down her tree pole, then walking across the yard and towards her for a cuddle, where the video promptly stopped. "See anything?"

Cole was well aware of Lucille's residual brain injury and coordination issues, but try as she might, she couldn't see anything out of the ordinary in the video. "No. Play it again."

Jodi complied. Together they reviewed the video several more times. "Okay, now I'll play the beginning part." At the start of the video, Pip expressed concern over Lucille, that something felt a bit off, but she couldn't identify anything definitive and therefore wanted a second opinion. "What do you think?"

Cole sat on the edge of Jodi's table and let out a held breath. "I honestly don't know. Does Lucille's behaviour look normal for a koala? No. We both know she is a special girl, but try as I might, I can't think of anything Lucille did in that video that was unusual for *her*." At a loss, Cole added, "But even though she couldn't put her finger on it, Pip senses something. And that's worth checking."

"Exactly." Jodi bit her lip, seemingly lost in thought as she watched the video again. A frown marred her features. Cole felt the wave of frustration coming off Jodi at not being able to see the problem and work towards a solution for Pip.

Cole reached over and closed her hand over Jodi's restless one atop the computer mouse. "It seems to me that no matter how many times you play that video, the answer isn't ready to be seen yet."

Jodi grunted and started to replay the video.

Cole brushed her thumb against the back of Jodi's hand, stilling her movements. When Jodi looked into her eyes, Cole saw a myriad of emotions race across her face—frustration, confusion, determination—and questions. Lots of questions. "Come take a break. Maybe when we come back we might have fresh eyes that see something." It was apparent that Jodi wanted to play the video again, to search for answers, to have something to try, but she also knew Jodi well enough to know she needed a break. "I'll be back in a minute."

Cole stepped out of the office briefly before returning. She stood beside the desk and held out her hand. "There's something I want to show you." Jodi hesitated and Cole knew she was reluctant to leave the puzzle unanswered. Cole held out her hand. "Please."

Jodi tilted her head in question, but Cole sensed that words would spoil things. She simply let her outstretched hand and gentle smile be encouragement for Jodi and hid her grin when it worked.

Jodi rose from her desk, took Cole's hand, and followed her through the office and out the back door. They paused only long enough for Cole to snag her handbag.

Jodi opened her mouth. But Cole silenced her by gently placing two fingers to Jodi's lips, then pointing to the passenger door of her Suzuki Swift. "In." She grinned in triumph as Jodi complied with the direction and folded her long frame into the compact vehicle.

"Where are we going?"

"You'll see." Cole started the engine and headed east away from the sun's glare and towards the ocean. Ten minutes later, Cole pulled into a secluded parking area and got out of the car, pleased to see Jodi mirror her actions. She opened the boot of the car and retrieved a bag, which she slung over her shoulder, before closing the lid and extending her hand for Jodi to join her along a pathway in front of the car.

"What are you doing?"

Cole trekked through the beachside vegetation of banksia and pigface that lined the sandy pathway with Jodi close behind.

"Do you remember last year when you made me office manager, on top of vet-nurse-extraordinaire-sidekick, I think were your exact words?"

"Yeah."

"Well, that's what I'm doing. Managing my office."

The pathway opened up onto beach frontage, empty of any living sole bar them. Cole walked to a sheltered spot to the right of the pathway, out of the wind and flying sand. She pulled a cloth from the bag, spread it on the sand, and sat down. Jodi joined her.

Cole retrieved two food containers from the bag, then two plates and some cutlery, and proceeded to serve up salad, chicken, cheese, and savoury fancy biscuits. She poured a sparkling soda water for each into tall plastic glasses. "You've barely eaten all day. Or taken a break. So consider yourself managed. And before you say anything, Mandy knows where we are, and we're only ten minutes away from the surgery if we're needed. But right now, you need to eat, and more importantly, Jodes, you need to *just stop* for a minute."

When Jodi opened her mouth to speak, Cole intervened by playfully shoving a small bread roll into Jodi's mouth. "Eat first, then you can rip me a new one." She winked before tucking into her own dinner plate of yumminess.

Jodi shook her head, and Cole was relieved to see her dutifully tuck into the prepared meal. In all honesty, Cole's stomach had been churning for most of the afternoon while she plotted the evening meal. Now that they were here, and Jodi was chewing away, seemingly contentedly, on the offerings, she began to relax.

Jodi finished her meal, got to her feet, and began pacing the perimeter of the blanket.

"A vitamin B complex and a light anti-inflammatory shot might tide her over until we have more information. We can do that after we get a blood sample from her." A grin broke out onto Jodi's face, the pleasure of having created a starting point for Lucille's care plan evident.

Cole knew Jodi's brain rarely switched off, but the clarity of time out of the office had helped right her thinking parameters. Lucille's care was slowly but surely unfolding into place.

While Cole prepared the medication for Lucille, Jodi retreated into her office and dialled Pip's number. Not surprisingly, her voicemail answered, so Jodi left her a message. "Hey, Pipsqueak. Sorry it took me a couple hours to get back to you. Cole squirreled me away for a fast picnic. It gave me a bit of time to have a think. My schedule is chock-a-block full today, so I can't get away. So I'm going to send Cole out with a vitamin B shot and to get a blood sample. She'll also have another syringe with an anti-inflammatory drug. I'll leave it for you to decide if you want to give it now, or wait until I get the blood results back. Anyway, hope you're not missing—"

Beep.

Jodi pulled the phone away from her ear and looked at it. Pip's voicemail had ended the call, but she was content enough, knowing she'd been able to tell Pip the important stuff. She shoved the phone into her back pocket and walked out into the reception area.

Cole stood chatting with Mandy, no doubt reviewing the upcoming patient schedule. A small Styrofoam cooler with the clinic's logo sat on the desk next to Cole's hand.

"I had to leave a message for Pip. She's more than likely home. Probably out feeding the masses."

Cole frowned. "I'm sure she's really feeling the load with Charlie away."

Jodi took a deep breath and nodded. "You better get going so you're home before the roos start moving." They both knew well enough the perils of driving in the country at dusk or dark with wildlife on the road.

"Right. See you tomorrow then." Cole collected the box and walked towards the entrance.

Jodi followed her to the door. Cole reached for the latch just as Jodi stroked her arm causing her to turn.

"Hey, I want to say thanks for the surprise lunch and…" Jodi paused to find the right words. "The emotional support. Sometimes I—"

"I know," Cole interrupted. "And you're more than welcome." She winked. "I've got your back." She turned and left.

Jodi tipped her head back for a moment and closed her eyes. Tingling warmth spread through her limbs. She opened her eyes in surprise, confused at the unexpected feelings. Somehow Cole had once again managed to release all the tension in her. A pleasurable shiver ran up her spine, baffling her further. She shook her head. She had clients to see. Work to do.

CHAPTER EIGHT

Cole blew a raspberry when she drove past Pip's well-concealed driveway, pleased that, even though she'd missed it initially, she was now aware of it to realize her mistake. She checked her rear-view mirror and backed up to correct her line of drive.

She pulled her car up and looked towards the house where she could just make out Pip in the window of the prep room. She paused briefly to wave.

Pip was wiping her hands on a dishcloth when Cole went in. She appeared a little tired but otherwise well in Charlie's absence.

"Hello, stranger—long time no see."

Cole laughed softly at the irony of it all, a second visit in only a handful of days after having never been to Pip's place. "Hello, yourself. How's it going? I imagine with Charlie gone you're flat to the boards."

Pip smiled and leaned against the counter. "Ah, well. You know yourself—when it comes to looking after animals, sleep is overrated."

"Have you heard from Charlie at all?"

"I have. She landed safely and caught all her connecting flights to where she had to be. She's busy getting stuck in to sorting things out."

"Can't be easy. On either of you."

Pip shrugged. "Sometimes you just gotta do what you gotta do."

"True enough that."

"You got time for a cuppa while you're here?"

"Absolutely."

"Great. Let's go and get the business done. Then we can come back and put our feet up and chew the fat for a while."

As Cole followed Pip to the koala enclosures, she marvelled again at how well set out Pip had her place. Each enclosure had its own space, and there was an abundance of native shrubs and trees which no doubt supplemented many of the animals' diets. Everything was superbly neat and tidy. Pip unlocked the gate to Lucille's pen, stepped inside, and closed the door behind Cole. They quietly watched Lucille as she sat in the Y frame of her perch.

Lucille raised her head slowly and swayed a little on her perch before climbing down and sauntering over to Pip. She raised her arms, asking to be picked up. Once in Pip's arms, Lucille put her head on Pip's chest and snuggled in.

"Is she eating?"

"Yes. And she still likes her milk in the morning, but she seems to be sleeping more and is very cuddly. More so than usual. It's almost like she doesn't want me to put her down."

Cole wasn't sure if she should be amused or concerned at how floppy and completely relaxed Lucille was against Pip's body. "Hm. Well, let's get some bloods. Jodi sent along a vitamin B shot and an anti-inflammatory dose. What would you like me to do?"

"I think we go with the vitamin B and I might get you to leave me the anti-inflammatory until we get the blood tests back."

"Jodi said you'd probably go that route, but she wanted you to decide." She knew koalas posed many veterinary challenges, with so much being unknown with regard to their care. Their liver and ilium were large and very proactive in order to process the toxins from eating eucalyptus leaves. Any drug in a koala's system had the potential to upset their digestive system, and could be fatal or be processed by the liver and passed out of their body at a rapid rate, before it had time to be effective.

Cole located a vein and drew a vial of blood from Lucille's arm. She followed up with the vitamin injection, noting that Lucille was extremely compliant throughout the process. Cole frowned. Pip had good reasons to be concerned.

Pip put her head on top of Lucille's and rocked her.

Cole gently brushed her fingers across Lucille's shoulder. "We're gonna try our best to get you sorted, my darling."

With a kiss atop her head, Pip walked over to the Y frame and urged Lucille to climb on, where she promptly went to sleep.

Back at the house, Pip held the kitchen door open for Cole. "If you want to go on through and wash up, I'll put the kettle on."

Upon her return, Cole found a plate of homemade oatmeal biscuits on the table, a teapot, and two steaming mugs of tea. "Ooh, yummy. Real tea."

Pip laughed. "It's nice to have someone to share it with. Charlie prefers coffee, so there's not much point in making a pot for one."

Cole sniffed the tea appreciatively. "This takes me back to growing up. My karani"—Cole smiled at the quizzical look on Pip's face—"my granny, we used to sit up after dinner and share a pot of tea and talk over the day. So thank you. This is really lovely."

"Truly my pleasure. So, how are things at the practice? Last time you were here, I got the impression you were a bit worried about Jodi."

Cole looked into the depths of her mug. "Mm. She's working all the hours that God made, and then a few more."

"She's always done that. Why is this different?"

Cole tried to find the words to describe what she felt. "I know. It's just that..." Cole chewed her bottom lip in thought. "It concerns me."

"Well, if anyone can make her see sense, it's you."

Cole shook her head and frowned. "I'm trying, but..." Thoughts and words jumbled around in her brain, confusion running rife.

Pip poured fresh tea into her mug.

Cole took a large sip and tried to settle her thoughts. "She's working too hard. Not sleeping. Not looking after herself like she should. She hasn't been swimming in nearly a week, and that *never* happens. I think it's time she started to look at getting in another vet to help with the workload. Then maybe she can take a break, or at least relax a little. Take better care of herself. She's lost weight, won't even take time off for a haircut..."

"You're worried about her."

"Of *course* I'm worried about her!" Cole grimaced apologetically at the unintended sharpness of her words.

Pip tilted her head. A soft smile tugged at the corners of her mouth as she topped her mug up. "Feel free to tell me to mind my own business, but I get the impression there's more to it than worrying about Jodi's working hours." Pip sat back in her chair, cradling the mug between her hands.

Cole's breath caught in her throat, shocked at Pip's implication. She squirmed in her chair. Could Pip see things that she didn't even fully recognize herself? She felt heat rise up her neck to steal over her cheeks. "I don't know what you're talking about."

"I think you do." Pip's voice was gentle. It held the promise of an open door for her, an unconditional safe space for her to voice her thoughts out loud.

Long moments passed before a tiny bubble of bravery rose to the surface. "How...how did you know that you were interested in women?" Cole whispered timidly, but it felt like something was screaming inside of her with fear and doubt at having uttered the words out loud. "I mean, are you supposed to be born knowing? Can you swap sides? Or does it…just happen?"

Oh, Charlie. Pip's heart warmed. While snuggling together late one night in bed, Charlie had voiced her thoughts on Cole and Jodi. *Looks like you were right, my love.*

Pip sympathized with Cole's confusion. She recalled her younger years and talking to her parents. Well, *trying* to talk to her parents. She knew enough about Cole's past to anticipate that the concept of falling for her boss, let alone a woman, must be scaring the crap out of her right about now. "Do you have any more calls to go to after here?"

"No." The fact that Cole couldn't even look at her spoke volumes.

Pip retrieved two wine glasses and a bottle of wine from the fridge. She held out her hand to Cole. "Good. Because I think this is a good cause for a girls' night in." Pip knew the pathology lab in town would be closed by the time Cole got back and she wouldn't be able to submit Lucille's samples until first thing in the morning. So she took a gamble that Cole might be convinced to stay for a while.

Cole grasped Pip's extended hand and rose, followed her over to the couch, and sat stiffly on the edge.

Pip poured them each a glass and curled up alongside Cole, feet tucked up beneath her.

Cole's hand shook slightly as she took a sip, quickly followed by a second, before carefully placing the glass back on the coffee table in front of them.

"I guess," Pip said, "thinking back to high school, I had boys who were mates, but none of them ever rocked my boat. But the girls did. And boy, did I have a crush on my English teacher. I would have walked a thousand miles on cut glass just to sweat in that woman's shadow. But it wasn't until I went to uni that I truly knew, and that I could say it out loud to myself. And of course, back then, it was a bit don't ask, don't tell, but there was a small group of us and we kept each other safe."

Cole took a few more sips of her wine and stared across the room.

"It's different for everyone. For some, there is no mistaking—they know right off the bat. For others, it takes a bit longer to recognize, act on, and be comfortable with their feelings. And for some people, it's not about which way you swing—it's about the *person* you're in love with." Pip let the concept that everyone was different sink in for a bit. "We're brought up in a predominantly heterosexual world. Some people fall in love with the opposite sex, as expected, only to discover later that something is missing, or something unexpected and different comes along that makes them question who they are, and what they're doing. There are a whole heap of differences of opinion about those few simple sentences. At the end of the day, it all comes down to who you love. You were engaged once, right?"

Cole nodded.

"And he was your boss too, wasn't he?"

Cole visibly winced.

"Phew. No wonder this is scrambling your eggs. It must feel like a double bunger of a dilemma for you."

Cole blew out a big breath. "It really is starting to do my head in. I mean, I loved my fiancé. And while the thought of being attracted to a woman never occurred to me before this, I...Well, I'm not opposed to it...and with Jodi...I *feel* things. Things I've never felt before. But the falling for my boss thing? Been there, done that. And that, more than anything, is scaring the shit out of me."

Pip laughed softly. "Oh, don't I know that feeling."

For the first time in quite a few minutes, Cole looked Pip's way. "Was it that way with you and Charlie?"

"You could say that. Once I got over the fact that she was a pain in the arse chained to my side for a year on an exchange program, we became friends." Pip smiled at the snapshot memories of small but pivotal moments when her relationship with Charlie had begun to change.

Cole tucked her legs up and mirrored Pip's posture on the couch, seemingly wrapped in what she was saying. "Jodi and I are friends."

"And that's special."

"But it's changed."

"Oh, yeah. And I don't mind telling you, it did my head in too. See, I was Charlie's boss. All sorts of moral and ethical red flags popped up for me. And truth be known, I didn't want to fall in love."

"You didn't?"

"Heck no. Then there was Kim, Charlie's ex, and, well, when she turned up, I thought, that's it. It's all over, Red Rover. But you know what?"

Cole shrugged.

"I reckon it was just meant to be. All *I* had to do was learn to relax, take my time, and be open for the ride."

"It was that simple?"

Pip snorted. "Hell no." She laughed. "If you remember rightly, Jodi had a big hand in getting me to *really* see what had been in front of me the whole time."

"She did, huh?"

Pip couldn't help but notice that Cole had not only relaxed, but that she was listening and seemed to be thinking as she sipped her wine.

"She did. Sometimes, it's the things closest to us that are the hardest to see." Pip could almost see Cole's thoughts rolling around in her head. "I'm a big believer that if it's meant to happen, it'll happen. Don't fret about labels. Don't sweat the past. Just take your time, and be open to whatever unfolds." Pip squeezed Cole's hand. "And if you ever need someone to talk to, well, now you know where I am, and the door is always open."

"Thank you."

"You're most welcome. Now, how about we throw something together for dinner so you can head on back before it gets too late?"

Cole smiled. And as they stood she reached over and hugged Pip before they made their way to the kitchen.

While she poured a cup of coffee, Mandy said, "Just a heads-up, Magnus is your last patient today. You've got fifteen minutes." Mandy giggled.

"Lovely." Jodi shook her head and smiled. "Have you heard from Cole yet?"

"No."

"Huh. Righto. I'm going to check on Rocky. Let me know when the big doofus arrives."

"Oh, you won't need me to tell you—I'm sure you'll hear him." Mandy snickered, referring to the massive Rhodesian ridgeback who never seemed to stop barking.

Jodi sipped her coffee as she made her way back to the kennelling area. She heard a moist cough when she opened the door. "Shit." She set the mug down quickly and went to Rocky's cage. She listened to his lungs with a stethoscope and heard the telltale signs of pneumonia. "Hey, little man. Let's stand you up for a sec." She gently set him up onto his legs and noted the wobbliness. To his credit, he tried to take a few steps before suddenly sitting down. She didn't like his laboured breathing and let his front legs slide forward so he rested on his side.

She closed his cage door to prevent any more of Rocky's precious oxygen from escaping. Upon checking his chart, she was dismayed to see that Mandy had found vomit when she cleaned the cage earlier. This didn't look good and she wasn't looking forward to talking to Roger tonight. She jotted a few notes onto the chart and finished her coffee.

Jodi stepped outside the back door. Although the sun was out, the August winds stole all the warmth. The tall palms stood stoic, the only thing moving the tufts of fronds at the very tops. The eucalypts, however, were taking a beating. Small branches and misfit leaves flew past her and scrambled across the expanse of green grass. She wondered briefly how Big Bird was making out, and then her thoughts drifted to Charlie and the effect of her absence on Pip. She'd have to remember to give Pip a call.

The crunch of tyres on the gravel out front of the clinic signified that Magnus had arrived. True to form, the dog's incredibly deep bark seemed to vibrate through everything. Jodi shook her head and went back inside to get ready for the canine lummox.

She'd just drawn the vaccine into the syringe when the examination room door flew open and slammed against the wall with a heavy thud. Magnus, eyes wide, drool hanging from his gaping mouth, dragged his helpless owner through the door on a tight leash.

As soon as Magnus saw Jodi, he sat and wagged his tail ferociously. His entire body wiggled with barely contained excitement. He began barking, with no stopping in sight.

Jodi knew it was no use trying to say anything to Tony Port, Magnus's owner. They'd been through this before. He wouldn't be able to hear Jodi, and Jodi certainly wouldn't be able to hear a thing he said. Although the ridgeback was loud, he was well-behaved for the most part. He just loved Jodi. A little too much, Jodi thought, not at all for the first time. She picked up the syringe, making sure the cap covering the needle was on securely. She raised her eyebrows to signal Tony to try and hold Magnus's head.

As she approached Magnus, she focused her eyes to the wall behind him. She knew if she made eye contact with him, all bets would be off, and Magnus would unceremoniously plop both of his enormous front paws on her shoulders. Avoiding eye contact was easy. It was the next part that the dog made nearly impossible. The injection.

Jodi moved as close to Magnus as she could without making any body contact. She bent over slowly and, knowing what came next, drew a breath and closed her mouth. As soon as she grasped a pinch of skin between her index finger and thumb, Magnus went at her. His too big saliva- and froth-covered tongue assaulted her entire face in a split second. She barely had time to breathe through her nose before he engulfed it with his tongue. The vet in her said to hold on to his hide, but the revulsion made her try to move her head away. The combination only enabled him to continue slobbering her face longer. Fortunately, the only things that moved on the dog were his tail and tongue. She flicked the cap off the needle with her thumb, put her index fingertip near the tip of the needle, and pushed it through his skin. She quickly depressed the plunger, removed the needle, and backed away.

To his credit, Tony didn't say a word until she'd wiped the sticky drool off her face with the surgical towel she'd brought into the room with her. When she looked at him, however, it was obvious he was trying very hard not to laugh.

"Bloody hell." Jodi pulled a tissue from a box on the counter and blew her nose. "I swear he's going to clean out my sinuses completely one day. It amazes me he can get that giant tongue into my nose."

Tony cleared his throat and bit his lower lip.

"Go ahead. You can laugh. I can't believe he doesn't do this at home."

"Honestly, it's only you, Jodi. He ignores my wife and kids most of the time."

"Well. Thankfully, that's the last of the needles for this year." Jodi wiped an eyelid with the back of a finger and made a note in his chart. "I promise he'll be—"

Jodi held her hand up. "Don't you make promises you can't keep, mate." She smiled, shook her head, and patted the now much calmer Magnus on the top of his head. "This dog is a needle junkie."

Tony finally laughed. "I believe you're right. And completely smitten with the only person who gives him what he wants."

"Mm." Jodi had to admit she really liked Magnus. He was everything a Rhodesian ridgeback should be. He was a muscular hound with a broad head that was flat between his medium-sized ears that were set high, drooping down, wide at the base, and tapering to a point. His red coat was short and dense with a clearly defined symmetrical ridge of hairs growing in the opposite direction down the middle of his back. All in all, he was a gorgeous specimen. She could even forgive his incessant barking if that bloody black tongue didn't always manage to find its way into her nostrils and mouth. Talk about an occupational hazard. She shook her head as she made her way back to the quiet kennelling area.

In keeping with his evening vigil, Roger was already sitting next to Rocky's cage, Popcorn in his lap. Lines of worry and sadness had deepened in his weathered face. He had one hand resting on Popcorn's back and a finger of the other hand inside Rocky's cage. In between panting, Rocky lovingly licked Roger's finger.

Jodi placed a hand on Roger's shoulder. "How're you holding up?"

"A bit better than my old mate in there, I reckon." Roger pointed to Rocky with a flick of his chin.

"I put him on some stronger antibiotics this morning. We'll see if that helps some." Jodi ruffled Popcorn's long coat. "I think this little fluff ball is the only one who's happy with this situation. She's sure appreciating your attention."

Roger looked up at her with wet eyes. "Rocky's not going to get better, is he, Jodi?"

The bluntness of his question momentarily knocked her for six. She flicked her eyes away from his for a second to find the courage to be honest with him. "I just don't know, Roger. I'd hoped he'd be on the other side of this by now. But I heard some signs of pneumonia. That's why I added the extra medication."

"Can he come back from that?" Roger's hand shook as he stroked Popcorn.

"Given all he's been through, I'm not very sure."

Roger's head drooped and he nodded to himself. "Maybe it's his time then."

"I'll be honest with you—most dogs wouldn't have made it this far. And Rocky's still hanging in there. Tell you what. Let's give him another day or so before we go down that road. I've only just started the new meds, and they need a bit to get going in his system."

"Righto."

Jodi suddenly brightened. "Hey, Roger, can I ask a favour? How would you feel about taking Popcorn home with you tonight? I've been that busy lately, I hardly get to spend much time with her, and she's getting pretty lonely back here. She's not Rocky, but she could sure do with a friend at the minute, and she's obviously very fond of you. Do you think you could keep each other company for the night?"

Roger swiped at his eye with three of his gnarled fingers. "You reckon that'd be okay?"

Jodi smiled reassuringly. "I do. It'd be good medicine all round. Doctor's orders."

❖

Jodi looked at her watch for the umpteenth time in the last hour. Cole hadn't rung or texted. And it was past nine p.m. She should've been back from Pip's hours ago. She'd sent Mandy home just after five and stayed back to sit with Roger before saying goodnight to him and Popcorn a little after seven. Visions of flat tyres, of Cole's car run off the road, crumpled in a ditch, or disabled in the middle of the road having hit a large animal flitted through her mind. If Cole wasn't back in the next half hour, she was going to go out looking for her. She distracted herself with tasks. The surgery was spotless and she had even resorted to straightening out the magazines in the waiting room when she heard a key in the back door and then the screen door slammed shut. She took a breath and calmed herself.

"You're still here." Cole smiled at her as she looked up from filling in the pathology request form. "I saw the light on and thought as much. Has someone new come in?"

"No." Jodi stood inside the doorway with her arms crossed over her chest.

"Oh. Is Rocky okay?"

"Not really, but he's doing his best."

"Okay. So, you're still here because…?"

"You, actually." Jodi took a small mark of pleasure as the smile faded from Cole's face.

"Me?"

"Do you know what time it is?" With a sense of determination that was quickly unravelling at the relief of Cole's return, Jodi kept her voice level, even though her heart was still hammering from the imagined images of Cole's car in a ditch.

Cole looked up at the clock. "Huh. It's later than I thought. Sorry."

"You left hours ago. Where've you been?"

"At Pip's, like you asked." Cole stood up and straightened, her voice and body language defensive. "Here, sign this please." Cole pushed over the completed form for Lucille's blood work, keeping an arm's length between them.

Jodi felt the tension in the room but could do nothing about it now that the adrenaline of fear was beginning to dissipate, only to be replaced by anger at Cole's frustrating flippancy at being so late.

"That was over five hours ago. You didn't think to let me know that you'd be late?" Jodi harshly scrawled on the form and slid it back across the bench top.

"No. You knew where I was and what I was doing. It was late. Pip asked me to stay for dinner, and I did. I knew I couldn't submit the bloods until first thing in the morning anyway." Cole transferred Lucille's samples into an overnight cooler and began restocking her kit bag.

Jodi paced the room, the energy within making her restless. "I don't think a text or a call would have been too much to ask."

"Was there something else you needed me to do?"

Cole's calm drove her crazy. "No."

"Do you trust me? To do my job, like you asked?"

Jodi stopped pacing. "Yes. Of *course* I do. That's not the point." She waved her arms in the air, not sure if she knew exactly what the point was.

Cole took two steps towards her until only a hand span separated them. "Then what is the point?" Her voice was soft, yet unrelenting in its inquisition.

"I was worried. Okay? Worried you'd had an accident, or broken down, or…just bloody worried. Okay?" Jodi rubbed her temples, the confusion of emotions all of a sudden giving her a pounding headache.

Soft hands enveloped hers, the heat suffusing itself all the way to her chest as her hands were lowered to her sides. Cole's gaze was unyielding as a soft half smile softened her features. "I'm sorry I'm late. Next time I will be sure to let you know."

"Thank you." Jodi heard her voice and mentally rolled her eyes. Her tone was almost teenaged in its sullenness and she hated herself for it but was powerless to recall it.

Cole put her bag across her shoulder and turned for the door. "I'm going to go home now. I'll see you tomorrow."

Jodi followed her to the door.

Cole turned around. "And for the record? You're cute when you're worried." She stepped forward and lightly kissed Jodi, the heat of her lips melting away any thought or resolve Jodi might have possessed.

Before Jodi had a chance to process what Cole had just said and done, she was gone, leaving Jodi to stand in the open doorway, her fingertips brushing lightly across lips that only a moment ago had been touched by something that defied scientific description.

Chapter Nine

H ave a great weekend," Jodi said as Mandy gathered her belongings to head home. It was Cole's rostered Saturday off, but the morning had passed smoothly enough.

"You too. Hope it's a quiet thirty-six hours."

"Shh. Don't say the Q-word." Jodi locked the door behind Mandy. She was alone and the office was quiet but for the hum of the fluorescent lights above. She switched them off and went into her office to regroup.

She knew Roger was in the kennelling area because his truck sat in the parking lot. Two days after Rocky was admitted, she'd started leaving the back door open for Roger so he wouldn't have to walk through the clinic each time he visited. It gave him the option to come and go as he needed and not be followed by inquiring eyes, especially on those days when his heart was heavy with worry.

Jodi wondered if today would be the day. When she'd initially suggested to Roger that it was Rocky's time, Roger had insisted on waiting one more day. And then the next, and the next. Sadly, Rocky wasn't improving at all. The antibiotics, while helping him battle the pneumonia, weren't effective against the paralysis tick toxin. He was an old dog, and it had been a valiant fight. She was going to do her best to keep him comfortable, but it was a battle they weren't going to win.

She tried to read one of the lab reports, but her eyes and mind wouldn't focus. She pinched the bridge of her nose and rubbed her eyebrows before getting up and emptying the last dregs of coffee into her mug. With a grimace she swigged the remains and turned the coffee machine off.

Roger was in his spot, in front of Rocky's cage, with Popcorn settled on his lap. He had the cage door open wide and was stroking Rocky's head. As Jodi watched from the doorway, Popcorn stood and put her front feet on the edge of the cage. She sniffed Rocky's nose and received a tired wag for her efforts.

"You're ready, aren't you, boy?" Roger sniffed and sighed heavily. He nodded to himself and turned around. When he spotted Jodi he rubbed the stubble on his cheeks and chin. "Okay, Jodi."

"I'm sorry I couldn't do more."

Roger shook his head. "You did plenty, girl. Above and beyond, I reckon. Can't have asked for any more."

"Would you like me to put Popcorn into a kennel so you can be with him?"

Roger sniffed. "No. If you don't mind, I'd like to hold her. I don't think Rocky would mind having a mate close by."

Jodi rubbed Roger's shoulder as his voice cracked ever so slightly. "I saw him wag his tail at her. I think he approves."

Roger nodded silently.

Jodi discreetly let Roger spend some more time with Rocky while she prepared the injection in the adjoining room. Her heart was heavy and she had a hard time blinking back her own tears. She took a deep breath and straightened her shoulders. "Damn, I hate this part of the job," she mumbled.

An hour later Jodi sat at her desk once again. A complete feeling of helplessness and defeat covered her like a blanket. She'd had too many losses lately and they had taken their toll. The only positive was that Roger had grown so fond of Popcorn and come to rely on the little dog so much in Rocky's absence that it didn't take much convincing for Roger to permanently adopt her.

Jodi suddenly felt an intense need to escape the confines of the clinic. She needed to get out of the building that had for years been her home away from home. She loved her work, but today, she'd had enough.

Her mobile rang and Jodi hesitated until she saw it was Pip.

"Hey," Jodi said, her voice barely making it past her tight throat.

"Jodi. Can you come out here?"

Jodi was instantly on alert. "I'll be there as soon as I can."

Having worked through the afternoon feeds, Pip had just enough time to take the quad bike out to gather fresh eucalypt leaves for the koalas, making sure to bring back an extra few helpings of Lucille's favourite. Chilli had enjoyed the ride on the back of the quad bike in a specially constructed seat, her tail wagging and tongue lolling in the breeze as she and Pip bounced across the home paddocks and back towards the pens with their leafy booty.

She turned the quad bike off and started to organize the gathered branches of leaves into species based buckets. As she placed the last of the branches into buckets of water, she froze on the spot as Chilli howled. Pip dropped a branch and ran towards her, the cry tearing at her very core. She checked the dog over, only to find that Chilli's distress was on another's behalf. She stood and scanned the pens. Her breath caught in her throat when she spied Lucille on the ground grunting and rocking slightly.

Pip threw open the gate and ran inside with Chilli close on her heels, whining quietly as she took her place beside Lucille's side.

"Good girl, Chilli. I've got her. Good girl."

Pip scooped Lucille gently into her arms and took off at a run towards the prep room. Chilli ran past and circled anxiously ahead of her. Lucille stiffened and dug her claws into her shoulder, something she never did. Her grunting intensified. Pip slowed and finally stopped when Lucille strained in her arms, her head pointing back towards her pen. Pip head swung back and forth from Lucille to the pen, to try to gauge what Lucille was looking at. Taking a chance, Pip turned and walked back towards the enclosure. Lucille's rocking intensified as if encouraging her. At the pen gate, Lucille looked off to her left. Following the koala's gaze, Pip turned left and took a few tentative steps, watching Lucille's reactions the whole time. As Pip came to the edge of the pen where the back wall faced the natural bushland, Pip could just make out a large tail lying in the grass against the back wall of the pen. Lucille stilled in her arms, as if relieved that her message had been received and understood. Pip drew slowly forward. She could now hear laboured breathing. She hurried the last few steps until she found the source. It was old Felix, the ousted ex–alpha male eastern grey kangaroo of the local mob of kangaroos that lived on her property. He had been one of her first ever rescues all those years ago.

Not long after Charlie had arrived at her place to start her exchange program, Felix had been bested by a younger, stronger male, and he had been relegated to the edge of the kangaroo mob's territory.

Pip slowly knelt and let Felix smell the back of her hand. He coughed and looked at her as if in recognition. Pip looked him over. He was thin and there were fresh scars on his flanks.

Lucille called out, surprising Pip, and received a laboured cough from Felix. Lucille clung to Pip tightly and tucked her head under Pip's chin.

"Is that what you've been trying to tell me, little one? Felix has come home?" Her voice cracked. A tear slipped from her eye as she stroked the old macropod's neck. He groaned and closed his eyes as she continued to stroke his thin fur.

She had to call Jodi, but she needed to explain what was going on. To do that, she had to gather herself as best she could. She grabbed the phone and slid to the ground beside him. She rocked Lucille in her arms, as much to comfort the koala as herself. She closed her eyes and fell into a rhythm. Breathe. Rock. Breathe.

After a minute she opened her eyes and focused on what needed to be done. She picked up the phone and hit Jodi's number on speed dial.

Jodi answered on the fourth ring. "Hey."

As hard as Pip tried to keep it together, she couldn't hide the fear in her voice. "Jodi. Can you come out here?"

"I'll be there as soon as I can."

Jodi's knuckles were stark white against the dark leather steering wheel. After a particularly bone jarring bump, she tightened her grip, ever more determined to get to Pip's as quickly as possible. As the driveway came into view, Jodi slammed on the brakes, the tyres desperately trying to grip the loose dirt surface. The Rover fishtailed through the gateway. With a grunt, Jodi changed down gears and ploughed on through. She brought the four-wheel drive to a skidding halt alongside Pip's house. Throwing the door open she flew out of the vehicle, retrieved two bags of equipment, and jogged down to the koala pen, where Pip had told her she was. The pen door was open, but there was no sign of her. "Pip?" She strained to hear for any sounds. Then she heard the breathing.

"I'm behind the pen."

Pip was on the ground with Lucille curled up in her arms. Lucille seemed fine although the nails of her left paw dug into Pip's T-shirt, blood staining the cotton fabric. The laboured breathing wasn't coming from her. Jodi's gaze shifted to the large male roo lying beside Pip, her hand resting on his shoulder. Jodi's heart plummeted, her guts roiling, as she began to see other signs.

Jodi swallowed her own fear, trying to be calm and brave for her dearest friend.

Apart from the location call, Pip hadn't uttered another word. Her face was as pale as the coastal dunes.

Jodi opened her bag, removed her stethoscope, and squatted beside the old roo. Gently, she listened intently to his heart, even though his breathing strongly hinted at what she had yet to formalize. She removed the stethoscope from her ears and wrapped the tubing around her neck, like she had done a thousand times before.

She grasped Pip's hands.

Pip looked up with a quivering chin. "It's his twilight, isn't it?"

"I'm afraid so, love."

Pip nodded and swallowed audibly.

Jodi cringed inside.

Pip stood and held Lucille close, rocking and weeping softly. She kissed Lucille on the top of her head and faced Jodi. "Don't let him suffer."

Jodi nodded. They had been down this road before, and no death was ever easy, but Felix was just that little bit more special. With heartfelt emotion, Jodi gave Pip's hand a quick squeeze, then discreetly opened her bag and removed a syringe and bottle.

She stayed with Pip for several hours, sharing a whisky toast to Felix followed by several pots of tea and many reminiscences. Midnight rolled around and as Jodi slowly pulled away from Pip's place, she watched as her friend began to turn the soil over for the makings of a new garden.

Jodi managed to hold it together until the clinic came into view. She knew she should just drive by and continue home. But her limbs had become too heavy to lift. All her remaining energy seemed to have left her. She licked her lips and tasted the remnants of the whisky.

She signalled and turned into the clinic parking lot. She stepped from the car and slammed the door shut, only to realize she had locked the keys inside. A raw cry of frustration tore from her mouth. She stumbled to the clinic's back door and unearthed the spare key she kept hidden in the pot plant hanging next to the rear door.

There was a bottle of Jack Daniel's in the bottom drawer of her desk, a Christmas gift a well-meaning client had given her two years ago. It sat unopened, waiting for an occasion to celebrate. While she was in no mood for festivities of any kind, her state of mind was as good a reason as any to crack the seal.

The security light in the waiting room cast dull shadows onto the floor, reflecting her mood. The room smelled of floor cleaner and antiseptic. Jodi left the door open. The scent reminded her too much of the fact that she was supposed to be a qualified vet. One who had graduated at the top of her class. Today it only emphasized her failures. Jodi clutched her middle as if trying to hold herself together. With lacklustre movements, she picked up a coffee mug on her way through and shuffled to her office. Her heart thudded dully in her chest as she dropped into her chair, opened the bottom drawer of her desk, and lifted the bottle out. She twisted the cap open and filled the mug to the brim. She sighed long and low before she brought the spirits to her lips. She took a sip and let the liquid burn its way to her belly, relishing the warmth as it spread through her body, washing away the sour taste that had built up in her mouth.

Her head was spinning. It had nothing to do with the whisky. It was the voices, the images of all the frustrations and subsequent rebuffs that streamed back into her mind: the mare and foal, Mrs. Rosa and Popcorn, Rocky, and now Felix, the final straw to break. It seemed no matter how hard she tried, how long she worked, it wasn't enough. In her mental fatigue, she worried she had disappointed so many others. She took a large mouthful of the golden heat and slowly swallowed it, willing to forget and hoping she would eventually be forgiven for her lapses and shortfalls.

She couldn't escape and go home; she couldn't get into the Rover. She lowered her chin to her chest and cried openly. She stared down at her hands, hands that were supposed to obey what her brain told them to do. But neither her brain nor hands had cooperated and given her the successes she needed for the people she'd loved, admired, and respected.

"Jodi?"

Jodi looked up with unfocused, tear-filled eyes. She blinked hard and shook her head slightly. "Cole? What are you doing here?" The office light came on suddenly. Jodi groaned and quickly covered her eyes. "Oh, shit. What'd you do that for?"

"I'm sorry. You're sitting here in the dark. What's happened?" Cole quickly flipped the light off, plunging them once again into the vague lighting.

"Just had a shit of a day." Jodi refilled the mug, lifted it to take a sip, and then decided against it. She licked her chapped lips and rubbed her eyes.

Cole disappeared briefly and came back with a bottle of water. She twisted it open and handed it to Jodi.

"Thanks." She took a long sip. The cool water was a welcome relief to the dryness the whisky had left in its wake.

"Do you want to talk about it?"

"No." Jodi drained the bottle and got to her feet. She swayed a bit and had to take hold of the desk to steady herself. "I just need to go home and sleep it off."

Cole met her at the desk and put her hands on Jodi's shoulders. "Look at me. You're in no shape to drive."

"You don't think so?" Jodi stood up straight and looked her in the eye.

"Tell me what happened, Jodi. Tell me so I can understand what's happening here."

Jodi took a deep breath and scrubbed her face with her hands. "I locked the bloody keys in the car."

"What?"

"I went out to Pip's, I thought to see Lucille. Turns out she's fine and it was an old kangaroo that was crook, and Lucille knew. She bloody well knew. I put the roo down, stayed with Pip for a bit, then came back here and locked my *fricking* keys in the car. I *can't* go home." Jodi's breath caught on a sob.

"Oh, sweetheart. I'm so sorry." Cole took Jodi's face in her hands and wiped her wet cheeks with her thumbs.

Jodi leaned in to Cole's palm and closed her eyes. Cole's touch was so soft, so comforting.

"What can I do?"

The enormity of Cole's question filled Jodi with more focus than she'd had in days. She let go of the desk and put her hands at Cole's waist, then met her gaze. "You can kiss me like you did the other day." She pulled Cole closer and inhaled the soft scents of shampoo and Cole.

"Jodi—"

Jodi pressed her lips to Cole's and drank in the rest of her words. The warmth and tenderness of Cole's kiss only served to fuel her need for more. She slid her hands to the small of Cole's back and pulled her close. She teased Cole's lips with her tongue and moaned when Cole opened her mouth, allowing their tongues to follow each other in a heated dance.

When Jodi released Cole's lips, breathing heavily, she pressed her forehead against Cole's. "What were you saying?"

"I don't remember."

They kissed for a while longer until Cole broke the intimate contact. "As much as I'm enjoying this, it's getting late and you need to go home."

Jodi held Cole close and rested her head on Cole's shoulder. Cole's hips and breasts pressed against hers and filled her with a desire she hadn't felt since...she couldn't remember. She forced it down, knowing they were tiptoeing on dangerous ground. This was Cole, for Christ's sake. Straight Cole. Cole, who *worked* for her. The same Cole who had always been there for her, looked out for her, had kissed her. On the lips. Her head was spinning. It had been right in front of her all this time. And it had taken until now, for her to completely lose it, for her to realize her attraction. The possibilities. And the problems. "You're right, as usual." She lifted her head and looked Cole in the eye. "What are you doing here anyway? Not that I'm complaining, mind you."

Cole rewarded her with that beautiful one hundred watt smile. "I was actually on my way home from a date. I went to the cinema. When I drove past, I saw the front door was wide open."

"How did the date go?"

Cole scrunched her nose up. "Not great. But it wasn't a wasted evening. I learned a few interesting things. But enough about that. Come on. I'll give you a lift home."

Jodi looked down at her feet and nodded, not really taking in much of what Cole was saying past the *date* statement. "Thank you for stopping by." Jodi squeezed Cole's hand lightly.

"Me too. Just look what I would've missed out on."

"I'm sorry." Jodi rubbed her burning eyes. "It was a hard day. Thank you for this."

Cole stepped back and crooked an eyebrow. "Don't you dare tell me that the only reason this happened was because you've had a bad day."

Jodi blinked slowly and smiled sadly. *Not even close.*

Charlie had been out of Australia and away from Pip for just over fourteen days, including a visit to her mom at the end of her trip, in her old hometown of Bangor, Maine. Now, from the boarding gate for her first flight, she did the quick calculation of the time difference in her head and engaged FaceTime, and waited for Pip to answer.

"Good morning, my lovely."

Charlie smiled upon hearing Pip's voice. "Hi, babe. It's great to hear your voice. Your accent always sends my heart aflutter."

"Oh, you only love me for my accent, do you?"

"There's so much more about you that I love, but yeah, hearing your accent in my ear gets me going. I miss you."

"I miss you too. And not just because I don't have enough hands to feed the six million magpies we have in, who all insist on being fed at the same time."

"Everything okay?"

"Yeah. Same old, same old. What time's your flight?"

Charlie checked the clock on the wall. "I have a couple minutes before we start boarding."

"I can't wait for you to arrive safely here."

Charlie sighed. "Me too. I'm so looking forward to coming home." Home. Warmth spread throughout her body. When she had arrived in Australia all those months ago, she never envisioned such a life-changing experience. But that's what Pip and Australia had become. Life-changing. And home.

"Oh. Before I forget. I've arranged for your bus ticket to be collected at the airport terminal when you get home. I'm sorry. I'm spewing I won't be there to pick you up."

"Sweet, neither of us knew there'd be a conflict when you agreed to that large mammal team conference call. As long as you're home when I get there, and I can hold you in my arms, I will manage."

Security had given her no trouble and Charlie passed through without incident. With the crossover of international timelines and dates, she was cutting it fine with her visa's expiry date, and she had spent far too much time fretting at each checkpoint, nervous that someone would stop her and tell her she couldn't go home. Her appetite was non-existent, but she decided she could still manage a cold beer, if only to calm her shredded nerves. Once she boarded the final plane, Charlie nearly wept with relief at the expectation of seeing Pip in about eighteen hours.

Ladies and gentlemen, as we start our descent, please make sure your seat back and tray tables are in their full upright position. Make sure your seat belt is securely fastened and all carry-on luggage is stowed underneath the seat in front of you or in the overhead bins. Thank you.

The flight was smooth and she'd slept through most of it. After collecting her bag she strode through the airport exit. The warm, humid air caused sweat to trickle down her brow. She was back in Australia. The bus ride was non-eventful. A wave of relief washed over her when she was deposited at the end of their driveway. She hefted her computer bag and dragged the duffel down the long path, excitement building with each step closer to home.

Charlie left her bags next to the front door and went in search of Pip. She found her in back with a garden trowel in her hand.

"Baby. My heavens, you've made the garden bigger." Charlie couldn't contain the grin that split her face. "I guess this means you must've missed me. A lot!"

Charlie's warm vocal timbre sent waves of relief washing through Pip, stealing her words away on the tide of emotion that rose and threatened to engulf her. Dropping the trowel, Pip quickly strode the two steps to meet Charlie, embracing her and holding her tight. She enjoyed a quick warm kiss before burrowing her head down into Charlie's shoulder, her grip around her lover's waist tightening. "I did, sweetheart. I did miss you."

"I can tell."

Pip heard the laughter in Charlie's words. Early in their relationship she had confessed to Charlie how parts of her extensive lush garden came to be, her way of expending an excess of physical energy and sexual tension. What she hadn't told Charlie was that in other parts of the garden, for each death in custody, a plant of significance to the animal or to the species was added as a part of their legacy. Pip patted Charlie's chest. "I did miss you, darling. But this garden isn't for you."

Cold air rushed in and replaced Charlie's body heat when Charlie pulled back and held Pip slightly away from her and looked into Pip's eyes. A frown settled on her face.

Pip wished there was an easier way to tell her but knew there was no such thing. Tears broke free, rolled down her cheeks, and free fell off her jawline to the dirt below. "This. This is Lucille's garden."

"Lucille? What do you...?" Charlie looked towards the pens. Lucille was sitting contentedly on a branch eating her favourite red gum leaves. "I don't understand."

"This is a garden for her friend, Felix."

"The old man roo, Felix?"

"Yes. He came back home. Back to where he grew up, to say goodbye to his old mate Lucille."

Charlie pulled her back against her and cradled her. "Oh, baby. When?"

Pip sniffed. "Not long. Probably just about the time you boarded the plane. Nothing you could have done, love. Nothing any of us could have done. It was his time."

A silence stretched between them as they held each other, until Charlie cleared her throat and asked, "Did…did he…?"

"No. Jodi came out."

"I'm glad. Glad that you each had a friend here."

Pip knew she should ring Jodi and thank her, but she wasn't yet ready to talk. She knew Jodi would understand.

With a deep breath, Pip reached up and gave Charlie another kiss, longer, with hints of more to come later. "Have you had anything to eat?"

"Not really. I just wanted to come home as soon as I could."

"Well, let's head on back to the house. I can make you some lunch and you can tell me all about your trip."

With arms wrapped around each other, they walked slowly back. Chilli barked cheerfully on the veranda, wagging her tail so energetically it made her whole body shake with joy. Charlie squatted and hugged and kissed Chilli.

Pip's heart ached for the loss of Felix. And yet there was a soft song that began to grow in it at Charlie's return. For the first time she had someone special who would help her build a new garden and honour the many more legacies to come.

A hard knock sounded on Jodi's front door and persisted. She squeezed her eyes closed tighter and ignored it, then grabbed the pillow and pulled it over her head. The knocking morphed into pounding.

She squinted at the clock beside her bed. Seven a.m. "Oh, for feck's sake." She threw the covers off and leapt out of bed, ready to rip whoever the fool was a new exit hole if this wasn't an emergency. She flung the door open and was temporarily blinded by the brilliant morning sun. But there was no mistaking the silhouette of the person who stood stupidly, unthinkingly, at her door at this ungodly Sunday morning hour. She growled. "This had better be good. You, of all people, know how rare a sleep in is for me."

Cole was seemingly unimpressed at her temper, or didn't care, as she walked straight past her into the house. "Oh, it is." Cole turned, smiled brightly, and threw some cloth at her midriff.

Jodi caught it and looked down. Puzzled, she tried to work out what stupid game Cole was playing.

"Get dressed. We're going swimming."

"Where did you…?"

"They're your spare pair, from the apartment. You haven't been swimming now for weeks and you need to get back to normal. Exercise, eating better, and getting some more sleep."

Jodi crossed her arms and tried to retain her grumpy facade. "And what makes you think I'm going swimming?"

Cole put down a basket she'd been carrying and looked Jodi in the eye. She proceeded to slowly remove her shorts, revealing long shapely legs that disappeared under the hem of an oversized T-shirt. Bending over slowly, she retrieved a sarong from the basket and tied it around her waist. She walked up to Jodi and planted a teasing kiss on her stunned lips before walking to the front door. She turned and paused. "Because I'm coming with you. I'll be in the car when you're ready."

Before Jodi recovered enough to close her mouth, Cole disappeared out the door.

CHAPTER TEN

A dmit it. It feels good to get back into the water," Cole said with a self-satisfied smile as she sat on the submerged ledge of the pool, swaying gently in the water.

Jodi anchored herself against the side of the pool, still in the water. She stuck her tongue out at Cole as she caught her breath. "Says you. How many laps did you do? All of three?" But Jodi secretly admitted to herself that even though her arms and legs felt like melted jelly, the hundred laps left her copacetic. Well, nearly. Cole dragging her out of bed on the Sunday morning, while not initially appreciated, had helped her begin to re-establish her morning routine. Here it was, on the Monday morning before work, and Cole had turned up again, just as she was about to get into the pool. It was a lovely motivating surprise, which helped her push to her set goal of one hundred laps.

"Maybe," Cole replied.

Jodi smiled at her. Cole was such a good friend. Friend. After that searing kissing session on Saturday night, Jodi wasn't as sure of Cole's orientation as she'd first thought. The air between them had certainly begun to change. Between the pair of them, she wondered who would be the first to bring it up. It scared her a little. They'd have to talk. There was no way around it. They had to discuss their changing relationship—otherwise they'd both spend all the hours ever made treading on thin ice until it came to a head. Jodi valued Cole as a vet nurse and colleague. As far as she was concerned, Cole was the best she could've ever hoped for. So if this thing between them didn't work out, there was every possibility she'd lose Cole as a friend and employee. It seemed like an awfully high-stakes gamble. Jodi would have to think long and hard about whether she'd want to risk that in exchange for a few kisses and...and what?

"Hey. Where'd you go?" Cole playfully splashed some water in her direction.

Jodi blinked and refocused. It was not the time or place to air the thoughts that were playing havoc in her mind. "Just trying to remember what's on today's schedule."

"Did the whisky over the weekend make your brain fuzzy?" Cole shuffled through the water to the ladder.

Jodi quirked an eyebrow. "Among other things." She caught a glance at Cole's reddening face just before she braced her feet against the pool wall and pushed out of the water.

"How about I meet you back at the clinic?" Cole said. "I'll go pick us up some brekkie."

"On the condition you let me give you some money."

Cole waved her away. "Don't worry about it. My shout."

Jodi shook her head. "You've got to stop doing this. I know for a fact that your boss doesn't pay you near what you're worth."

Cole laughed. "I'm sure my boss will make it up to me someway." She winked and disappeared through the entrance gates.

Jodi shook her head and wondered what was going to come of all this.

She showered quickly to rinse the salt off, got dressed, and headed to her car. The headache that had resided behind her eyelids had disappeared with the exercise. But her eyes were still a little sensitive to the bright sunlight. She slid her sunglasses on and drove to the office.

The smell of antiseptic enveloped Jodi when she walked through the clinic doors. The endorphins that had flooded her bloodstream in the pool and on her way to work disappeared, and left adrenaline in their place. She went straight to her office and sat down heavily in her chair. As she rubbed a hand through her damp hair, she tried to figure out why her chest had suddenly tightened, and a sinking feeling started in her stomach. She'd been staring at the framed doctor of veterinary science certificate. She broke her gaze when Cole walked in with two cups of coffee and a bag that smelled suspiciously like a toasted bacon and egg sandwich.

"You feel okay? You look a little pale." Cole handed her a wrapped bundle and set a coffee in front of her.

Although Jodi's stomach growled she didn't feel like eating. "I'm fine. My sugar is probably low because I had to drag myself out of bed—no coffee."

Cole put her hands on her hips. "I think you're getting sugar and caffeine mixed up, Doc." She sat down, unwrapped her sandwich, and took a big bite. "Yum." When Jodi didn't make a move, she said, "You better get a move on. Your first appointment is in twenty minutes."

Jodi grimaced and shook her head slightly. She picked up her coffee and took a long drink, ignoring the intense flow of heat that travelled down her throat. She forced herself to take a bite of the sandwich and chewed slowly. Cole finished her meal before Jodi had swallowed her second bite.

"I'll go set up the exam room. Eat up."

Jodi felt like she was operating in slow motion, her thought processes foreign and disjointed. She glanced at the lab reports on the corner of her desk. Instead of piqued curiosity, she felt indifference. Instead of excitement to start the day, she searched for energy she couldn't muster. She finished the coffee in a long gulp and rose to her feet. She went to the closet and took a scrub top off the shelf and slipped it over her head. When she turned around to face the door, she took a deep breath. Whatever this was, she needed to shove it aside and get on with the day. Her patients and their owners were counting on her to turn up in body *and* mind.

Penny Thornton and her Border collie, Teal, were already in the exam room waiting for her.

Jodi scanned Teal's chart as she walked in. "Good morning." She stroked Teal's head. "And hello to you, big girl. Just a heartworm test today?"

"Yes, please. I need to get her tested before she can have the monthly pill, right?"

"That's correct. If she did have heartworm and was given the preventative, the worm load in her heart would die and possibly clog her heart as they let loose. So we want to make sure she's good and healthy before we do that."

Jodi slipped a tourniquet onto Teal's forearm and tightened it. She palpated the large raised vein and wiped it with alcohol. Holding the 5 ml syringe in one hand and Teal's leg in the other, she placed the needle on top of the bulging vein. Suddenly her mind went blank and the hand holding the syringe quivered. She swallowed hard and tried to concentrate. But an action she'd done countless times before suddenly felt alien.

She loosened the tourniquet and set the syringe on the counter. "Would you please excuse me for one second? I'll be right back." Jodi opened the door and walked out. She leaned against the wall and held her hands out in front of her. They still shook. She clenched them into fists and then slowly relaxed them, to no avail.

"Jodi?" Cole approached her from the waiting room. "What's the matter?"

Jodi shook her hands out and then clasped them together. "I don't know."

Cole gently took Jodi's hands and unfolded them. "Try to relax. It's probably just the caffeine hit. You did drink that coffee pretty fast."

"Maybe." But Jodi wasn't convinced. Cole could be right about the shaking. But not feeling comfortable taking blood was entirely different. "No, you're probably right. Would you mind getting the sample and testing it?"

"Of course not."

"Thanks. I'm going to get a bottle of water and sit outside for a minute to clear my head. Just tell Penny I had to take an important call or something." Cole's eyes showed concern and Jodi appreciated the look of compassion. "Thanks, Cole. I honestly don't know what I'd do without you."

"Good thing you'll never have to find out." Cole quickly kissed her cheek and moved past her into the exam room.

Jodi sat outside in the shade with her legs crossed. She twisted the bottle cap open and took a long drink, relishing the coolness in her throat and enjoying the fresh breeze. A mob of eastern grey kangaroos grazed a short distance away. A couple of joeys hung out of their mums' pouches. She envied the fact that the little things didn't have a care in the world. Four yellow-tailed cockatoos flew over, calling to each other in their plaintive *plee-erk* voice. They reminded Jodi of thick bushland with eucalypts that reached high into the sky. She missed her weekend hikes. With full weekend schedules and emergencies that inevitably cropped up, she had reluctantly traded off several hikes. After a while, it was all too much effort and she had just stopped going. Jodi sighed. *That has to change. For my sake.*

When Cole joined her fifteen minutes later, she handed Jodi another bottle of water and a granola bar. "Shakes gone?"

Jodi flexed her hands and nodded. "I've never had that happen before."

"Well, like I said, it was probably the coffee and you only ate half your breakfast after pushing yourself in the pool."

"Mm."

"Look, we have a very light morning until surgery. I can handle stitch removal and refilling scripts. You just take it easy. Relax and rehydrate."

Jodi looked up. "That's all there is? I didn't think to look at the schedule when I got here." Truth be told, she hadn't even thought about it, let alone cared to look.

"You should know by now that I try not to cram the mornings with appointments on surgery day."

"And here I always thought it was a fluke." Jodi held her hand up and Cole helped her to her feet.

"The only flukes around here are attached to dolphins and whales." Cole leaned back as Jodi stood up. She didn't let go of Jodi's hand when she was upright, but rather used it to pull her close. She wrapped her arms around Jodi's waist.

Jodi smiled and glanced around to see if anyone could see. Thankfully not.

"You okay now?" Cole pushed a strand of hair behind Jodi's ear.

Jodi placed a soft kiss on Cole's lips. "I'm good. My hands have stopped shaking. Must be time for another coffee." She winked at Cole.

"Not until after lunch when you have more in your stomach."

"Yes, boss."

Cole tapped Jodi's nose. "Someone has to keep you on the straight and narrow."

Jodi spent the remainder of the morning reviewing lab reports and X-rays. It seemed that whatever had overtaken her earlier had passed.

The office closed for regular appointments at noon. Surgery day meant she might be able to go home at a normal time unless an urgent call came in. Or she might find herself leaving a lot later.

Cole strode in with fish and chips and two bottles of water. She set them on Jodi's desk and took a seat. "Whiting and flathead were on special today. I got one of each so we could share."

"Did you get me a coffee?"

"Nope. Just two waters."

"Come on, Cole, you know I like coffee with lunch."

Cole pinned her with her gaze. "Do you really think it's a good idea for you to have caffeine, given what happened this morning?"

Jodi rolled her eyes. Mainly because she was frustrated and also because she knew Cole was probably right. "Fine."

They ate in companionable silence until the only things left were the copious amount of chips that the co-op always added.

Jodi wiped her mouth with the serviette and guzzled the rest of her water. "What's on the surgery schedule?"

"Just two things. I've already set up for them. The first is a bladder stone removal and the other is a hematoma ear tacking. Easy stuff." Cole smiled at her and Jodi wondered why she'd never really noticed how pretty she was, with her dark eyes and hair and tanned skin, a stunning reflection of her grandmother's Maori heritage.

"I recognize the ear tacking. That's George Schmidt's dog. But I don't remember a patient with a urinary calculi."

"Oh, you wouldn't. Frank Hodder had a new kelpie flown up from Melbourne. He brought all his vet records when he dropped him off."

Jodi finger-tapped the desk and clenched her jaw. "I would've appreciated a heads-up on this one." *Shit. Anybody but Frank.*

Cole shoved a chip into her mouth and looked surprised. "I didn't think it'd be a big deal. You've done heaps of these procedures. And as you always say, in and out, easy-peasy."

Jodi rolled her eyes and stood up. "I'll go read his records while you get him on the table."

"Righto."

Jodi pulled the dog's X-rays from the envelope and held them up to the light. The uroliths sitting in the bladder were unmistakeable. As with the skeletal system, the rock-like collections showed up clearly on the film because of their mineral density. There were only three, easy enough to remove.

After donning a surgical gown, Jodi scrubbed her hands and watched Cole through the window. The dog was already on the table, anesthetized and intubated. All four legs were tied to the corners of the surgical table. Cole plugged in the clippers and began prepping the surgical site. Jodi knew by the time she walked into the surgery room, Cole would have already scrubbed the site with an iodine solution and pinned sterile drapes around the dog's abdomen.

Sweat broke out on her brow. The same empty feeling rolled in and took its place in the pit of her stomach as it had this morning. She licked her lips and tasted salt. She swallowed hard, suddenly thirsty.

Jodi avoided Cole's eyes when she walked into the surgery. She unwrapped the sterile surgical gloves and slowly pulled them over her fingers. The clamminess of her hands made it difficult despite the powder inside.

The slow steady beat of the dog's heart filled the room when Cole attached the heart monitor. Jodi tried to slow her own racing heart to match the dog's.

"All set and ready for you." Cole stood by the anaesthesia machine and seemed to study her as she walked to the side of the table and looked down at the dog.

Jodi closed her eyes and willed the butterflies to quiet. This wasn't the first cystectomy she'd ever performed, for Pete's sake. She picked up the scalpel and mentally drew the incision she would make in the abdominal wall.

"Jodi?"

Jodi looked up at Cole and her breath caught in her chest. What if something went wrong? What if—?

"Aren't you going to catheterize him to drain his bladder?"

"Oh. Shit. Yes. Sorry, I don't know where my mind is." Jodi picked up the packet of tubing Cole had left on the surgical tray. She opened the sterile envelope and fed the tubing into the dog's penis until a steady stream of urine flowed into the catch bucket at the end of the table. She removed the tubing, dropped it into the garbage can next to her, and picked up the scalpel again.

"Aren't you going to change out your gloves?"

Jodi mentally slapped herself. "Yes. Yes. Of course." She flipped both off, tossed them in with the catheter, and pulled on another pair.

"Are you sure you're okay?" Cole dumped a fresh scalpel out of a packet onto the surgical tray and then returned to the head of the table.

"I'm fine." Jodi rolled her neck. She picked up the new scalpel and once again held it over the dog's belly. As she lowered her hand to make the incision, her hand began to shake and she pulled back. "I'm—" Sweat trickled between her shoulder blades and down her back. The fish roiled in her stomach. She looked at Cole. "Maybe we should send this one over to Angourie."

"Whatever for?"

Jodi looked down at the dog's exposed abdomen.

"What's going on? What's bothering you? Talk to me, Jodi."

"I just don't think I can do this." Jodi put the scalpel down and stepped back. She blinked in total confusion. What was happening to her? Why did she feel so…so *what*? Her heart clenched when the realization of what she felt hit her. Scared. She felt scared.

Cole came to her immediately and put her hands on her shoulders. "Babe, look at me." Jodi met her eyes and chewed her bottom lip. "You look scared to death. You're as pale as a ghost. What's the matter?"

"My mind is blank. I can't remember what to do. And I'm sure as eggs gonna screw it up."

Cole blew out a breath and nodded. "Okay. It clearly wasn't the coffee. I guess I should've let you have some."

Jodi let out a half-hearted laugh and then peered at the ceiling. There was just no way she could do this surgery today. In fact, she wasn't sure she ever wanted to operate again. Right now the thought of it scared her too much. "I need you to call Frank and tell him he needs to schedule this surgery with Mel at Angourie. And while you're at it, send the ear tack over there too."

"Jodi. I think you might be overre—"

Jodi pulled her gown off and dropped it on the floor. "Stop. Just do as I ask. Please." She closed her eyes briefly. When she opened them, she said, "I'm sorry. I just can't."

Despite Cole's attempts to call her back, Jodi grabbed her keys and bag and walked out of the clinic. She threw the bag on the passenger seat of the Rover and got in. Her body trembled uncontrollably as she reversed out of the parking lot and drove away.

CHAPTER ELEVEN

Having made the necessary arrangements for the animals requiring surgery, Cole sat stunned in the empty waiting room, trying to work out what had gone so horribly wrong that had prompted Jodi to up and leave.

They'd started the morning with a swim, come to work, eaten, then set about getting into the day's work. True, Jodi had seemed a tad off, but then she had come good again before totally unravelling in surgery. Jodi was a rock. Steadfast. With reserves of iron. But not today. Today something broke, and Cole couldn't for the life of her work out why.

Her mind whirred over and over, back and forth, across everything she could remember saying or doing, trying to work out what upset Jodi, trying desperately to find what Jodi's trigger might have been, but she came up empty.

She rang Jodi's mobile and home phone but they rang through each time. She left several messages but was left stranded in the echo of resounding silence.

The phone rang and Cole nearly jumped out of her skin. Her heart raced as she hurriedly picked it up. "Hello?" Her voice cracked. She cleared her throat and tried again in an attempt to sound slightly more confident. "Hello."

The voice on the end of the line was comforting in the familiarity, but Cole was gutted that it wasn't Jodi. "Oh. Hi, Pip." She swallowed hard. "No. She's not here." Cole knew that Pip was perceptive and wasn't at all surprised when she asked what was wrong.

Cole traced her finger along the edge of the desk. How could she explain what she didn't really begin to understand herself? She took a breath and relayed the morning's events. "And she won't answer her phone. I've got no idea where she is, or if she's okay." She sniffled and hastily scrubbed an errant tear. "I've never seen her like this. I don't know what to do."

She drew comfort from Pip's offer of advice and help. When Pip rang off, although still deeply worried, she no longer carried the burden alone and the knots loosened slightly in her stomach.

Jodi didn't react when Pip appeared and sat down beside her on the otherwise deserted sand dune.

"You know, I'd almost forgotten about this place."

Jodi stared into the fading light hovering over the ocean. "It's been a while." This was their place—the place they would come to when the world pressed in too hard, back when they had both started out all those years ago. They would meet up here to work through things together, or else come here on their own and allow the surroundings to help them let stuff go, or at least give them space to be able to breathe.

Pip huffed softly. "Feels like half a lifetime." Wordlessly she handed over a silver flask.

Jodi raised it to her lips and took a sip. She grimaced as the liquid burned a white hot trail of searing spirited lava down the back of her throat. It landed heavily in her largely empty stomach. She took another sip, this time embracing the discomfort, like a punishment deserved. She handed the flask back to Pip and wiped a hand across her mouth. "Something to be grateful for, I s'pose."

"Hm." Pip nabbed a sip from the flask before handing it to Jodi who held it between her fingers, her arms outstretched across bent knees.

Pip added a few more branches to the fire. The smoke, crackling of twigs, and hissing of gases released to the open flames were the only sounds aside from the roll and boom of the ocean's waves.

Jodi took another swig and allowed the burn to circle her mouth before swallowing. "You been talking to Cole, then?"

"I have. She's worried about you. Funny thing is, I rang to see how you were doing. Turns out I only missed you by a few minutes."

"You always were a tinny thing."

"Except when it came to Charlie."

"Ha. Yeah. Except that. You were a bit thick over that."

Pip laughed softly. "Well, lucky for me, I have a friend who is as subtle as a brick through a window, and who intervened and helped me see sense."

Jodi smiled wryly.

Pip reached behind her and retrieved a bag. Within a few minutes she had jaffles toasting on the open fire in a jaffle iron press. When they were cooked, she handed the freshly toasted hot cheese and ham sandwich to Jodi. "Compliments of Charlie."

Jodi hadn't realized how hungry she was until Pip handed her the steaming package. Her stomach growled. "You're a hell of a team, you two." She took a bite and closed her eyes at the pure sensory pleasure of it all.

"So are you and your Kiwi bird."

Jodi took another bite of her sandwich. They were a hell of a team, her and Cole, but the ground beneath them was beginning to change. This new path was unknown and treacherous.

They finished the rest of the meal in an easy silence, Jodi always grateful for the comfortable company they shared. Pip had come all the way out to find her, no questions asked, and she knew there'd be no pressure for her to spill her guts. But she felt bad leaving Pip in the dark about what was going on. She took a sip from the flask and swirled it around her mouth before swallowing.

"I think I hit a wall."

"Uh-huh."

"I couldn't draw blood. I couldn't stop my hands from shaking." She downed a swift disgusted swallow. "My damn mind went blank over the simplest of procedures. Ones I've done a thousand times in my sleep. Total bullshit."

"It happens."

Jodi turned on her friend. "Not to me, it doesn't."

"Well, today it did."

"It's bullshit. I can't do my job. And if I can't do even the simplest of things, I might as well chuck it all in." Jodi picked up a stick and hurled it off into the darkness.

"You can't be perfect all the time, Stretch."

"People expect it."

"No. People expect you to do your *best*. There's a difference."

Jodi opened her mouth to protest but Pip held up a hand. "Hear me out, Jodes. You've been running the wire, stretching yourself tighter and tighter and doing it all on your own now for a long time. I reckon you're right when you said you hit a wall. You're exhausted, physically and emotionally, and you've had a crap run of late, but every call, every appointment you have, you've always done your best. That hasn't changed."

"Nice try. But there's a string of deaths that poke holes in your theory, Pipsqueak."

"No. They don't. And when you stop shredding yourself to pieces and dissect each case clinically, you'll come to the same conclusion. You gave them *all* your best. Every. Single. One. And in doing so you gave gifts of love and total care to all of your patients and their owners. Not even you can stop the inevitable when someone's time is done."

Jodi tried desperately to hear Pip's words in her heart as well as her head.

"We all keep coming back to you because we trust you with things that are most precious to us. You have never let any one of us down. Ever. So I want you to go home, get some sleep, and stop this pity party. Take a break. Rest, go hiking, get drunk, whatever you need to do to blow out the cobwebs. And then come on back. We'll wait for you."

Jodi leaned in and accepted a hug. Pip kissed her on the top of the head, then stood and pulled her upward. "Go home, Jodi. I'll look after this. Go home and get some rest."

With a gentle push from Pip, Jodi got into the Rover and pointed it towards home.

When Jodi turned into her driveway, the truck's headlights washed over the veranda of the Queenslander house she'd bought several years ago. It was high set on timber stumps, constructed of wood with a corrugated iron roof. Although the pitch was steep, it still allowed for the moon to illuminate the front of the house. Originally built with a single veranda in the front, she'd hired a tradesman to continue it around the entire house to cater for the long hot summer months. A set of large wicker chairs decorated the area immediately to the left of the french doors. A shadowy figure occupied one of them.

She silenced the truck with a flick of the key and sat for a moment to collect her thoughts. She had no doubt it was Cole who sat up there. A wave of guilt flooded through her and she took a deep pain-filled breath. She pawed a hand through her hair and bit her bottom lip. She owed Cole an explanation, but she wasn't even sure she could find the words for it. Cole had gotten to her feet and was now waiting for her at the top of the steps.

Jodi opened the door and slid out of the truck. She shuffled over on leaden feet to the bottom of the veranda. She cast her gaze down, purposely not meeting Cole's undoubtedly worried eyes. She lifted her foot up onto the first step and was instantly engulfed in Cole's arms.

"Cole, I—"

"Shh." Cole squeezed her close and nuzzled her head into Jodi's neck. "Don't talk. I'm just glad you're home safe."

Jodi snaked her arms around Cole's waist and nodded against her chest. "I'm sorry I worried you."

Cole kissed her gently. "I don't know what's wrong, or why you felt the need to run. But I do know we'll get you through this." She slid her hand into Jodi's and led her to the door.

Jodi fingered the house key into the lock of the stained glass door, while Cole rested her hand on the small of Jodi's back. The warmth from that single touch set off an ebb and flow of peacefulness and arousal. She had no desire to be anywhere else, and suddenly she was living in the moment, not acknowledging the past or future.

She swung the door open and automatically flicked the light switch on. The elaborately pressed metal ceiling reflected the light, creating animated shadows that seemed to dance with every little movement.

Suddenly a need so primal, so passionate engulfed her. She pulled her hand from Cole's and framed Cole's face with both of hers. She held Cole's gaze and in a slow deliberate movement, captured her lips. The softness of Cole nearly brought her to her knees with desire. Jodi teased Cole's lips apart with her tongue and met Cole's in a heated dance. Her taste and scent made Jodi heady.

Jodi broke the kiss, both of them breathing heavily. She rested her forehead against Cole's. "Cole, please let me make love to you."

"Oh God. Jodi, yes."

Jodi led Cole by the hand to her bedroom. The moonlight sparkled and danced through the leaded windows. Jodi's heart beat steady and strong. She hadn't been this sure of anything in weeks. She wanted this woman. Physically and emotionally. And Cole had said yes. Her heart swelled with adoration and the need to feel Cole's body against her own.

She turned and faced Cole, gently placing her hand on her heart.

The beat of it traded places with deep breaths. Jodi slid her hands down Cole's arms and linked their fingers. "Are you sure?"

Cole kissed her hard and fierce in reply.

Jodi lifted Cole's shirt up and over her head, revealing lovely breasts, peaked to attention. Just for her. She lifted one, relishing the weight of it, and caressed a thumb over the nipple.

Cole took in a quick breath and closed her eyes. "You have no idea how many times I have fantasized about this. Jesus."

Jodi smiled, dipped her head, and took Cole's rigid nipple into her mouth. She circled it with her tongue and was rewarded with a deep moan from Cole.

"How many times?" she asked playfully and unhurriedly rolled Cole's other nipple between her thumb and index finger. She heard Cole's quick intake of breath and smiled. She had one desire. To make Cole feel good. Loved. Somehow the day's events faded as soon as she'd seen Cole waiting for her. So many emotions had taken their place. And it was those that were beginning to make her feel alive again.

Cole held Jodi's head to her breast. "More than the number of stars."

"Lie with me." Jodi wrapped an arm around Cole's waist and helped her to the bed where she slowly undressed her. The smell of Cole's heat was intoxicating. Holding Cole's gaze, she removed her own clothing. The fabric still held a trace of the ocean's flavour, wild and untamed. Her hands were steady and eager to touch every inch of Cole. She took her time, stroking, caressing, and kissing Cole's dark skin. When finally her fingers found Cole's most sensitive parts, they slid into her slick wetness. Jodi moaned in delight. Cole arched up to meet Jodi, silently asking for more. Jodi carefully entered Cole and within seconds felt the stirrings of an orgasm.

Cole breathed in and her body trembled uncontrollably with pleasure. Jodi kissed her neck, sucked her earlobe, and returned to once again claim Cole's lips. They held each other for a long while, and Jodi revelled in the majesty of the closeness, before falling into a dreamless sleep.

Cole woke to the whisper of fingers caressing her thigh. She smiled with the realization of just whose fingers they were. She opened her eyes and was greeted by the softest of early morning light filtering through the lace curtain, outlining naked limbs entwined together.

"Good morning."

"This is incredible." Jodi continued to trace the tattooed pattern that held pride of place along the top part of her thigh, sweeping up around her hip.

"I like it," Cole said.

"I sense a story behind it. Tell me."

"Remember I told you that I carry a piece of my grandparents with me always? Well, this is it. The silver fern represents my grandmother's Maori heritage. One half of the leaf is traditional for her, and the other half of the leaf is Celtic knotwork, for my Scottish grandfather."

"The detail is so fine and meticulous, yet there's a powerful simplicity about it."

"I worked with the tattoo artist until we came up with this design. It was perfect. No matter what I do, or where I go, they are with me."

Jodi kissed the tattoo before sliding up to feast on Cole's lips. "Do you think they'd be okay...with this? With us? Are you okay with it? Shit. I didn't pressure you into..." Jodi tensed and started to withdraw.

Cole needed to let Jodi know how she felt but didn't think words could convey her thoughts and feelings well enough. She had to show Jodi just how much she meant to her. She captured Jodi's lips, effectively silencing any lingering doubts. "Has anyone ever told you that sometimes you think too much?" She might not have known much about pleasuring another woman, but she knew what pleased her and was more than willing to experiment and learn as she went. She coaxed Jodi onto her back. Jodi's nipples fascinated her. As she brushed her fingertips across the surface of one peak, the skin puckered and the nipple rose from the soft pink areola bed. She caressed the now ridged surface and was rewarded with a groan from Jodi. She licked her lips, momentarily unsure if what she wanted to do next was right. Jodi arched up into her. With a shiver, she remembered the pleasure of Jodi's mouth. She savoured the nipple before her and was rewarded with a whimper. Jodi rested her hand against the back of her head, holding her close, encouraging and silently granting permission for more.

She moved her attention to the other breast. It was like starving to death, only to find an oasis of satisfaction before her, feasting for all she was worth. Jodi moved beneath her. She lifted her lips from Jodi's breast. "I don't know what to do."

"Trust yourself," Jodi whispered. She found Cole's hand and guided it down to her heated centre.

The warmth and wetness fascinated Cole. She followed the folds, mesmerized as Jodi's hips rose and fell, meeting her movements.

"Please," Jodi breathed.

Cole claimed Jodi's lips as her fingers ventured in. Jodi clenched and held her in tight, moaning and moving in total synchronicity to her fingers' commands. She felt the tension grow beneath her as Jodi's breath quickened. She pulled back and watched Jodi's face flush with desire, her mouth open, hips writhing beneath her fingers as she increased the pace. Jodi's thighs trembled, she arched to meet Cole as her breath was seemingly stolen, and she lay, rigid, arched, pulsing around her fingers for the longest of moments until finally she fell back onto the bed, trembling.

Jodi kissed her and pushed her thigh into her own sensitive centre. Their kiss deepened. Jodi pressed high and tight against her and tingles ran from her toes, up her legs, through her spine, to flower in her brain. Cole responded by pressing and grinding against Jodi. A need older than time consumed her as she rocked. She rose and sat astride Jodi, her hips grinding deep and slow. Jodi reached up and squeezed her breasts. Cole arched her back, her need becoming more urgent. She tossed her head back as she allowed her body to answer the primal call, until lights flashed behind her closed eyelids and she fell, boneless, along the length of Jodi's sweat-soaked body, both of them shaking, breathing heavily, their hearts pounding quickly.

Jodi tucked a stray curl behind Cole's ear. "You okay?"

"No." Cole smiled at Jodi's stricken look. "I'm not okay. I'm… *exquisite*."

"Exquisite?" Jodi's expression changed to a pleasantly surprised one.

"Uh-huh." Cole grinned and stretched like a feline.

"Is that right?"

Cole rolled onto her side, took Jodi's hand, and tenderly kissed her fingertips. "I've had sex before and enjoyed it, but I think it's fair to say that today is the first time that I feel I have truly made love." Cole kissed Jodi, letting her know with every fibre of her being just how wonderful she felt.

Charlie woke to the sound of heavy rain pounding on the tin roof. She pulled the Doona higher, covering herself to just below the shoulders, and Pip up to her neck. Pip snuggled in closer, her naked body draped over Charlie's. Pip's head rested on Charlie's chest, her arm curled around Charlie's belly, hand tucked just beneath the small of her back. Pip slid a leg over Charlie's, and the slight brush of her sock-clad foot made Charlie smile contentedly. Pip never went to bed without socks on, no matter what the temperature was inside or out. Her diabetes affected her circulation, leaving her feet often feeling cold. It was just one of the endearing qualities about Pip that made Charlie fall more in love with her every day.

"*Skeek mest ew,*" Pip mumbled into Charlie's breast.

Charlie shifted her boob with her free hand so she could understand Pip, plus avoid the drool that had pooled at the front of Pip's bottom lip. "I have no idea what you just said."

Pip swallowed and licked her lips. She had yet to open those gorgeous blue eyes. "Squeak missed you when you were gone."

"I missed her too." Squeak was the first macropod she'd been charged with caring for when she first arrived in Australia. Now the once tiny swamp wallaby was nearly full-grown and in the soft release pen. "That's a funny thing to say before you're even fully awake." Charlie lifted her shoulder and tried to wake Pip. "Hey, sleepyhead, are you dreaming?"

"No."

"I don't get—" A rumble of thunder rolled across the sky and Charlie finally understood. "Ah. My turn to feed the penned joeys then, is it?"

Pip yawned and slowly nodded.

Charlie sighed. "Fine. You're going to lose your pillow, though, princess." She flung the covers back and slid sideways. She had a moment of satisfaction when Pip's head and upper body slid off her and onto the mattress with a quiet thud. But that quickly disappeared when Pip merely rolled over and pulled a pillow to her chest. Charlie knew her lover was already sound asleep again and covered her back up.

She dressed quietly in cargo shorts and singlet top. Some days she missed the winter season and all the clothes that went with it. She could stay comfortably warm in them. Even with the barest of clothing, it was sometimes—truthfully, often—impossible to stay cool in the Australian heat.

Chilli followed her out the door, and she headed towards the prep room and Chilli into the rain to do her business. They'd built a covered wooden walkway from the house to the door, which allowed them to keep all their wet-weather and dirty field gear on hooks and stands outside the prep room.

Charlie flipped the kettle on and measured out the milk for the three joeys. She stretched the teats over the bottle tops, put them in the ceramic tray, and waited for the water to boil. She was tempted to make a cup of coffee but knew she'd never make it to the pen without spilling it. Steam finally rose from the spout and she heard rumbling from within, signalling an impending boil. She slid her arms into a raincoat and pulled the hood over her head. Once she'd poured the water into the tray, she headed outside.

The rain had subsided a little. At least it wasn't pouring any more, just a steady shower. Droplets of moisture rolled off the eucalypt leaves high above and drummed against the ground, blurring into one long whirring noise.

By the time Charlie had walked the ten minutes it took to get to the huge pen, the noise had lessened and the drops faded into a musical chime. The steel-grey clouds had begun to lighten. The sun popped out and cast slanted beams of light across the lightly covered tree grove. She clucked to the joeys, who wasted no time in hopping towards the gate. All except for Squeak, who was content to hang back and wait for Troody and Brooce, two eastern grey kangaroo juveniles of a similar age, to have their feeds and move off. Squeak had somehow figured out she'd get more attention and pampering in exchange for a slightly later breakfast, although Charlie was sure her hissing was her way of telling the others, *Hurry the hell up.*

She sat on the feeding bench and held a bottle in each hand, offering them to the pair. It took less than a minute for the two of them to suck down the entire contents of the bottles, after which they nuzzled her for more. That quickly came to an end when Squeak shoved her body between them, clearly having lost her remaining patience. She hissed a warning at which the other two macropods quickly scarpered off.

Charlie laughed. "You are a little psycho sometimes, my darling." She ruffled the soft fuzz on Squeak's belly with one hand and offered her the bottle with the other. Squeak grabbed the teat and sucked voraciously. She grasped Charlie's fingers with her little black paws. Charlie had often thought they looked like she had bicycle gloves on. "So, how's my little girl? Rumour has it you missed me. Did you give

Pip a hard time?" Charlie snickered knowing she had. Pip had told her that her little darling had attacked the other two before they were done with their feed. Apparently all hell had broken loose and there'd been spilt milk too. "Good girl. My mom always told me to take what I wanted."

"Like mother, like psycho then." Pip sat next to her and handed Charlie a steaming cup of coffee, which she accepted gratefully.

"Oh, she's not that bad. Are you, Squeak?" Charlie rubbed Squeak beneath her jaw.

"Uh-huh. You weren't here when I had to go make up more milk because Squeak hit the others so hard the bottles went flying. Quite a tanty chucker, your girl."

Charlie laughed.

"Or when I had to spend an hour trying to get them to come in to feed because she kept herding them away. Damned near got carried away by the mozzies before I was done."

"Guess you should've put on some repellent before you came down then."

Pip rested her hand on Charlie's thigh. "It's a good thing I love you, Yank."

Charlie kissed her lightly on the lips. "I love you too, short stuff." She took a sip of her coffee and groaned in appreciation. "Thank you for this."

"I figured I'd be nice since I sent you out into the rain."

Charlie looked up at the sky. "Looks like it'll be a nice day, though."

"Humid. But nice." Pip picked a blade of grass and offered it to Squeak. She sniffed it once and turned her attention back to Charlie. "Cheeky bugger."

"What's on your agenda today? I have to work on my immigration application, so I won't be of much help." Charlie gathered the bottles and stood.

Pip stretched her legs out in front of her. "I don't know. I may just sit here all day and leave you to toil away." She grinned at Charlie. "Just kidding. I'm going to give Jodi a call and see how she's doing. I'm a bit worried about her."

"I understand completely. I just can't imagine her losing her edge like that."

"Stress will do it. You know a bit of what that tastes like."

"Yeah, do I ever. Give her my love when you talk to her. Now how about breakfast before we both keel over?"

"Thought you'd never ask."

Jodi woke just at dawn when she felt Cole get up out of bed, and the bathroom light turned on. The steady sound of rain against the tin roof matched the buzz running through her body. If she wanted to be poetic, she could almost say she was purring. Last night, with Cole, had blown her away in ways she could never have previously imagined. Their connection and fit, whether in the throes of passion or afterwards, snuggling and talking, sometimes dozing in each other's arms, felt almost unreal and out of this world, such was the uniqueness of it. It eclipsed any other experience in her recent memory, and she closed her eyes, savouring the flashbacks and the flush of warmth they created.

A piercing squeal shattered her equilibrium. In a single movement she threw the covers off, leapt from the bed, and ran across the room to find Cole cowering in the corner of the bathroom, a bath towel held in front of her.

"What the…?"

"Jesus! Come here!" Cole grabbed her as she entered the doorway and hastily yanked her against her, replacing the soft-shield towel with Jodi's full naked length.

"Cole. What's going on?" She tried to turn around but Cole held her tight and didn't allow any swivel room. Cole pointed over her shoulder to the door lintel and guided her focus to the assailant.

High on the wall, sitting in the crevice where the ceiling met the wall above the door, sat a five-inch-wide huntsman spider with its long hairy legs spread-eagled.

Cole being trapped in the bathroom by a measly old spider was the perfect remedy for her pounding, panicked heart. Jodi smirked. "Oh, don't mind him. That's Wolfie. He often comes in when it rains. He won't hurt you. He'll be gone in the morning."

"No. Way. I am *not* moving while he's there."

Jodi shrugged. "Okay. I'll make you a coffee and bring it in here, then."

"*What?*"

Jodi struggled to keep a straight face. "Well, you said you wouldn't come out. So I'll just bring breakfast in here. Shall I?"

"Shit. No. You can't leave me in here all alone with it."

"Sweetheart, he won't hurt you. He just doesn't like getting wet."

"Nuh-uh. Get rid of it. Kill it. Put a saddle on it and ride it out of here—I don't care what you do. Just get it the hell away from here. Please."

Cole trembled in her arms. Her face was pale with fright. Even though Jodi thought it was funny, Cole clearly was struggling, and she took pity on her. "All right. Just give me a minute."

It took a bit of convincing for Cole to let her go, but she finally released her, reverting to her original towel shield grip.

Jodi slipped out of the room and retrieved a broom and a plastic container. She expertly wrangled the spider from the ceiling and into the box. She walked through the house, opened the sliding glass door onto the veranda, and released the spider outside. "You can come out now," Jodi said as she closed the door behind her.

"You promise it's gone?"

"I do."

Jodi tried valiantly to keep a neutral face as Cole crept out, inch by wary inch, scanning the ceiling and walls for any other creatures. Jodi was aware of Cole's phobia for creepy crawlies and decided, for all concerned, to impart a safety message. "You okay now?"

Cole was still pale, but nodded.

"Good. Good. Just a heads-up—you might not want to use the loo out the back on the veranda while you're here."

Cole shivered. "Do I want to know what's in there?"

Jodi pulled on her earlobe. "Yeah. Um, maybe not. Probably best just to steer clear of that one for the time being."

Cole groaned weakly.

"Cheer up, love. If I'm not here, you can always trust that your shield of quality cotton will save you." Jodi gave Cole's towel a gentle shake.

"Oh, get stuffed."

The giggle started slowly and built in Jodi until she laughed openly, while her new lover, naked, frowning, and trying her best to look indignant, clutched the towel and tried to look anything other than ridiculous and nervous.

Cole finally gave in and laughed along with her until they gasped for breath. Cole punched her lightly in the arm. "You might be good in bed, but you're still a shit."

Jodi wiggled her eyebrows playfully. "A sexy, *exquisite* shit, who just happens to have rescued your sorry arse from a wild and ferocious arachnid. So don't you forget it, cutie."

"Pfft." Cole waved her hand vaguely in the air.

"How 'bout I go and put the kettle on? Fancy a cuppa?"

"Mm, please."

As Jodi put the jug on to boil and set some plates out for breakfast, her phone rang.

"Got it." Cole waved her back to her culinary duties and picked up the handset. "Hello?" Cole straightened and squinted her eyes. A tidal line of pink blush slowly crawled up Cole's neck and fanned over her face. "Oh, hi, Pip." Cole closed her eyes. "Yes. No, no, it's not too early." Cole opened her eyes and looked at Jodi, her gaze silently pleading for help. "Uh-huh. Yes, we got some nice rain too. Same time, around dawn." Cole must have realized what she had just said and grimaced, having given away enormous clues that she'd spent the night. She raised her hand and wildly gesticulated for Jodi's help.

Jodi leaned against the kitchen bench, enjoying herself. The view of Cole trying to gain some dignity, attempting to wrap the towel around her naked torso while on the phone with Pip, was quite entertaining. She toyed with the idea of letting Cole squirm just a little longer before taking over the phone. But a wild wave from Cole made her chuckle softly and relent. She padded across the room and relieved Cole.

"Hey, Pipsqueak." Jodi wrapped her free arm around Cole, who snuggled in close and buried her face in her neck. "Yeah. Cole's here." Jodi could almost hear the wheels turning in Pip's mind as she put two and two together. Jodi knew her best friend had pegged what was going on. And she couldn't think of anyone else, apart from Cole, she wanted more to know of her news. "She says hi. Or she would if she could stop blushing long enough."

Cole snapped her head up, a shocked look upon her face. She slapped Jodi on the upper arm.

"Ow!" Jodi laughed. "Yup. A definite good morning." That earned her another slap, which only made her laugh more. She pulled Cole close, softly kissing her lips and forehead. "Thanks for last night and the kick in the butt." Jodi softened her voice. If there was one person who she'd listen to, then it was Pip.

Jodi blinked as lips traversed the length of her neck and the line of her collarbone and fingers danced along the length of her sides. *And maybe now Cole.* She involuntarily shivered as Cole's fingers left tangible tingling trails. She almost lost what Pip was saying. "Uh-huh. No. We're pretty good here for the minute, I reckon."

Cole's towel dropped to the floor and she closed the gap between them. Jodi gasped as the full lengths of their bodies met and morphed, one into the other, every square inch seeming to delight in the sensory overload of skin on skin.

"Uh-huh. Yep. Sure. I'll call you." Jodi vaguely registered Pip chuckling before the phone slipped from her fingers and fell to the floor. "I reckon breakfast can wait." She stole a kiss as Cole raised her face from its attentions along her jawline.

"I reckon you might be right."

Jodi gave in and answered the call of Cole's sensuous lips and slowly tango-walked back to the bedroom.

CHAPTER TWELVE

Charlie ran her finger down the checklist of information and forms that she had to supply to the Australian Department of Immigration. It was a daunting task, but after months of working on it, the number of items needing her attention now numbered only two. Unfortunately, they were ones requiring the most work and time to complete.

"Friggin' hell. This thirty page form is going to take me forever to fill out." She felt the beginnings of an anxious sweat and wiped her brow with the back of her hand. She licked the salt from her lips and took a deep breath to steady her galloping heart.

The kitchen table was the perfect place for her to set her laptop and spread out. Coffee was always readily available and a gentle breeze flowed in from the front door. But it was also the busiest area in the house as Pip came and went for snacks and phone calls, which made it hard to concentrate.

She was vaguely aware that Pip was on the phone with Jodi, overhearing snippets of Pip's responses and her laugh now and again.

"Charlie?"

"Hm?" Charlie tapped a few keys and downloaded the huge form into her immigration folder.

"Did you hear what I just said?"

"Uh-huh." She scrolled to the bottom to see how many pages there were. Crap. Thirty-four. What a waste of paper.

She felt a hard tapping on top of her head. She waved it away like a pesky fly. But it continued. She swatted at it hard and connected with Pip's hand.

"Ow!"

"Sorry." Charlie riffled through the personal papers that she kept in a plastic file.

Tap. Tap. Tap. Tap. Tap.

Charlie looked up at Pip, annoyed and nearly out of patience. "What? Sweetheart, can't you see I'm busy?" She located her résumé and set it down next to her laptop.

"So you don't want to hear about Jodi and Cole?"

"What about them?" She scrolled back to the top of the laboriously long form and typed in her name and address.

"I think they slept together."

"That's nice." Charlie rubbed her lip with her thumb. She raised her hands to begin typing again when the weight of what Pip had just said sank in. She looked up and stared at Pip. "Wait. Did I hear you right? They slept together?"

Pip tittered. "Well, I can't be sure, but Cole answered Jodi's phone. It's too early for them *both* to be at the clinic."

"There might have been an emergency."

Pip laughed. "I think the only urgent *thing* going on was satisfying their libido. Apparently Cole was blushing quite a lot."

Charlie shook her head in disbelief. "Holy hell. It's about time. Cole has had the hots for Jodi for a while."

"What? You knew? Did Cole talk to you, too?"

"No, I haven't had a one-on-one chat with Cole in a while. But it's quite obvious if you ask me. Cole hangs on every one of Jodi's words and she has that look in her eye. You know, that soft expression you get when you look at me when you think no one is looking?" Charlie sighed. "I just don't want either of them to get hurt."

"What do you mean? You don't sound happy for them. I think what's happened between the two of them is fantastic."

"I am, sweet. But let's face it. Their timing probably isn't the best. I just hope Jodi isn't using Cole as a distraction for whatever is going on in her head professionally."

"But what if she is? What if this is what Jodi has needed all along? Support, someone who makes her feel loved. Hooking up with Cole might be just the thing to help her gain her confidence again."

Charlie pursed her lips in thought. "I guess we'll just have to wait and see. I hope you're right for their sake. You know, I only want what's best for them."

Pip kissed Charlie on the head. "Aside from being the most beautiful woman I've ever known, you're also the most genuine. And I love you for that." She turned towards the door. "I'm going to feed the magpies. They should be awake by now."

"They're sure not morning people, are they."

"Not when they're young. I'll leave you be. I'll be out back if you need me."

"Do you have enough snacks in the prep room fridge?"

"I'll be fine, lovely. You just keep ploughing away on that application. It'll be done and submitted soon enough."

Charlie took a deep breath and blew it out slowly. She smiled and nodded at Pip. "Love you, babe."

"Love you, too."

Charlie faintly heard the door slam. She was already focused on the computer screen.

Monday morning. Typically Cole's least favourite day of the week. She yawned while opening the shutters of the clinic and then turned the answering machine off. She checked the voicemail messages and took notes in between sips of strong black coffee. She was normally a tea drinker, but this morning deserved coffee. She had woken at four, made love again with Jodi, and by five thirty was showering and heading home to pick up some fresh clothes for work, leaving Jodi to go off to her early morning swim.

She yawned again. She was dog-tired and would so love another day off. But happy. So much had happened in the last few days. Where their relationship was headed yet was anybody's guess. Right now she was going with the flow, and it admittedly felt pretty damn good. Better than she had even hoped. She was, for the most part, happy, but a part of her brain clutched at a kernel of nervousness. Jodi was not only her boss. She was her best friend. And now her lover. So much more was now at stake since they'd crossed that line. She'd never intended it to happen, but here she was, sitting nestled between the devil and the deep blue sea.

She took a breath and stretched to loosen up, attempting to shake the memories of the last forty-eight sensuously delicious hours into a safer place. It almost worked. Until a vision flashed before her eyes of Jodi, naked, serving up coffee in bed and feeding her croissants, one finger-licking mouthful at a time. She shivered and hit replay on the answering machine message.

The back door opened and closed, and a wisp of nerves ran across her spine. She concentrated on taking notes off the answering machine as the footsteps came closer. When an arm snaked around her waist and pulled her in close, she hummed out loud, the aroma of soap and sea salt still fresh and lingering on Jodi's skin. "I think I now know what summer smells like."

Jodi nuzzled her neck and shoulder line. "Mm. And what would that be?"

Cole turned around slowly, took Jodi's face in her hands, and kissed her warmly. "You." She kissed Jodi again, simply because she could. Her doubts began to dissolve and settle just a little. They could do this. They just needed a plan. Cole straightened Jodi's scrub top. "You ready for the day?"

Jodi blanched ever so slightly and winced. "I don't honestly know."

"All right." Cole laced her hands behind her head. "Let's just take it one step at a time. Several reports from pathology have come in— they're on your desk. You have a litter of puppies coming in at nine for their six week health check and vaccinations, Harold the golden retriever coming in at half nine to have some lumps checked out, and a new client appointment at ten."

"Okay."

"One appointment at a time. And just remember, I'll be there every second if you need me to be."

Jodi nodded, swallowing audibly. "Right."

"You go and check on your reports and I'll bring you in a coffee."

"Thanks."

Cole watched Jodi shuffle off. A ball of nervousness took hold in her stomach. She briefly closed her eyes and took a calming breath. She had hoped, after the weekend, that maybe Jodi might feel better, more confident somehow. But in only a matter of moments, as soon as they started to talk work, Jodi's demeanour changed and she became withdrawn and tentative.

She mentally slapped herself. Who did she think she was that after one night—okay, a very *long* night…and most of the early morning hours really—she had made enough of a difference with Jodi that her previous insecurities could be erased?

Stupid. Just plain stupid. And arrogant.

She was ready to apply a full internal dressing down to her ego when the familiar *moo* of the surgery's front door alarm announced itself. The owner of the puppies had arrived, with seven liver-coloured curly coated retrievers. She held a washing basket full of puppies in both hands and a lead with mum retriever looped around her wrist.

"Sorry to be early, but quite frankly, they are busting the house down this morning. So I thought it better to be here than at home."

Cole plastered on one of her *no problems* expressions—the lady was technically half an hour early. Who knew? Perhaps the extra time would provide a much-needed catch up for them later in the day. She led them into the examination room and left them there to get settled while she summoned Jodi.

She stood in the doorway and gazed across the room to where Jodi sat at her desk. A frown etched Jodi's brow as she studied the path results while tapping a finger on the table. She scribbled some notes on a piece of paper.

Cole cleared her throat. "Your coffee might be a bit delayed. Your first appointment is here."

"Oh."

"I've put them in the first room."

Jodi got up, straightened her shoulders, and tugged her scrub top straight. Her smile seemed forced. "Let's go."

Cole rubbed her back as she passed on her way to the surgery, where seven bouncing mounds were rambling around, snuffling and yipping, leaping on the spot, and slip-sliding along the linoleum floor with the pure abandon that fat happy puppies exude in abundance.

Jodi opened the door, only to have the chubbiest puppy run straight into her leg and tumble over. She picked it up and held it close to her face. "Well, hello there. Who do we have here?"

Cole released the breath she'd been holding as Jodi cuddled and cooed softly at the puppy trying to eat her earlobe.

"That's Bonza." The owner was visibly proud of her male pup. "I called him Bonza because, well, look at him. He's the biggest boof head of the group. He really is a bonza lad."

Jodi lowered him to the examination tabletop. "Indeed you are, Bonza. So let's start with you first, shall we?"

Jodi made out a vaccination card for each puppy. She was the consummate professional as she palpated each puppy, listened to the their heart, looked at their teeth, into their ears and eyes, flexing and testing elbows and hips, and offering the full body scrutiny.

Cole had drawn up a vaccination dose for each puppy. She doubted the owner noticed, but she certainly couldn't mistake the tremor in Jodi's hand at the first set of injections.

With each pup assessed, Jodi now turned to the mother, examining her teats, checking temperature, and assessing her weight and condition.

Seemingly satisfied, Jodi suggested a supplement be added to her diet to cater for the extra calcium being leached from her body by the pups.

At the conclusion of the consultation, Jodi bid the owner and her hairy entourage farewell and left the billing and details up to Cole to finalize. Cole knew they had twenty minutes before the next appointment and silently watched as Jodi disappeared out the back as she held the door open for the puppies' owner.

When Cole followed in Jodi's direction, she heard retching sounds coming from the bathroom before a toilet flush. She busied herself doing a drug cupboard stock take.

Jodi emerged, pale faced, still wiping her mouth with the back of her hand.

"I left you your promised coffee on your desk. We have some time before the next patient."

"Thanks." Jodi walked straight into her office and closed the door behind her, something she rarely ever did.

Cole's heart sat heavy. That had been an easy consultation and Jodi clearly struggled. She really didn't know what else she could do to help her.

She didn't have long to ponder before Harold the golden retriever and his owner, Ellen, came in. Harold was getting on in years, and typical of his age and breed, had a history of throwing benign fatty cysts, particularly in his abdominal area. Ellen had made an appointment because a new lump had recently appeared on the base of his chest and it was growing fast. She thought it felt different to previous lumps.

Cole showed them into the second examination room. Within a minute, Jodi entered the room, still pale faced but professional, smiling and greeting both dog and owner. She read the dog's chart and conducted an exam. Quietly she pulled her stethoscope out of her ears and looped it around her neck, her fingers trailing through the dog's blond hair.

"Harold looks good enough, considering his age. His heart is good and lungs clear, but I agree, the lump feels more fixed than the previous ones. At the very least, it's worth a biopsy and potentially a removal, given the speed of growth you've described."

Ellen took a visible steadying breath. "Okay. When can you do it?"

"I'm afraid our anaesthetic machine is out of action. We're waiting on a part to come from England, so we won't be able to remove the lump here. I can refer you to Angourie or Maclean. It's probably best if they do the test. That will help them determine how or what they need to do when the results come in."

Although Cole had her back to them, she did a mental double take. She was stunned at the lie Jodi had offered to avoid doing the surgery. She was so shocked, she barely registered Jodi and Ellen concluding the consultation and walking out.

Cole didn't have time to have a discussion with Jodi between clients coming in requesting flea treatments, worm tablets, and advice on microchipping. She had no sooner closed off the last inquiry account than a new client, Greg, walked in with Sophie, a standard poodle. Sophie had lost a leg in a car accident when she was two years old. Now seven, Greg was concerned about a lingering limp in her remaining hind leg since a tumble in the park several weeks earlier. Jodi had been highly recommended by Greg's previous vet in Sydney.

Cole fussed over Sophie and offered her some liver treats while Jodi read her records. Jodi sat on the floor with the poodle and undertook the physical exam at the dog's level. Cole had seen her do this before, especially with animals who'd had long medical histories. Jodi's aim was to help them feel less anxious throughout the examination process, while she obtained valuable facts and evidence.

Sophie curled up in Jodi's lap and allowed her to massage her scalp and neck. She extended her neck, eyes closed, and rested heavily into Jodi's embrace, a study in complete comfort and pleasure.

"I am not going to lie to you, Greg. Having read Sophie's medical history, I think your concern is a reasonable one. The joint is loose, swollen, tender to the touch. I suspect she has a torn cruciate ligament in her knee. I would recommend further investigation, starting with some X-rays."

"If..." Greg swallowed audibly. "If it is, can you operate?"

Jodi shook her head. "My advice is to wait and see what the X-rays tell us first. It may be a spur—a bone stress fragment related to the extra strain on the joint due to her amputation. I don't think it's worth jumping to conclusions just yet, but I think, given her background and her tumble, we do need to be cautious and prepared."

"But, if need be, you can do the operation here, right?"

"No. Sorry. I'm afraid our anaesthetic machine is out of order and will be for some time while we wait for a part to come from America. In the meantime, Cole will refer you to the Angourie vet who will be more than happy to look after Sophie. She's an excellent vet. I have no hesitation in recommending her for Sophie's follow-up treatment."

"I was told you were the best in these parts. So I'm happy to trust your counsel."

"Thank you, Greg. I'll call straight after our appointment and make sure you and Sophie are made a top priority."

"Thanks, Doc. I appreciate it."

"You're more than welcome. It's the least I can do, under the circumstances. And this consultation is on the house—on the proviso you and Sophie come back sometime soon and let me know how you're going."

If Cole felt stunned at the previous consultation, she was left nearly speechless after this one. It didn't take a genius to see that Jodi was doing everything in her power to avoid any form of surgery whatsoever, even to the point of giving free consultations to appease the clients for her lack of full service.

She went into the tea room and boiled the jug. While she mulled over the morning's events, Jodi walked in. They each prepared their own beverage, wordlessly, and Cole poured hot water into both their cups. She handed Jodi hers while she removed the tea bag from her own and added milk. She leaned against the counter and studied Jodi.

"So. This fictional part for the anaesthetic machine. Where exactly is it coming from again? England or America? And when exactly can we expect it to arrive, do you think?"

Jodi glared at her, grabbed her coffee, and headed back into her office. She closed the door firmly on any reply Cole might have hoped for.

Jodi sat down hard in her chair and set her cup next to her, ignoring the fact that it sloshed onto some lab reports. She rested her elbows on the desk and laid her head in her hands. What the hell was she doing? She was completely disgusted with herself. The excuses, the outright lies, and her treatment of Cole were inexcusable. Her clients would never know the real truth behind all of it. How she'd lost every ounce of confidence in herself. Truthfully, if Cole hadn't been in the room with her, offering her strong, silent support, Jodi wasn't sure she would've even gotten through the examinations without bolting. Just the memory made her sick to her stomach with doubt and abhorrence of her behaviour.

Jodi sniffed and swallowed hard. Her throat burned and a sour tang rose into her mouth from the depths of her stomach. She sat up quickly, pulled the wastebasket closer, and dry-heaved over it. She broke into a cold, clammy sweat, and even though she was sitting, her knees felt weak and full of jelly. Jodi covered her ears, the incessant ringing becoming too loud. She bent over again, hyperventilating, unable to focus or gain some sort of control.

Cole was there in an instant, rubbing her back and mumbling reassurances. Cole was always there. Jodi turned into Cole, pressed her head into Cole's stomach, wrapped her arms around her, and sobbed. She cried until completely spent. She gave in to the exhaustion and let her arms drop to her sides. Cole hugged her close, still holding on tightly. Still supporting Jodi. Always. Her crutch. Her anchor. Her lover, who deserved so much better.

"I'm so sorry, Cole."

"Shh." Cole kissed the top of Jodi's head. "Just relax for a minute. Don't think about anything."

Jodi took a deep breath and let it out haltingly. "Fuck. I don't know what's wrong with me. I've lost the plot."

"Tell me what you need, sweetheart."

Jodi shook her head against Cole's stomach. "I have no idea. It's like there's this huge disconnect between my brain and hands. But today…Christ, today my scalp started burning and I couldn't think. The buzzing in my head was too loud."

Cole held Jodi by the shoulders. "Part of me says that you need a break. But I'm afraid that if you take that break, you'll never come back. Babe, this is your life. I've never seen a better vet than you."

Jodi wiped her eyes. "Yeah, some vet I am. I'm afraid of my own hands, I don't trust any of my decisions. Unless it's to tell the clients to go away."

"Your talent with animals is unsurpassed as far as I'm concerned. And everybody always talks about your beautiful bedside manner. People keep bringing their animals back to you because of *you*. They trust you to tell it like it is and not beat around the bush like some vets do. You aim right at the heart of the problem and treat it with a single purpose: to give that animal a longer or better quality of life. You do that, Jodi. *You*."

Jodi leaned back in her chair and ran her hands through her hair. "You sound like Pip."

"You should listen to her. She's much wiser than me."

"Tell me what to do. Because I sure as hell don't know."

Cole knelt in front of her. "Look, you've been working non-stop for as long as I've known you. How about we back down on your schedule for a bit. Maybe only take appointments three days a week. We'll send all the surgeries over to Angourie. They'll appreciate the extra business."

Jodi bit her lower lip. She could use a break. And what Cole was suggesting might possibly mean she wouldn't lose any clients. "Okay. I'm willing to try it."

Cole smiled reassuringly. "And on your days off, you're going to swim, and hike, and just bloody well relax."

"And make love with you."

Cole wiggled her eyebrows. "Well, that goes without saying, darling."

Jodi only just managed to get through the next day's appointments. Cole spent the entire day in the examination rooms with Jodi, helping her any way she could. Jodi trusted her to give vaccines and draw blood under her guidance, which thankfully covered the majority of the day's business.

While Cole cleaned the exam table, Jodi drew vaccines into syringes and laid them out in preparation for the nine working kelpies a cattle farmer was bringing in.

"Watching you give the injections and doing the blood draws is actually very relaxing." Jodi laid the charts side by side on the counter so they could apply the numbered stickers corresponding with each vaccine to each dog's chart.

Cole shot her a grin. "And why is that, Doctor?"

"Well, mainly because I don't have to do them at the moment." Jodi screwed her nose up at her own absurdity. She was the vet, for heaven's sakes. *She* should be performing those functions. But for now, she would go with the flow. And Cole's suggestion that she let Cole do as much as she was able to was admittedly a good one.

"In time. You'll be back at it in time." Cole put the cleaning supplies away under the sink. She put her hands on her hips and looked around. "Well, after we're done with the kelpies, that's it for the day."

Jodi looked at her watch and was amazed to see it was nearing five o'clock. "Wow. The day went quick."

"Yep. Sure did. Oh. By the way, will you pick me up tomorrow morning?"

Jodi shook her head in confusion. "What are you talking about?"

"After your swim, would you drop by my place?"

"Yeah, I guess. So you're not spending the night?"

Cole kissed her lightly on the cheek. "Not tonight, sweetness. I have a few things to take care of."

Jodi wrapped her arms around Cole's waist. "Like what? What could possibly be more important than snuggling under the sheets with me?"

Cole rolled her eyes and sighed dramatically. "Okay, fine. I'll tell you." She tapped Jodi's breastbone with her finger. "Tomorrow we're going on a picnic. But not just any picnic. You see, after we eat, I want you to take yourself off for a hike. So keeping that in mind, make sure you dress appropriately."

Jodi grinned. "Really?"

"Yes. Really. When you get home, spend some time thinking about where you'd like to spread a blanket on the ground as well as a place that puts you in a Zen spot."

Jodi rubbed her nose against Cole's. "You're spoiling me. You know that, right?"

"Yep." Cole turned Jodi away from her and gave her a little shove towards the door. "Go greet your next appointment, and make it snappy. I've got errands to run."

The ocean invigorated all of Jodi's senses as she freestyled through the thirty-metre ocean pool in Yamba the next morning. All the muscles in her body worked in unison to propel her against the waves breaking over the wall facing the seasonal swells.

Built into the rocks, the pool was cleaned regularly by the changing of the tides. When a southerly raced up the coast, it would oftentimes cast small sea creatures and fish into the pool. Jodi saw a myriad of them, made all the more clear by her swimming goggles. Three starfish clung to the rocks while a school of butterfly fish skittered away beneath her. A crab crawled sideways along the bottom, alternately picking up pieces of food with its claws and shoving them into its mouth. All of it made the hundred laps go faster.

Jodi got out and showered. She retrieved her bag of clothes from the Rover and went into the bathroom to dry off and change into her hiking gear. She knew exactly where she wanted to take Cole for the picnic. Purgatory Trail. She hadn't been back since Big Bird's release, and it'd been even longer than that since she'd taken the time to hike the area. She was going to change that today.

Cole walked out of her house as soon as Jodi pulled up. She wore a short-sleeved Karolina shirt that sculpted an airy and fluid silhouette, accentuated by skin-hugging shorts. Jodi gawked. *Man, she's gorgeous.* She then realized she should probably help carry the huge basket Cole had in one hand while juggling two travel mugs in the other. Jodi quickly got out and relieved her of the basket.

"Strewth, this is heavy. What's in it? The entire contents of your fridge?"

"You'll see," Cole sing-songed.

Once they were in the truck, Jodi leaned over and Cole met her for a lingering kiss.

"I missed you last night. I hope all your errands were worth it," Jodi teased.

"That remains to be seen. Oh, wait! I forgot to leave a note for the lawn guy. I'll be right back." Cole shoved the mugs into Jodi's hands, slid out of the truck, and rushed back to the house.

While she waited, Jodi took a sip of the hot coffee and had a good look at Cole's house. Naked was the best word she could come up with. The entire house, it seemed, was surrounded by nothing but very short grass. There were no gardens, trees, or even a potted plant on the veranda.

"Okay. Ready," Cole said, hopping back into the truck.

"How long have you lived here?" Jodi ducked her head to peer out the windscreen.

"Five years. Why?"

Jodi shook her head. "No reason, really. I was just wondering why you haven't planted anything to make it more natural."

Cole shuddered. "No way. Natural equals nature. And nature means bugs and other things that I don't get along with."

Jodi laughed. "They'll still find you, you know."

"Shh. Let's get out of here before they hear you."

Jodi shook her head in amusement and turned the key. "We're a pair, aren't we?" She glanced at Cole before turning out of her driveway. "I love nature, everything about it. And you absolutely abhor it. It strikes me funny that you'll actually handle any native beasties that come into the clinic."

"Feather and fur, baby girl. I don't mind them."

"What about mice? They have fur."

Cole visibly shuddered. "Except for them."

"Antichinus?" Jodi said, referring to the tiny marsupial.

"Meh. Pushing it. Those things look too much like a mouse with a long snout." Cole stuck her tongue out and shook her head.

"But they're interesting little things. Did you know that the male actually kills himself through sex?"

Cole looked at Jodi in disbelief. "Really? Hm. Maybe I could tolerate them then. But they still look like mice." She looked out the side window. "Where are we going?"

Jodi grinned. "We're going to Purgatory Trail."

"Isn't that where Charlie released Big Bird?"

"Yep. It's a beautiful spot. My boots have left a lot of tracks on the trails up there."

"I'm glad you're going hiking today."

Jodi met Cole's eyes and smiled. "Me too." She took Cole's hand in hers and squeezed. "Thank you."

The rest of the drive went quickly, despite little conversation. Jodi relished the warmth of Cole's hand in hers and held it continually. Even when shifting gears necessitated she let go, she didn't hesitate to quickly relink her fingers with Cole's thereafter.

The turnoff was even more disguised than the last time she was here by vegetation that had grown towards the middle, each side reaching to mingle with the other's leaves.

"Wow. How'd you ever find this place?" Cole leaned away from her side of the truck as branches tried to press their way in, even though her window was closed.

"It's not as overgrown in winter. But it was this time of year when I first came here," Jodi explained. "I must've driven by the blasted road half a dozen times before I finally saw it." She slowed the truck, shifted into low gear, and engaged the four-wheel drive.

"How far in does it go?" Cole seemed to relax a little.

"A fair bit. But we're not going as far back as the release site. There's a perfect little picnic spot close to the river that I want to show you."

The truck had no problem going through the rutted and bumpy area. Jodi silently thanked the Land Rover for being tenacious and rugged. Just before the road rose up into the mountains, Jodi edged the truck onto a nearly imperceptible logging trail. She navigated over river rocks, through a small stream, and into a small clearing on the opposite side where she braked to a stop.

"Okay. We're here." She beamed at Cole and flung her door open. "Isn't it beautiful?"

Shards of sunlight pierced the lowest branches of the trees like golden swords.

Cole got out and joined Jodi. "It's so quiet."

"Come on down to the water for a minute. I want to show you something."

The trail soon gave way to the trickling of water. They ventured down the embankment to where the river joined a stream that swirled and churned over rubbles of rocks.

Since Jodi's hiking boots were waterproof, she didn't hesitate to walk right into the shallow water. She stretched her arm out and beckoned to Cole. "Come on. Take my hand."

"Nope. I'm not setting one foot in that water. I saw the cows we passed just before the turnoff. They probably pooped in here. There's no telling what kind of nasty shit is floating around in there."

Jodi rolled her eyes. "Really?"

Cole stood with her feet firmly planted on dry ground.

"Fine. Suit yourself. Just don't go anywhere, okay?"

"I won't."

Jodi bent over and scanned the bottom of the clear running stream. She reached into the water, ran her fingers through the myriad of rocks, and waited for it to clear. She repeated the action several more times. When nothing of interest showed up, she sidestepped a few feet upstream.

"What exactly are you looking for?" Cole fanned a fly away from her face.

"I'll know it when I see it," Jodi said, resuming her search. Her efforts finally revealed a small stone. Exactly what she was looking for. She plunged her hand into the water and grabbed it between her thumb and index finger.

Holding her prize tightly lest she drop it, she waded back to where Cole waited.

"Have a look." She opened her hand for Cole to see.

"What is it?" Cole picked it up and twisted it between her fingers.

"It's a raw garnet. Put it up real close to your eye. Closer. Good. Now hold it up towards the light and look through the very top of it. That's called the table. What do you see?"

Cole played around with the stone, changing its angle. "Oh, wow! A rainbow! How cool." She looked at Jodi. "How'd you know what to look for?"

"My dad used to take me fossicking when I was a kid. The first time I came up here, I spent hours looking into the water. I have a couple big ones at home."

Cole held the rock up to the light again. "This is just beautiful. Wait. I don't see green or yellow in the rainbow."

"Wait! What? Give it here a second." Cole handed it to Jodi, who held it up to inspect it. "I'll be damned."

"What? Tell me."

"It's not a garnet at all." When Cole's face fell with disappointment, Jodi divulged her secret. "It's a ruby."

"Bloody hell! You found a ruby?" Cole looked back at the stream. "I don't care what's in the water any more. Let's look for some more." With her hands stretched out at her sides for balance, Cole waded in, exchanging grins with grimaces.

Jodi threw her head back and laughed. She pocketed the gem and joined Cole in the water.

CHAPTER THIRTEEN

Cole had laughed more in the last hour looking for precious stones than she had in ages. But more amazing than finding the stones was seeing glimpses of the old Jodi begin to uncurl and relax, shining as she should in the great outdoors that she loved so much. Each precious stone they found together not only held amazing colours within its hardened structures, but it also captured and held their moments of love and joy, each pebble safely stored away in their pockets, a treasured rich memory in and of itself.

It was only through the stark contrast that Cole realized how on tenterhooks she had been of late, watching over Jodi and the client workload. Not that she minded, nor would she trade for an instant, but it was good for both of them to be away from the practice, if only for a little while.

The weather was kind, the sun was out, and although humid, under the canopy of the sclerophyll forest, the air was pleasantly cool. With pockets full of precious stones, they sat on a large boulder, midstream, their knees bent, fingers entwined, resting against each other in peaceful bliss. Jodi sat behind Cole, arms wrapped around her. Who was leaning against whom was debatable as they moulded against each other.

Cole felt more than heard Jodi humming in her ear. The sound was barely audible, but the buzzing resonance of it was soothing. She closed her eyes and allowed her body and mind to melt into Jodi, with total trust and abandon—something she didn't think she had ever truly given, or offered in kind, to anyone else. This thought surprised her and made her think about not only what she and Jodi had shared as friends, but also where and how their relationship was metamorphosing.

"Hey, sleepyhead." Jodi's voice tickled in her ear. "Shh. Don't make any sudden moves. If you stay very still and open your eyes, you'll see a platypus off to your right."

Cole stiffened as she digested Jodi's message.

"Shh, now. Just open your eyes."

Cole supressed the sudden need to move, instead taking a slow, deliberate, measured breath before willing her limbs to stillness. As if anticipating Cole's move, Jodi tightened her arms briefly in an acknowledging hug. "Just off to the left, under that large willow branch overhanging the water. There's a half-submerged rock. Just watch. Keep your eyes on the rock." Jodi's voice was so whisper soft that it made her shiver.

Cole stared so hard she felt like her eyeballs were going to dry out. A head emerged, the bill scuttering across the surface, testing and tasting. Cole knew patience and stillness were the keys to potentially witnessing something wonderful.

In a most astounding moment, a tiny head appeared next to the emerged adult's. Both Cole and Jodi took in surprised breaths when the parent platypus raised its head, tasting the air at the significant change and influence they, as intruders, brought to the quiet creek.

After what felt like an eon, the adult appeared to appreciate their non-threatening presence and relaxed, dropping its head, taking turns preening itself and its offspring.

Cole leaned back and whispered. "That's amazing."

"I know. I can't believe what we're seeing. In all my years, I have never seen anything like it."

The awe in Jodi's voice reverberated in Cole's heart. If she could bottle this moment, she would gladly do it a thousand times over in order to have Jodi so happy and enthralled.

They sat transfixed for half an hour, watching the adult and baby platypus play. It was fascinating watching the youngster swim and dive and clumsily preen itself. With a last dive, they disappeared under the water and both Cole and Jodi sighed.

Jodi stretched behind Cole. "I don't know about you, but I think my bum's gone numb. I need to stand. You up to stretching your legs?"

"That was mind-blowing. But next time, remind me to bring a cushion."

Jodi laughed as she stood and held out her hand, pulling Cole up on stiff legs. "Come on, princess."

Hand in hand they stepped on rocks, manoeuvring through the stream back onto the grassy bank and to the Land Rover. Cole looked at her watch. "How about you go off on your bush toddle while I set things up here. I'll have lunch ready when you get back."

Jodi turned and encircled Cole's waist with her arms. "Why don't you come with me? We can both set up when we get back."

Cole shook her head. "The bush is your thing, bub. Go off and have some fun."

"Won't you get bored?"

"I brought a book that I've been dying to finish. I'll be plenty happy here."

"What time's lunch?"

Cole kissed her softly on the lips. "Whenever you're hungry."

"You're sure?"

"Positive. Go on. Off you go, love."

Jodi retrieved her backpack, pulled out a palm-sized device on a carabiner clip, and hooked it to her waist.

"What's that?" Cole asked.

"It's a personal satellite tracker. Whenever I go hiking, I always take it with me. It works where a lot of phones won't. If I get in trouble, I can hit this button here and it sends off an SOS message to emergency services and a grid reference so they know where to find me. And it tracks where I've been, which can sometimes be fun to look back on."

Cole was taken aback that such a small device could do all that, but not really surprised that Jodi had one. Jodi was a thinker and a planner and to own such a device was the responsible thing, as she hiked on her own almost as much as she did with her hiking group. "So it's kind of like an EPIRB device?"

"Exactly."

"I'm glad."

"I'm pleased you approve."

Cole kissed her because she could. "I do. Now get out of here while you still can." She turned Jodi around and gave her a light shove towards a wooded pathway.

Jodi gifted her with a gentle laugh and a quick wave before being swallowed up by the bush.

Cole sighed and hugged her middle. She wished she could bottle this happiness. She retrieved the picnic basket from the car and shook the blanket out onto the ground. As she unpacked the basket of goodies, and with each item laid out in place, a plan began to unfurl in her mind. Each item unlocked a planning step as to how the practice could stay open regular hours, while keeping the pressure off Jodi until she was confident and ready to take on her regular load again. Cole hummed tunelessly as the puzzle began to take shape.

❖

Jodi crossed the stream that she and Cole had had so much fun in earlier, hopping from rock to rock. She turned right onto the road and followed it towards the mountains.

The track was an easy walk at first. She soon realized that she had unconsciously lengthened her stride on the flat and slowed to take in her surroundings. The dry open eucalypt forest rose twenty-five and more metres above her. The interlocking canopy afforded her shade with rare glimpses of the blue sky above. The floor on either side was covered with various types of grasses, ferns, and shrubs.

A goanna ambled across the path. Jodi paused to watch it, but when it caught sight of her, it quickly scrambled into the low growth. Soon after she heard vigorous scratching and glimpsed flakes of tree bark fall to the ground as the lizard climbed to safety.

The terrain rose and with it came stark reminders of a long-ago bush fire. Numerous trees had large holes burnt into them or were streaked where the flames had tried in vain to reach the tops where a flock of yellow-tailed black cockatoos now called from.

Jodi welcomed the burn in her calf and thigh muscles as she walked. Swimming had helped increase her stamina, but it couldn't prepare her for adapting to the rise in elevation. Sweat poured down her face. Her heart rate increased and she heard every breath she took. It felt good even though she knew she'd feel it the next day. Although she loved her morning swim, her passion was the outdoors and immersing herself in it by hiking. There was something about being on the trail, feeling the wind brush against her skin and the sun beating against her back. Nothing else really mattered when she was trekking up a mountain, down a gorge, or around a loop. The world seemed to come to a standstill when her next step was the only thing that really mattered.

She never knew what she was going to encounter when she started a hike. She might find any sort of wildlife along the trail and that, along with challenging her body in nature's amphitheatre, was what blew her hair back. This was her drug, her release.

Jodi checked the GPS and the landmarks around her. At the rate she was travelling, she could make it to one of her favourite spots, Lyrebird Rock. The sun was still high in the sky and, barring any change in weather, she could make it to the open granite outcrop within the hour.

She followed a ridge, which made a gradual descent to the south and finally came at length to the brow of the massive cliff. It was an impressive lookout point. The main valley spread to the east. To the west, the land fell away in gullies and precipitous ravines as far as the eye could see. A small waterfall, the result of recent heavy rains, streamed down rocky walls, arching away from them as it descended.

Green catbirds and bellbirds called from the thick vegetation behind her. The varied flora and fauna that lived on Lyrebird Rock were more protected from bush fire than the creatures that inhabited the land below. However, they were exposed, day and night, to all the elements: rain, wind, sun, and even snow sometimes over winter. A strong breeze whipped her hair about her face. She tried in vain to tuck it behind her ears, but the wind had other ideas.

A shadow blocked her sun. Jodi looked up just in time to see a huge bird glide overhead, casting a moving silhouette over the granite. She shaded her eyes with her hand and studied it. Based on size and the unmistakable tail shape, she was sure it was a wedge-tailed eagle. The bird dipped a wing and circled, catching a thermal to take it higher. The sun reflected off its dark wings as it banked. Jodi blinked hard. Was that a white feather on the right wing? Could that be Big Bird? She quickly unzipped her pack and pulled out her binoculars. But by then the bird had climbed higher still, making it impossible to have a better look, even magnified.

Even so, it *could've* been Big Bird. She grinned and turned around to head back. She couldn't wait to tell Charlie when she got home.

Jodi made great time on the way back. The downhill slope made the walk much easier, although she felt it in her knees when the terrain flattened. She turned onto the path leading to the stream, crossed it, and walked to the truck. Cole was lying on the back seat sound asleep, legs crossed, her book resting on her chest. Jodi's stomach fluttered and she flashed a silly grin. Was this what falling in love felt like? She gently opened the back door and kissed the sleeping lips. She sure hoped so.

It was late afternoon when Jodi parked in front of Cole's house. Cole didn't want to get out of the car. She didn't want the day to end and hoped Jodi felt the same. Suddenly shy, Cole nervously plucked at the seat upholstery. "Um, would you like to come in? Although I'd understand completely if you just wanted to go home. It's been a big day, and you must be tired. You'll probably want to go to bed early, and—"

Jodi's laughter surprised her and, thankfully, stunned her long enough to stop the prattle that seemed to be tumbling out like an overflowing bubbler.

"I'd love to. Besides, you're gonna need help carrying all the picnic gear back into the house."

Cole winced. "I may have over-catered just a tad."

"Babe, we won't have to worry about preparing any food for about…oh, three days, I reckon."

Cole released her seat belt, opened the door, and stepped out of the car. Jodi took the basket of food to carry inside while Cole grabbed the wine cooler, thermos, and another box of unopened goodies. "I wasn't sure what you wanted, so I figured I would just bring it all. Besides, you forget, I know how good a chewer you are. I'm confident nothing will go to waste."

"Especially those melting moment biccies."

Once inside, Cole started putting things away while Jodi hovered nearby. "Feel free to wander about and take a look. I can hear your mind ticking over from here."

Jodi grinned in answer to her offer and could be heard wandering around the living room, an odd tinkle from a couple of piano keys giving away her position in the house.

"I didn't know you played." A few more keys tentatively sang out.

"Not as much as I used to." Cole leaned on the door frame.

"Why's that?"

Cole looked at her. "Been a bit distracted, I guess."

"Because of me, you mean?" Jodi dropped her gaze.

Cole walked around the piano and took her by the hand. "Come with me a minute." She led her down a brightly lit corridor into her office. She stood back and watched Jodi take in the large room. She called it her office, but the label was a disservice to its size and contents. There was a stunning stone wall, complete with water feature, against the far end of the room. Tribal artwork and carvings adorned the rammed earth walls, and a handwoven rug covered much of the polished hardwood floor. A large framed painting of the Scottish Highlands presided over an oak table that was covered in several of her sketches, only a handful of which were completed.

Cole wrapped her arms around Jodi from behind and drew her close against her. She rested her chin on Jodi's shoulder. "You are *definitely* distracting." Jodi stiffened in her arms. Cole kissed the outer edge of her ear, nipping it lightly to emphasize what she was about to say. "But in the most delicious way." She smiled, pleased when Jodi shuddered ever so slightly. "But I also get a little restless this time of year." She released Jodi and strolled over to reverently run her finger along the frame of a photograph of an elderly couple. They were smiling and laughing at the camera. "This time of year is a little bittersweet. Both of their birthdays fall this month. This was their favourite time of year. Flowers in bloom, going into the city to visit art galleries on Sundays, eating ice cream in the park, picnics on the back lawn, and quick thrown together dinners as we drove to the beach to watch the storms gather out to sea."

"You miss them."

"Some days I do. Terribly. And others, I feel their comfort as they walk beside me."

"What do you feel today?"

"Envious. And a little nervous."

Jodi moved beside her. "Why?"

"Because." She took a calming breath. "Because theirs was the most amazing love story ever. And I want what they had."

"Oh."

"And I kind of thought I had it. Once."

"I see," Jodi said quietly.

Cole frowned. Jodi was clearly retreating back into herself. She needed to make herself clearer. She took the framed photograph and handed it to Jodi to study. To see. To hear the words she needed to say out loud. "No. I don't think you do. I *thought* I'd found that sort of love, and when it all fell apart, I was devastated. I had to rebuild myself and my life. I had to start again. But I *needed* to do that. It was important, because without it, I would never have found you. And coming to love you, I am now only just beginning to see *this* is the sort of love I have been looking for." Looking down at the photograph of her grandparents and thinking back to today's picnic, there had been numerous moments where they had laughed and hugged and loved, just like her grandparents. She gently disengaged the picture from Jodi's fingers and set it back in its place. She took Jodi's hands in hers and held them to her chest. "And so," she said, dropping her voice to a whisper, "that leaves me feeling nervous. Scared that I'll screw this up, that I'll lose you."

Jodi glanced briefly to the picture of her grandparents and returned her gaze. Jodi kissed the backs of Cole's knuckles with tender lips. "Then I guess we better hold on tight to each other."

A sniffle escaped from Cole. "Uh-huh."

❖

"Come on. Where the hell are you?" Charlie muttered to herself. She'd already driven over ten kilometres looking for the kangaroo that'd been reported being hit between Lawrence and Grafton on the Summerland Highway. Frustratingly, they hadn't given any mile markers or landmarks as to the exact location of the downed roo. And the thick fog wasn't helping her efforts either.

Pip and she had been right in the middle of morning feeds when the call came in. Since Pip had been up most of the night with a sickly orphaned eastern grey kangaroo joey, Charlie volunteered to go alone. Now she worried that the injured roo might've managed to drag itself off the road and out of sight. With no idea as to where the collision had occurred, she wasn't too keen on having to drive on the shoulder the entire thirty-three kilometres both ways, with the fog limiting her visibility to boot.

Charlie's back and neck complained as she strained to see out the windscreen. She rolled her shoulders and rocked her head to ease some of the discomfort. A dark form darted out in front of her. She hit the brakes hard, dreading the impending thump. Thankfully none came. "That's why you silly things get hit. You have no road sense whatsoever." She shook her head in disbelief that the kangaroo had managed to avoid the bull bar on the Hilux.

The fog cleared ever so slightly as she came to the top of a rise. There! A dark form lay motionless on the side of the road just barely over the white line. That had to be it. She signalled and stopped the ute just behind the animal. She engaged the emergency flashers and checked for traffic out the side view mirror. Seeing that it was all clear, she opened her door and quickly stepped out. Getting hit by another driver while checking animals on the road was a risk. It was also her biggest fear. Aside from snakes, that was.

The smell of death assaulted her nostrils as she walked up to the bloated animal, and her heart fell when she realized it wasn't the roo she was looking for. The red-necked wallaby had been dead for at least a day. It didn't take long for decomposition to begin in the heat. "Might as well get you out of the road, you poor thing." As she bent down to grab a leg, she was saddened to see a tail and two hind feet protruding from the dead mum's pouch. "Aw, hell." Suddenly a leg moved. "Holy crap!" She grasped the tail in one hand and the feet in the other and pulled. The feet kicked in her hand and she nearly lost her grip. But with a sudden lurch the joey came free of the tightened pouch.

Charlie held the just-furred joey by the tail, holding tight while she pulled the body off the road. The joey kicked and hissed at her in fright and annoyance. She noticed one leg seemed to be weaker than the other. She quickly carried it to the ute, opened the back, and retrieved a cotton pouch. She held it open with one hand and lowered the little boy into it. She secured the pouch with a cable tie and put the bundle into a canvas bag attached to a special frame to suspend it off the ground.

She continued her search for the kangaroo. Fortunately, she didn't have to travel much further. There wasn't anything she could do for the young eastern grey buck except pull him off the road like she had the other one.

Once back in the truck, she phoned Pip to let her know she was heading to Yamba to have Jodi examine the joey and turned around towards the coast. Unfortunately, the fog once again hindered her as she descended the hills onto the flatter terrain. But the wind coming from the ocean soon dissipated it as soon as she crossed the Clarence River in Harwood. She was finally able to drive the speed limit.

There was only one car in the parking lot when Charlie turned into the clinic's drive. Hopefully that meant Jodi wasn't too busy and could have a look at the joey without a long wait.

The telltale *moo* announced her entry into the clinic. She held the pouched joey snugly against her chest, keeping it warm and giving it a sense of comfort by imitating the close confines of the mum's pouch.

"Hi, Mandy," Charlie said from the doorway. Her voice echoed in the empty reception room.

"Hey ya, Charlie. How're you going?" Mandy stood and went to the filing cabinet. She opened the second drawer down and pulled out a thick file. Charlie knew they were the WREN documents, which were considerably thick and varied.

"Good. Busy. But that never seems to change. I have a little red-necked joey I'd like Jodi to have a look at if she has the time. I think one of its back legs is injured."

Mandy ran her finger down the scheduling roster. "Righto. If you don't mind waiting a bit, she can see it right after the current appointment who's in there now."

"Wonderful. Thanks." Charlie took a seat away from the door and in the quietest spot she could find. Any loud noises would stress the joey and could cause stress myopathy, potentially killing the young animal.

Twenty minutes later, a tired looking woman with twin toddlers walked out. Cole followed them, carrying a cat carrier. None of them looked happy and from the sound of the cat's howling, it seemed to share the sentiment.

"Hi, Charlie." Cole waved enthusiastically as she set the small crate next to the reception desk. "Mandy, will you help Mrs. Chatwin?"

"No problem."

Cole radiated happiness. Her eyes danced and sparkled when she focused on Charlie again. "You're out and about early. Head on back and I'll bring you a cup of coffee."

Charlie yawned in response. "Thanks. We've had a couple of long nights."

Cole rubbed Charlie's back as she followed her as far as the coffee machine. "Yeah. I know what you mean."

Since Cole didn't elaborate before disappearing into the kitchen, Charlie walked towards the back, through the kennelling room, and into the area that Jodi had converted into a quiet space for hospitalized wildlife. She'd spent untold hours in here with Big Bird while he convalesced from surgery.

A few minutes passed and still no Jodi. Cole pushed the door open with her bum a short time later, holding three steaming cups of coffee. Charlie hurried to relieve her of one, while Cole set Jodi's on the counter.

Charlie took a sip, closed her eyes, and moaned. "Some mornings it's certainly harder to get motivated than others."

"Oh, don't I know it. Some days I don't know whether I'm coming or going."

"Things going good for you two then?" Charlie hid her smile with her mug.

Cole grinned. "We're taking it one day at a time."

"And one night at a time?" Charlie couldn't resist teasing her a bit.

Cole blushed brightly, even in the dim light.

Jodi appeared to rescue Cole at that very moment. Charlie hadn't seen Jodi in a few weeks and the difference was startling. She was gaunt, her face drawn and pale. And if Charlie wasn't mistaken, Jodi looked like she was sick to her stomach. "Jodi, are you feeling all right?"

A look passed between Jodi and Cole. Jodi nodded. "Yeah. Fine."

"What do you have here, Charlie?" Cole quickly changed the subject.

Charlie cut the cable tie with the pair of scissors she'd pulled from one of the drawers. "I may be imagining it, but this joey's left leg seemed a bit off when I pulled him. I just want to make sure it's okay before I take him home." She lifted the wiggling creature out of the bag and held him so Jodi had easy access to the suspect leg. Much to her surprise, Jodi didn't touch the wallaby. Not once.

"Cole, let's just get an X-ray, shall we?" Jodi rubbed her tired looking eyes with her thumbs.

"Yep," Cole said with complete lack of emotion.

Charlie slid the joey back into the pouch and handed the bundle to Cole, who then walked out of the room.

"Jodi, shouldn't you—"

"Oh! Hey. Cole and I went down to Jackadgery yesterday. I'm pretty sure I spotted Big Bird while I was down there. I was going to call you last night, but I spent the night at Cole's and well…"

"What? You're kidding?"

Jodi lifted one shoulder. "I can't be a hundred per cent sure it was him. He hit the thermals pretty quick not long after I first noticed him. But I could've sworn I saw a flash of that white wing feather."

"No way. What are the chances he's still in the area?"

Jodi shrugged.

"Where'd you see him? In the field where we released him?"

Jodi shook her head. "No. Just a little bit away. I hiked to a lookout called Lyrebird Rock. You can see forever up there."

"Does Pip know where that is?" Charlie bounced up and down on her toes, barely able to contain her excitement.

"She might, although it's a bit remote. But I'd be happy to take you up there."

Charlie grabbed Jodi's arm. "Really? When?"

Jodi frowned. "Probably not for at least a week at the earliest. There's more rain coming in."

"Right, okay. We'll have to make plans."

Cole walked in with the pouch cuddled against her chest. "The image should be up on the computer," she said flatly.

Jodi opened up the laptop and tapped a couple keys, and a skeletal image appeared on the screen. She studied it for a few minutes. "Doesn't look like anything serious, Charlie. I'd wager it's just bruised badly. Heat and quiet should help make a difference over the next fortnight."

Charlie took the joey from Cole, completely flabbergasted that Jodi had still not touched him. "Okay. I'll have Pip call you. She sends her love to both of you, by the way."

"Back at her." Jodi sculled the remainder of her coffee and moved towards the door. "Good seeing you. I have to get going. Mandy'll have the next client waiting in the examining room." She opened the door and left without another word.

"Is she going to be okay?"

Cole blew out a sad breath. "Your guess is as good as mine. But I'm hopeful. There're some things in the works, fingers crossed, that should help. Anyway, I'd best push off and give her a hand."

"Okay. See you." Charlie showed herself out of the clinic. She secured the joey in the bag and pointed the ute towards home. She wondered what Pip was going to make of all this.

Pip was washing the mid-morning feeding bottles and bowls when she heard Charlie arrive home. A few moments later she entered the prep room.

Charlie greeted her with a soft kiss. "Hey, babe."

Pip smiled. "Hey, yourself. What's in your goody bag?"

Charlie laid the bag on the table and opened it. "You mean the joey pouch? I swear it's going to take me half a lifetime to come to terms with your Aussie lingo."

"You're presuming, of course, that you'll live a long life. We're a complicated mob, you know?"

"Don't I know it." Charlie took the joey out of the bag, a frown creeping over her features.

"Walk me through your morning."

After Charlie regaled her with the morning's events, Pip examined the joey, running her fingers along limbs, stretching out joints, testing and looking for contusions or signs of trauma. Meantime, Charlie had her hands and fingers deftly weaving in and out of Pip's as she took tail and hind leg measurements, recording all the details as she went. Their seamless teamwork still surprised and delighted Pip, having spent quite a few years doing everything on her own.

"And there it is," Charlie concluded. "Just a plain weird kind of morning. I tell you, I still can't get over Jodi. In fact, the more I think about it, the more it bothers me."

"Even though I didn't see the X-rays, for what it's worth, I think

Jodi's probably right." Charlie blinked hard. Pip stroked the back of Charlie's hand. "I know, love. It's not right. More importantly, you're right—it's so not Jodi. But let's break it down—the joey, the results, and Jodi."

Charlie pulled in a breath. "So, the joey—initially we'll keep it quiet, support the joint, and assess swelling, circulation, and movement at regular intervals."

"Uh-huh."

"And Jodi?" Charlie put the joey back into a brushed cotton wrap, a woollen lined pouch, and then into a secondary heavy duty bag that she hung off a frame.

"I'm not sure I have a big enough pouch for her," Pip said. "But I suspect the treatment won't be dissimilar to the joey here."

"What do you mean exactly?"

"We can see signs and symptoms of something not quite right."

"Correct."

"And so we'll aim to keep what we can calm around her, we will assess each situation as it arises, and we'll be supportive. We will monitor reactions, as best we can, at regular intervals, and we will consult with Cole and compare notes, where we think it's deemed reasonable."

Charlie blew out an exasperated breath. "So. We do nothing."

Pip wrapped her arms around Charlie's waist, drawing her in close. She kissed the tip of her nose. "On the contrary."

Charlie visibly struggled with the concept of passive, supportive assistance. "I don't get it."

"I think you do. Probably more than most, I'd hazard a guess." Empathy softened Pip's voice naturally.

"What?"

"Your panic attacks, sweet. Largely, they were the result of a long series of built-up events. The triggers of an episode could range from something major to almost insignificant individual events or isolated occurrences."

"You're saying Jodi is having panic attacks."

Pip tilted her head slightly. "In a sense, yes." Pip was especially mindful that Charlie might feel reactive to the emotive comparison to her past situation. She knew she was taking a gamble that it might work in her favour, with Charlie the most likely to understand some of where Jodi's reactions and feelings were coming from.

Pip ran her fingers lightly through Charlie's hair. She always loved how Charlie's curls lazily tumbled through her fingers, their strands as soft as silk. She sensed, more than felt, the slight shudder that passed through Charlie's body. She waited and was finally rewarded by Charlie's clear-eyed glance, ricocheting straight to her heart. Pip had come to know that look. That look signified Charlie had not only embraced the learning that came from a new situation, but she also relished the challenge.

Chapter Fourteen

They spent the day at the beach, with Jodi teaching Cole how to snorkel the clear sandy depths. Cole, as was fast becoming her tradition, had brought a mountain of food along, most of which, by mid-afternoon, they greedily consumed. Cole's body hummed in unimagined satisfaction. The days away from the office were wonderfully, delectably decadent, but she knew it couldn't last. There were business decisions to be made, clients to look after, and of course, there was the giant elephant in the room—the decrease in the amount of money coming in.

As the person who did the banking and once a month helped Jodi balance all the books, Cole knew the financial state of the business. And while Jodi might enjoy the temporary working reprieve, the lack of clients wouldn't sustain the business in its current format for too much longer if there weren't some changes made, and soon.

Her dilemma was how and when she could find a moment appropriate to have such a discussion with Jodi. Her head ached with the tension of the predicament of looking after her lover and helping to look after the business.

She packed the last of the lunchtime containers into the picnic basket. Jodi had pretended to struggle under the weight of it. And Cole had playfully ignored her. She smiled now, knowing that the basket would be a great deal lighter for their trek back to the Rover.

Cole slathered another layer of sunscreen on her shoulders, face, and arms, opting to cover her legs with her sarong while she read her book. She still hadn't finished it.

She was left in a peaceful solitude, as Jodi was keen to explore the headlands. With Cole's encouragement, some water, and a snack, Jodi had headed off to navigate the landscape.

Cole's book sat unopened in her lap. They were so different, on so many levels, and yet, they were kind of like a key and a lock—two very different shapes and patterns, but somehow they complemented each other in their differences. That anomaly was alien to her, and yet here she sat, completely at ease, excited for Jodi's return, yet pleased knowing that Jodi was off doing something she loved and neither needed, nor expected company, happy in the knowledge that Cole would be waiting for her. And Cole was happy that she felt no pressure to join her and endure the marathon slog through coastal heathlands, to land back limp and exhausted, pretending to enjoy what was effectively a nature-fest marathon.

She nodded to herself. Yep, a key and a lock. That's what they were. Her analogy, although surprising, somehow filled her with joyful confidence and a sense of peace in its discovery.

Jodi came back several hours later, sweaty, grinning, and a touch pink from the sun. They quickly packed up and headed to the car. On their way home, Jodi recounted her hike along the headlands, including sitting on some rocks on the ocean's front and having four kangaroos come down to the beach. They'd stood in the water not more than two metres away from where she sat on the tidal rock shelf, the surf breaking against their tummies and long muscular back legs.

After a quick wash, Cole set about chopping up some salad vegetables while Jodi took her turn in the shower. She covered the salad bowl and put it in the fridge. They had bought a cooked chicken on the way home, which sat cooling on the bench.

Jodi emerged, smelling of soap, in a tank top and loose cargo shorts. Cole couldn't be sure, but by the loose fall of the clothes she guessed that Jodi wore nothing underneath. She swallowed as a rush of heat stole up her neck and across her face.

Cole opened the fridge door and looked inside. "Dinner's a way off yet. Would you like wine, beer, water, juice, or something else?"

Cole barely had time to register Jodi closing the fridge door. "Something else, please." Jodi drew Cole against her. A slow simmering kiss stole whatever dinner plans had been formulating in Cole's mind.

"Mm. And what might that be, pray tell?" Cole wrapped her arms around Jodi's neck and kissed her smiling mouth.

"I'm thinking I might fancy an entrée." Jodi kissed her lips, her nose, and her neck.

"Oh?"

"Oh, yeah. I fancy me some rare sumptuous Kiwi bird." Under Jodi's guidance, Cole walked backward down the hallway into her bedroom.

"Is that so?"

Between Jodi's kisses and free roaming hands, Cole had just enough sense to register that her shirt had gone missing, as had one of her slip-on house shoes. By the time they reached the edge of the bed, Cole was barely aware that Jodi was negotiating the knot at her hip that held her sarong in place. She felt it give way and whisper against her legs, to lie in a pool of cloth around her now bare feet. They tumbled to the bed and relished the slow and languid taste of each other's lips.

It was apparent that Jodi had had a good day. Cole caressed Jodi's shoulders as she kissed her way down her body. Her fingers traced a sun kissed arc across the midline of her biceps. "You caught some sun today."

Jodi rose briefly and kissed Cole on the nose, and across her cheeks. "So did you."

Cole took a breath. "Honey?"

"Hm?" Jodi seemed intent on exploring her clavicle and neckline.

"Today was wonderful. Thank you."

Jodi sensuously rubbed her cheek along the under curve of Cole's right breast. "You're welcome. I loved it, too."

Cole sucked in a sharp breath as Jodi toyed with her nipple with a lightning quick suck, followed by a feather-soft kiss, before retreating to explore the valley between her breasts. She mentally shook her head trying to regather her thoughts. "You know I love our days off."

"Me, too." Jodi slid a few inches lower, seeming to count every one of Cole's ribs with her lips and tongue.

"But we need to talk about work."

Jodi slid lower again, her tongue playing along the line where her abdomen met her pelvis. "Not now."

"But...oh." Cole's breath shortened as Jodi gently parted her thighs. "We..." She swallowed. "We do need to get our heads around it at some point."

Jodi slid ever lower until she lay nestled between Cole's legs, her breath hot. Close. Making her shiver with each exhalation. "I'd say"— Jodi ever so slowly, with a single long, slow motion, stroked the full length of Cole's sensitive centre with her tongue—"my head is in the best position it's been in a long time."

Cole slid her hands towards Jodi's head. "No. Really. I mean... *oh.*" As Jodi's lips claimed every square inch of her, Cole could barely breathe. Jodi's mouth rendered her near speechless with her continued close attention.

"We really should…oh my God." Cole's moan effectively finished her sentence. Jodi was destroying any chance she had of having a sensible and serious conversation as she drew her ever closer to the point of no return, the heat of her lips smouldering in the attention.

"Don't want to talk about it," Jodi mumbled between kisses.

"But we…" Cole cried out as Jodi entered her.

"What is there to say?"

As Jodi's lips encircled her clit and sucked her in, Cole's hips moved beyond her control to meet the mouth that held her on the precipice of absolute wonder. Her fingers, twined in Jodi's hair, held her tight against her centre, the need to be close driving all careful plans from her mind, her voice a strangled whisper. "Don't stop." Cole arched her body, gathering Jodi closer still, her head thrown back as the lights behind her eyes exploded outward, lighting up every fibre in her being.

She barely registered Jodi's chuckle.

"That's what I thought."

Charlie tucked a strand of hair behind her ear and took a sip of coffee. Her eyes remained trained on the visa checklist. For every document she pulled from her pile and slid into the large Express Post envelope, she checked the corresponding box on the list. The next one destined to join the growing pile in the mailer was the form declaring Pip's sponsorship of her application. She put an X over the box and slid her finger down to the next one: Pip's statutory declaration. Charlie riffled through the remaining papers. But it wasn't there. Shit. She looked towards the door. She hadn't seen hide nor hair of Pip and Chilli since breakfast. She glanced at the wall clock. Eleven twenty. She had an hour and a half before the post office closed. She quickly took stock of the remaining papers. Nope. It wasn't there. "Where the heck did it go?" She looked up suddenly, realizing that she hadn't actually *seen* one. "I'll bet she hasn't even written it yet. Dammit."

She pushed her chair away from the table, grabbed two apples from the fruit bowl, and went in search of her lover. The soft breeze that met her on the other side of the door smelled like rain. The sky had clouded over since the morning feed. She wondered how long it'd be before everything was wet again.

The prep room was empty but for Pip's sickly little joey, who was tucked into a bag in the warmest part of the room, and the joey she'd recently rescued hung right next to it. The frame from which he was suspended jiggled a bit as he readjusted himself, but then became quiet again. As usual, everything was in its place, not a bit of clutter or dirt anywhere. The room exuded cleanliness and had a nearly sterile appearance.

Movement in the window caught her eye. Pip drove the four-wheeler along the garden, towing a trailer filled with new branches for the koalas. Chilli sat on the seat behind her, perfectly balanced and happy.

Charlie knew Pip would come directly to the prep room looking for a snack and drink to replenish her energy reserves. Gathering branches was hard work, especially in the heat, and Pip had to make sure her blood sugar remained stable.

She shined one apple against her shirt, took a bite, and rubbed the other one while she chewed. The apple was half gone by the time the door opened and Chilli ambled in, followed by a flushed and sweaty Pip.

"Go sit. I'll grab you a drink." Charlie quickly retrieved a Gatorade from the fridge and cracked it open while Pip plopped down into the thick lounge cushions.

"Gonna rain soon." Pip took the proffered bottle and proceeded to down half of it.

"Mm. It definitely has that feel about it." Charlie sat next to Pip and handed the apple to her.

"Thanks, sweet." She took a bite, laid her head back, and chewed with her eyes closed.

Charlie nudged her. "No time for sleeping. You need to write up your Stat Dec so I can get everything in the mail."

Pip pointed to the computer with her chin. "It's done. Just have to print and sign it."

Charlie scrubbed a hand over her face. "I wish you'd told me that at breakfast."

Pip blinked innocently. "Sorry. Didn't think about it."

"Sweetheart," Charlie said, trying hard not to clench her teeth, "really?" She pushed up from the lounge and woke the computer from sleep mode. There in front of her was Pip's Stat Dec. She was just about to send the document to the printer when a few odd words caught her eye. She stared in disbelief as she read what Pip had written: *To whom it may concern, Pip Atkins here. Charlie Dickerson is my partner. She's good in bed and a bloody hard worker. She's afraid of snakes. But so am*

I, so don't hold that against her. But the main reason I think she should be allowed to stay in Australia is that she's tall. And I sometimes need her to reach things for me. Sincerely, Pip Atkins.

"Is this some kind of joke, Pip?" Charlie slammed the lid of the laptop down and spun around. She glared at Pip who still sat with her eyes closed. A whisper of a smile graced her lips, which nearly sent Charlie over the edge. "I asked you to write up one thing! *I* did everything else and all *you* had to do was write up one little thing. *One!*"

Pip remained motionless.

"Well? Aren't you going to say anything?"

Pip opened those gorgeous blue eyes and met Charlie's.

Charlie softened a little. Pip's eyes were very often her undoing.

Leaning forward just a bit, Pip pulled an envelope from her back pocket and tossed it onto the table in front of her. "Maybe this one will suit you better?" She leaned back and closed her eyes again.

Charlie snatched the envelope, pulled out the paper, and unfolded it. Her patience had worn thin over the past couple of days. Her mouth fell open. The story of how she had come to Australia and details of how they had fallen in love and were in a committed relationship were written in almost poetic form. Pip had signed it at the bottom and it was sealed by the Maclean justice of the peace. The backs of her eyes burned as tears formed, welled, and spilled down her cheeks.

Charlie sniffed. "I'm so sorry, babe. I owe you a huge apology. I'm just—"

In a blink of an eye, Pip rose and wrapped her arms tightly around her. "I only did the first one to make you smile that lovely smile of yours, you goose. I know how important this is."

Charlie held Pip tight. "I'm so scared that immigration won't let me stay."

"Shh, now. You've done absolutely everything you can. All you can do is done now. Post it, then let it go. Don't even think about it. If something happens that you don't get it, well, we'll work something out. Promise."

"It's all I think about."

"I know. But whatever happens, nothing changes. This is about you and me. Okay, mostly you, but I'm not going anywhere. You and I…we're supposed to be together. I feel that in my bones. We've just got to do whatever it takes to make that happen."

Charlie glanced up at the wall clock and wiped her eyes with the backs of her hands. "I have to get going. This is the last thing I needed to put in the envelope to get this application sent off."

"Then you'd best tuck it in there fast and get your cute butt to the post office."

Charlie sniffed again and nodded. "Okay."

"We'll celebrate tonight, love. That's a big thing you've done—putting that monster application together. You should be right proud of yourself. I know I'm indescribably proud of you."

"Thanks." Charlie pointed over her shoulder. "I need to—"

"Go. I'll be here when you get back."

That was all Charlie needed to hear. Her heart swelled with adoration for her Aussie.

Jodi was up and undoubtedly off swimming by the time Cole got out of bed. As she stumbled into the kitchen, she saw that Jodi had laid out breakfast for her—bread for toasting, a cup of tea, and a bowl of freshly cut fruit. A small note sat on top of her bread, a hand-drawn love heart with a smiley face inscribed into the middle.

Cole put the message under a fridge magnet, her fingers brushing lightly across the paper face. She turned the kettle on and put her toast in to cook. Today she would really need to sit Jodi down and talk to her about work, whether Jodi liked it or not. She nodded once, resolved in her determination of her day's plan, and quickly finished breakfast.

With a brief shower and a change into clean scrubs, Cole set off to work, a bag of food packed for Jodi's breakfast tucked under her arm.

When she'd first moved into her home, the drive to work felt like forever, especially at the end of a long day or late night. But now she loved it as it provided her with the perfect amount of time to plan the day, or unwind from a big one, so that she arrived relaxed and ready to face whatever was waiting for her. This morning it also gave her extra time to reflect on the previous day and the night. Her skin tingled, and she found herself humming a tune, her heart singing along silently.

Opening up the surgery, she went through the regular routine, turning on lights, sterilizers, computers, and the all-important coffee machine in preparation for…She waited and smiled as the telltale jingle of the bells on the back door announced Jodi's arrival. She knew by the time Jodi had finished getting changed that the coffee would be ready. With a quick flourish of pen on paper, Cole left a similar note to Jodi's in her breakfast bag in the kitchen.

Pleased with herself, she reviewed the day's appointment book to see what opportunities she might have to collar Jodi and talk work and her plan. There was a small break before midday which could work, and that would also afford Jodi some time to think about what she might like to do. Cole quickly penciled in a block of time for a meeting.

She heard Jodi in the kitchen pottering about, and moments later she came out with two steaming mugs in her hands, one her usual coffee mug and the other a fresh cup of tea for her. Handing the mug over, Jodi leaned across the bench and captured her lips in a soft, slow kiss.

"A good swim?"

"Perfect. Thank you. And thank you for my brekkie."

"My pleasure. And thank you for my note this morning." It warmed Cole to see a blush creep up Jodi's neck and spill onto her cheeks. "And speaking of notes, Anna from Angourie has emailed over some reports for a couple of last week's patients we referred over to her. They're on your desk."

"Ah, thanks." Jodi went to her office just as the phone rang. Cole answered it and was delighted to hear Charlie's voice on the other end. "How's your little joey doing?" Cole listened to Charlie's report. "I'm glad." She looked down and fiddled with a pen as Charlie spoke. "I know. I'm sorry. It's complicated. But she's working through it." Cole mindlessly drew circular doodles on a scrap piece of paper. "I'd forgotten you told me about your panic attacks. It might be nice for her to have someone to talk to about it. You know, someone who knows what it's like. And if you had any advice, or ideas to help her, that might be handy. I'm sure she'd appreciate that." Knowing that both she and Jodi had Pip and Charlie in their corner was a treasure. She lifted her chin in thought at a question from Charlie. "Hang on and I'll ask."

Cole held the phone to her chest as she walked to Jodi's office and tapped lightly on the door frame before entering, "Hey, bub, Charlie wants to know if we'd like to come out to their place on the weekend, maybe head out to see if we can spot Big Bird, then come back for dinner. She's celebrating submitting her immigration application."

Jodi looked up and smiled. "Sure, love to. Just let us know what time and what to bring."

Cole pushed off from the door frame and sauntered over to the front door of the surgery, turning the sign to *Open* and unlocking the door. "We'd love to, just text me through the details of time and what you want us to bring." She'd no sooner turned her back and reached the counter when the first client arrived. She waved them in. "Uh-huh. Okay. Yep, just text me. You too. Bye."

The first appointment was closely followed by two people wanting flea and tick treatments. The morning had started with a rush. Cole was keen to see how Jodi was getting on in the first examination room but was quickly swamped by clients coming in or the phone ringing. In an hour, Jodi had trimmed dog toenails, pulled out a grass seed from a cocker spaniel's ear, and referred a terrier to Angourie for a nasty eye infection that would necessitate the eye being removed. Cole had only managed to briefly put her head in on a couple of the consultations, and she could see the tension beginning to build on Jodi's face and in the stiffening set of her shoulders.

Jodi headed towards the kitchen to get a fresh cup of coffee as Cole walked into the pharmacy room to retrieve some arthritis drugs for a dog whose owner was at the front counter, when the front door *moo* sounded again. Jodi waved at her as she walked past. "It's all right. I got this one."

Cole came back with the meds in her hand and heard a familiar voice calling out a greeting.

Jodi stood at the counter. "Cate. What a pleasant surprise."

With her sharply cut bob framing her beaming face, Cate Fletcher waved excitedly. "I know. I was on my way back from Brisbane. Thought I'd call in. Say hi. I hope you don't mind."

Cole winced when she saw Jodi's back stiffen.

"That's quite a drive. Why don't you head on out the back and make yourself a cuppa. You still remember where things are?" Cole noticed Jodi's forced smile. "One of us will be out to join you in a minute."

"Oh yes. Thanks." Cate's face was flushed and she all but bounced to the kitchen.

Cole quietly handed the replenished stock of drugs to the client and wished them a good day.

Jodi hadn't moved.

Shit.

"When is the next appointment?"

Cole cringed internally as she glanced over the appointment book. "Not for another fifteen minutes."

"Good. Lock the front door, turn the answering machine on, and meet me in my office."

Turning on her heel, Jodi left, taking the air out of the room with her.

Cole's stomach somersaulted and bile threatened to rise up and choke her. She swallowed it down and did as Jodi asked before standing in her office doorway. Her insides trembled.

"Shut the door."

The fact that Jodi's voice was deadpan flat sent shivers up her spine more than if she'd yelled at her. She desperately wished she *would* yell at her.

"Did you know Cate was going to call in?"

"Not exactly. But that's what I've been trying to talk to you ab—"

"What?"

"I've kept in touch with Cate. Since she did her last prac stint with us."

"Go on."

"I said, you know, if ever she was in the vicinity, she was always welcome to call in. I didn't think you'd mind."

"I see."

"She's not doing anything at the minute. And maybe if she doesn't have any set plans, she might be able to help out for a while. Help take the pressure off a bit. You said she had promise and the clients already know her, so it's not like she's a total stranger, and she got on really well with everyone before when she was here for her last rotation before graduating."

Cole knew she was talking too fast but she had to get out as much as possible before Jodi shut her down. "The practice can't afford to cover the overhead, only being open a couple of days a week and what with our clientele going over to Angourie and Maclean. This way we can stay open, with normal hours, the money comes in, and Cate can do the surgeries. You can still have your days off, but Cate can help share the load for a bit, until you're back on your feet."

"And the days that I am here?"

"Consultancy. Both for Cate and the clients. You're an excellent teacher and clients love you. That way your head stays busy, but your hands get a break. You can do as little or as much as you feel comfortable doing." Cole took a breath.

"Looks like you've got it all sorted."

"No. I've been *trying* to talk to you about the *concept* of thinking about getting some help in, to give you a much needed break, but now that she's here, it would be silly not to talk to her at least. See what her plans are. If you think it would help, maybe consider a trial? What do you think?"

Jodi held her hand up. She slowly stood and walked behind her. Cole stood frozen in place. She could feel Jodi's breath on the back of her neck.

In barely a whisper, Jodi said, "You might be the practice manager, but see that plate on my desk?"

Cole nodded.

"That is my name. And this is still my business."

A cold sweat formed on Cole's brow. She grounded herself. "Yes, you're right. But I happen to care about you. And I can't stand idly by and watch you drive yourself into the ground, or see the business you've worked so hard to build crumble beneath your feet because you're too proud to ask for help. Please, Jodi. At least talk to her. See what you think."

A large heavy silence sat between them. It was a push-pull moment. Cole held her breath, not knowing which way Jodi would go.

"I'll talk to Cate. You will go out, open up, and maintain the desk. When I'm finished, I will be leaving for the day."

Cole turned and looked at her. Jodi's face was pale, her face devoid of all expression. A shadow seemed to pass across Jodi's eyes. A cold fear crept into Cole's heart. "What do you want me to do with this afternoon's appointments?"

Jodi blinked slowly and tilted her head briefly to the side. "Seems to me you're on a roll." Cole strained to hear her. "I'm sure you'll figure something out."

Cole never heard her leave the room. She shivered and wrapped her arms around her body in an attempt to ward off the cold that consumed her from the inside out.

CHAPTER FIFTEEN

Jodi managed to hold in check every single emotion that coursed through her until she arrived at the dunes. Up until then, she'd purposely shut down so as to not let them have their way with her. She wanted to analyse them one by one.

She'd gone home in a self-imposed daze and grabbed the gear she always kept at the ready. Food, extra clothing including a raincoat and her trusted Akubra, her swag, and toiletries all went into the back of her Rover. At the last minute, she tossed a bottle of whisky onto the passenger's seat, figuring she'd need a stiff drink in order to process all that had gone down at the clinic.

Jodi turned off the main road and onto the sandy path, shifted into four-wheel drive, and followed the deep grooves. As soon as she hit the firm sand of the beach, she turned left, away from the main beaches, and drove until the dunes surrounded her, effectively secluding her from the rest of the world. She parked close to the massive hills of sand so that she was hidden from sight. In automatic, brisk movements, she unloaded everything and left it in a heap while she walked to the water. She needed the healing energy of the ocean. The ebb and flow of the waves washed her ankles as the tidewaters receded. She fixed her eyes on the skyline and watched clouds drift across the blue with almost imperceptible slowness. The sea spray misted her face with gentle fingertip-like touches, as the sky changed to a mauve colour. Cumulus clouds gathered on the horizon and crept across the changing sky. She took a deep breath, smelling the fishy, tangy, and slightly salty scent of the ocean.

Tense muscles slowly relinquished their knotted hold. The burn and ache were suddenly missed. At least she'd been able to concentrate on the pain, instead of the tangle of thoughts roiling around in her head like misguided tumbleweeds. *Not ready yet.* Jodi turned with a sudden flurry of quick movements and set up her camp, going from one chore to the next on automatic pilot.

Within an hour, she had smoothed out a three-by-one metre section of sand and set her swag on it. She tucked her rain gear and a change of clothes inside and zipped it up tight. She swiped sand aside and created a small hollow for a fire. That done, she went in search of firewood. Soon after, a crackling fire reflected off the sand dunes. Waves of heat brushed against her skin when the wind died.

Jodi sat down by the fire and crossed her legs. She opened the whisky bottle and took a swig. She wiped her lips with the back of her hand as the gold liquid burned its way to her stomach. It was time. She couldn't put it off any longer. She'd spent the last two hours pushing herself into near exhaustion. Her body was pleasantly weary, but her mind was far from tired. *It's time.* She needed to process.

She took another long swallow of whisky and began the slow dissection of the day. Layer by layer, like she would do in surgery. Well, like she *used* to do in surgery. Jodi sighed. She needed to get back to the vet she knew. Somehow. Even though that felt like it was a million miles away. But right now, she had other issues to deal with.

Had Cole overstepped the mark? Jodi felt anger grow again. Heat flushed through her body and she clenched her jaw. She couldn't believe the audacity of the woman! Was it pre-planned, or was Cate's arrival purely coincidental? Jodi threw a piece of wood into the fire so hard that sparks raced upward and fled in all directions.

The fact that Cole had been in contact with Cate and told her she could call in anytime without asking grated. Was she pissed because she had been out of the loop? Had she given Cole too much authority within the practice? Or had Cole's overconfidence been born of the fact that they were sleeping together? "Dammit! Frickin' libido." Jodi shook her head, disgusted with herself.

Poor Cate. Before leaving, she'd managed to have a nice long chat with her. It'd been good to catch up, but she wondered if Cate hadn't felt the tension. *Hell, you could've cut it with a knife.*

She wasn't surprised to learn that Cate had graduated from vet school with high honours. During the months Cate spent working in her surgery, Jodi had seen so much promise. The woman had sure hands, was open to trying new things, conventional or not, and above all, every single animal she laid her hands on had absolutely loved her. That was something that couldn't be learned, no matter how smart you were.

When Jodi originally designed the clinic, she'd incorporated plans for a future second vet. The room that served as a kitchenette was in actuality another examination room. But since the two existing exam rooms sufficed for her needs, she'd turned the space into an eating area. It'd be easy to convert back.

Jodi looked out onto the ocean, surprised at the thought. Would there be an advantage? Another vet would be an added drain on the income. But at the moment, the income was limited because of her… personal issues. Could the practice sustain another vet? She tossed another piece of wood on the fire. The ensuing crackling and smell of smoke were comforting. Before her world had come crashing down and she'd started to turn away business, the days that she'd been run off her feet had been steadily increasing. Wasn't that why she'd given up swimming and hiking? Work had become everything, an all-consuming entity, leaving her with no time to herself. Of course her clients were more important than her taking a stroll in the bush. There was no question. She snorted derisively. "Yeah, see where that got me."

The idea of having Cate come on board was appealing. She was witty and had an insanely good sense of humour. Jodi remembered many occasions, laughing so hard her sides hurt. The clinic atmosphere had beamed with an unspoken energy as soon as Cate walked through the door. She would unquestionably be a good addition.

Cate was lucky. The only reason she was open to the idea was that she knew Cate. Frankly, if anyone other than Cate had shown up at the clinic, they would've been politely turned away.

Jodi considered the possibilities. Cate had proven she could work alone, but she had no qualms about asking for help or a consult. *This might work.* While a large part of the clinic work was hands-on medicine, there was also a certain percentage that consisted of only consultation. Jodi could easily fill that role. Since Cate was basically still a rookie and would be for a few years, she'd have to work under some supervision. Especially in surgery. All the tension in Jodi's body was suddenly released. She had an innate desire to remain completely still and let…what?…sink in. Relief? That's what it was. If Jodi hired Cate, she would be afforded the time to somehow fix the disconnect between her brain and hands. And she wouldn't suffer from the anxiety and pressure to get back to the vet surgeon she had been, and hoped to be once again.

Jodi raised the bottle in the ocean's direction, saluting the horizon because it hinted that there were good things out there. And she was on her way to finding them. She took another sip, closed her eyes, and took a deep breath, allowing the resolution, the whisky, and the ocean to wrap around her.

Cole's image suddenly appeared behind her eyelids and her mood darkened once again. Despite her decision to hire Cate, she found she was just as hurt and angry with Cole as she had been several hours earlier.

Jodi swigged a rough mouthful of whisky. Would she have agreed it was a good idea if Cole had just talked to her before contacting Cate? She wasn't sure. No. Probably not. It was her surgery, and her decision to make. Period. Her mind hadn't ventured to that level of contemplation involving another vet—effectively getting in help.

Over the past few weeks, she'd fallen in love with Cole. But right now, she felt betrayed. Cornered. Pressured. The boundaries between work and her heart had blurred. Although it was irresponsible of her, a dark part of her decided to not go into the surgery tomorrow. Cole would just have to rearrange the appointments on her own, since she was so smart.

Jodi let the fire die down. It was dark out, but for the millions of stars overhead. She waved one mozzie away, knowing that within minutes of the fire burning low, there'd be an onslaught of the bloodsuckers hovering around her, waiting for any opportunity. She stood, stretched, unzipped her swag, and got in. Tomorrow she'd hike to an area where there was mobile reception and give Cate a call. She was the only person Jodi needed to talk to for the next thirty-six hours. She fluffed her pillow, snuggled down, and let the whisky and the rhythm of the ocean's waves carry her away to sleep.

"Aw crap, Cole." Charlie cringed in empathy when Cole relayed what had happened.

"I know! I know." Cole paced back and forth in Pip and Charlie's lounge room, distress falling off her in waves. "Oh, dear Lord. I've screwed up, big time. Shit, shit, *shit*."

"Okay. Here's what we're gonna do." Pip stood at the kitchen cooktop, stirring a large pot of vegetable soup. "I have a load of mulch that desperately needs spreading out in the far wallaby pen. If you two can make that happen, by the time you finish, come back, and wash up, I'll have dinner on and we can sit and mull things over."

Cole barely slowed her pacing. She didn't care. She had enough distress-fuelled energy flowing through her veins at the minute. One mountain of mulch or sixteen, she didn't much care. She welcomed mind-numbing activity and spreading out mulch sounded just fine to her.

She'd spent the afternoon calling clients and rescheduling appointments. Her biggest fear was that she wasn't entirely sure when, or even if, Jodi would come back to the office—the fear she'd pushed her too far loomed large in her mind. A cold sweat spread across her body and left her feeling sick in its wake.

Charlie showed her the pile of mulch and she attacked it like a demon. She pushed and pulled the shovel through the mix mechanically. The movement barely contained the threat of the bile of betrayal that sat heavy at the base of her throat. Her intentions had been good, but the execution had come horribly undone. She had so badly wanted to make things easier for Jodi. Cate was a person she knew Jodi would not only feel happy working with, but would be a comfortable fit both for the practice and, most importantly, for Jodi's clientele.

There had been only a small window of time between when she'd come up with the idea and when she'd made contact with Cate. Time. Her arms strained under a particularly heavy load of mulch. She'd thought she would have time to talk to Jodi about it. To see what she thought. To be guided by whatever she wanted. Instead, things had coalesced at a speed that was beyond her control. She hadn't managed to find an opportunity to collar Jodi long enough to talk about work. Then Cate had turned up early. And she had inadvertently put them all in it. She would never forget the look of utter hurt and betrayal on Jodi's face when she put two and two together. And poor Cate, the complete and utter innocent bystander in all of this.

Cole dropped her shovel and strode across the enclosure. She bent over the side of the pen. The bile that had threatened all afternoon needed release. She was vaguely aware of Charlie holding her hair back as she vomited over the fence.

When her stomach was as empty as her heart, she slid to the ground. Charlie guided her down, holding her safely in an embrace, as sobs wracked her. Except for her hiccupping breaths, there was silence, something her heart and her mind needed.

Charlie helped her up, walked her to the house, and guided Cole to the shower. Afterwards Cole found Charlie had left her some fresh clean pyjamas to change into.

Pip had made chicken and vegetable soup, and under normal circumstances she would have begged for the recipe, such were the explosions of flavours in her mouth. Tonight, its main power rested in soothing her stomach and her soul after such a tumultuous day. When she'd eaten all she could, she allowed Pip to put her to bed.

Cole lay with the sheets pulled up under her chin. Pip stroked the hair away from her forehead. A box of tissues had magically appeared on her bedside table.

"Time. That's what you both need."

Cole cried. "Time can't heal what I've done. I've ruined it. I'll never learn."

"Shh, now. We'll talk more in the morning, but know this: While your execution might have been a tad off, your intention wasn't. She's gonna sting and hurt for a bit, but she's smart. She'll eventually see the love and thought behind what you did."

Cole shook her head. "I let her down. I made it look like I don't trust her or her decisions."

"*Do* you trust her?"

Cole fixed Pip with her teary gaze. "With all my heart." Never a truer statement had she uttered. "I just wanted to help her, to take the load off and give her space to come back to her old self."

Pip handed her a tissue. "I know that. And eventually Jodi'll know that too. But right now, she needs some time and space. You've had some huge lessons thrown in your faces. She's had a truck full of emotions run right through everything she knows. Give her some time to find her inner compass, and to work her way through what she needs to do. Don't push. Just be there for her when she needs it. It's not going to be easy." Pip smiled wryly, a smile born of years of friendship with Jodi. "But trust me when I say you need to hang in there." Pip wiped Cole's tears. "Do you love her enough to do that?"

"I do."

"Then let it be your anchor." Pip kissed her on the forehead before rising from the bed and turning out the light.

Jodi parked next to Cate's Holden ute when she arrived at the clinic on Monday. She'd phoned her Saturday afternoon to ask her to join the practice. Cate was ecstatic, and Jodi'd offered her the apartment above the clinic as an interim measure, until she found a place of her own. Cate jumped at the chance and asked if she could start Monday morning. Although it meant leaving her dune sanctuary early, Jodi had met Cate at the clinic on Sunday to give her a key.

Cate's enthusiasm was infectious. Even though it was early Monday morning, Jodi was already looking forward to the day and beyond. She juggled the keys in her hand as she walked around to the back entrance. When she found the door already open, she went in. The lights were on inside and Cate's bum stuck out of one the big cages.

"What *are* you doing? Don't you know it's too early to start work?" Jodi bumped Cate's foot with her own as she walked by.

"Just seeing if I'd fit in this cage in case you needed the apartment in an emergency."

Jodi laughed. "It's yours until you don't need it. It's been sitting empty for a while anyway, so it's a good thing you moved in. I needed someone to clean it."

"Well, mate, you coulda left me a six-pack in the fridge and I wouldn't have even noticed."

"Mm. When you're done checking out your new digs, want to join me in my office for a cuppa? I want to go over a few things with you before the front door opens."

"Righto. Black, no sugar."

Jodi quirked an eyebrow and smiled. "I remember."

"Good bosses do," Cate said as she backed out of the cage. She fluffed make-believe long hair. "I'll be along in a minute. I just have to fix my face."

"Not touching that one!"

Cate was back and Jodi knew she'd made the right decision. Surprisingly, the banter they'd exchanged in just the few minutes she'd been around somehow increased Jodi's willingness to take back control and lead on.

Cate was already sitting in front of Jodi's desk when she came in with the two mugs of coffee. "Just keep in mind that the only reason *I'm* bringing *you* coffee is because it's your first day."

"Still the same old slave driver, I see." Cate smiled over her mug before taking a sip. "Ah, nectar of the gods."

"See, that's why I hired you. You worship the same entity."

"Caffeine?"

"Is there any other?" Jodi took a sip and set the mug down. "So here's the thing. I couldn't really go into what I'm planning when we talked on the phone."

"Not sure what your plan was?" Cate shot her a devilish grin.

"I knew *exactly* what it was. I just didn't think I could talk over your squeals of excitement."

"Pfft." Cate flicked her wrist at Jodi, motioning her to go on.

"I've put a lot of thought behind this."

"Five seconds."

"Yeah. Shut up and let me talk." Jodi rolled her eyes. "You know I wouldn't take this abuse from just anyone."

"Oh, so you're saying I'm special? Thank you very much, Doctor."

Jodi reached into the top drawer and brought out a roll of duct tape. "I still have this, you know."

Cate's eyes widened. "Shit. I'd forgotten about that." She made a motion with her fingers to zip her lips.

Jodi chuckled. They'd once made a bet Cate couldn't stay quiet for longer than fifteen minutes. Jodi had assisted her by applying a piece of tape over her mouth. She still had to pay Cate for losing the bet, but it was worth it.

"I'd like to try something for a while."

"Sh—"

Jodi lifted the roll of tape. Cate put a hand across her mouth and nodded.

"In the past year or so, I'm finding I'm spending a lot more time on consultations. Which, unfortunately, I either have to cut short, or the next client has to wait longer. For the time being, I'd like you to have the hands-on portion of the day, which will free up my time for consults. I'll still shadow you in the exam room when I can, and of course maintain the supervisory role in surgery. Think you can manage that?"

"Can I talk now?"

Jodi pushed her tongue into her cheek, raised her eyebrows, and nodded.

"Can I listen in on consultations if I'm free?"

"Of course. I think that'd be advantageous to us both."

A shadow darkened the office doorway. Cole. She didn't return Cole's smile. She kept her face emotionless. She had to create an emotional barrier between the two of them. It was the only way she'd be able to heal and learn to trust her again. "Good morning, Cole."

"Good morning. Sorry to interrupt, but Cate, would you excuse us for a minute? I'd like to talk to Jodi." Cole fidgeted and bit a fingernail.

"No worries," Cate said as she got up. "I want to have a look at today's appointments anyway."

Jodi checked the time. "Sorry. Time to open the doors. You'll have to learn to fly by the seat of your pants, Dr. Cate."

"That does have a certain appealing ring to it. At any rate, I need to run upstairs and get my stethoscope." She smiled at Cole and left.

"Is Mandy out back?" Cole took a step inside the office.

Jodi stood and fixed her with a cold stare. "No. She's not here. You'll be managing the front desk."

"Oh. Okay. Well, if you need me in the ex—"

"Cate and I can manage, thank you. Would you please open the front door?" Jodi walked past Cole, went to the closet, and pulled out a set of clean scrubs. Cole was still standing there when she turned around. "If you don't mind?"

The day flew by at lightning speed. And the clinic was insanely busy. Jodi was pleased to see that her short hiatus hadn't affected appointments. The phone rang constantly, and much to her delight, she spent over three hours all told on the phone giving advice to other vets as well as clients.

Cate rose to the challenge and gained the trust and confidence of every patient and owner who walked in. Jodi didn't see dissatisfaction on the faces of anyone who passed through the door. For that, she was grateful for Cate and the obvious trust her clients had in her ability to run a vet surgery. Regardless, it had been a long day, Jodi thought, while locking the front door.

"Want to come up for a beer?" Cate said as she followed her into the kennelling area. "Oh. That's right. I don't have any." She winked at Jodi.

"How about we rain check that idea and walk down to the fish and chips place?" Jodi rolled her eyes. "I'll even shout you since you won't get your first pay cheque until next week."

"Yeah, I gotta talk to my tightwad boss about that. But all the same, I accept your offer."

Jodi pointed to the door. "We might as well head out the back. I need to grab a jumper."

"Meet you at your car then. I'll go get mine."

Jodi knew well that Cole would be up front, getting the desk in order, putting away files, and pulling those for tomorrow's appointments. Most afternoons she used to have a cup of coffee while waiting for Cole to finish. Tonight was different. It felt easier to escape, rather than face Cole and the feelings and thoughts she had yet to process.

Cole heard them go. She closed her eyes briefly and held still as she willed herself to breathe through the pain in her chest. After a few deep breaths she opened her eyes and finished organizing the files for the following day. Her movements were slow, mechanical, and measured. Her mind went only as far as the next file.

Pip wasn't kidding when she said it wouldn't be easy. Cole had loved and lost before, and there had been dark days, but nothing compared to the chasm of hurt that had opened up in her heart now. Jodi's reaction to her was like a spear to her guts. She was alive enough to breathe and move, but each emotionless look, each brush-off, each time she approached a consulting room only to have the door close on her resulted in one thrust after another. Cate was turning out to be what she had hoped. She just didn't envision the part where she became redundant.

Both examination rooms were set up identically, since Jodi liked to be able to put her hands on things without looking for them, regardless of where she was. So Cole didn't feel the need to add anything additional to what was fast becoming Cate's room, confident that all would suit her well for whatever she encountered.

At the reception desk, Jodi and Cole had, over the years, created a record sequencing of upcoming patient appointments, history, and pathology reports in a single system. Cole created a second system for Cate—again identical, in case Jodi needed to quickly check or qualify something in Cate's absence. Cole laid out Cate's client files in preparation for the early morning start.

Lastly, she washed the floors and hung out the laundered towels and cloths. When nothing more could be done, she activated the answering machine and alarm, turned off the lights, and locked the door behind her. Her footsteps were heavy in the gravel. She drove home, not ever really remembering any part of the journey to get there, and sat in the car until the daylight faded.

Her limbs felt as heavy as her heart. She showered, then stood in her office. She remembered showing Jodi through the room only days before. Her eyes fixed on the photograph of her grandparents' smiling faces. Disappointment and shame ran from her conscience like rain off a tin roof. A wave of cold settled into her bones. Silently she closed the door in a vain attempt to distance herself from the emptiness that echoed within her.

She had no appetite. Broken, with nothing else to do, she went to bed, curled up tight, a pillow clutched to her middle.

As each day drew to a close, Jodi marvelled at how satisfied she felt. Although she still didn't trust herself to do any surgery, her mind was beginning to reignite, engaging and relishing in the challenges of working through cases as opposed to wading through the mental fog that had previously settled around her mind and confidence, choking it ever so slowly.

The only downside was Cole. Just as Jodi was becoming more and more invested in her work and reinvigorated, with every day she was conscious of Cole withdrawing further and further away.

As she pushed herself in the pool, lap after lap, images of Cole flashed in her mind. Her open smiling face and easy laugh had been replaced by a pale, tense gauntness and dark circles under her eyes.

When Jodi entered a room, Cole no longer looked at her for any length of time and left as quickly as was polite. Still as ever proficient in her job, Cole made sure that neither she nor Cate lacked for professional support, but for all her efficiency, the Cole she knew was fading before her eyes, leaving a feeling of hurt and unrest to sit low and heavy in her gut, knowing she had been the cause of a lot of Cole's change.

Jodi finished her laps and pulled herself out of the pool, her gaze automatically going to the bench where Cole would often be waiting for her with a coffee or tasty treat on hand. The sight of the empty bench hit her in the middle of the chest, stunning her briefly. She walked over and sat on it, analysing the feeling. The diagnosis, in the end, was fairly simple. She missed her friend. And her lover.

Cate was fun, challenging, and stimulating, and to her honest surprise, Jodi found herself enjoying the role of being a teacher and mentor to someone as bright and as receptive as Cate.

But Cate was not Cole. Cole nurtured the soul of the practice. And since she and Cole had become distant, she sensed that a warmth had disappeared from the practice. From her. From them.

Jodi stood and briskly wiped herself down. She couldn't miss Cole. She was still angry with her. Shrugging off the melancholy, it felt easier to go back to feeling affronted and manipulated. And yet, here she was with Cate on board, enjoying work again, and most importantly, relishing in the satisfaction of her clients, two legs and four.

Was she being pigheaded and proud, for the sake of saving face? No. She was still angry with Cole.

Jodi arrived at work a little later than normal, having been up half the night helping to deliver some Jack Russell terrier puppies. Thankfully, there hadn't been any complications and the little mother whelped them herself. It felt good to take her time, enjoy her swim, knowing there was another vet there to open and not feeling pressured to get up five minutes after she had gone to bed, needing to grind her way through the following workday horrendously sleep-deprived.

She entered through the back door and was greeted by silence. She walked out front and found Mandy at the counter, working on a drug stock-take order.

"Oh, hi, Jodi."

"Where is everyone?"

Mandy motioned with her head. "Room one." A grimace briefly flashed across her face. "Not a good start to the morning. Mrs. Jones brought Tiger in. She found him in the gutter out the front of her place this morning. Looks like a hit and run."

"Is he…?"

Mandy shook her head. "It doesn't look good," she whispered.

"Right then. I'd better—" Before Jodi finished her sentence, Cate came out of the room and shut the door behind her. Her face was flushed with a contrasting pale outline around her mouth and nose. Her jaw was clenched tight, the muscles jumping under the glare of the fluorescent lighting over the counter.

"Is everything all right?"

Cate scrubbed her hand across her face and up into her hair, holding it up off her forehead. She blew out a breath. "I. No, Mrs. Jones…" Cate gesticulated her hand towards the closed door. "No." She shook her head and frowned. "I mean, yes, but no."

"I think you need to stop. Collect yourself"—Jodi pulled out a chair and motioned for her to sit—"and tell me, clinically, what the situation is and the course of proposed treatment."

Cate relayed that Mrs. Jones's sixteen-year-old cat had what appeared to be massive internal trauma, presumably from being hit by a vehicle. Given Cate's description, and knowing Tiger quite well, Jodi saw the outcome unfolding in her mind even before Cate stated the medically obvious.

"And what are your treatment options, Dr. Fletcher?"

"I can euthanize straight up. Or prep for surgery and hope he survives, which I doubt he will, given his age and circumstances."

"Or?"

"Mrs. Jones has opted to keep him comfortable, with pain relief, and to sit with him."

"They were all sensible, viable options to present. So why do you look like you're unravelling?"

"I hate this part of the job. I completely suck at it. I didn't know what to say, how to sound believable, how to be *connected* yet dispassionate enough to help her. I just…I got lost in the moment and I…thank God for Cole. She really saved my bacon in there. She knew all the right words. When to talk, when not to." A dark wry half grin tweaked the corner of Cate's mouth. "I found myself blabbering like an idiot, just to fill the space, even though I knew it was wrong. But Cole…" Cate shook her head and looked up at Jodi, a gleam of awe in her eyes. "She's brilliant." Cate started to stand. "I need to get back in there."

Jodi stopped her rise with a hand on her shoulder. "Why don't you take five and grab yourself a drink. I'll pop in and see how they're doing."

Relief poured off Cate. "Thanks, Jodi."

Jodi nodded, smiled softly, and shooed her to the back kitchen. She remembered all too well the early years, starting out, learning to deal with losing patients and supporting the owners in their grief. Like it or not, it was a part of their job. In time she knew Cate would find her own way of managing that part. But for now, her young learned colleague could do with a break.

Jodi quietly opened the door and stood silently in the doorway. Cole had found Mrs. Jones a chair and a stool for herself. There were tissues on the stainless steel bench. Cole helped support Mrs. Jones, as Tiger lay wrapped in a soft cotton blanket in her lap, her gnarled fingers stroking lovingly through his thick, soft apricot coat. Their heads were close together and Jodi could just make out their murmurings.

Jodi stepped forward and put a light hand on Cole's shoulder, leaving it there when Cole met her eyes. Her other hand rested on Mrs. Jones's shoulder. "Cate told me about Tiger. I'm so sorry."

Mrs. Jones sniffed and dabbed at her wet eyes. "He was a brave lad. Your girls made sure he felt no pain. I shall miss him terribly." Her shoulders shook with her grief. The three of them stood, connected physically and through the love and care for an old, much-loved cat. "I think I'd like to take him home now, if that's all right?"

"Yes, yes. Of course." Jodi looked about the room wondering what arrangements she needed to set in place to get Mrs. Jones and Tiger home.

"If it's all right with you, I'll take Mrs. Jones home," Cole said softly.

"Yes. That's fine. Take your time. We've got things covered here."

Cole wrapped her arm around Mrs. Jones. "Let's get you home then."

Jodi lifted Tiger from the old lady's arms and followed behind her and Cole as they went discreetly out the back door, away from curious eyes in the waiting room. After Mrs. Jones got into the car, Jodi gently laid Tiger's body in her lap, while Cole got into the driver's seat.

Mrs. Jones grasped Cole's and Jodi's hands. "Thank you. Thank you both."

Cole gave the old woman's hand an ever so brief squeeze. "You're welcome. You and Tiger are family."

Jodi carefully closed the car door and watched as they drove away. Cole had uttered just a few simple heartfelt words that summed up everything—the trust between a caregiver and a client, and a client and their much-loved pet.

In that one moment, as the car disappeared from view, Jodi stood alone and forgot why she was angry. She was reminded of the beauty at Cole's core. Something that her stubbornness had blinded her to. She realized, in that moment, she could forgive Cole almost anything.

CHAPTER SIXTEEN

D oing anything fun for the rest of the weekend?" Cate said as they watched the last Saturday client walk out the door with their toy poodle in tow.

Jodi stole a glance at Cole, who was on the phone scheduling an appointment for next week.

"Yeah. As a matter of fact I am. Do you remember Pip Atkins, the wildlife carer for WREN?"

"Um, short in stature, but not in giving you a hard time, with a cute yellow Lab?"

"The one and only. Her partner, Charlie, spent some time working here last year and rehabilitated a wedge-tail eagle that came in with a broken wing. She released him some months ago and I think I spotted him on one of my hikes. So the four of us"—Jodi pointed to Cole with her chin—"are going out to see if it really was him."

"Cool. It's supposed to be a gem of a day on Sunday, but then maybe thunderstorms later."

"We'll be back well before then."

Cole was still talking to the client and writing notes.

"Will you tell Cole I'm heading out to Pip's and I'll see her there?"

"No dramas. Enjoy your time in the bush and don't forget your mozzie spray and sunscreen."

Jodi waved over her shoulder as she walked into her office. "Already in my backpack." She changed out of her scrubs, shoved her feet into her hiking sneakers, grabbed her keys off the desk, and headed out the back.

There wasn't a cloud in the sky and certainly not one hint of the rain Cate had mentioned. Jodi got in the truck, turned the key, and backed out of the clinic's drive. As she drove through town, she decided to stop at the liquor store and buy a nice bottle of wine for Pip and

Charlie. Once on the road again, she rolled the windows all the way down and let the smells of the countryside wash through. She left the scents of the ocean and headed inland where sugar cane fields had been burnt the night before. The tall bright green stalks had been reduced to leaning yellow and black rods, giving off pungent sweet and sour odours. Black kites, sea eagles, whistling kites, cattle egrets, and crows stood vigil nearby as the cane was harvested, giving them access to bugs and other food.

Jodi put a Pink CD into the player and sang along, not caring that she was mostly out of tune. It had been a very long time since she'd done that, or even hummed for that matter. But today, she felt light and happy, such a stark contrast to the heaviness she'd felt as of late. Although she and Cole hadn't really reconciled, things seemed to be getting back to a more normal ambiance at the clinic. She'd let go of the anger, finally admitting, only to herself, that Cole had been right all along. She should've hired someone a long time ago. But, to be fair, Cate had only just recently graduated, and she was glad she had waited for her, albeit unintentionally.

Charlie was coming out of the house when Jodi drove up. She rolled the window down and handed Charlie the bottle of wine.

"Here's a little prezzie for you. Congrats on sending in your application."

Charlie rolled her eyes. "I'm so glad to have that thing done and dusted." She looked at the empty passenger seat. "Where's Cole?"

"She'll be along. She had some things to finish up. So what happens with your visa now?"

"I wait. And of course worry."

"Nah, you'll be right."

"Pip started on the feeds about fifteen minutes ago. Why don't you go throw your stuff in the cabin? She should be done by the time you get back." Charlie raised the bottle. "And this might even be chilled by then."

"Sounds good."

"Hey, are you and Cole okay with sharing the cabin? I mean we can—"

"We'll be fine. But thanks for asking." Jodi winked and put the truck in gear. But as she drove off, she knew she'd sounded a lot more confident than she felt. In actuality, when Cole did arrive, it would be the first time they'd been together outside of work. So much had changed. Or had it? She just couldn't be sure. Nor did she really know what would happen once they were both under the same roof in a very intimate location.

She pointed the Rover down a barely perceptible path, which she knew would bring her to the cabin. After several minutes of driving in first gear, she cleared the thick shrubbery and the cabin appeared just beyond.

Large smooth-barked gums with tall canopies surrounded the structure and took over as far as she could see. The cabin was built on a hillside and completely supported on stilts. Wide slabs of nearly black wood covered the sides. Moss coated the eaves, contrasting nicely against the dark-toned tin roof. A magnificent staghorn fern clung to a large tree, level with the window. A railed ramp with a lot of air underneath and a barely discernible incline led to the front door. A window looked out on either side of the walkway and an overhang protected the entrance.

She'd only been in the cabin once, and that was years ago when Pip had given her a quick tour on their way past to the big joey pen. At that point, it'd only been about half done as Pip was building it by herself. Since its completion, life had gotten in the way and they'd never had an occasion to revisit the structure. So Jodi had no idea what to expect.

Jodi grabbed her duffel from the back of the truck and stood for a moment on the ramp. Yellow-tailed black cockatoos called from the branches above. Her eyes were drawn to rustling down the hill. She smiled as three red-necked wallabies paused their eating of the tender grass and watched her. Jodi had no doubt these were ones Pip had raised or were offspring of those she had.

The door opened easily and she stopped short to take it all in. The interior was painted white and very stylishly decorated. The main feature, which she'd forgotten about, was the gum tree growing through the floor, its trunk extending through the highest part of the cabin. The trunk was wrapped in heavy rubber top and bottom, where it grew through the floorboards and ceiling. Pip had painted the ceiling to look like a canopy of leaves with glimpses of branches.

The kitchen, although small, was still impressive. The granite benches were wide and there was plenty of storage space. The stove and refrigerator sat at opposite ends of the benches, which were divided by a spacious sink.

A two-shelved bookcase sat atop a desk, one shelf crammed with various field identification guides for mammals, insects, birds, reptiles, trees, and flowers. The other shelf held stacks of folded maps.

"Wow." Jodi tossed her bag on the queen-sized bed, which sat upon a foundation of drawers. It was situated beneath a skylight. She walked through to the far end and out the door. A wide porch extended out and wrapped around the left corner. She grasped the railing and looked over the seemingly endless entanglement of canopy.

Jodi's musings were interrupted by the sound of the front door closing. She turned around and smiled because she was sure she had worn the same expression of amazement as Cole did this very minute.

"Nice, hey?" Jodi called from her spot against the railing.

"Holy smokes. I would never have dreamed the inside would look like this." Cole set her bag down next to the lounge that sat to the left of the door.

"I know. Come out and have a look. It's incredible." Jodi turned, braced her arms against the parapet, and continued to admire the scenery. She felt more than heard Cole come up beside her. It seemed Cole was conscious of keeping a fair bit of distance.

Silence stretched between them.

"Are you okay with me staying here with you?" Cole said without looking at her.

"Yeah, sure. Why would you ask?"

"Well, for one thing, there's only one bed. And then there's—"

"Cole, don't worry about it. We're both adults."

Cole sighed deeply. "I kind of thought, maybe hoped, we were more than that."

Jodi turned and rubbed Cole's arm. "Come here." She pulled Cole into a hug. "I just need some more time. Can you give that to me?" Cole nodded. "I promise that after we get back from this hike, you and I'll sit down and have a heart to heart. I know we need to talk about us and what happens next, but I just don't think this is the time or place, y'know? I want to get back to being simple, for us to enjoy this, and being here with each other and with friends."

Cole sniffed and pulled back. "Yeah, I'd like that." She smiled and Jodi's heart melted a little more.

"You ready to head up to the main house? I know for a fact there's a nice bottle of wine chilling in their fridge."

"Do we have to walk?" Cole fidgeted a bit. "I mean, we'll be coming back here after dark and there might be…things…on the path."

Jodi threw her head back and laughed. And it felt so good. "Come on. I'll drive."

"Oh, thank God."

"What time can we head out tomorrow?" Charlie refilled everyone's wine glass. She was so excited to possibly get a glimpse of Big Bird. Would he remember her and maybe fly in closer? Her heart sped up just a little at the thought.

Pip snaked an arm around her waist and squeezed. "If you guys drink any more, it won't be until afternoon, sweet."

"Aw, come on. We're celebrating me finally mailing the damned visa application. One more won't hurt."

"Are you immune to the effects of alcohol, Pip?" Cole raised her eyebrows.

"Not at all. But then, I've only had a smidgeon compared to you lot. I just want to make sure you three get out of here early enough to make it home before dark."

"What do you mean? You're not coming?" Jodi put her empty glass on the table.

"No. We've got two joeys that are still on five bottles a day. At this point they're too young to be skipping feeds."

"Well, wait a minute," Cole said, sitting up straighter in her chair. "How about I stay behind and take care of them? Then you can go too."

"Thanks, Cole, but I wouldn't want to burden you with them." Pip smiled wryly.

"Trust me. It wouldn't be. I'm not really into trekking around in the wilderness anyway." Cole visibly shuddered, getting a laugh out of all of them. "And I can have dinner ready for when you all get back. I'll be much happier pottering about in the kitchen than getting all hot and sweaty running up and down hillsides."

"If you're sure." Pip glanced at Charlie, who nodded her approval.

Charlie heard her phone vibrate on the counter behind her, signifying an incoming email. She chose to ignore it for the moment.

"Believe me, it's no drama," Cole said.

"Well, if you're going to stay, do you mind keeping Chilli company? What with ticks and snakes, I'm not real keen on letting her romp in the bush in this warm weather." Pip stroked the dog's back.

"Absolutely." Cole bent down and ruffled the fur on Chilli's neck.

"We'll have a lovely time, hey, girl?" Chilli wagged her tail and huffed at her.

Charlie watched this interaction with affection. She was so pleased that Pip had been convinced to come on the hike. Not that she didn't want Cole along, but Pip had been instrumental in getting the big aviary built that had been so vital to Big Bird's recovery, so in a sense, Pip had as much invested in the eagle as she. She trusted that Cole would take excellent care of the animals while they were out for the day.

"Thank you, Cole. With that settled, I'm rather looking forward to a long walk in the bush. I haven't been up that way in years, other than when Charlie released Big Bird. But even then, we didn't walk the trails much."

Charlie picked up the empty potato chip bowl and took it to the counter to refill it. She remembered the incoming email, so picked her phone up and scrolled down past two spam messages. And saw it. An email from the Australian Department of Immigration. She broke out into a cold sweat and her knees grew weak.

"Charlie? Sweet, you look like you've seen a ghost." Pip came to her side. "What is it?"

Charlie looked at her and opened her mouth to speak, but nothing came out. She handed Pip the phone.

"Oh. Shit. Do you want me to see what it says?"

Charlie swallowed and held her elbows tightly against her sides. A mixture of dread and nervousness flowed through her veins as an anxiety attack threatened. She felt nauseous and tried hard to control her breathing. She nodded.

"Babe, sit down before you fall down." Pip grabbed her elbow and helped her back to her chair.

Charlie glanced at Jodi and Cole, seeing mirrored looks of concern.

Pip cleared her throat. "Dear Charlene, we are pleased to inform you that you have been issued a bridging visa. You are no longer required to leave the country every three months. However, if you wish to leave Australia before a decision has been made on your defacto visa 801, you will need to request permission from the ADI. Attached is a copy of your interim visa 820. Sincerely, blah, blah, blah."

It took a minute for it to sink in. Charlie looked at Pip in disbelief. "That's really what it says?"

"Like I'd dick around about this." Pip gave Charlie the phone and smiled broadly. "You did it, babe. We're halfway there."

Charlie read the words over and over until the disbelief faded and was replaced by sheer elation. She let out a whoop. "I don't care if we leave a little late tomorrow. I'm opening a bottle of champagne!"

Jodi, Cole, and Pip all yelled, "Hear, hear!"

Cole was grateful Jodi had given in to her subtle suggestion to drive to the main house. Through the dark, the headlights glared off the stunning white mottled bark of the all gums lining the pathway down to the cabin. Unknown creatures and insects flickered in and out of the light as they meandered down the bush track.

The evening had been delightful, full of cheerful banter and anticipation of the day ahead. Pip offered a tour of the kitchen, pantry, and vegetable garden the following morning, which she was secretly looking forward to. The bush walk had worried her a little, but she'd been prepared to suck it up and go along. Thankfully, she now had an out, and the weekend suddenly promised alignment with things more suited to her comfort zone. Except one thing. Tonight.

During the last few days, Cole's heart had lightened to see glimpses of the old Jodi returning. But the two of them were still distant. She had stuffed up and betrayed Jodi. She couldn't blame Jodi for her anger. She deserved it. It was something neither of them would forget in a hurry, if ever. She had breached the tenuous bridge of trust between work colleagues and lovers, creating significant damage in the process. There was no going back—nothing could be the same again. If she could turn back time, she would, and make more of an effort to sit down and talk with Jodi. But she couldn't. Things had rushed out of control and smashed headlong into a wall called reality.

But they were at least talking again. And Jodi said she was okay with sharing the cottage. And one bed. Cole had mulled it over and over in her mind on the slow drive down to the cabin but failed to feel quite as confident.

When they arrived at the cabin, the solar lights came on, illuminating the ramp to the doorway. Cole stood back as Jodi opened the door. Jodi might profess to be okay, but her own guts were definitely churning at the prospect of the evening ahead.

Now that they were alone, she didn't know what to talk about. The silence weighed heavy. "Fancy a cuppa?"

Jodi closed the door and shoved her hands deep into her trouser pockets. "I'm just going to throw myself in the shower, but I'd love one. I won't be long."

Alone, Cole took the time to explore the cabin. It really was a marvellous piece of craftsmanship. The tree, centre stage, was breathtaking. She looked at the painted leaves on the ceiling and had to school herself that the leaves were painted features and not real, and certainly not home to a legion of outdoor critters. She shook her head in amusement. It was light, earthy, and very comfortable. One could even call the cottage intimate. As the jug heated to a boil she checked out the sofa and found that it could unfold out to a double bed. Hm, could be a good backup plan. She was looking for spare linen when Jodi came out of the bathroom, wearing a loose pair of sleep shorts and a T-shirt, and towelling her damp hair.

Cole swallowed and had to look away. The sofa suddenly held a lot more merit.

"What are you doing?"

Cole handed Jodi her coffee, trying desperately to seem casual. "Just looking."

"For anything in particular?"

"Um, linen." Cole weakly gestured to the sofa.

"Mm, thanks." Jodi wrapped her hands around her coffee cup. "Don't be silly. There's plenty of room in the bed over there. And I won't bite."

Cole tried to gauge Jodi's expression, but she took her coffee outside. She stood on the wide veranda and seemed to gaze out towards to the dark forest habitat below.

It was late and Cole's nerves were strung tight. Sleep would be hard enough to come by as it was, and she didn't think a cup of caffeine would be a wise move for her before bed. Perhaps if she got in bed first and pretended to be asleep when Jodi came in, it might work.

"I might have a shower myself and turn in. It's been a big day. I guess I'll see you in the morning."

Jodi turned and leaned on the balcony railing. She raised her mug in salute. "Goodnight then. Sleep well."

Jodi's voice was quiet and her face hidden half in shadows so Cole couldn't work out her expression. All she could do was take the words at face value. She looked down and nodded once. "Goodnight."

She didn't dally in the shower, quickly washing the day away and changing into pyjamas. She virtually threw herself in bed and turned off her bedside lamp.

It was a good hour later when the mattress dipped with Jodi's weight as she slid onto the bed. Lips softly brushed against her temple.

She desperately wanted more but knew she didn't deserve it. Cole lay still, eyes firmly shut, faking sleep. She held her breath as Jodi turned out her bedside light, casting the cabin into darkness. She didn't dare move a muscle. She lay frozen, immobile, for what seemed like forever before Jodi's breathing deepened and lengthened, indicating she had crossed the realms to sleep. Then and only then did she relax. It was going to be a long night.

Jodi spent some time out on the balcony admiring the millions of stars that blanketed the sky. The Southern Cross showed brilliantly in the absence of the moon. A Powerful Owl's slowly uttered, rather mournful *woo-hoo* carried across the tops of the trees. She imagined it hunting from its perch, its prey the slow-moving mammals and unsuspecting large birds which they plucked from their roosts.

She sipped her coffee slowly. The bitter flavour washed the aftertastes of wine and celebratory champagne away. Charlie had sported a wide grin the entire evening. Her sparkling eyes and throaty laughter brought out the woman she'd been before all that immigration stuff had started. Pip was so lucky to have her. Jodi knew Pip must've been just as worried, but of course, Pip being Pip would hide it well, always putting forth a positive word for Charlie's benefit.

Cole had been quite generous bowing out of the hike and insisting that Pip go in her place. These days, what with the animals they had in care requiring multiple feeds a day, Pip and Charlie rarely got to go anywhere together for any length of time, unless it was a quick run into town or roaming the back blocks on the property with the quad. But Jodi was sure they loved their life as much as they did each other.

It'd been delightful laughing and sharing yarns with the three of them tonight. The distance between her and Cole had decreased just a bit more. She missed what they'd had. And to be honest, she truly hoped they could rekindle the passion and close relationship they'd been well on the way to cementing.

The mozzies finally found her and drove her into the cabin. Bloody things. Jodi swatted at a few of the pests whining about her ears. She stole a quick glance at her watch. Eleven thirty. She'd best try to sleep. Tomorrow would come early and be a long but very enjoyable day.

Jodi washed her cup in the sink and set it on the bench to dry. She set her alarm for six a.m. That would give her plenty of time to put herself together and join Pip and Charlie for breakfast, and they could be on their way.

When she got into bed and pulled the covers over her, the familiar smell of Cole settled into her senses. Nostalgia, desire, and deep affection rose into her chest. Yeah. They needed to fix this. She missed Cole. A lot. She leaned over and gently brushed her lips over Cole's temple, resisting the temptation to go further. Jodi sighed quietly, rolled over onto her side, and emptied her mind, letting sleep take over.

Pip nestled her body against Charlie and wrapped an arm around her waist. "Did you have a good time tonight, love?"

Charlie snuggled as close as possible. "I did. It was made even better by having Jodi and Cole to share it with."

"Indeed." Pip squeezed Charlie's middle.

"Do you think they'll reconcile? They're so good together."

"Who knows, but I've got my fingers crossed. They seemed pretty comfortable with each other tonight, and did you check out the stolen glances, when each thought the other wasn't looking? There was a lot of love in those looks."

"I hope so." Charlie laced her fingers with Pip's.

"I'm so proud of you, lovely."

Charlie smiled. "It's only the first step. The application could still be rejected."

"It won't be. I can feel it in my bones. This is the beginning of us living the rest of our days together."

"Thank you for being so optimistic. It helps."

"I know." Pip kissed the back of Charlie's neck. "Now, go to sleep. Tomorrow'll be here before you know it."

"Night, baby." Charlie grinned. Pip was already asleep.

CHAPTER SEVENTEEN

The foursome shared a leisurely breakfast together, picking up where they'd left off the night before, with easy, witty conversation flowing back and forth.

"Lucky for us we have some trekking ahead of us today. Girls, that was a breakfast fit for a king." Jodi leaned back and stretched. Pip and Cole had double-teamed in the kitchen and come up with pancakes, fresh fruit, and maple syrup, with bacon and eggs on the side.

"I am so full." Charlie snagged an arm around Pip's waist as she passed. "I'm not sure if I want to go out and conquer the world after such a magnificent feast, or curl up in a ball and go to sleep. You two in the kitchen are mind-blowing."

"Well, seeing as you both wolfed down third helpings, how about you two start by cleaning up so I can run Cole through all the feeding paraphernalia and any last minute instructions?"

"And then can I get a grand tour of the garden and pantry so I can work on concocting some culinary magic for you all for when you return?" Cole rubbed her hands together excitedly. She really had enjoyed working with Pip in the kitchen. They chatted, swapped food preferences, and worked happily side by side, preparing a simple but filling meal for people who were special to them. This was, in her mind, a recipe for happiness. She deliberately didn't delve too deeply into this thought, appreciating and accepting it on the surface for what it was at just this moment in time.

"Absolutely." Pip put her arm around Cole's shoulders. "I can't thank you enough for today. It's like a spontaneous holiday. And I am so excited about dinner. Although part of me feels a tad guilty for taking your place on the walk."

Cole huffed and waved her away as the pair of them made their way out to the prep room. "I love to cook. Cooking for one"—she waggled a hand with a slight grimace on her face—"doesn't quite cut the culinary mustard for excitement, if you know what I mean. You have no idea how excited I am to look after the babies, and to dip into the freshest of ingredients from this reportedly fabulous garden of yours. I feel like *I* have been given the ultimate treat." Cole smiled freely.

Pip stopped short in the prep room and looked at her incredulously. "You really are happy at the swap?"

Cole chuckled. "Oh, I really, really am. You have no idea."

Pip gave her a sideways hug. "Then we are truly both very lucky today."

"We most certainly are."

"Right then, let's get through the notes I made up this morning for the little furry ones, then we can mosey on down to the garden."

Cole listened attentively to Pip's instructions, impressed by her detail and preparedness. She was no stranger to bottle feeding macropods, be they kangaroos or wallabies, or birds, and if need be, she could also feed the possums and koalas from the bountiful food supply Pip had on hand. All she had to do was give a midday feed, followed by a late afternoon feed for the little ones. Pip and Charlie would be home to look after the subsequent, later evening feeds. Large blocks of the morning would be hers to explore, with the afternoon taken up by preparation for dinner. By then the troops would be back and the evening would unfold, no doubt with talk of the day, which she was looking forward to hearing all about. There was also the promised, much needed conversation between her and Jodi to come, but she shelved that, concentrating instead on the aspects of the day ahead.

Pip and Charlie's vegetable garden was everything and more than Cole could ever have dreamed of. Nearly every seasonal vegetable was there, completely available at her fingertips. She ran through several recipes in her head, and she spent a wonderful half hour with Pip picking fresh food ready for the evening.

With hands laden they walked back to the house and deposited the vegetables in the sink. Jodi and Charlie had cleaned up the breakfast dishes and were leaning over the kitchen bench top studying a map.

Three backpacks sat on the floor by the table. Pip sidled up behind Charlie and wrapped her arms around her, leaning over to get a glimpse of the map that lay on the table. "You two know where you're going?"

Charlie turned in Pip's arms, grinning, and kissed her on the lips. "Puh-lease."

Cole rearranged the vegetables in the sink as Pip's soft laughter floated across the room. A small pang of jealousy bit deep. She wasn't sure what she and Jodi had any more, but it wasn't what Pip and Charlie had, or her grandparents. She took a breath and steadied herself, focusing on and hanging on to the positive things that were before her in the day.

Jodi folded the map and put it into the front pocket of her pack. "We're all sorted. You about ready to go, Pipsqueak?"

"Soon. I just need to throw some lunch and snacks together."

"All done, love. Water, snacks, and lunch. Do you want to check and make sure everything's okay?"

Pip grabbed a bag and stood on tiptoes to give Charlie a kiss on the cheek. "Nope. If you're happy, then I'm happy. I reckon we're as good as ready to rock 'n' roll."

Charlie picked her backpack up and casually slung it over her shoulder, almost bouncing on the spot with excitement. "Time's a wastin'."

As the threesome headed outside, Cole followed in their wake with Chilli by her side. She and Chilli stood at the veranda as they got into the car. Jodi seemed to hesitate in the driver's seat before getting out. With purposeful strides, Jodi walked back to where she and Chilli stood.

"Did you forget something?"

"I did." Jodi held one hand behind her back. She carefully picked up Cole's hand and placed in her palm a light pink and white rosebud that was just beginning to open.

Cole peered down at the soft bloom and brought it to her nose. The delicate perfume tickled her senses. She looked up at Jodi, and her breath caught in her throat at the vulnerable openness that Jodi displayed with a simple look. "Thank you." Cole couldn't help but smile as a blush stole across Jodi's cheeks.

Jodi brushed tender warm lips against hers. "I'll see you tonight."

Cole nodded. Her throat closed over with emotion as she fought to rally a whispered acknowledgement. "I'll be waiting."

With a last chaste kiss, Jodi turned and was gone, leaving Cole and Chilli to watch the threesome head out down the dusty driveway.

By the time they got to Grafton, almost an hour's drive later, Pip was sound asleep in the back seat.

"I could use a cuppa, how about you?" Jodi put her blinker on and turned into the local Macca's.

"Sounds good to me. It might counteract the carb crash I'm starting to feel." Charlie reached into her pack for her wallet. "I'll shout you."

"Ta."

Charlie giggled. "You know, the first time I ever handled Australian money, I was so confused. Pip tossed her wallet to me and asked me to get seventy cents out for her. I just stared at the pile of coins and told her I didn't even know what seventy cents looked like. I'll never forget her laughing at me."

"American money is that different, hey?"

"Yeah. There aren't any gold coins and we have pennies, which are one-cent copper pieces."

"Think Pip would want a tea or something?" Jodi glanced in the rear-view mirror.

"Probably not. Let's let her sleep. She can use the shut-eye more than the caffeine."

Jodi navigated the Rover into the drive-through and within minutes was turning onto the main road again, two coffees sitting in the console to cool a bit before either of them dared take a sip for fear of burning their tongues.

"I'm really looking forward to this. Even if we don't spot Big Bird, just getting out is something Pip and I both need."

"Yeah, you guys have been going flat out. I'm surprised you even have the energy, but I suppose the possibility of seeing your overgrown budgie would inspire you."

Charlie picked up her coffee and blew over the top of it before venturing a sip. "Almost cool enough." She set it back down and nodded. "While that's a big incentive, to be truthful, in all the time I've been in Australia, I haven't had much opportunity to explore. Between all the rescues and the visa thing, when we have a chance to finally relax, we end up trying to catch up on sleep. Plus, there's always the fear that if we get out of signal range we'll miss a critical call-out."

"What changed for today?"

"Pip called Teresa early this morning and asked her to divert as many of the calls to one of the other members. While we have the main care facility, there are a couple of people who will attend rescues if we get in a bind."

Jodi grinned. "I'd say this is as good an excuse as any."

Charlie took a drink of her coffee. "Ah, this is heaven." She handed Jodi her cup and smiled when Jodi groaned in agreement. "Being outdoors is one of those restorative things. The peace, the quiet, the sound of the birds, and even the sound of your own footsteps can be quite cathartic. I'm glad we're heading out fairly early so we can beat the worst heat of the day."

"Trust me, once we get higher in elevation, you may wish for some of that heat. It can get pretty chilly up there."

"I'm not worried. I suppose as long as we keep moving we'll be okay." Charlie peered out the windscreen at the sky. "Plus, the sun is out, so that should help." She sat back in her seat and studied Jodi for a moment. "So," Charlie said, letting the word drag out. "Things better with you and Cole?"

Jodi shrugged. "We're working on it."

"Giving her that flower was really sweet."

"As mad as I was at Cole, there's just something about her that…" Jodi blew out a breath. "I guess the best way of saying it is she completes me in places where I didn't know pieces of me were missing."

"Trust me. I get that. Pip does that for me. When I'm away from her, it feels like part of my soul stays with her."

Charlie suddenly twisted around in her seat. "Hey, wasn't that where you were supposed to turn off?"

"It was, but I got to thinking. There's an area called the Dandahra Crags that is an amazing hike, plus the trail comes out onto some major granite outcroppings where you can basically see forever. If there's any chance of you seeing Big Bird, I think it'd be from there."

"Okay. You'd know best."

"Not really. I only found that by accident while looking at the trails on the web."

"Oh, well, then you get to go someplace new too. Good on ya."

They passed the huge gum tree log with Gibraltar Range and the insignia of the national parks carved into it.

"Gibraltar is such a fitting name for these mountains." Charlie drained the rest of her coffee.

"This range is listed as a World Heritage site for rare forest plants that have existed since Australia was part of the Gondwana supercontinent."

"Wow. Find that little factoid while on the web too?"

Jodi winked and tapped the side of her head. "One can never stop learning."

"There's always room in the bean for that."

Jodi slowed when a small sign with a hiker and Gibraltar-

Washpool Heritage Walk lettered beneath it appeared on the left side of the road.

"This is where we turn off." Jodi pulled onto the dirt road and shifted into four-wheel drive.

It was fairly easy going for about a kilometre and Charlie began to wonder about the necessity of the four-wheel drive. That is, until they rounded a bend and forged through a rocky, rushing creek. The other side was steep and very rutted.

"Are you sure there's a road on the other side?" Charlie grabbed hold of the dashboard, turning her knuckles white.

"Only one way to find out." Jodi gunned the truck and the engine roared its protest.

The bull bar hit the bank hard on the other side and for an instant Charlie saw nothing but blue sky.

"Where the hell did you learn how to drive?" Charlie giggled nervously.

"I'd like to know the same thing, Stretch." The backpacks had flown loose across the cabin and onto Pip, who hurriedly picked them up and tossed them back onto the floor of the Rover. "Bloody hell, where are we anyway?" Pip leaned forward, grasped both seats, and held on.

"Ah, finally awake are you, Pipsqueak? Well, you'll soon find out." Jodi grinned devilishly.

"If we live that long," Pip muttered, making Charlie laugh.

"Oh, hush, you back-seat driver, you. Sit back and enjoy the scenery. Oh. Sorry, I forgot to bring along the raised seat for you."

"Funny. Not." Pip playfully swatted Jodi on the arm.

Although the road did continue on the other side, it was rutted and in some places, Jodi had to carefully navigate around huge puddles where the depth was questionable. That was all they'd need, to get helplessly stuck in the middle of nowhere and have to hike out for help.

"Ever think about putting a winch on this thing?" Charlie tightened the seat belt around her waist.

"Only when I get to driving in this kind of stuff." Jodi moaned as one of the tyres hit a large rock protruding from the middle of the rut they were in. "Thankfully, I have a spare tyre in case of a flat."

They hit another bump and all three of them grunted. The backpacks once again bounced around in the footwell, tumbling over each other like beans.

"Are you sure your spare is inflated?"

"Now that you mention it, nope. Didn't have time to check that either."

"Jesus, Jodi," Pip and Charlie said together.

Jodi took one hand off the steering wheel and waved nonchalantly at them before grabbing it again in a death grip when the truck lurched to the right. "Shit. It can't be that much further."

"We can only hope," Charlie said.

A few minutes later, Jodi eased the Rover to a stop. "I'm thinking we should hike the rest of the way in. The trail entrance shouldn't be far."

Charlie craned her neck to look around them. "How are you going to turn this around? There's not a lot of room. Anywhere."

"Meh. I'll figure that out when we come back. I want to get going so that we're up on the crags before the thermals kick in."

They all got out of the Rover and donned their backpacks. Jodi locked the truck before leading the way down the road.

Charlie smiled at Pip, who jutted her chin in Jodi's direction and rolled her eyes. "There's no one like that one."

The only sign indicating the trail was a large white arrow painted onto a gum tree. Even so, part of the white paint had peeled off with the shedding bark. If they hadn't been paying attention, they would've missed it.

The tall open eucalypt forest was the major feature for the first two kilometres they hiked. The grassy understory featured grass trees and tree ferns. Many of the trees sported blackened scars from numerous fires over the years. They mostly hiked in silence and spoke in quiet tones when they did.

Charlie stopped frequently to admire the unique vegetation and prolific wildflowers, and glanced upward in hopes of seeing her eagle. But all she saw was blue sky with a sparse cloud here and there. The ground was alive with birdlife such as small scrub wrens, elusive log runners, and an occasional brush turkey.

Their hike skirted past an enormous and strangely beautiful swamp. They took a break there and had a snack and some water while admiring the scenery.

"What is this place? It's kind of eerie looking." Charlie turned in circles and gazed out at the expansive fields of red and gold reeds. Low banksias fringed the edges, sporting their colourful flower spikes, providing wonderful contrast to the forested area.

Jodi unzipped her backpack. She pulled out the map and unfolded it over Pip's back. "This is Surveyor's Swamp."

Great swaths of densely growing grasses and sedges waved in the breeze and the sound of frogs suddenly became nearly deafening.

"We should probably get moving again." Jodi refolded the map and stored it in her pack.

In single file, they moved past the swamp. Eventually, dramatic rock formations including outcrops and balancing tors rose all around the track.

"Jodi?" Charlie called from the back. "Do you know anything about those huge round boulders? They're almost too perfectly symmetrical."

Pip stopped and turned sideways. "I can answer that. I learned something about this in a geology class I took a million years ago. It's called onion peel weathering. Water enters cracks in the rocks and then freezes overnight. The water turns to ice, expands, and sheets of rock just slide off like an onion skin."

"Show-off," Jodi said with a grin. "Isn't this all the product of ancient volcanic activity?"

"Correct. Followed by faulting and uplift and onion skin. If I'm correct, we're only on the fringe of it. I'm thinking the crags should be up ahead a little ways."

"It's kind of like a scene from *Lord of the Rings*. I wouldn't be surprised if Gandalf himself suddenly appeared." Charlie shoved her water bottle into the elastic netting of her pack.

"Ready?" Pip shouldered her pack once again and started off.

The huge boulders became more numerous the further they hiked. Some were stacked precariously. Charlie marvelled at the incredible formations. She had a hard time tearing her gaze from them and paid the price by stumbling more than a few times.

Heath and grasses grew all around. Some of the huge tors sported vegetation growing on their tops. Charlie looked around for identical plants on the ground but couldn't spot a one.

"How unusual," Charlie muttered.

"What's that, sweet?" Pip asked.

"What's so special about the tops of those rocks that stuff will grow up there, and not down here?" Charlie shaded her eyes and peered up.

"It's not what's up there—it's what happened down here. Those rocks protected those plants from fire. They probably did grow on the flats but were eliminated eons ago. Up there is the only place they can survive." Pip flashed her a smile.

"We need to do this more often, sweetheart. I've already learned so much." Charlie stole a quick kiss.

"I promise we'll make a more concerted effort once the silly season ends." Pip rubbed Charlie's arm up and down.

"Hey, you lovebirds!" Jodi called from up ahead. "Have a look." Charlie and Pip looked in the direction she pointed.

"Can we try to climb them?" Charlie studied the rock surface.

"We can give it a go, anyway." Jodi's voice echoed with the excitement of a challenge.

They dropped their packs, and with the help of a few naturally occurring hand- and foot-holds, they started to climb.

About three quarters of the way up, Charlie paused for a breather and looked back from where they'd come, across the swamp and into the distance. They'd hiked further than she had thought. She'd obviously been distracted by her surroundings and hadn't paid much attention to the kilometres she'd put under her hiking boots.

They managed to climb to the top. Huge blocks of ancient weathered granite formed a shady and sheltered place to rest. Grass trees and wild flowers grew here and there. A cool breeze wafted throughout.

Charlie walked over to a grass tree and looked closely at the flower stem that towered over her head. Tiny white flowers covered the woody stem.

Jodi and Pip joined her and each plucked a flower off and popped it into their mouths.

Pip picked one for Charlie and handed it to her. "Try this. It's as sweet as honey."

Charlie placed it on her tongue and closed her mouth. The flavour was subtle, but pleasing.

"This is quite a useful plant. You can soak the flowers and make a sweet tea, and the root is even edible. The Aboriginals used to boil down the resin to make a type of glue. Nowadays, people just like them as an ornamental. I have a few in my garden." Jodi piled a small handful of flowers into her mouth and chewed slowly.

Charlie followed suit and looked out onto the expanse. She couldn't have described the cathedral splendour with words. The views were incredible in every direction.

"Hey, babe, have a look over there." Pip indicated the direction with her chin.

Charlie scanned the horizon over the large, freestanding rocky outcrops that rose abruptly from the surrounding gentle slope of the ridge crest. "What do you see?"

"Crouch down a bit." Pip walked behind her and pointed over her shoulder. "See where I'm pointing? Wait. Hold on. I can't see it. Oh. Yeah. See it now? Think that's your eagle?"

At the mere mention of Big Bird, Charlie's pulse sped up. She squinted and strained to see. All she saw was a black silhouette. "That might be a wedgie. I don't know."

"Given the distance and the fact that we can see him, I'd bet it is." Pip rested her head against Charlie's. "What do you think, Jodes?"

"Unfortunately, my binoculars are down in my pack. But look over to the right. If I'm correct, that's Raspberry Lookout you can see when the mist clears. It's a climb to get up to it, but I think you'd have a better chance of catching a look. The fact the bird is staying in that area could mean its aerie is close."

Charlie bit her lip as her mind raced through the possibilities. "Is there a way to get over there, without having to do much backtracking?"

Jodi narrowed her eyes in thought. "Let's climb down and have a look at the map."

Charlie followed Pip and Jodi down. By the time she hopped from the last rock to the ground, Jodi had her map spread open on a rock and was tracking a route with her finger.

Jodi blew a big breath from her cheeks. "We'll have to hike back about a K. A lot of these treks can be joined and exited at numerous points along the heritage loop. This one will be a bit of a challenge, but"—she met Charlie's and then Pip's eyes—"I think we can do it." She pointed to a dotted trail on the map. "If we take this one and make tracks to here, we can bushwhack to this trail here." She tapped the map. "When we pick this trail up, it's only a short distance to the lookout, but it'll be a helluva climb. If we drop our packs here at the junction, we can make better time and won't be bogged down by their weight."

Charlie offered Pip a questioning gaze. "How are you feeling?"

Pip gave her a reassuring smile and patted her insulin pack. "All good. If you want to do it, I'm not going to hold you back. I'm not even sure a herd of wild horses could at this point."

Charlie nodded as Pip spoke and licked her lips with cautious hope. She glanced up at the sky. A few clouds had moved in, but it was still a beautiful day. "Okay. Let's do it."

They donned their packs and, in a silent march, hiked back to where Jodi had indicated, leaving the rocky outcroppings. It took a few minutes to find the tiny trail marker partially hidden in the trees.

"They don't like to make it easy, do they?" Charlie muttered under her breath. She hated wasting precious time. Every minute counted. The bird could move on at any time. She rubbed the back of her neck, anxious to keep moving.

It took the better part of two hours to push their way through the bush to get to the trail that would lead them to the lookout. Charlie thanked her lucky stars she was staying in the back, for Jodi was frequently flapping her arms in front of her, knocking down spiderwebs before she walked into them. Before they pushed through a wet peaty area, they applied mosquito repellent. The high-pitched whine of the insects could be heard above their breathing. They all knew they'd have to pick up their pace to get through unscathed by the hungry bloodsuckers. It was hard work trying to maintain good progress while swatting at the mozzies, pushing branches aside, and trying to avoid tripping and falling in the mushy uneven surface.

Charlie guessed they had to be getting close when exposed granite became more frequent as they walked. They finally broke through onto what they guessed was an unmarked trail.

Jodi stopped and looked around. "Let's leave the packs on the other side of that log. I don't think they'll be seen if anyone happens to come through."

They all shoved their water bottles into the waistbands of their shorts to free up their hands for climbing. Charlie tossed a muesli bar at Pip and took one for herself. She noticed Jodi stuffing one into a pocket as well.

The climb up the rocks was arduous. Charlie knew she was leaving bits of skin and blood from scraping her knees and elbows against the jagged and scabrous rock surface. She caught up to Pip, who stood in front of the last portion.

"You okay, babe?"

Pip sighed. "I really hate to admit this, but I don't think I can reach that next ledge. You guys go ahead and I'll wait here."

"Not on your life, sweetheart." Charlie laced her fingers together and crouched next to the rock. "Step onto my hands and I'll boost you up. I should be able to lift you high enough to get there."

"But—"

"Quit giving her short excuses and arguing with her, Pipsqueak. Come on. The view is amazing up here." Jodi, having already reached the top, stood looking down at them with her hands on her hips.

"Tell me again why we're friends?" Pip frowned at Charlie. "I don't want to hurt you. Tell me if it gets too hard, okay?"

Charlie growled at her. "It'll be fine. Just do it, Pip." She knew that every minute sitting down here was time lost for spotting Big Bird.

Pip put a hand on Charlie's shoulder and her right foot in Charlie's hand. Charlie lifted her easily as she bounced up, grabbed hold of the ledge, and pulled herself up. She received a little help from Jodi, who grabbed the back of her shorts and yanked her up.

Once Pip was safely on top, Charlie quickly scrambled the rest of the way up.

"Wow," Charlie said in between trying to catch her breath. "This. Is. Amazing. I think we can see forever from up here."

The day had turned partly cloudy. The sun threw a moving patchwork of cloud shadows over the mountain range.

Jodi turned to her and smiled. "Welcome to Raspberry Lookout. What you're looking at is the entirety of the Bindery-Mann Wilderness Area. Pretty impressive, hey?"

Pip sat down and leaned against a rock three times her size. Charlie crouched next to her. "Hey. Are you doing all right? You look a little pale."

Pip rolled her shoulders. "I'm fine. Just out of practice. A bit of food in the old tank and I'll be right as rain."

Charlie pulled the now mushed muesli bar from her back pocket. "Here. Eat mine too. And don't argue with me."

Pip shook her head and accepted the bar.

Charlie walked over to Jodi, who stood gazing towards where they'd last seen the eagle.

"See anything?"

"No." Jodi pointed downward. "And by the looks of things, we won't for a while."

A heavy morning mist crept slowly up the valley and obliterated any views below. Within minutes the wind brought it to where they stood. Charlie shivered at the loss of sunlight. The muted silence within the cloud felt alien as it engulfed them, isolating them from the rest of the world. She looked over at Pip, aware that their morning of high-energy bushwalking would impact the calculations to her food and insulin routines. "You doing okay?"

"All good."

The swirling mist cleared as quickly as it had come in. The sun's rays reached down and caressed them and the rock, lighting up two grass trees growing in front of them.

Charlie welcomed the return of the warmth. She'd heard about Australian bush tucker but up until now hadn't had much chance to explore and experiment. But here she was now, deep inside a rich national park. Jodi's example of the grass tree's flowers had piqued her curiosity. She looked around but nothing appeared edible. "Hey, Jodes, if this place is called Raspberry Lookout, where are the raspberry bushes?"

Jodi shook her head. "Not raspberry as in food. Raspberry as in the type of spur the Aboriginals and stockmen used in their decent to the Mann River."

"Well, that's not very helpful."

"Sorry."

Pip softly poked her in the ribs. "Sweetheart, I said I'm fine. You packed us a truckload of food. I've got this. Stop fussing." Pip waved her away. "Go look for your budgie."

Charlie sighed deeply. Pip was right. She'd been managing her diabetes for decades. She knew what she was doing. She needed to relax and stop worrying every five minutes.

"At least she's little, if we have to carry her out." Jodi bumped Charlie with her shoulder.

Pip wagged her finger pointedly at Jodi. "Not funny, Stretch."

"Charlie! *Look*." Jodi pointed towards the east. The unmistakable form of a wedge-tailed eagle rounded the side of the mountain.

Charlie stepped forward but wasn't satisfied. She walked ahead a few steps and surveyed the possibilities. The rock they stood on was adjacent to an even larger one, which seemed to jut out further, and only part of it was submerged into the thick vegetation. If she could get on that one, it was possible the eagle, if it was Big Bird, would see and recognize her. There was only one problem. A deep cleft separated the two rocks. It was less than a metre wide and quite jumpable, although the thought made her heart skip a beat. She walked to the edge and gauged her own abilities. She peered over to see how far she'd fall if she didn't make it. An empty feeling formed in the pit of her stomach. The thought of falling down there and becoming completely stuck where it narrowed towards the bottom wasn't appealing at all.

Charlie swallowed hard and took a deep breath. It was the only way. She backed up three big steps.

"Charlie, you're not really going to—"

"Charlie, no!" Pip pushed herself up.

Charlie winked and said, "Yup," before she lost her nerve. She ran at the divide and pushed off as hard as she could with her right foot. She landed safely on the other side and flashed Jodi and Pip a victorious grin.

While Pip held a hand to her chest, Jodi shook her head and said, "Bloody hell, Charlie!"

Charlie scanned the sky but it was empty but for the clouds. She strained to see anything in the giant eucalypts where they'd first spotted the bird. At first she thought it a shadow, but when the eagle spread its wings and took flight, her breath caught in her throat. The eagle rose high in a thermal, seeming to avoid the human disturbance. She watched as it circled overhead. The sun's intense glare made it impossible for Charlie to see if there was a white feather on the eagle's wing. On a whim, she raised one arm straight up and the other perpendicular to her body. This was the signal she used to give Big Bird to fly to her. She held her arms still and hoped if it was her eagle, he'd remember the sign.

Jodi watched, completely enthralled by Charlie's determination. She looked back and forth between Charlie and the eagle. She shaded her eyes with her hand and squinted. Was it her imagination, or did the eagle seem to be flying closer?

"Well I'll be buggered," Jodi said under her breath. "It *is* him." She stepped back, remembering Big Bird's possessiveness over Charlie.

Big Bird swooped closer, the white feather, the only sign to indicate he'd once had an injury, quite evident now. Charlie didn't move. He chirped three times and then rose higher.

Jodi vaguely noticed Charlie swat at her leg before resuming her position. Her eyes were glued to the bird in the sky.

Suddenly, Big Bird screeched like he did when he objected to someone other than Charlie. He tucked his wings and dove towards Charlie at breakneck speed.

"Charlie!" Jodi and Pip yelled at the same time.

It was then that Jodi noticed the huge brown snake lying near Charlie's foot. It reared back and struck Charlie's leg.

Big Bird pushed his talons forward and dove towards the snake. It seemed like time stood still at that moment. Just as the snake prepared for another strike, it was suddenly encased in Big Bird's giant talons. It writhed and wiggled beneath him.

Jodi met Charlie's terrified eyes. "Oh, Jesus."

"Pip. Jodi. Help me!"

CHAPTER EIGHTEEN

Pip's stomach lurched. Her heart beat so hard that stars swam before her eyes. For long moments she stood frozen, staring into Charlie's terrified eyes, knowing that her own showed nothing but complete fear. If she was going to help Charlie, she had to change that. And now.

Snakebite. Back to the basics. Charlie's life depended on her ability to stay calm and focused. But she needed to work quickly, being mindful not to increase anyone's sense of panic, particularly Charlie's. "Honey. Sweetheart. Look at me." Charlie's chest rose and fell as her breathing increased along with her adrenaline and fear. "Charlie. Look at me." Charlie's terrified wide eyes locked onto hers. "I need you to listen to me and do what I tell you. Okay? It's really, *really* important." Charlie nodded once. "I need to you lower yourself down to the ground. Slowly. And sit with your back against the rock behind you. Put your legs out in front of you, and then sit very, *very* still. It's really important you don't move, love. Can you do that for me?"

Charlie stood frozen in place.

"Honey? I *really* need you to sit down. Please." Pip held her breath for several heartbeats until Charlie did as she was told. Pip turned to an ashen-faced Jodi. "There're rolled and triangular bandages in my backpack. We need to wrap her up and splint her leg as soon as we can, to slow the spread of poison. You'll be faster than me. Can you scamper down and grab our backpacks and bring them on back? There's bandages in each of them that will do what we need to do."

Jodi spun around. "On it. And I've got a satellite alert on my backpack. I'll trigger that off to get help on its way. I'll be as quick as I can." In a blur Jodi took off and scaled down over the edge of the rock face they had not long ago all ascended.

Pip shielded the bright sun from her eyes with a hand. She needed to keep Charlie calm, yet focused, so she targeted the one thing she knew would tap into Charlie's shocked thoughts. "Where's Big Bird, love?"

Pip was met with silence.

"Charlie, where's Big Bird?"

"He's…" Charlie licked her lips. "He's here. With me."

Big Bird had landed not far from Charlie. His feathers were puffed out. His stance was exaggerated and upright. He was strung tight as a bow—clear signs of alert and distress.

"What did he do with the snake?"

"He dropped it over the edge."

"So it's gone?"

"Yes."

"Well, that's a good thing. How's he look? Big Bird. How's he look to you?" Pip knew she had to keep Charlie busy until Jodi returned.

"Good."

"How good?"

"He's bigger. Filled out."

"Uh-huh. What else?"

"He recognized me."

"He did, didn't he."

"He came down. To help me. He grabbed the snake."

"He sure did. He's a good bird, that one."

"Yeah. He is."

Pip noticed Charlie staring off into space. She needed to bring her back. "He looks a bit stressed to me. What do you think?" Pip waited for a response and didn't get one. "Charlie. Big Bird needs you." Pip smiled at a flicker of Charlie's response to her statement. "You need to talk to him. Calm him down."

Charlie looked at Pip briefly before focusing on Big Bird. She was pleased to hear Charlie cluck to the eagle, quietly murmuring to him. Slowly she raised her hand and brushed the back of a finger across his chest. Pip had come to learn that this was their kind of hug or cuddle. Ever so slowly the bird and Charlie relaxed in each other's company.

Another bird circled high overhead.

"Hey, babe, I think your giant budgie has a girlfriend."

Charlie raised her eyes to the bird lazily looping in the thermals above them. She clucked and rubbed Big Bird's chest some more. "You got an eye for the cute ones. Just like your momma. Who's a clever boy, huh?"

"Keep talking to him. I think it's working. He looks better, don't you think?"

"Yeah."

Charlie said a few more things to Big Bird that Pip couldn't hear, but she knew by looking at them both that their heart rates would have begun to settle.

Hearing scrambling noises behind her, Pip turned to see Jodi come up over the rock edge, with all three backpacks slung over her shoulder. Her face was grim. "That's not a happy face, Stretch. Talk to me." Pip knelt down and started gutting her and Charlie's bags, pulling out the bandages and putting them to one side.

"The satellite device I always carry when I go walking..." Jodi's voice was low and quiet.

Pip looked up at her, not sure if she wanted to hear the rest of the statement or not.

"I got it out of the pack a minute ago."

"Uh-huh."

"I went to turn it on and it was already going. There's hardly any battery life left. I don't have enough charge left to set off and sustain a signal. I don't understand it—I checked it last night before we left. It was at full capacity."

Pip's mind flashed back to the bags flailing around in the Rover. That was hours ago. "The bumpy car ride in must have activated it. Do you have any spare batteries?"

"Yeah. Back in the truck." Jodi pulled at her hair and looked to the sky, obviously berating herself.

"Okay."

"What do you mean *okay*? It's not *okay*. I fucked up."

Pip stuffed the bandages and a food parcel all into one backpack. "No, Bowman. You did everything right, but sometimes shit just happens. We've all just had a small moment of being horrendously human. So we now move to plan B."

"And what the frig is that?"

"We're still gonna wrap Charlie up. That hasn't changed. And then we work out how to get her off that rock. Then, plan B."

"Which is?"

"You get to enjoy another hike back to the car and set off your device thingy. Charlie and I will follow you, somewhat more sedately. And then we wait for help to arrive."

Pip eyed the backpack contents strewn across the rock face. Both she and Jodi had a small length of rope in the bottom of their bags. A jumper. Jodi had a small roll of fluorescent tape. Her mind began ticking over.

"And I suppose we sing camp songs and tell jokes while we wait?" Pip recognized an edge of hysteria to Jodi's words. She needed Jodi now more than ever. "No. Not you. I've heard your singing. You suck. You're only allowed to tell jokes." She stood and faced her friend. She held her steady with her gaze. "We got this, Jodes. But we need to work together. And fast. You with me?"

Jodi closed her eyes. Pip imagined she counted to ten before staring back at her. "Sorry. I'm being an arse. Talk me through the plan."

"We need to wrap and splint Charlie's whole leg. Get her off that rock and somehow make some kind of travois. Once we do that, you head off back to the car. Mark the trails as you go and we'll follow as best we can so we're closer to help when it arrives."

Jodi looked at the bag contents Pip had laid out and then over to Charlie. "One small problem. Or, rather, one large, feathered problem."

Pip grimaced. "I know. I'd love it if you could think of another easier solution but we don't have time. I gotta get over there. Now." Pip hefted the backpack of bandages onto her back.

Jodi stopped her with a hand on her arm. "Do you want me to do it?"

"No. I need you to tell me to get my arse over there. Then really make tracks to get help if the budgie rips me to shreds."

"Shit."

"I know. Once I'm over there, can you scout around and see if you can find some branches that we can tie together somehow? You're much cleverer than I am at that sort of thing."

"Okay. Will do. Good luck. Now go rescue your girl."

Pip swallowed once and ran at the rock face. She leapt into the air before her courage gave out. She held the jumper in front of her and tossed it over Big Bird's head, just as she landed right next to the angry and very, very protective screaming eagle.

Charlie must have tweaked to her plan. She reached over and snared the eagle to her side, effectively securing him, talking to him all the while. Pip mouthed, "Thank you." She knew if Big Bird heard her voice at this moment, that not even Charlie would be able to hold him. So she made as little sound as possible. She was vaguely aware of Jodi scrabbling back over the rock, intent on her own part of the mission ahead.

Pip whipped the backpack off and tipped out the contents. Grabbing a pocketknife, she slit Charlie's pant leg all the way up to her hip, revealing the bite and giving her maximum access to her limb.

She unlaced Charlie's boot and took it off, throwing it in the now empty bag. She grabbed a wide, heavy cotton bandage and, starting at Charlie's toes, wrapped, in firm concentric circles, all the way up to where she had been bitten. She put a light piece of gauze pad over the wound and continued wrapping, leaving one corner of the pad sticking up, like a marker flag, indicating the bite site. When she ran out of bandage, she grabbed another one and wrapped all the way up to Charlie's thigh. Three bandages in total encased her limb. Next she unfurled a SAM splint and immobilized Charlie's limb by securing it to her other leg.

Finished, she sat back on her haunches and breathed heavily, shaking with the effort of staying calm. It was done. She had slowed the poison down and bought Charlie some much needed time.

Cole fed the baby joeys their lunch and late afternoon feeds, with all going smoothly in the process. In between feeds, she and Chilli took several strolls around the grounds. When she came across Lucille's garden, she picked some flowers and laid them on the granite stone that bore Felix's name.

Chilli looked at her and wagged her tail. Cole leaned over and kissed the dog's head. "Let's go on back and start getting some dinner together for the adventure crew." Chilli offered up a single bright bark. "Don't worry, bub, I have something special planned for you too, my friend."

A cheese and fresh fruit platter was sitting in the fridge, which Cole had made up earlier, with strawberries, kiwi fruit, and apricots from Pip's garden. But it was the main meal that she spent the next hour and a half preparing. She chose a variety of vegetables from Pip's garden and made one big, and several small, chicken and vegetable pies. The process of making the puff pastry by hand was slow but cathartic. It reminded her of growing up and helping her grandmother in the kitchen.

Cole turned up the oven, making sure it was hot to ensure the pastry would puff up before the butter melted and ran out. She filled the pies and lowered the tray so Chilli could see what she had made. "See that one? That one's special—that one's yours, Chilli dog." She laughed softly as Chilli woofed.

"And then we set the timer...and now, we wait. My money's on them being back about four. So if all goes well, you and I can catch a snooze on the couch and still be as fresh as a daisy for when they all come tumbling through the door."

Charlie closed her eyes against the headache that'd started to encircle her brain. It seemed to increase with each beat of her heart. "Didn't see it."

"What? The snake?" Pip whispered. She eased herself down next to Charlie mindful of Big Bird, and laced her fingers with Charlie's.

Charlie nodded.

"Sneaky bastard."

Big Bird screeched a warning.

"It's okay, buddy." Charlie lolled her head towards the eagle. She opened her eyes carefully, squinting against the bright sun. *He's gorgeous.*

Big Bird chortled quietly.

"Sweet," Pip said, barely above a whisper.

"Mm." Charlie rolled her head to the other side and instantly regretted it. A sharp spear of pain penetrated her skull. She moaned.

"Try not to move. Jodi and I are—"

Big Bird screeched and tried to flap his wings. One of his huge taloned feet reached out and blindly tried to take hold of something. Finding nothing, he lowered it and sat still again.

"Pip. You have to move away so I can let him go. It's the only way. He's getting too strong for me to hold."

"Kay."

Charlie felt, rather than heard, Pip move away. She instantly missed her comforting presence.

"Let him go, Charlie."

Charlie slowly relinquished her hold on him. He stood still with the jumper over his head. When she eased it off, he shook his head to resettle his feathers and stared defiantly at Pip.

"Go on, buddy." She nudged him away from her. It broke her heart to have to push him away. But at this point, her life was dependent on keeping Pip and Jodi safe from her protective eagle.

He rubbed close to her and then turned. A gust of wind flowed over the outcrop. He bent low, spread his wings, and leaned into the wind. Within moments he was circling above, floating on the early afternoon thermals rising from the valley below.

Jodi and Pip sprang into action. Jodi had managed to drag two medium-sized poles up top. Charlie watched through half-lidded eyes as Pip removed the belts on the backpacks.

"Jodi, lay the poles side by side over the gap, about a body width apart."

Jodi slid them over the crevasse towards them.

Pip tightened the shoulder straps on both packs as tight as they would go and then tied the ends into the securest knot she could manage. She then wove one of the belts through the straps at the bottom of each pack, effectively joining them together. She tied the end of one of the ropes to the handhold at the top of the pack and then repeated the process with the other. Pip pulled on each strap and rope end to make sure there wouldn't be any slippage with Charlie's weight. She then slid the pole ends through the looped straps. When she was done, she checked the knots one more time. The sling was crude, but one that would hopefully get Charlie over the gap and safely to the other side.

"Okay, Jodi. Grab the end of this rope." Pip tossed it to Jodi, who handily caught it. "Stand on the ends of the poles and try to keep them from moving. We're going to try to slide Charlie over on top of the packs."

"Sweetheart, I need you to help me out now."

Charlie opened her eyes. "Thirsty."

Pip unscrewed the cap of her water bottle and held it to Charlie's lips. "Little sips, babe. Don't overdo it."

Charlie swallowed. "Okay."

"As slowly as you can, I need you to slide yourself over and onto the backpacks. It's not going to be the most comfortable, and will probably feel awkward, but it's the only way we can get you over onto the other rock. Can you do that? I'll try to help you as best I can."

Charlie put her hands flat on the rock and pushed herself over to the packs. She made the mistake of looking down into the gap and nearly vomited. She stopped and took some more deep breaths before dragging her bound legs behind her. When she lay flat on the packs, she closed her eyes. She was exhausted and cold sweat covered her body.

"Jodes, when you're ready, slowly start pulling her across. I'll steady her on this end with this rope."

Charlie felt a sharp tug and then felt the backpacks start to drag over the surface. The rings of the packs screeched against the rock, as inch by inch the makeshift sling upon which she was suspended moved in jerks and starts. Suddenly all movement stopped.

"What's wrong, Jodi?"

"I think one of the straps is caught."

"Crap."

Charlie felt a tug in the opposite direction.

"Try now."

The sling moved a few inches and came to an abrupt halt again.

"Charlie, can you very carefully rock yourself from side to side?"

"Can try." Charlie pushed up onto her elbows and leaned her weight to one side and then the other. There was a single moment when the left pole shifted and she thought she was going to flip the entire sling upside down and fall into the crevasse. But somehow the sling righted itself. Jodi pulled her the remaining distance without incident. As soon as her shoulders met the rock on the other side, Jodi slid her hands into Charlie's armpits and dragged her completely off the sling and onto solid rock once again.

"Charlie, my love, you did great. Now lie still while we fashion a way to get you down onto the ground. Oh, hey, look up. Big Bird's still here. I think he's watching over you."

Charlie blinked hard as two enormous birds circled just metres above her. They were so quiet she thought she might be imagining them. Pip and Jodi scurried around her. She didn't pay them any attention. She just couldn't. Deep down she knew she was suffering from shock. She tried hard to forget the moment when she'd turned around and saw the huge snake lunging at her leg. But the vision kept repeating itself over and over. Her heart sped up and she came close to hyperventilating.

Pip appeared at her side once again. "Deep breaths, my love. You need to slow your heart rate down or you'll push the venom deeper into your body."

Charlie nodded and looked into Pip's calming eyes. Pip was her anchor. She needed to trust what she said. Do what she was told to do. Pip would not let her down.

While Pip tended to Charlie, Jodi untied the rope from the packs. She ran one end around the base of a huge round rock. She then fashioned a sort of harness at the other end and brought it over to Charlie. Pip helped Charlie push her arms through the knotted loops and used one of the pack belts to secure the rest of the line around her waist. It was a crude harness of sorts, but it would do the job. She then threw the backpacks down on the main trail.

"Okay," Jodi said, taking the play out of the rope. "Charlie, we're going to lower you down feet first. Pip will guide you from below while I let the rope out a little bit at a time. Just relax. Let us do all the work."

Pip grazed Charlie's forehead with her lips before standing up and disappearing below the edge of the rock.

Jodi held the rope behind her back and leaned against it. She put one foot in front of the other and braced herself. "Okay, Charlie, slowly scoot towards the edge. Pip is down there and will guide your legs and support you as you go. If you need to take a break, just say so."

Charlie nodded and pushed her legs forward to the edge.

As Charlie's legs rocked downward, Jodi held on tight, gritted her teeth, and grunted with the effort. Her hands burned as the rope slid through them. She silently wished she'd brought a pair of gloves. Suddenly the rope went slack.

"Is everything all right, Pip?" Jodi took up the slack rope.

"All good. Charlie is having a rest. We'll be good to go in a sec."

Jodi relaxed for a few moments until the rope went taut again.

By the time Charlie was finally safely on the ground, Jodi's hands were red and on fire. Blisters had formed, popped, and bled. She slowly unclenched her stiff fingers from around the rope, fighting back tears as it ripped more skin from her wounded hands. The pain was excruciating. She clenched her fists and, using the meaty part of her wrist and palm, started to climb down the rock face.

She managed to make her way about halfway down by bracing her body and arms against opposite rocks. There was only one more onion skin rock to navigate. The rest of the way would be loose rocks and sand. She stopped, looked down, and tried to make a plan of descent. Blood dripped slowly out of her clenched hands. She'd just have to open her hands to grip the tiny ledges on the rock face. She bent her knees and lowered her right foot, reaching out with her right hand to push against the rock. Her feet slipped out from under her—she'd miscalculated. She stifled the cry when she felt a painful pop in her ankle as she hit the rock surface below, the jar reverberating all the way to her teeth. She held her breath and bit her lip, trying to ignore the white-hot pain shooting through her leg. She slid down the wash on her bum. She didn't even have to look—she'd sprained her ankle badly. She made a silent vow to not let on to Charlie and Pip. They had enough to worry about. All of them did.

"Jesus, Jodes, look at your hands." Pip grasped one and gently opened it. When Jodi winced, Pip carefully folded Jodi's hand back into a fist again. "We need to attend to those hands before we go any further."

"No." Jodi shook her head adamantly. "I don't need them to walk, and we certainly don't have that kind of time. A few hours won't make a bit of difference to these mitts. I'll help you put the travois together and then I'm heading out."

"Jodes, your hands are so important. I can't—"

Jodi stood quickly and wished she hadn't because she'd carelessly put more weight on her ankle than she'd intended. An involuntary grunt passed her lips before she could help it.

Pip scrutinized her and frowned. "Are you sure you're okay?"

"Just a little stiff in places that I'd forgotten about. Let's get moving."

Although Jodi couldn't move her fingers that well, she was able to help Pip assemble the travois by holding the poles between her wrists while Pip tied the backpacks to them again. This time, however, she used Jodi's pack as well to produce a makeshift bed between the two poles. With a leftover belt strap, Pip managed to attach each end to a pole. They got Charlie situated on the travois and then Pip stepped inside the harness, between the two poles. She grasped a pole in each hand and, by leaning into the belt, was able to drag it quite easily.

"You good?" Jodi took a long drink of water from her canteen.

"Yep. Except I don't know the way out of here."

Jodi stopped to think. "I only have a little fluorescent tape to mark my trail." She put the back of her hand to her forehead and partially covered her eyes to think. "Okay. It won't be a problem. In the trees, I'll just bend some branches over. In rocky areas, I'll build a little cairn and line up three or four stones in the direction I'm heading." She looked up at the sky. The clouds were on the increase, but so far they weren't the heavy dark ones indicative of impending rain. "All right. I need to get going." Jodi gave Pip a quick hug, then walked to the back of the travois. "You just relax and let Pipsqueak do all the work. We'll get you out of here. I promise." Jodi kissed Charlie on the cheek.

"Don't worry about us. We'll be ready when help arrives." Charlie reached up and squeezed Jodi's forearm. "Take care of yourself, and be careful."

"Will do, sweet." Jodi nodded to Pip. "Okay. I'm off." It took everything Jodi had within her to bear the pain in her ankle and not limp. Fortunately, there was a curve in the trail not long after she left Pip and Charlie. She stopped and took a quick rest. The effort took her breath away. She wiped the sweat from her brow with the back of her wrist. She looked around and found a stick she could use as an improvised cane. One more drink from her canteen and she was off.

She had to backtrack a couple of times when it occurred to her that she'd forgotten to mark the trail. Thankfully, she'd been able to keep ahead of Pip.

Her thoughts eventually turned to Cole. She missed her. She could almost hear Cole reading her the riot act for worrying her. They were most definitely going be late getting home, and she had no way of warning Cole, or asking her to send help. Jodi limped her way over to a tree and laboriously tied a fluorescent tag on it, leaving enough free to blow in the wind and attract Pip's attention.

At work Cole had always seemed to read her mind and anticipate her every need. Jodi hoped that Cole could anticipate her needs once again and raise the alarm to send help. Jodi swapped hands on her support stick and limped on. Even though they were miles apart, she needed Cole and her intuition now more than ever.

Charlie woke at a jolt. Pip had stumbled and nearly dropped the frame she was resting on. She felt far from great. Her headache was still very much present and her stomach continued to roil like a small boat on the ocean. But she surmised she was no worse, at least that she could tell. Pip, on the other hand, was tripping and stumbling along an unseen pathway. "Pip." Her voice barely carried. She cleared her dry throat and tried again. "Pip. Can we stop and take a break?"

"Huh?"

"A break. Can we just stop for a minute, please?" Charlie wanted to get a look at Pip to gauge how she was doing. Charlie guessed, from the angle of the sun, that they were heading into late afternoon. She must have fallen asleep. She couldn't remember seeing Pip have lunch, and given the way the travois had been lurching about, she wanted to make sure Pip stopped and refuelled.

Pip stopped. Charlie waited for her to put the frame down, but after half a minute, she found herself still suspended in mid-air. "Pip. Put me down, babe. On the ground. That's it." She winced as her head met the earth a little more suddenly than she had expected. "Come round here and sit next to me." She patted the earthen floor beside her. From the corner of her eye she saw Pip turn and totter slightly her way, sinking to her knees, then her bottom, to rest beside her. Charlie rummaged around in the bag that was tied to the frame she was resting on, and pulled out a ham and cheese sandwich. She searched around for more food but came up empty. She unwrapped the lone sandwich and handed Pip one half. "Chew on that for a minute." Pip stared at her, slightly glassy eyed. She held the sandwich out again. "Eat."

Pip reached for the bread with a shaky hand and put it in her mouth. Slowly, she took a bite and chewed in a laborious, mechanical way.

"That's the way. Good job, love." Each time Pip lowered her hand, Charlie nudged her arm and raised the sandwich back up to her lips to take another bite, until at last, the meal was finished. "Well done. Better?"

"Thank you." Pip yawned.

"Tired?"

"Mm."

Charlie held her arm out wide. "Come lie down for a minute."

Pip shook her head. "Can't. Need to keep going, while I can." She got up clumsily. "Only got a handful of hours of daylight left."

Charlie ignored her headache for a moment to look around at where they had stopped, trying to mentally orientate where they were. "I can't see any pink tape."

"I think Jodi's run out. Been following stick marks and footsteps in the dirt and some rock markers for a while now."

"Oh." Charlie felt disorientated from time and tried to process what had happened and where they were. "Can I ask a question?"

"Sure."

"Why is there only one sandwich in the pack? There should be at least two."

Pip looked a little shamefaced and rubbed the bridge of her nose. "Ah. Well. A funny thing, that."

"How so?"

"Turns out your budgie likes ham and cheese sandwiches."

"Come again?"

"I had to stop and retie a couple of the straps on your frame. Big Bird decided he would come down and supervise. Make sure I got it right, I suppose."

"Uh-huh." Charlie sipped at the bottle of water Pip offered her.

"And, well, he kind of insisted on being close. *Real* close. So I tore up one of the sandwiches and threw him pieces to keep him busy."

"I see. And the snacks?"

"I ate one and shoved one into Jodi's jacket, along with her sandwich, before she left. There should be another couple of snacks in there."

Charlie delved back into the pack and searched around. She undid the two zippered compartments, each time coming up zero before turning the bag inside out. Turning the pack upside down she spied a hole in the bottom of the bag, the threads torn and loose. She put her fingers through the hole and held up the bag, wiggling her digits at Pip. "Looks like we caught the bag on something. I think we've lost the snacks overboard. Apart from the water bottles, there's nothing else in here." Charlie bit the inside of her lip trying to estimate when Pip would need more food, but her headache was making her calculations stall. "How long have you got, babe? Till you need something to eat?"

Pip stood up and brushed her hands on her trousers. "Plenty of time for Jodi to get back and organize some help to arrive." Pip brushed a quick kiss on the top of her head. "But we need to keep pushing on while we still have light." Charlie felt, more than saw, Pip walk past her head and step into the frame. She lifted her up once again. "Ready to go, love?"

Charlie knew Pip was deflecting her concerns and trying to remain positive for her sake. She'd have done the same. "Ready when you are."

Charlie's body jolted as Pip surged forward with the frame along the dirt track. Charlie closed her eyes. There wasn't much she could do now except lie back and worry enough for both of them.

Cole woke as the timer went off. The house was filled with the mouth-watering smells of home cooking. She opened the oven and tested the pies. Her grandmother would be proud. They were lightly golden, moist, and cooked evenly right through. With the vegetables all cut and sitting in a pot of water in readiness, all she'd have to do, once the mob returned, was heat the pies and cook the vegetables and serve.

She put the pies on the bench and covered them with a tea towel to cool. Checking her watch, she frowned. Time was getting on. It had gone past five, an hour later than she had expected them to return. With nothing left to do before the last of the dinner preparations, she decided it wouldn't hurt to replace the koala leaves with fresh branches and make sure the possums and birds had plenty to eat for the evening. It would be one less thing for Pip and Charlie to worry about after their big day.

By the time she got back to the house, it was half past six. Knowing how important the regular feeding patterns were for the joeys, Cole mixed up some fresh milk and gave them the first of their evening meals.

By the time she finished and cleaned up, having noted all the pertinent feeding details, the clock read half past seven. A kernel of worry began to settle and grow in the pit of her stomach. She tried ringing first Jodi's mobile number, then Pip's, then Charlie's, all without success. She assumed they were still in a mobile reception black spot up in the hills. It was now well and truly getting dark and she knew they'd intended to be home well before that happened.

She headed to Pip's study, where she remembered seeing a UHF CB radio. Jodi had a radio in her Rover which she kept tuned to UHF station 12. She tried calling Jodi on that, only to be greeted with an empty static-filled wall of no reply.

Eight o'clock rolled around and still there was no sign or message from the girls. Cole had lost count of how many times she picked up her phone, hoping for a blinking blue light to indicate a message—they'd had a flat tyre, or run out of fuel, or some sort of mechanical difficulty, and they would be home soon. But each time she looked, the screen was blank. No messages, no calls, no indication of contact whatsoever.

She pulled out one of Pip's maps and tried to remember what she'd heard Jodi and Charlie planning. She traced various routes with her fingers along trails, roads, and creeks, hoping that something would trigger some memory of where they said they were going. She had a vague idea of where Big Bird had been released and where Jodi had thought she had spotted him only recently, but Cole knew how big the area was. Precise details were what she needed if she was to be of any help. Her breath hitched and caught. She really didn't know exactly where they had gone. If she had to call someone to help look for them, she wasn't even sure where to suggest they start.

By ten o'clock she went looking for Pip's phone book. They were now well over six hours overdue. She wasn't sure where exactly she needed to look, but something deep inside her gut told her she needed to make a start, and now.

CHAPTER NINETEEN

Jodi concentrated on the placement of every step, and at the same time tried to remember to set the markers for Pip. The area around her ankle where her hiking shoe rubbed her skin was tender from the swelling. Her ankle felt wobbly and unstable. Yeah, she'd done a good job on it. She hobbled along, leaning on the gnarled stick for support, muttering to herself about how screwed up this entire day had gotten. She wished more than once that she'd taken the five minutes and had let Pip wrap her hands before setting out. The makeshift walking stick she was using was only making her torn and raw hands worse, the stick slick with blood.

Swapping the stick from hand to hand to provide the smallest modicum of relief was no longer working. Several times she had leaned heavily on the stick to step over roots or rocks, only to have the stick slip from her hands, tearing skin as it went. She had no choice. She had to stop. She untied the light Gore-Tex zip-up jacket she had tied around her waist and cut it into large strips. She used the sleeves to wrap around her hands and the longer lengths to bind and support her ankle as best she could, albeit in a crude fashion. She found the sandwich and snack Pip had stowed away. Shoving the sandwich down her shirt top, she quickly scarfed the snack. She rose tenderly to her feet. Everything hurt. Time was getting away from her. She needed to push on.

The daylight had disappeared quickly with the thickening of clouds. Hour by hour the cloud deck grew lower and thicker and darker. A southerly breeze picked up, bringing with it cool remnants of the Antarctic from where it likely originated. Gooseflesh peppered her skin. For just a brief moment she regretted cutting up her thin jacket, but it was a useless thought as the deed had been done. She tossed the thought aside and hoped the rain would hold off until morning, but her hopes dwindled when she heard a mutter of thunder in the distance.

She strained to see what was in front of her in the waning light. Was it a branch in the trail or, heaven forbid, a python stretching itself across the metre wide expanse? After the day's events, she couldn't afford not to be extra vigilant. She stomped the end of her cane into the ground hoping that if it was indeed a snake, the vibrations would encourage it to move on. But it remained motionless. She couldn't waste any more time deliberating, so she hobbled ahead, taking one tentative step at a time. She felt a small rock roll under the heel of her good foot. She lifted her injured ankle off the ground, bent the knee of the other leg, and found the golfball sized piece of granite. After straightening up and regaining her balance, she used her best softball underhand pitch and tossed it in the stick-or-snake's direction. When the rock bounced off with a low thud, she breathed a sigh of relief. Stick.

Jodi looked around and tried to gauge where she was. But it was too dark to make out any landmarks. Even the ground had become flat and monotonous. She paused to slide her mobile and her pocketknife that had a compass built into the handle out of her pocket. She'd have to use the torch app sparingly to save the battery, as well as maintain some amount of night vision. She flicked it on and held it in front of her for a few seconds. She checked the direction she was heading and the area around her before extinguishing the light. If she'd only packed a regular torch…But she'd set it aside when she was loading her pack with day hike essentials. In her mind's eye, Jodi could see exactly where it was, sitting right next to the small pile of dehydrated food she'd forgotten all about. Now she wished she had those packets as well, her carefully stowed sandwich having been lost. Her stomach clenched with fear and hunger, and was tinged with a bit of nausea from overexertion.

Thunder rolled overhead, seemingly rumbling towards her, through the darkened clouds, spreading out into the night with the promise of rain. Jodi looked at the sky behind her. Short, dim flashes of lightning seemed to play in the clouds. By her best estimation, the major part of the storm was still creeping up the valley. She'd have to hurry. Once the cloudburst became more organized, it would undoubtedly pack a wallop. And Pip and Charlie were right in its path.

She shifted her weight to turn, lost her balance, and fell. Her opposite foot slammed into her ankle, twisting it painfully. "Shit!" Jodi grabbed her ankle and rocked back and forth, a sob bubbling up from within. She let it out, not caring that it scared a flock of birds that voiced their annoyance with loud squawks. "Shut up!" Anger formed and grew hot in her chest. Heat flushed through her body and she took strength from it. She struggled to her feet, muscles quivering in her legs and arms, and pushed on.

The throaty cough and growl of a brushtail possum disturbed by her presence mingled with the singing of what sounded like a million frogs. She must be close to Surveyor's Swamp. Jodi flicked the light on and then off, relieved to see the reeds and high grasses of the marsh. Not far now. A drop of rain fell on her shoulder. What she had mistaken for a breeze wafting through the trees, rubbing the leaves against each other, was actually the slow encroachment of the rain.

Jodi quickly changed the position of her walking stick. She held it against the leg with the sprain and let it take most of her weight. She imagined her gait to be a combination of hobble-hitch-limp. If she wasn't trying to outrun the storm, with Pip and Charlie still behind her, she might find it comical. And maybe one day they *could* all laugh about what had happened. But her friends were relying on her to get help. With a strength born of pure love and determination, she forged on.

The rain became steadier and louder and harder. Before she knew it, she was moving through what seemed like a wall of water. The ground became treacherously slippery and she fell. Once. Twice. The rain washed the grime from her face. The cold slowly sapped her strength. She struggled blindly forward. Her vision was cut to only a couple of metres in front of her, leaving her only able to guess that she might be on the trail. She gave up trying to leave signs for Pip and Charlie to follow, hoping they would recognize the swamp like she did.

Blackness, interrupted by flashes of lightning and deafening thunder, surrounded her. She wildly looked around. For a brief moment she didn't have any idea where she was. Panic bubbled inside her. Jodi paused next to a huge gum tree taking refuge beneath its expansive canopy. Her teeth chattered as she grew increasingly colder. She had to keep moving or risk hypothermia. But where the hell was she? She turned in circles, trying to see something, anything that would give her a clue.

She cringed and almost closed her eyes when lightning forks exploded across the sky, looking for something to clasp in their white, hot clutches. Quick flickers of light danced across her eyes and the landscape, briefly reflecting against the smooth grey bark of the trees. But not everything was vertical. A large black form seemed to huddle against the tree line. Jodi squinted into the dying flash of light. She wanted to believe but was too scared to. Was it her Rover? She only had to wait a split second before she got her answer as another booming flash exploded overhead.

Cole tried each of the girls' phones and the UHF radio every half hour, in between conversations with the local emergency services. She had the map spread out on Pip's dining room table and had marked several places of likely interest. She was waiting for the local State Emergency Service coordinator, Garry Knight, to finish liaising with local police and get back to her with a plan of action. She paced the living room and tried the mobiles once more. Still no answer. She tried the radio, anticipating the same response, just as her mobile sounded.

"Garry? Yes, hello. What's the latest?"

Cole listened with a heavy heart. Helicopters didn't fly at night up in the mountains, and the rain that had started to fall would surely only further hamper rescue efforts.

"Are you saying you can't do anything until morning? I'm telling you, something is wrong. We can't afford to wait. We need…"

Static sounded from the radio. Cole missed what Garry was saying, her focus keenly attuned to the CB speaker. She waited. There. It happened again. She dashed over to the table and keyed the mike. "Jodi? Jodi? Is that you? It's Cole. Come in, Jodi."

Static crackled back at her.

"Jodi? Are you there? It's me, Cole." Cole held her breath as the silence grew around her.

Nothing. Her shoulders slumped and she raised the mobile phone back up to her ear. "Sorry, Garry, I thought—"

"*I'm here.*"

Cole froze. Did she really hear a voice? Or was it the sound of desperation and the trickery of her brain telling her what she desperately wanted to hear?

"*I'm here.*" The voice was strained and mixed with static, but it was there.

With a sob, Cole picked up the mike. "Jodi, love, I'm here too." She released the mike and held it to her forehead as she shook with relief. *Oh, thank you, God.* "Where are you?"

"Near Surveyor's Swamp."

"Are you all right?"

"No. Need help. Charlie's been bitten by a snake and Pip is with her. Had to leave them behind to get help."

Cole was frantically trying to find Surveyor's Swamp on the map when she remembered she had left Garry waiting on the phone. "Hang on a minute, bub, I've got someone who'll know where you are— it's Garry from the SES." She quickly relayed Jodi's message. Garry wanted more details than she could offer so she picked up the mike.

"Jodes, Garry wants to ask you some questions. Hang on and I'll put you through." She lined up the phone and the mike. "Go ahead, love, tell him what you know."

"*Garry, I'm near Surveyor's Swamp. I've just set my SOS device off—you can get the exact grid reference coordinates from that. We need urgent medical help. I've got one snakebite victim and an insulin dependent diabetic. It's pouring with rain up here and there's a wind-chill factor that's making life uncomfortable.*"

Cole listened to Jodi's voice as she relayed details to Garry's questions. Nobody could read Jodi better than she, and while Jodi might appear to be calm in the giving over of helpful information, Cole could hear the underlying tremor in Jodi's voice. If she could transport herself there magically and wrap her arms around Jodi, she would do it in a heartbeat, but all she could do was wait, and that was almost as hard as the unknown.

A search party had been mobilized and dispatched along with a remote area paramedic crew. Garry promised to keep in touch with Cole and she with him.

"Jodi, love, you still there?"

"*Yeah. Still here.*"

Cole heard Jodi's teeth chattering over the radio. "See if you've got a space blanket in your first aid kit."

Cole waited, but now that she was in contact with Jodi, the silence was just time and space. It didn't hurt as much as the eon of emptiness of before.

"*Got it.*"

"Okay. Wrap yourself up in it. It'll warm you up in a few minutes."

"*I need to get back to Pip and Charlie.*"

"Sweetheart, you need to stay in the car so the search party can find you. Then you can lead them to the girls."

"*They're still out there...*"

"I know, but you're the link. Just stay there, love."

"But I feel bad leaving them."

"You're not leaving them. You'll be bringing help *to* them. Just promise me you'll stay there till help arrives. It won't be long, love. They know where you are."

Jodi didn't respond right away.

"Jodi?"

"Yeah."

"You've done a great job. Help's on its way."

"I have to go. Need to save the battery."

"All right. Just promise you'll stay." Cole fidgeted. She wanted to keep talking to Jodi but understood the need to conserve the car's battery power. "Promise me."

"I promise."

"Okay. I'm looking at the clock. It's nearly one in the morning. I'm going to call you every half hour. So sit back and get warmed up and I'll talk to you soon."

"Love you."

Cole had to swallow past the lump in her throat at Jodi's quiet statement. "I love you too, bub. Now rest. Talk to you soon."

"Bye."

Cole sat down heavily in the chair as relief weakened her knees. They were in trouble. Her instincts had been right, but she took no satisfaction in that. Her peace would come when she saw them all home safe. But they were a long way yet to that happening, with help still hours away.

At first Charlie thought she was still asleep because of the darkness, but she caught glimpses of lightning flashing in the distance, and she realized night had fallen. The travois bounced unevenly. She could just make out Pip mumbling. She tried to decipher what she was saying but Pip seemed largely incoherent to her.

"Pip."

There was no break in Pip's rambling to indicate she'd heard her. Charlie tried harder to project her voice. *"Pip."*

Pip stumbled and fell to her knees. She crawled a few steps before regaining her feet, swaying left and right. She stepped forward and tripped and fell back to the ground. She crawled a few paces and struggled to stand again. Her mumbling continued.

"Dammit." Charlie realized Pip was slipping into a hypoglycaemic episode and was rapidly becoming unresponsive. "Pip!" she yelled. It seemed to work. Pip stopped struggling to get up and sat heavily on the ground staring off into space, still mumbling.

She was effectively immobile, and Pip lay just out of her reach. Charlie knew she had to get closer to her to make sure she didn't wander off into the dark to end up who-only-knew where. She shivered. She was highly aware of how high up they were and how treacherous the Australian wilderness could be in the daytime, let alone in the middle of the night, in pitch dark, with diminished mental faculties.

Pip got to her feet and drunkenly weaved several steps forward, straight into a tree. She dropped onto her bottom once again. Charlie knew she had to take the chance now or she ran the risk of losing Pip. She untied herself from the travois and dragged herself, commando style, on her stomach, digging her hands and elbows into the ground, pulling and heaving herself to where Pip was. She half rolled onto Pip to hinder any more movement and swallowed hard. She knew she couldn't hold Pip if she decided she wanted to go. Looking around, there were very few options available to her, especially as she had rolled away from the travois and the ropes. There was only one obvious choice left, and it came with a risk. But Pip was declining rapidly, no longer aware of her surroundings. In order to give them both a chance, she had to act fast and try to keep them together. She unwrapped the top bandage along her thigh. She got to the end and removed it altogether. She wiggled her way down to Pip's feet and tied one end around one ankle and then wrapped both feet and ankles together, continuing up to her mid-calves where she made a knot. She tied the loose end to her left wrist, effectively binding them together.

Charlie gathered Pip in her arms and encouraged her to lie down. She tried to connect with Pip's consciousness on some level in an attempt to soothe her by running shaky fingers through her soft hair.

When Pip's breathing slowed and lengthened, Charlie lay back and tried to be as still as possible, breathing slowly in an attempt to slow her own heartbeat down and to bleed away the adrenaline rush the effort had cost her. She had removed a third of her bandages and needed to stay still now, more than ever. In order to keep Pip safe, she had compromised her own safety. There had been no other choice.

As the first fat, heavy drops of rain began to fall, Charlie squished her eyes shut against the wet onslaught. Pip lay oblivious to the change in conditions. Charlie tightened her arms and pulled Pip as close along her body as she could manage, to try to preserve both of their core temperatures. She raised her head and kissed Pip on the forehead. "Jodi's getting help. Not long now, love. Just hang on for me. Rest. Not long now." With nothing else to do, Charlie lay back and closed her eyes as her headache tightened around her skull with every pound of her heart.

Jodi woke with a start. She remembered closing her eyes when she'd started to warm up, thanks to the space blanket. Her muscles had finally relaxed when the cold had relinquished its hold on her and her teeth had stopped chattering. She ached all over. Somehow she'd managed to keep her ankle immobile and for the first time in hours felt only a dull throb.

But she'd never meant to fall asleep. Cole had said help was on its way. It was up to her to direct them to Pip and Charlie. She was the only one who knew where they were. Worry wormed itself through her. Guilt tightened her chest and rose painfully to the back of her throat. She was warm and had shelter. They were no doubt out in the open and cold to the bone. Tears spilled down her cheeks. She should've gone back.

Pale white mist floated lightly around the truck. Jodi suddenly realized it was nearly dawn. The rain had stopped, but clouds still darkened the sky, making it difficult to judge how close daylight was. How long had it been since she'd spoken with Cole? Was help on the way yet? Jodi turned the ignition key to power the radio. She took the mike out of the holder and pressed the send key. "Cole? You there?"

"*Yes, yes,*" Cole answered immediately.

Jodi smiled at the familiar voice. "Were you sleeping?"

"*Not exactly. Let's just say this radio makes for a horrible pillow. How are you, sweet?*"

"Better now that I'm warmer. What time is it?"

There was a short pause. "*Nearly five thirty.*"

"It's been what? Almost three, four hours? Where's the SES? Charlie and Pip are still out there." Panic rose sharply in Jodi's chest.

"*They should be there anytime.*"

"They've been out there too long. I have to go to them."

"*Jodi, no. Stay put. Give me a minute and I'll ring Garry to get an update. I'll be right back.*"

It felt like hours before Jodi heard the telltale static of the radio coming to life.

"*Babe? Sorry it took me so long. Garry and the crew should be close. The weather held them up a bit. The good news is that a helicopter's on standby and will be flying in as soon as Garry can give them coordinates of where Charlie and Pip are.*"

Jodi sighed in frustration. The urge to leave the Rover and go looking herself was so strong she nearly gave in to it.

"*Don't you dare.*"

Jodi shook her head. "How did you know what I was thinking?"

"*After all these years, you really need to ask?*"

Jodi snorted. "No. I guess not."

The inside of the Rover was suddenly engulfed in white light with flashes of yellow and blue. Jodi looked in her rear-view mirror and was blinded by a vehicle's headlights.

"They're here. Baby, I gotta go. I love you."

"*Okay. Let Garry and his crew do their job. And, sweetheart? Don't raise a fuss when they want to look you over.*"

"Yes, dear. I'll try to call you as soon as I hear something."

"*I love you, Jodi. I'll be waiting.*"

Jodi swung the Rover's door open just as the four-wheel-drive sports utility vehicle pulled up alongside her. *Ambulance Service NSW* was lettered in red on the side. A folded gurney was strapped to the roof racks. Two white and orange SES four-wheel-drives drove up. Orange jumpsuited men and women piled out of the vehicles, strapping on helmets and donning backpacks as they disembarked. A short stocky man in orange with several pips on his epaulettes walked towards her.

"Jodi? I'm Garry."

"You're here." Nearly disbelieving, she took a step out of the truck, faltered, and grabbed onto the door for support. She gave up trying to stand and rested against the seat.

"Don't move. One of the crew will help you." Garry was a muscular, short man with eyes that gleamed. His roundish face sported a thin dishevelled moustache that stuck out from under the tip of a rigid nose.

"I'm fine. You need to find my friends."

Garry handed her a topographical map of the area just as another off-road four-wheel-drive ambulance drove up behind the convoy. "Can you give me an idea of where you think they are?"

Jodi quickly pointed to Surveyor's Swamp. "Best guess is that they've made it this far. If you can get yourselves to the marsh, I've marked the trail from there. I just couldn't..." Her voice faltered and cracked.

Garry put a meaty hand on her shoulder. "You're the reason we *will* find them. One of the ambos is going to examine you while the rest of the team search for your friends. I'll send word back when we've located them."

Jodi's throat was so tight with emotion that she couldn't speak. She nodded quickly.

Radios crackled and six men and women organized themselves in preparation for the long trek in. With packs at the ready, the blue jumpsuited paramedics and the orange suited SES team were gone in the span of only a handful of minutes.

"Hi, Jodi, I'm Dan. How about I have a look at you while we wait for the others to get back?" A complete opposite to Garry, Dan was clean-shaven, tall, and lanky.

"I sprained my ankle."

"Okay. Let's get you into the back of the ambulance and I'll have a look at it."

A short while later, Jodi lay on a stretcher with an IV drip in her arm to treat her for dehydration, pain, and shock. Dan had cut her shoe off and stabilized her swollen and discoloured ankle with a pillow splint.

"It doesn't look like you've broken anything, but I can't rule out a fracture. You'll be going to the hospital for an X-ray for that."

"Can we wait until we've heard something?"

Dan smiled at her compassionately. "Your vitals are all good, so yeah, we can wait. But if anything changes, we're outta here. Deal?"

"Thank you." Jodi started feeling groggy with the pain meds on board. She finally gave in to sleep.

Jodi woke to gentle rubbing on her shoulder. She blinked heavy-lidded eyes and worked her tongue in her dry mouth. She suddenly became aware of where she was, and worried, she searched Dan's eyes for answers.

"It's okay. It's okay. They found your friends. A chopper is on its way to take one of them out."

"One?"

"Yes, Garry is bringing the other out. That's all I know. I have instructions to transport you to the hospital. Your friends will be taken there as well."

"I need to radio Cole." Jodi tried to sit up, but Dan applied pressure to her shoulder. She was too tired to offer much resistance.

"Is that the person who raised the alarm?"

"Yes."

"She's been notified by dispatch. She'll undoubtedly be waiting at the hospital for you."

The sound of frogs reverberated painfully in her raw brain. *Shut up.* Charlie groaned. Even thinking hurt. Behind closed eyelids she thought she could discern a light but was not prepared to brave any more pain by opening her eyes. Her tongue felt swollen, there was a strange metallic taste in her mouth, and her lips were dry and cracked. Her stomach rolled with nausea and intermittent cramps. On a scale of one to ten, she felt a miserable eight. Everything seemed to hurt. She was soaked and cold, her thoughts slow and unclear.

Charlie wanted to sit up and check on Pip but she couldn't move. The weight was still heavy on her chest, so she guessed Pip was still there.

Her mind wandered, words and thoughts falling hopelessly away, finding no connection to anything substantive. She thought she heard voices but couldn't be sure. She tried to move her head in the direction of the noise but quickly stopped when her headache increased to the screaming point. She licked her lips and tried to dispel the coppery taste on her tongue.

The noises got closer.

"Found them!"

Air moved around her. The weight was lifted from her chest. She took a deep breath and instantly regretted it as her stomach contents rose within, bile burning the back of her throat. She turned her head to the side and spluttered wetly. Hands were on her and rolled her gently to the side which helped stop her feeling like she was going to choke on her own spit. She chanced cracking her eyes open and was greeted by blood-flecked spittle. She moaned weakly at the sight knowing it couldn't be good.

"Shh, it's all right. We've got you."

"Pip."

"She's right here beside you. The guys are helping her too."

Snatches of conversation washed over her. A doctor. Ambulance. Something about a basket and priorities. She barely registered the IV line going in, with brief conscious hints of her hand rising and falling and the touch of fingers on the back of her hand.

"Seizing!"

Charlie turned her head to the side and saw people crowded around Pip.

"Pip." Her voice barely registered out loud. She could see Pip's legs shaking but not much else for the crowd around her. "Pip."

A soft hand brushed against her forehead and a woman in a blue uniform smiled at her. "Your friend's having a diabetic seizure, but a doctor is with her. They're loading her up with IV glucose. See? She's settled again. Oh, hey, look, up in the sky—looks like you've drawn a crowd. There're two eagles circling us. How cool is that?"

"Big Bird."

"They're big all right. Amazing."

Charlie didn't really have the time or energy to correct the paramedic so she let it go and revelled in the fact that the eagles were still with them. "He is."

Charlie thought she detected a soft moan from Pip. "Pip," she called, her voice raspy. But there was no answer.

She closed her eyes to shield herself from the increasing light and movement around her. Hands up and down the length of her body lifted her and settled her back down again. A wonderfully warm blanket was wrapped around her, and she felt the pressure of straps being tightened across her body.

"Charlie, can you hear me?" A man's voice broke through her rapidly fogging awareness. "My name's Allan. I'm one of the paramedics. In a few minutes it's going to get a bit windy and noisy because you and I are going to go up on a hoist and go for a helicopter ride. In a minute, I'm going to put some glasses on you so you don't get dust in your eyes. I'll also put some earmuffs on you to shield you from some of the noise when the helicopter comes in. I'm going to be with you all the way."

In Charlie's mind, Allan's head seemed overly large, but then she realized he was wearing a helmet. Her mind wobbled back and forth over what this meant. It was all so surreal. She needed to mentally hang on to what she could. "Pip." Charlie tried to raise a hand to point to her partner, but her arm was strapped down.

"The SES boys and girls are going to carry her out to an ambulance that's waiting back down the track where your friend is."

"Jodi?"

"Uh-huh. She says hi by the way, and *See you soon.*"

Charlie's lips quivered. *Good. Help. Jodi made it. Thank you.*

Charlie heard another louder moan from Pip and some mumbling.

"Pip."

"Okay, time to put your glasses on, Charlie." Allan slid the plastic frames over her ears and settled them across the bridge of her nose just as the wind began to pick up and her hair blew back and forth across her face. The radio sounded from his helmet and Charlie winced at the loudness of his voice as he responded to someone. "It's time to go, Charlie. All you gotta do is just lie back, close your eyes, and relax. I'm right here."

Dirt and dust whirled around them as the helicopter appeared above. A cable crawled down from the hovering beast. She saw Allan reach up for it, finally grasping it and clipping it on them both and on the lift wire attached to the basket she was strapped in.

As Allan bent to put her earmuffs on she heard Pip's raised voice. She shook her head away from the earmuffs, unable to use her hands to push them away.

Pip's voice grew louder. She was screaming now. "Don't touch me. *Hands off me.* Don't. Charlie...*Charlie!*"

Charlie strained against her bindings. She needed to get to Pip.

Earmuffs slapped down on her head. Allan frantically waved his hands in an *up* signal.

She couldn't leave Pip. She tried desperately to sit up only to feel Allan pull the bindings tighter around her. But all Charlie's efforts achieved was to make the basket spin in mid-air as the hoist on the helicopter pulled them up into the bright blue sky. Her eyes and taxed mind couldn't cope with Pip's cries of help still ringing in her head, the world spinning violently around her, and the brightness of the day stabbing through her eyes, straight into the deep recesses of her brain. The stimulus was too much. And with the echoes of Pip screaming out her name imprinted forever in her mind, she was blessedly kidnapped by an encroaching darkness.

CHAPTER TWENTY

I think, Ms. Bowman…"

"Jodi."

"All right, Jodi. I think you would feel more comfortable in a cast."

"Can't swim in a cast. If you can just strap my foot, then I'll be out of here."

The young orthopaedic registrar sighed.

Jodi couldn't blame him. He'd given it his best shot, but she just wanted the hell out of the hospital. Or more correctly, she wanted out of the room and to find out what had happened to Pip and Charlie. "Can you do me a favour?"

The registrar folded his arms and squinted at her. "Depends."

"Can you find out how my friends are doing, and see if I can see them? Please?"

"On one condition. You agree to let me strap your foot and put you in a moon boot. With crutches. And I want to see you again in three days."

Jodi waved a freshly bandaged hand at him. "Fine. Yes. Can you find out about my friends first?"

He grinned at his victory. "I'll make some calls, then come back and strap you up while we wait for some more information."

Jodi grunted softly. "Fair trade." She lay back on the pristine white sheets of the hospital bed and waited as the young doctor made some phone calls from a discreet distance away.

It was a fine line between trying to rest and giving in completely and falling asleep. She knew that one of the girls had come in via the rescue chopper and one had followed behind her in the second ambulance, but which was which she wasn't sure. The fact that all of them had to be rescued and shipped out bothered her, but she put her personal thoughts aside. Right now, she just needed details. Details and answers.

She felt around in her trouser pockets. She had no idea where her mobile ended up. She wanted nothing more than to call Cole. It felt like forever since she had talked to her and seen her. Cole could help her find Pip and Charlie, and then maybe they could *all* go home.

The doctor returned and told her he was waiting on a call from his colleagues upstairs where Charlie and Pip had both been rushed for intensive treatment.

"Can I ask one more favour? Can I borrow your phone for just a minute? Please?"

He sighed, handed over his phone, and then busied himself with setting up a tray with several rolls of tape, foam padding, and bandages.

As she dialled Cole's number, Jodi ignored what was going on at the bottom of the bed as the doctor measured her foot, presumably for the protective boot he was going to lumber her with.

Jodi's heart hitched as Cole hesitantly answered the phone. "Cole. It's me. I've borrowed a friend's phone."

Jodi smiled sweetly at the surprised look on the doctor's face at her reference to him. She winked at him and looked away. "Where are you?" Jodi nodded. "Hang on and I'll see if they can buzz you through."

The doctor swivelled on his stool and asked an attending nurse to let Cole into the emergency treatment area. Jodi mouthed a thank you to him. He smiled and went back to the task at hand.

"They're gonna let you through. See you in a bit." She hung up and held out the phone. "Thank you. I really appreciate it."

"You know, despite being a pain in my side, I heard about what you and your friends went through. I figured you could do with a break."

Jodi accepted the gift he offered solemnly. She wasn't ready to replay and digest the past twenty-four hours. She needed to gather all the facts first, see what the situation and prognosis were, and then go from there.

A buzz sounded from the other side of the bed curtain as a door opened. Within a breath the curtains were parted and Cole poked her head through. As soon as they made eye contact, Cole's face lit up. Two steps and Cole was pulling her warmly into her arms. Safe arms. Arms that told her she was home even though she was in a foreign, far from ideal environment.

Cole released her hold and straightened. Sniffling as if she'd been crying, Cole ducked to kiss her on the lips, and when she was finished she brushed hair out of Jodi's eyes, then frowned and slapped her on her upper right arm.

"Ow!"

Before Jodi could protest any more, Cole put her hands on Jodi's cheeks and kissed her again. Jodi closed her eyes, disappearing in the refuge of Cole's mouth. Just as she started to reciprocate, Cole pulled back. She slapped her again on the upper arm. "Wha?" Jodi sat back, stunned at the swing of Cole's attentions. "What was that for?"

"For scaring me half to death."

"Oh. Is that all?" Her glib comment earned her another light slap. "Hey-up. Steady on. I'm only joking."

"Well I'm not, Jodi Bowman. I've never been so terrified. When I couldn't find any of you, I thought…" Cole's voice was choked with emotion.

Jodi took pity on her and held her arms out. Cole fell into them and nuzzled her shoulder.

Jodi was unsure of who was getting the most comfort, Cole or her, for the pure physical satisfaction of having Cole close. She was tired, her nerves and emotions raw and close to the surface, and holding Cole helped soothe everything and gave her the space to just breathe.

"I'm so sorry. So sorry. Everything was fine, and then boom, it went pear-shaped."

Cole put her forehead to Jodi's and stroked down the side of her jawline. "It's okay, love. You made it. You all did. That's all that matters."

Jodi shook her head. "I shouldn't have—"

Cole put her finger over her lips. "Don't you dare. Sometimes, sweetheart, crazy shit just happens. It's thanks to you that you were all found and brought back safely. You stopped things from going horribly, horribly wrong. And I for one won't let you forget it. Okay? So no more blame game, or so help me, I *will* slap you again."

The doctor glanced up after smoothing down the last strip of tape up her leg. "You know, I'd listen to her if I were you."

Jodi held her bandaged hands up in surrender.

The doctor's phone rang. He excused himself to answer it, coming back several minutes later. "Okay, the update on your friends—they're both upstairs in ICU. The one who came in on the helicopter, the snakebite?"

Jodi sat up straighter in the bed. "Charlie."

"Right, Charlie. She showed positive signs of envenomation and has been treated with the CSL brown snake antivenom. They're going to keep her in ICU overnight and monitor her coagulation profiles and renal function. It's a wait-and-see game for the minute, but considering the immediacy of treatment she received out in the field, and the length of time that has passed since envenomation, the doctors are feeling optimistic for a positive outcome."

Jodi and Cole exchanged relieved glances.

Jodi gave Cole's hand a gentle squeeze. "Good. Good. And Pip? She came in the other ambulance, same as me, so she's doing okay too, huh?"

Jodi didn't like the subtle shift in the young resident's face. She was a clinician too. She knew he was bracing himself, and them, for a less than happy update.

"They're struggling to stabilize her diabetes. When paramedics found her, she was in a hypoglycaemic coma. She was given several doses of glucagon and placed on a dextrose IV en route to the hospital."

"And it worked. I heard someone say earlier that she was conscious when they carried her back and loaded her in the ambulance."

"Yes, but she's been vomiting ever since. They're going to sedate her and put in a nasogastric tube to try and replenish her liver glycogen stores and stop her from going into secondary hypoglycaemia."

Cole squeezed her hand. Jodi sympathetically winced on behalf of Pip, knowing she'd be hating all of what was going on. "Can we see her? Can we see them both?"

The resident shook his head. "Only family at this stage."

Jodi swung her legs over the bed and sat on the edge. "We *are* family."

The doctor folded his arms across his chest and frowned.

Cole stood beside Jodi and flung an arm over her shoulders. "We're sisters."

The doctor quirked a disbelieving eyebrow. "Oh, *really*?"

Jodi slid off the bed and stood, her face straight, her voice droll. "Yeah. Our father got around. Now, are you going to tell us where they are, or do we just tear this place apart until we find them?"

The doctor stared stony-faced at them for all of thirty seconds before bursting out laughing and shaking his head. "I figure, damned if I do and damned if I don't give in to you two." He picked up Jodi's boot. "Sit."

Jodi stood defiantly.

He sighed. "Please sit, Ms. Bowman."

"Jodi."

"Jodi. Can you please sit so I can fit your boot, *then* I will go off and see what I can manage?"

Cole held her hand out for the boot. "I'm a nurse. I've fitted these before. How about you leave me to do this while you go off and work your magic so we can visit our *sisters. And* I promise to make her behave until you get back."

The doctor handed Cole the boot and raised his hands in supplication, effectively giving up and walking out, a playful smirk on his face.

Cole expertly fitted the boot around Jodi's foot and ankle, Velcroing the straps firmly into place. Her fingers were strong and quick, and she knew how to loop and tie off the lengthy straps. Jodi had to admit, having the extra protection and stabilization around her injured ankle and foot made her feel more comfortable and secure, all things considered.

"Feel okay?"

"Uh-huh. Thanks, *sister*."

Cole giggled. "I had to say something. It was the first thing that came to mind. And *I'm* not the one who intimated that our father was a tart."

Jodi grinned mischievously. With the relief of tension, a wave of weariness washed over her. She yawned and went to rub her face with her hands but pulled up short when the stark white bandages reminded her that this might not be a good, or comfortable, idea. She slumped. "Damn."

"Come here." Cole wrapped her in her arms and she leaned unashamedly and completely against Cole.

"I should be holding you. I at least got to doze in the ambulance on the way here. You've been up all night."

"When we get home, we can hold each other."

"I'd like that."

The curtain opened. The resident had returned with a wheelchair and a pair of crutches. "I can get you both five minutes, and no more."

Jodi and Cole exchanged conspiratorial grins. Cole helped Jodi stand and manoeuvre into the chair. "We'll take it. Thank you."

The doctor took them around several corridors, up a lift, and down several more passageways with Cole following behind carrying Jodi's crutches. Finally they stood outside a secured doorway. He pressed an intercom button and announced them. A buzzer sounded and the door clicked open, allowing them entrance.

Numerous beds were lined up, and Jodi was wheeled to the end of the row, to the last two beds. Charlie was nearest the wall and Pip in the bed off to her left.

The doctor pushed her up to Pip's bedside, bent down, and whispered in her ear. "Five minutes." Jodi nodded, only half listening.

Pip lay on the bed, looking extremely pale. A tube came out of her nostril across to her cheek, where a strip of tape anchored it in place. It disappeared down her neck and shoulder and off the side of the bed to one of the many hanging bags. Several monitors ticked and beeped beside her. Jodi brushed her fingertips along Pip's cheek briefly and then rested her hand on Pip's shoulder. "We did a right royal number this time, hey, mate?"

Jodi wiped a tear away. "Charlie's here beside you. And Cole too. So you just rest up now and get your shit together, huh?" She sat silent for a few minutes.

Cole quietly came up behind her. "Charlie's asking for you, and the nurse over there is giving me the evil eye, so we better be quick." Cole reversed Jodi's chair and wheeled her over to Charlie's bedside.

"Hey." Charlie's voice, although tired and weak, was like magic to her ears.

"Hey yourself. I heard me a rumour you got a first class ride back here, while we had to bounce our way on the Pony-not-so-Express. What's the name of your travel agent?"

"I believe it's *Pseudonaja textalis*."

Jodi laughed softly at Charlie's reference to the scientific name for the eastern brown snake. "Right you are. Remind me to avoid her in future."

Charlie blinked slowly, obviously tired. "Consider it done. How's Pip?"

Jodi put her hand on Charlie's arm. "She's in the bed beside you. She's sleeping at the minute."

"I can see that. Jodi, I need to know. How is she?"

Jodi knew exactly what Charlie was asking. If she was in Charlie's shoes, she'd want a straight answer too. "She was in a bad way, but help got to her in time, and she got the necessary injections and IVs to bring her around again. Unfortunately she's been vomiting since then."

Charlie nodded and looked in Pip's direction. "The glucagon injection made her sick last time too."

"Apparently they had to give her a couple when they first found her, and she's been chucking up since. They've given her something to sleep and put in an NG tube to get some food into her while she's sleeping."

"But she's okay?"

Jodi leaned forward so Charlie would hear her words clearly. "Until she wakes up and starts getting some food into herself, you know it's a balancing game. But she's here, so are you, and you're both safe and in good hands. *And*, most importantly, if she's asleep while that revolting looking juice goes into her, then she can't bitch about how bad the food is."

Jodi was relieved to see Charlie smile.

"Ain't that the truth."

Cole gave Jodi the wind-up signal. "Now you rest up and feel better. Cole and I are gonna head on back to your place and feed all your monsters. We'll call in and see you later."

"Jodi." Charlie grasped Jodi's wrist. "I can't thank you enough."

Jodi patted Charlie's hand with the back of her other bandaged hand.

"Pip is everything to me. And you and Cole…we came close to losing all that. You saved us."

Jodi tried to wave her off.

"No. I mean it. You saved us. I'll never forget that, Jodi."

"Time, ladies." A nurse stood diligently close.

Jodi waved to the nurse in acknowledgement. "Yes. Yes. Of course. Thank you." She turned and looked over at Pip before leaning over to kiss Charlie's forehead. "Sleep well. We'll see you both later."

Cole wheeled her out of the hospital to her car. After Cole returned the wheelchair, they headed off to Pip and Charlie's.

Cole's hand rested over the back of Jodi's. "Close your eyes, bub, and rest. I'll wake you when we arrive."

Knowing Pip and Charlie were in the best hands and that she could do no more, and having Cole beside her, their fingers warmly entwined, Jodi finally felt safe enough and settled enough to let go and close her eyes, knowing that Cole had both her hand and her heart.

Charlie was only able to doze lightly, attuned to her half hourly observations and Pip's too. The nurse had just finished taking Pip's blood sugar reading and was writing up her notes. "How is she doing?"

"Good. Her numbers are coming up, and they're starting to hold. If she keeps this up we should be able to lighten her sedation."

Charlie sighed with relief.

The nurse straightened Charlie's sheets. "And your results are looking positive too. Why don't you try to close your eyes and get some sleep. If there are any changes, I'll be sure to let you know."

"Promise?"

"Cross my heart. Now close your eyes and rest—it's the best medicine there is. For both of you."

Charlie didn't remember falling asleep, but she must have because when she woke there was a new nursing shift on. A mature nurse with short hair, liberally flecked with steel grey, smiled in acknowledgement of Charlie's open eyes.

"Well, hey there, Sleeping Beauty. Nice to see the insides of your eyes. How are you feeling?"

Charlie squinted and read *Phyllis* on the nurse's ID badge clipped to her shirt pocket. "Okay, I guess. How's Pip doing?" Charlie pointed to the bed next to hers.

"Your friend's vital signs are good, and she was weaned off her sedation at three this morning. She's been dozing comfortably since."

"And her BSL?"

"Is good. In fact, you two are doing so well the doctor is thinking of releasing you downstairs to a normal ward later this morning."

"Is the food any better?" Charlie shuddered in memory of the cold creamed rice pudding dessert she had been served. Two mouthfuls of the soggy dish had been one and a half too many.

Phyllis laughed softly and patted the blanket at Charlie's knee. "Shh. The food's our strongest motivating factor to getting everyone well and back home in their own beds."

"Heh. It's a solid ploy. What time do you think we'll get moved?"

"The talk is somewhere around ten. So after the doctor sees you both."

Charlie nodded. Downstairs was one step closer to them both getting home, and right now that was high on her list. "You hear that, babe? We're getting a new room."

Pip grunted softly. "Hope it's quieter than this one," she mumbled into her pillow.

Overjoyed at hearing Pip's voice, Charlie waited until Phyllis had returned to her station and carefully slipped out of her bed. She leaned over as far as her IV and machine lines would allow and kissed the back of Pip's extended hand, which was outstretched, reaching for her. Charlie couldn't contain her smile.

"Excuse me, we were told Pip Atkins was in room forty-three, but there's nobody there." Cole had tracked down a harried nurse at the nurses' station on the medical ward after they failed to find Pip.

The nurse consulted a folder on the counter. "Pip Atkins?"

"Yes, room forty-three."

"Ah, yes." The nurse rolled her eyes. "She is *supposed* to be there, but keeps ending up in room forty-seven."

Jodi, who had been leaning on her crutches, snickered behind Cole. "Don't tell me. That's Charlie's room."

"We've been chasing her out of there most of the night. In the end, we simply gave up."

Jodi straightened and took a firmer hold on her crutches as she hobbled to turn. "Smart move."

"Thank you." Cole waved briefly at the nurse who had already turned away to answer the phone. "There it is, on the right." With her hand at the small of Jodi's back, they walked tentatively into the room.

They paused in the doorway. It might only have been a single bed, but Pip was curled up asleep against Charlie's right side, her head on Charlie's chest, tucked up under her chin. Charlie's arm was around Pip, chin resting on the top of Pip's head. Both appeared to be sleeping.

"How cute is that?" Jodi murmured.

Cole rested her fingers comfortably at Jodi's waist. "I know. Maybe we should come back later." Charlie cracked one of her eyes open and Cole waved her fingers at her. "Hi there," she whispered.

Charlie stretched like a cat, not once relinquishing her hold on Pip. "Hi, yourself, you two. Come over here and give me a hug."

Cole tiptoed over and lightly kissed Charlie on the cheek. "We didn't want to wake you."

"It's okay—it's nearly lunchtime anyway. This sleeping business is very decadent."

Jodi pointed her chin at them. "How you both doing?"

"We're great. All our test results are solid and Pip's eating and bitching about the food and the noise, so I'd say we're getting back to normal. We might, if we're lucky, get out tomorrow."

"Pip bitching. Yup, definitely sounds like things are looking up." Jodi snickered.

"I'm not bitching. I'm just not a morning person," Pip mumbled into Charlie's gown.

"'Cept it's not morning, Pipsqueak," Jodi noted. "It's nearly lunchtime."

"I'm not a lunchtime person either."

Cole covered her mouth to stifle her giggles. "You three are music to my ears." A lump rose rapidly to lodge in her throat. "I don't care if you all complain for a week. I'm just so damn happy to have you all here, safe…I…"

An awkward emotionally loaded silence settled on the group.

Pip sat up and rubbed her eyes. She pointed at Jodi and Cole and patted the bed.

Cole helped Jodi to sit and took her crutches and rested them against the visitor's chair. She stood to the side.

Pip crooked her finger at her. "Nuh-uh. You too, Kiwi bird. Get up here."

Cole sat behind Jodi and rested a hand on her shoulder.

Pip extended her hands and got them all to do the same. They interwove hands and arms in the middle, fingers and palms intertwined. "We're here because each and every person contributed to a plan greater than themselves. We each had moments and doubts, and we all overcame them so that we can be here. All of us. Together. We make a hell of a team."

Charlie kissed the back of Pip's head. "Hell, yeah."

They squeezed each other's hands in love and recognition of the enormity of what they had shared and how they had come out the other side. Cole marvelled at the complete understanding they exchanged without any words having been spoken. Pip was right. They were a heck of a team.

"Now please tell me one of you two brought me in something decent to eat."

The moment passed, and everybody chuckled at Pip's longing for home-cooked food.

CHAPTER TWENTY-ONE

Three weeks later

"Good news," Charlie said quietly as she eased the door open to the prep room.

Pip looked up from feeding a koala joey and smiled. "What's that, sweet?"

"The osprey is eating better." She went to the sink and washed her hands.

"That's great. Hopefully her bruised wing will heal quickly and she can be on her way soon." Pip set the now empty milk bottle down and cleaned the little koala.

"It is, but it also means we're now out of fish."

"We'll go over to the Maclean co-op and see if they have any extras they'd like to give us."

"I have a better idea." Charlie joined Pip on the lounge and reached over to stroke the joey. "Hey, cutie."

"Are you talking to Monkey, or me?"

"Monkey." Charlie shot Pip a mischievous grin. "And you of course."

"Good comeback. So what's your idea?"

"Let's get some bait and go fishing. Chilli will love playing on the beach while we catch dinner for us and food for Grace."

Pip rolled her eyes. "I still can't believe you named the osprey Grace. She hardly looked graceful dragging that wing behind her in the cane field."

"It's to encourage her to heal faster. Anyway, what do you say?" Charlie flashed Pip her most endearing smile.

"Ha! How could I resist that look?" Pip got up and put the koala in the nursery pen they'd set up in the corner of the room. She turned to Charlie and held out her hand. "Come here, you."

Charlie walked into Pip's arms.

"A month ago, I would've said we didn't have time, and we should just go to the co-op. But after what happened up in the mountains, I've learned that we need to take advantage of the life we have on this earth."

"Being philosophical, are we?" Charlie kissed her on the cheek.

"Not at all. More sensible, I think. Near death experiences'll do that to you. From now on, I want to take time to do the things we like. Even if it's only for a few minutes, or a few hours. But I'm telling you now, if you or I want something, then we'll do our best to make it happen. If we want to do something, same thing. I think we both had a major focus readjustment—we have no idea if we'll be granted another life to fix any regrets from this one. So I reckon we make the best of what we've got."

"Does this mean we're going fishing?"

Pip laughed. "Yes. It means we're going fishing. If you get the gear together, I'll go pack us some lunch."

"Hear that, Chilli girl? We're goin' fishin'." Charlie did a little jig out the door.

Chilli happily pranced beside her and woofed her excitement. But the dog stopped in the doorway as Charlie knew she would. Ever since Pip had been released from the hospital, Chilli refused to leave her side. She'd always been attentive to Pip's every move, but in the three weeks since their ordeal, Chilli had been even more vigilant.

Charlie thought about Pip's words as she gathered the beach rods, tackle bag, landing net, and a five gallon bucket to hold what she hoped would be a lot of fish. The nightmare of getting bitten by one of the deadliest snakes in Australia and Pip going into a hypoglycaemic coma and seizures was something she never wanted to repeat. One or both of them could have died a horrible death in the mountains. Cole and Jodi were the true heroes, and she and Pip would be forever in their debt. Especially Jodi. She wasn't sure she would've had the fortitude to cover the distance Jodi did on basically one leg, and in terrible pain, to get help. They were also lucky to not suffer any residual effects, although she would probably always wear the scars from the bite, and Pip would have to be extra diligent in monitoring her sugar until her doctor was satisfied and gave her the all clear.

Pip was right in wanting to savour every breathing moment. Charlie was willing to live with only one regret: not having found Pip earlier in life. But she imagined all their experiences, prior to them meeting and falling in love, had made them the women they were today.

Charlie sighed contentedly. To this day, she couldn't quite believe she was in love with and loved by such an amazing woman as Pip.

"The fish aren't going to jump in the bucket by themselves, my love," Pip called from the truck.

Charlie emerged from the shed with the rods tucked under her arms, bag over her shoulder, and her hands full with everything else. "I feel like a walking tackle shop."

"A cute one though." Pip met her halfway and relieved her of the bucket and one of the fishing rods.

"Flattery will get you everywhere." Charlie smiled at her.

"I'm hoping that'll be the case for later." Pip winked and slapped her playfully on the bum.

Pip had already opened the door for Chilli, who wasted no time in jumping into the back seat. As soon as the gear was securely stowed in the bed of the truck, they headed to a popular beach fishing spot in Iluka.

Jodi moaned in appreciation as she took a sip of her favourite dark roast coffee while sitting at her desk. It was her fourth cup of the day, and she relished every single drop. She'd only just begun drinking coffee again since spraining her ankle. She loved drinking coffee. But when her ankle was at its worst and the doctors recommended staying off it, she quickly realized it was just too painful and too much work to have to get up and pee fifty times a day.

Now that her foot was encased in a moon boot for support and protection, she could stand for longer periods of time and even walk short distances. The only disadvantages were it felt hot and wasn't ideal for sleeping. But her ankle was on the mend.

"You're going to float away if you keep drinking all that coffee," Cate said from the doorway.

Jodi closed her eyes and sighed. "I don't care. It tastes so damn good."

"You'll only have yourself to blame if you're up all night." Cole suddenly appeared next to Cate.

Jodi wiggled her eyebrows at Cole. "That's not all bad, is it?"

Cole blushed beet red. "It'd be fine if it weren't for that bloody boot." She lifted her pant leg to reveal a series of light bruises.

Jodi rolled her eyes. "I told you we could switch sides of the bed, but you won't sleep next to the window."

Cate looked at Cole. "I would think that would be the perfect place on a hot night to catch any cool breeze coming in."

"It would be, if Jodi would get rid of the huntsman spider that lives in the corner of the window."

"Hey, you leave Windex alone. She keeps all the other bugs from coming in."

Cate laughed and shook her head. "I'll leave you two to figure out your sleeping arrangements. I'm heading out to Byron Bay for the afternoon and then leaving for Brisbane for the weekend from there. I've got a herd of polo ponies to vaccinate and write health certs for. You'll be right to handle the rest of the afternoon?"

Cole replied, "We should be fine. It's been quiet all day."

"Righto. I'm off then."

"See ya when we see ya." Cole sat down across from Jodi and crossed her legs. "She's good value, hey."

Jodi shook her head. "I honestly don't know what we would've done without her after all this," she said, indicating her ankle.

"How's it feeling? You've been off it most of the day."

Jodi tapped the boot. "Yeah, good. I've whacked it against the desk a couple of times. The first time I did it, I cringed, waiting for the pain, but this thing is worth its weight in gold."

Cole glanced at her watch. "There're no appointments scheduled from here to close. How about I duck out and get us some lunch? You need something to soak up all that caffeine you've been ingesting."

"Beaut. Thai?"

Cole rose from her chair. "Ha. You don't ask much. I have to go all the way to the other end of town to get that. But," she said, walking around to Jodi's side of the desk, "you're totally worth it." She bent down and kissed Jodi.

Jodi closed her eyes and wrapped her arms around Cole's middle. She teased Cole's mouth open with her tongue and moaned when entry was granted. Their kiss was warm and wet, and Jodi felt the stirrings of arousal in her centre.

Cole broke the kiss and drew back. She wagged a finger at Jodi. "You are a dangerous woman."

"You inspire me."

Cole stroked Jodi's cheek and rubbed her lips with her thumb. "Mm. I'll see you in a while. What are you going to do while I'm gone?"

Jodi indicated a pile of lab reports and X-rays on her desk. "Work on these. I'm hoping to have at least half done by the time my gorgeous woman arrives back here with lunch."

"I'd best get going then. I wouldn't want to miss her." Cole kissed the top of Jodi's head and rubbed her back gently. "Love you."

"Love you back."

Jodi stared after Cole as she left her office. While things had started to get better between the two of them before the trip into the mountains, they were happily back to normal now. They'd had long talks into the night. Cole had held her as a captive audience because she sure as hell hadn't been going anywhere fast. Her life was as complete as she'd ever wanted it to be. They hadn't made love yet. Cole insisted that Jodi be one hundred per cent first because, as she put it, she had plans for her.

Grabbing the first lab report on top of the pile, she read the top line, and then stopped. Cate had stepped up and worked harder and longer hours than Jodi would have ever expected. She'd kept the client base very happy. Her progress in surgery was outstanding, just as Jodi knew it would be. Although Cate was quite skilled with her hands, she still needed experience with the delicate surgeries, such as cruciate ligament repairs and arthroscopic procedures. And Jodi wanted to be the one to teach Cate these skills. However, she hadn't tested herself surgically since she'd been back to work. She wanted to keep the consultant role for now, despite that the desire to pick up a scalpel was starting to take seed. But right now she needed to focus on getting these reports read and noted.

Pip turned off the Pacific Highway onto the road leading to Iluka. Charlie loved the drive, taking them through the heart of Bundjalung National Park. She'd only been to the area a handful of times, but there'd been no opportunity to explore the beaches or the variety of other habitats there, such as the rainforest and coastal cypress stands.

The familiar smell of the beach wafted through the open windows, briny, sulphury, and fresh, all rolled into one.

Chilli whined from the back seat.

Pip looked in the rear-view mirror. "Almost there, kiddo."

"Aren't we going all the way into Iluka?"

"Nope. Too many tourists. We're going to Shark Bay to fish."

"Um, that sounds kind of ominous. Are you sure we should go there, especially with Chilli?"

"Meh. They call it that because the reef is the perfect habitat for the reef shark. We'd be lucky to see one though. It's a great spot for flathead and bream. I think we'll have more chance of filling up that bucket with fish. It's a beautiful bay. You'll love it."

The small sandy parking lot was deserted but for their ute. Charlie heard waves hitting the beach on the other side of the tree line, which made her all the more eager to get moving. They gathered their gear and walked the short distance through a small picnic area that the parks department kept nicely mowed. Chilli seemed barely able to refrain from running ahead. But when they reached the path that led right onto the beach, Pip encouraged her to go. Chilli looked at Pip, then towards the beach, then back to Pip.

"Go for it, Chill. Run like the wind, girl. You deserve it."

Chilli didn't need any more convincing. Sand flew up behind her as her paws found purchase in the loose sand. She was gone in a flash, leaving them laughing in her wake.

A moment later, the trail emptied them out onto the beach. They were alone except for a fisherman out in his boat about a half kilometre out.

Charlie stopped short. "Wow." The bay was surrounded by hills in the distance and low growing bush. To the right was wide-open water, leading out to the ocean. The beach was strewn with driftwood of all sizes, with patches of seaweed littering it elsewhere. A breeze blew in from the ocean, tousling their hair.

"The beach is usually a lot cleaner than this. Looks like that storm front the other night chucked all this up on the wash. I'd be willing to bet that after a couple high tides it'll be back to its pristine self again." Pip pointed to the right. "See that point down there? It's where the reef starts and juts out about three hundred metres. That's where all the fish are."

"Well then, that's where we should go." Charlie started walking in that direction, eager to wet her line and see what grabbed it.

"Come on, Chilli. This way."

Charlie laughed as Chilli raced past, her face one big smile, tongue lolling out the side.

Pip caught up to Charlie quickly and they watched the dog dart in and out of the water, chasing waves and making splashes of her own. "Yeah, definitely have to do this more often, babe. Gem of an idea.," Pip said.

Once they reached the point, it didn't take long for them to tackle up and make their first casts into the water. The waves were small and wouldn't change until the tide started coming in.

Charlie stood barefoot in the water, rocking back and forth as the ebb and flow of the water shifted the sand beneath her feet. She took a deep breath, checked the slack in her line, and held it gently with a finger next to the reel. She focused on the feel of the line and what it did on top of the water.

"Hey, Charlie, look!" Pip pointed up. Three pelicans circled above them and seemed to be looking to land.

"Looking for a free meal?"

"Or spilt bait."

"Chilli won't let them steal our bait, will you, girl?" Charlie patted Chilli, who'd lost interest in the water and was staring intently at the huge birds that quickly landed a ways down the beach.

Suddenly something snatched the end of Charlie's line. She jerked the rod up to set the hook and then turned the reel to pull out the slack. She tightened the drag a little, dropped the tip down a bit, and reeled. As she raised the rod again, she backed up, hoping the waves would help her land the fish. Charlie was vaguely aware that Chilli had left and was trotting up the beach.

Pip arrived at her side. "Do you know what it is?"

"No. It hit hard and then took off." Charlie patiently played the fish.

"Could be a nice flathead. Fingers crossed, that'll be our dinner. I caught a couple bream for Grace."

Charlie grunted with the effort of holding the rod steady.

Pip laughed beside her. "I guess Chilli decided she didn't want the birds on her beach. She—"

"Pip, I need you to help me."

"Okay, okay. You have my undivided attention."

"What I need is the net. I'm worried this flatty might break off before I can get him on shore."

Pip ran to the higher part of the beach behind them and retrieved the net. She waded calf deep into the water alongside Charlie's line. "Okay, steady. Don't loosen up the line or he'll be able to crank it and your line'll break."

Charlie dipped the rod slowly and pulled in some more line. She backed up two steps and then braced herself against the fish's pull. The dark brown flathead broke the surface of the water briefly before slapping its tail and attempting to pull off the hook.

"That's a nice lizard, baby!" Pip reached forward with the net, but the fish narrowly avoided it.

"Lizard?" Charlie grunted with the effort of fighting the fish. "I thought you said...it was a...flathead."

Pip waded further into the water and netted the fish. She laughed gleefully. "Same, same. Ooh, that's a keeper, for sure. He's a ripper! Well done, my love!" Pip needed two hands to carry the wiggling flathead out of the water and up onto the beach. "Be careful. It'll try and nail you with those spines. Would you go get my filleting knife out of the bag, please?"

Charlie set the rod down, grateful to relieve the strain on her arms. She rolled her neck and shoulders to ease the stiffness, and walked to the shaded spot where they'd left the bait and tackle bag. She rummaged around and found the knife. On her way back, she looked for Chilli, surprised the Lab hadn't been right there with them. And then she spotted her, standing still, looking in the opposite direction. Something about how the dog was holding her head didn't sit well with Charlie. "Hey, Chilli! Chilli girl, come here." Chilli remained motionless. *That's odd. She should've been able to hear me. The wind is blowing from me to her.* Charlie returned to Pip and handed her the knife, her focus still on Chilli. "Babe, can you whistle for Chilli?"

"Yeah. Why?"

Charlie pointed with her chin. "She's just standing there. I hope she's not staring down a goanna or something."

Pip whistled. But Chilli still didn't react.

"That's just weird. You good here?" When Pip nodded, Charlie said, "I'm going to go see what she's looking at."

"Yep. No worries. I'll be here when you get back."

Charlie strolled the hundred metres to Chilli. "Chilli? What're you doing?"

Chilli whined mournfully and panted hard, her sides heaving with the effort. But she still didn't move.

Charlie trotted the remaining distance to the dog and her heart stopped. Chilli had impaled herself on a sharp piece of driftwood. "No." Charlie dropped to her knees next to her. "No, no, no." The branch had entered the lower part of Chilli's chest, in her right armpit, with the pointed end sticking out at her flank. "Oh, baby girl." Charlie was afraid to touch her. She stood up and yelled for Pip, waving her arms frantically. But to no avail. So she ran down the beach as fast as she could. "Pip! Pip!"

Pip looked up with a smile on her face, which quickly disappeared. She stood up and ran to Charlie. "What's the matter?" She looked over Charlie's shoulder in Chilli's direction.

Charlie worked to catch her breath. But fear, panic, and the run made it hard for her to breathe and talk. "It's Chilli. Hurt bad."

Pip took off at a run. Despite her burning lungs, Charlie jogged to keep up. By the time she got there, Pip's face had paled and tears streamed down her cheeks.

"What do we do? We can't pull her off it." Pip dropped to her knees and consoled Chilli. "Oh, sweetheart. We're going to fix this." Chilli whined. Her eyes rolled back into her head.

"We still have the handsaw in the back of the truck?" Charlie asked.

Pip nodded and stroked Chilli's head. "Steady, girl. It's all right, love. Stay nice and still for me, bub. Nice and still."

Charlie took a deep breath and ran up the beach, down the trail, and to the truck. Blood pounded in her ears and her heart nearly beat itself out of her chest. The muscles in her legs quivered and threatened to cramp when she finally stood at the back of the truck. "Where is it? Where is it?" She threw rescue gear left and right. And then she spotted the saw pinned up against the side of the bed. She grabbed it and ran as fast as she could, back to Chilli and Pip. "Keep her still, Pip. I'll try to be as gentle as possible. When I'm close to cutting through, you'll have to support her." Pip stared at Chilli vacantly. "Pip! Did you hear me?" Charlie shook Pip's shoulder. "Pip, snap out of it. You have to help me. We need to work together." Charlie lifted Pip's chin and raised her eyes to her own. "We can do this."

Pip finally nodded and, to Charlie's relief, stood up and put one arm under Chilli's neck and the other under her haunches. "Okay. I've got her."

Charlie pushed and pulled the saw through the cement-hard driftwood as fast as she could. Sweat dripped down her brow and into her eyes. She blinked against the sting and focused on one thing—cutting through the branch.

Chilli moaned when the branch finally gave way. Pip picked her up and together they walked as quickly and gently to the truck as they could manage, mindful of moving Chilli's body and the stick as little as possible.

Charlie helped Pip step into the truck with Chilli in her arms, trying hard to ignore the poor dog's whine. She couldn't imagine the pain she must be in. Charlie raced to the back and retrieved three large blankets, which she rolled up and put around Chilli to help Pip keep her immobile. "Hold on tight." Charlie got in the driver's seat, started the truck, and sped off towards Yamba. Jodi was the only one they trusted enough to save their beloved Chilli.

"Oh, my word. This is so good," Jodi said as she put another forkful of gang massaman into her mouth. She closed her eyes, savouring the peanut and cinnamon flavouring in the unbelievably tender chicken. "You done good, babe."

Cole wiggled her eyebrows as she devoured her green chicken curry. "I did, didn't I?"

Jodi took a drink from her water bottle and patted her stomach. "If I eat another bite, I'll explode."

"I don't know where you put it all anyway."

Jodi plunked her booted foot up on the desk. "I have spare room, in here."

Cole shook her head.

There was a sudden commotion from the reception area. The door slammed open, hitting the wall with a loud crash.

"Jodi! Come quick! We need help!"

Jodi glanced at Cole. "That's Charlie." She slid her leg off the desk and hobbled out of her office.

Cole, being quicker, was already out there. She took a very limp Chilli into her arms. Charlie helped Pip to a chair.

Jodi glanced at the seemingly lifeless dog. "Cole, take her back and start an IV drip wide open and put an oxygen mask on her." Jodi sat down next to Pip. "What happened?"

"We were at the beach, and she must have been chasing the birds. She ran into a piece of driftwood. Jesus, Jodi, it went right through her." Charlie cleared her throat and swallowed hard.

Pip turned to Jodi and with pleading eyes said, "Jodi, please help her. Don't let her die."

Jodi took a deep breath and rose to her feet. "Stay here. I'll assess her and send Cole out to talk to you if I can." She took two steps when Charlie touched her arm.

"Jodi. Please. It's Chilli."

Jodi nodded and squeezed Charlie's hand. "I'll do what I can." She left her two best friends and hurried to the surgery.

Cole had lain Chilli on the surgery table and placed rolled towels under the ends of the protruding wood to keep them from damaging anything further. An IV of lactated Ringer's ran through the tubing and into a vein in Chilli's front forearm.

"I gave her a mil of Valium to settle her a little." Cole covered Chilli's muzzle with an oxygen mask.

"Cole, this doesn't look good." Jodi scraped a hand through her hair. The Thai food rolled grossly around in her stomach. She reached for the phone. "I'm going to call Angourie."

Cole was at her side in an instant. She took the phone from Jodi's hand and hung it up. "Jodi, Chilli doesn't have that kind of time. You have to do this."

"Cole, I—"

Cole took Jodi's face in her hands. "Babe, you *can* do this. You are so capable and have done surgeries more intricate than this."

Jodi looked down at her hands, amazed that although they were sweaty, they were steady.

"Sweetheart, come on. This is your watershed. You can do this. I'll be right by your side. I have every confidence you can find that wonderful connection between your beautiful brain and your hands. And if you need help, if you tell me what to do, I'll—"

"Okay. I want an X-ray, from this angle here." Jodi indicated the position with her hand. "Then prep her for surgery." The words tumbled out of her mouth before she could think twice.

"That's my girl."

Jodi pulled out fresh surgical scrubs from the cupboard and changed into them. By the time she'd disinfected her hands, Cole had clipped the surgical area and placed sterile drapes over the dog. The requested X-ray was up on the wall-mounted monitor behind the head of the table. All the surgical equipment Jodi would require was at her elbow in readiness. Cole helped Jodi intubate Chilli, and after opening a packet of sterile gloves for Jodi, she took her position as anaesthetist.

Jodi held her hands shoulder high and alternated between looking at the X-ray and the dog's wounds. "There's no external bleeding. It's all internal." Jodi closed her eyes briefly and pictured the anatomy of a dog—muscles, arteries, organs, and bones. She took a deep breath, picked up her scalpel, and with the steadiest hands she'd had in months, made the first incision.

When Jodi exposed the wound around Chilli's shoulder, she was encouraged. The stake had missed her thoracic organs but had pierced her diaphragm. The only reason Chilli was still alive was because the wood had acted as a plug, and Pip and Charlie had done such a good job of keeping it immobile in transit. Jodi made another incision at Chilli's flank and retracted it to examine her ribs. "She already has massive amounts of bruising here." She stepped back from the table and closed her eyes again.

"You okay?"

Jodi paused before answering. *I can do this.* Although she was confident with the surgical plan, she wasn't at all confident Chilli could survive it. But she had to try.

"I have to go in through her belly to remove the wood and repair the diaphragm. It's going to be tricky. Give her a little more gas and monitor her carefully. The slightest change, I want you to yell."

Cole nodded and adjusted the oxygen to nitrous oxide mix. She put the stethoscope to her ears and listened to Chilli's heart. "Good to go."

Jodi swallowed hard and went to work. Now, more than ever, she needed to scale and conquer that precipice of doubt. Cole was right. This needed to be her turning point. She gritted her teeth and forged on.

Two hours later, Jodi finally sent Cole out to talk to Pip and Charlie. She was so exhausted that she didn't think she could face them at the moment. Her ankle throbbed all the way to her hip. The boot felt tight, and she knew her foot had swelled grossly from standing way too long alongside the surgical table. She slid to the floor and let tears fall. It had been a near impossible surgery. Chilli's heart had stopped beating briefly when she'd eased the stake out of her thorax. As she'd suspected, blood had pooled in her chest. The dog had had only minutes to live. She'd worked hard to save Chilli's life. But she had done it. It might have been her hands and her skill that had performed the surgery, but it was Chilli who had saved her life as a vet.

Chilli whimpered as she began the slow process of coming out from under the effects of the anaesthesia. Jodi leaned over to kiss a velvet ear and stroke Chilli's golden head and whispered, "Thank you, dear girl."

CHAPTER TWENTY-TWO

O kay, which one of you is going to spill it?" Pip eased back into one of two oversized cane lounge chairs on the cabin's veranda. Cole sat nestled, her back against Jodi, on the other, Jodi's arm casually draped across the back of the chair.

Jodi took a sip of beer and discreetly yanked on Cole's shirt with the other hand as a signal to play along with her. "I have no idea what you're talking about, Pipsqueak."

"Well, for one, you two have a look about you," Charlie said. She leaned against the veranda railing, winked at Pip, and cocked an eyebrow at Jodi and Cole.

"A look."

"Yeah." Pip tapped her lips with her index finger. "I can't quite put my finger on it."

Jodi smirked. "I reckon it's the same kind of look you and Charlie had when you got together."

Pip waved a dismissive hand in mid-air. "No. That was lust."

Charlie choked and she and Cole turned red.

Jodi shook her head.

"It's like you're nesting or something." Pip squinted and studied them.

"Nesting? Well, I can tell you neither of us is up the duff."

"Bet you've been trying though." Pip smirked and pushed her tongue into her cheek.

Jodi rolled her eyes and put her hand up. "Okay, okay, Cole and I do have some news."

Pip leaned forward and nodded.

Cole laughed and said, "Oh, cut it out—it's not like it's any juicy gossip. Jodi decided that Cate and Mandy would permanently work Saturdays so we could have weekends free."

"Oh," Pip and Charlie said simultaneously.

Charlie scratched her head. "Well, we did wonder how you managed to get Jodi out of the clinic so early on a Saturday. I thought maybe you cancelled any appointments."

Cole smiled smugly. "Oh, that's not the case at all. As a matter of fact, the clinic is busier than ever. Cate is doing a wonderful job. It seems all the local lesbians purposefully make appointments on Saturday so they can see Cate."

Laughter danced around the group.

"What else?" Pip demanded.

Jodi remained silent and hid behind her bottle of beer.

"Stretch. You know I'll drag it out of you one way or another."

Jodi sighed.

Cole twisted around and smiled. "We might as well tell them. You know how she is."

Jodi leaned her head to one side, agreeing with Cole's assessment. "Yeah, you're right." She licked her lips and took another sip of beer.

"Waiting." Pip scooted forward a tad further.

"You're gonna fall off that chair, ya little terrier." Jodi wrapped her arms around Cole. "You can tell them, sweet."

"You're sure? I don't want to steal your thunder."

"No, it's okay."

"You know, once I start—"

"Sweetheart, we talked abo—"

"Bloody hell. I'm going to get another beer." Pip got up and stormed into the cabin.

Charlie giggled. "You know she can't stand waiting. She's hell on Christmas Day, let me tell you."

Pip re-emerged a little while later with four fresh beers and Chilli at her heel.

When Chilli saw Jodi and Cole, her tail wagged so fast it was a blur. She trotted to them, put her front feet up on Jodi's leg, and took turns giving Jodi and Cole sloppy kisses.

"I was wondering where you were, Chilli girl!"

"She was sound asleep in the truck when I drove up. I didn't have the heart to wake her." Pip watched on with a bright smile.

They all laughed when the Lab started acting silly. She chased her tail and ran out of the cabin.

Charlie peered over the railing. "She's looking for the perfect stick for you to throw."

"I can't believe the difference. Her incision is barely noticeable and her coat is growing back so fast." Jodi wiped slobber off her face with the back of her hand.

"Comes from having the best vet around." Pip sat back down. "All flattery aside, what's going on with you two?"

Jodi laughed. "Get right to the point, hey? All right. Cole and I have decided to move in together."

Pip bit her lip, clearly disappointed. "Is that all? Boring. We figured you'd do that eventually. The question is, which house are you keeping?"

"Neither. We've decided to build."

"Really? Where?" Charlie crouched next to Pip and grabbed the stick Chilli had brought in. She tossed it over the side and Chilli disappeared outside to retrieve it.

"We think you guys might like this. Well, if you don't, I guess it'd be too late at this point. You know your neighbour, Robert Fischer, had his three hundred acres up for sale?"

"Money-hungry old coot. He wants an arm and a leg and maybe some toes for that place." Pip cocked her head. "Wait! You did not buy that place."

Cole smiled brightly. "Yep. We did. He's owed Jodi a lot of money over the years. So he came down on price to avoid Jodi taking him to court."

"You're going to live right next to us?"

"Well, not *right* next to you. There's a fair amount of bush between the houses."

"What the hell are you going to do with all that land?" Pip stretched her legs out in front of her.

"I'm not going to do anything with it. But I figured you might have a use for it. Maybe put up some joey pens or something. And there's a huge stand of grey gums, tallowwoods, and ironbark for your koalas too."

"Holy shit. I can't believe it!" Charlie gave Jodi and Cole a combined hug. "That's so exciting!"

"And there's a jetty onto the Clarence River too. So plenty of fishing will be had by all. Oh! Which reminds me. I have some gear of yours in the back of the Rover. Two rods, a tackle bag, a net, and a bucket."

Pip furrowed her brow. "How'd you get that? Not that it matters, but we figured it all for a loss when we finally remembered we'd left it behind when Chilli hurt herself."

"Nah. The guy said he was out on a boat, fishing, saw you guys leave in a hurry, and came back and picked it all up. He found your fishing licenses but couldn't figure out where you lived. There was also a WREN pin attached to the bag. So he figured I'd know who you all were and dropped the stuff off at the surgery. End of story."

"If you ever see him again, please be sure to thank him for us. That was very lovely of him."

Charlie put her arm around Pip. "I got some news today too. About my visa status."

Pip looked at her incredulously. "You did? When?"

"While you were napping with Chilli."

"Well? Do tell!"

Charlie sat up straighter and Jodi didn't think she'd ever looked happier.

"Your boss, Terese, knows someone down there, I swear. Anyway, they fast-tracked it through. I'm here for good."

After the cheers quieted and hugging was done, Pip said, "I can't believe you were able to keep quiet about that until now. I would've figured you'd be jumping out of your skin."

Charlie shook her head and laughed. "Remember I told you I went for a walk earlier?"

"Yeah."

"Well, I was so excited, it was more like a march. And when I got out to the end of the driveway, out of your earshot so as not to wake you, I screamed and danced and jumped all around. I'm sure the drivers of the two cars that went by thought I was having a seizure of sorts."

Pip wrapped her arms around Charlie's shoulders and drew her in close. "Oh, sweetheart. I am so very, very happy for you. For us. For the future." Pip cupped Charlie's face and they shared a long, sweet kiss.

Jodi cleared her throat. On the one hand, it was beautiful watching her best friend and Charlie so damn happy, but on the other hand it seemed such a private moment—both amazing and a tad uncomfortable to witness.

Cole elbowed her in the ribs. "See this? It's sweet. It's romantic. You could learn something from this."

"I can be romantic. I just tend to err more on the side of practicality is all."

Cole chuckled and shook her head. "And never a truer word has been spoken."

Jodi looked to Pip. "So now what do we do?"

Pip blew out a breath. "I'm not sure."

"The playing field's changed a bit since we—"

"I know."

Jodi mused, "It seemed like a good idea at the time."

Pip pursed her lips thoughtfully. "I know."

"Kind of feels like the thunder's been stolen or lost a bit now, don't you think?"

"Yeah."

Cole sat up straight and stared at Pip and Jodi. "What the heck are you two jabbering on about?"

"Pipsqueak and I went shopping."

Charlie sat upright in disbelief. "You two? Shopping?"

Pip waggled a hand mid-air. "It has been known to happen."

"Yeah." Jodi swigged a mouthful of beer. "Two birds, one stone, so to speak."

"But now with your news"—Pip pointed at Charlie—"and then Jodi and Cole buying land and planning to build and live together..." Pip waved vaguely.

Jodi drained her beer bottle. "Kind of feels like a moot point now."

Pip sighed loudly.

Charlie looked back and forth between them. "I swear, if you two don't cut the bull and spill the beans, Cole and I may be forced to kill one of you or, at the very least, do some serious harm."

Cole raised her beer to Charlie. "Right on, sister. What she said."

A weighted silence sat between them for the briefest of moments before Jodi broke it. She looked to Pip. "So. You gonna?"

Pip shrugged. "Might as well. And you?"

"I'll do it if you do."

"Fair enough."

Cole stood up. "Oh, for pity's sake! *Someone* put us out of our misery. Please."

Pip turned to Charlie in the chair. "When the Parliament of Australia started to look like they were going to pass marriage equality, Jodi and I had a thought that maybe, to help with the visa thing and all, it might be worth considering. But now your visa is through, well, I guess this"—Pip pulled a small velveteen box from her trouser pocket and with deft fingers opened it one-handed to reveal a band of white gold, sparkling with diamonds—"can wait for another day."

Charlie was able to put two and two together—the ring, marriage, the visa. Jodi'd never seen Charlie so rattled before. Her hands shook as she wrapped them around Pip's smaller ones as they held the ring case together.

"Are you asking me to marry you?"

Pip fingered the box. "I was going to, but then—"

"Yes!"

The smile fell from Pip's face. "What?"

"You heard me, Pip Atkins. Yes. Yes, yes, *yes*."

Jodi was conscious of Cole's hand squeezing her thigh harder and harder as she waited to hear Charlie's answer. Jodi leaned forward and hugged her.

Cole held out her hand and waved it at Charlie. "Show me! Show me." Charlie obliged and they held their heads close to admire the shine and setting.

Cole swivelled to face Jodi with a smile like a thousand-watt bulb, her excitement bubbling over. "Did you see it? Oh. Isn't it beautiful?"

Jodi scrunched her nose up and struggled to keep her face impassive. "Yeah. It's nice."

Cole whipped around and stared open-mouthed at her. "Nice. Really. You couldn't be a *little* more enthusiastic?" Her voice was a dramatic whisper.

"Well, I could, except for two things. I went shopping with Pip, so I've already seen it."

"Yeah, but…"

"And it's nice. But"—Jodi squirmed in the seat until she had what she was looking for—"personally, I think mine is nicer." She flipped open a matching velvet box and held it before Cole—a white gold ring with intricate knotwork, the centre of each knot inlaid with a ruby.

Cole looked back and forth between her and the ring. One hand flew to her chest. "Oh my God."

"No. Just me. Cole Jameson, will you live with me, love me, marry me, and help me to make as wonderful a relationship as your grandparents had?"

"Wha—?"

"Will you be my wife?"

Cole looked at Jodi, then to Pip and Charlie, who nodded and smiled at her. She stared wordlessly at Jodi, the stretch of silence almost doing Jodi's heart in as she waited to hear the one thing she suddenly realized she had been waiting most of her life to hear.

"Yes."

Jodi never gave Cole another breath's chance to say anything else before sealing the answer with a crushing kiss. She couldn't think of anything more perfect than to celebrate life and love with the people who were most important in her world, who knew the preciousness and precariousness of life, and who now, more than ever, had the blessing and light to shine on a love that was boundless.

Cole and Charlie compared rings, grins and shining eyes full of emotion. Behind them Pip and Jodi grinned and raised fresh beer bottles in toast of their success and cunning plan. "We should go shopping more often, Pipsqueak."

"I reckon that's a cracker of an idea, Stretch."

Epilogue

Jodi stepped out of the caravan perched on the hill slope. She had a chilled bottle of white wine in her hand and a plate of cheese and cracker biscuits in the other. She leaned over Cole's shoulder to top up her wine glass.

Cole raised her head as Jodi bent down to pour the wine, a smile lingering on her face. "Thank you, sweetheart."

Jodi moved closer and captured Cole's lips in a soft and lingering kiss. "You're welcome." She sat down on the camp chair next to Cole. Their hands met and fingers intertwined as they sat side by side, leaning slightly into each other, looking over their new block of land with the perfect river view.

"I think you're right—this is the perfect place and outlook for the new house." Jodi gave Cole's fingers a gentle squeeze. They had been coming up each weekend for the past month and walking the property to work out the ideal place for their house. It was Cole who'd found the place where they were now camped out.

On a whim, they had bought a vintage caravan and towed it up the small hill to where it was now parked. They had spent the day stepping out and making plans for their new home, as witnessed by a series of pegs in the ground around them and the van.

Cole gestured in front of her. "Can we have a big sweeping veranda—one that goes all the way around the house?"

"Can't see why not."

"I want to put some nice chairs and a table on it, so we can sit out here in the evening, like now, and look over the river, the sun setting over the water, and watch the boats go by."

"That sounds perfect." Jodi relaxed into her chair as she looked at the scenic vista before her. The sun glistened with the last of the day's brilliance on the river's surface. She turned her head to gaze fondly over at her fiancée. A gentleness and peace stole over her. The depths of warmth was surprising. But whereas once she would have shied away from acknowledging it, now she felt settled. Composed. Whole.

Cole turned her head, her eyes dark and solemn. "I've changed my mind."

Jodi jerked her head at the change. "Sorry?"

"I don't want chairs on the veranda."

Jodi sat up. "Okay."

Cole put her glass down and stood, drawing Jodi with her. Cole relieved Jodi of her glass. "I was thinking about a lounge, but it's not big enough."

"It's not?"

Cole stepped into Jodi's space and pressed along her full length, one arm wrapped around Jodi's neck. She traced Jodi's jawline and eyebrow ridges with soft, sensuous fingertips. "I want a bed out here."

"You do? A bed."

"Uh-huh." Cole drew Jodi's head closer until only the whisper of their breath separated them. She leaned in the last inch and stole any words Jodi might have uttered as their lips came together. Jodi couldn't help but smile into the kiss as she heard Cole hum. "Because then I wouldn't have to stop doing this"—she stole another kiss, her tongue lingering on Jodi's upper lip, the kiss ending in a playful nip—"in order to take you to bed and show you how much I love you."

Jodi chuckled softly. Cole pulled back slightly to look at her, somewhat bemused.

"You do realize we would be eaten to death by mozzies the moment we got our kit off."

"I'm sure you could be motivated to think of something to solve that."

Jodi's hands stole down to cup Cole's waist and draw her close. She felt the warmth coming up from the land, through their feet, rising up to embrace them both.

A month earlier, doubt and anxiety had been her constant shadows, but now she was gifted with light and warmth, its nexus centred around the woman in her arms. She began to walk them backward towards the van door. "I'm beginning to feel motivated now."

Cole purred as Jodi skilfully relieved her of her clothes as they stepped inside. "I do love a creative mind."

Jodi let the door close behind them. "And I love nothing better than a challenge."

About the Authors

Mardi Alexander:
Mardi lives on a farm high up on the mountain tablelands of the Great Dividing Range in New South Wales along with her partner, a myriad of cats and dogs and prerequisite farm animals.

When not working full-time, Mardi is also a firefighter, firefighting instructor, and a member of a local wildlife rescue service looking after orphaned, sick, and injured native Australian animals. Her current specialties include koala wrangling and raising joeys.

A finalist in the Golden Crown Literary Awards with her debut book *Twice Lucky*, Mardi delights in sharing the richness of Australian culture and heritage in her works.

Laurie Eichler:
Originally from the US, Laurie Eichler now calls the northern rivers of coastal New South Wales, Australia, home. She lives in a small town alongside the Clarence River with her three dogs, and as a member of a local wildlife rescue organization, more often than not, she has one or more orphaned kangaroo joeys and an assortment of native birds in her care. Recently, she has been able to return to one of her greatest loves, working with horses, specifically Thoroughbreds.

Laurie has co-authored two books with Mardi Alexander, *To Be Determined* and *Precipice of Doubt.*

In addition, she wrote *A Kiss Before Dawn* (2016 Rainbow Award), *Right Out of Nowhere*, *Positive Lightning*, *In the Stillness of Dawn* (2015 Rainbow Honorable Mention), *After a Time* (YA) and *The Day Cagney Lost Her Wag* (Children) under Laurie Salzler.

Books Available From Bold Strokes Books

Captive by Donna K. Ford. To escape a human trafficking ring, Greyson Cooper and Olivia Danner become players in a game of deceit and violence. Will their love stand a chance? (978-1-63555-215-7)

Crossing the Line by CF Frizzell. The Mob discovers a nemesis within its ranks, and in the ultimate retaliation, draws Stick McLaughlin from anonymity by threatening everything she holds dear. (978-1-63555-161-7)

Love's Verdict by Carsen Taite. Attorneys Landon Holt and Carly Pachett want the exact same thing: the only open partnership spot at their prestigious criminal defense firm. But will they compromise their careers for love? (978-1-63555-042-9)

Precipice of Doubt by Mardi Alexander & Laurie Eichler. Can Cole Jameson resist her attraction to her boss, veterinarian Jodi Bowman, or will she risk a workplace romance and her heart? (978-1-63555-128-0)

Savage Horizons by CJ Birch. Captain Jordan Kellow's feelings for Lt. Ali Ash have her past and future colliding, setting in motion a series of events that strands her crew in an unknown galaxy thousands of light years from home. (978-1-63555-250-8)

Secrets of the Last Castle by A. Rose Mathieu. When Elizabeth Campbell represents a young man accused of murdering an elderly woman, her investigation leads to an abandoned plantation that reveals many dark Southern secrets. (978-1-63555-240-9)

Take Your Time by VK Powell. A neurotic parrot brings police officer Grace Booker and temporary veterinarian Dr. Dani Wingate together in the tiny town of Pine Cone, but their unexpected attraction keeps the sparks flying. (978-1-63555-130-3)

The Last Seduction by Ronica Black. When you allow true love to elude you once and you desperately regret it, are you brave enough to grab it when it comes around again? (978-1-63555-211-9)

The Shape of You by Georgia Beers. Rebecca McCall doesn't play it safe, but when sexy Spencer Thompson joins her workout class, their